TWO OF A KIND HEART

TWO OF A KIND HEART

Nanci Griffith

JRP BOOKS | SHARON, VERMONT

The everlasting earth, a home, a place for the heart to come to,
the earthly mortal love, the love of a woman, who, it seems to me
belongs to the earth and is a force that makes men wander,
that makes them search, that makes them lonely,
and that makes them both hate and love their loneliness.

— THOMAS WOLFE

Maybe all people who hurt inside are alike in that regard.
Maybe just two of a kind heart, we are. Not sharing the same mind,
just sharing the same pain.

— KERRY FOSTER

The Quartet

"EDGAR, WAKE UP. We're in San Angelo. You said we could stop here and grab a bite to eat. Come on, now, wake up for Chrissakes."

It was Richmond's voice coming through the fog Edgar was lost in, and it was the last voice he wanted to hear.

"Dadgum you, Richmond. Can't you see I'm sleeping here? Why couldn't you just drive on awhile and let a man get some sleep?"

When Edgar finally opened his eyes, they were in the parking lot of a drive-in restaurant in the middle of a minor dust storm. It was late September and the dust storms always came along just before the first blue norther blew in. Edgar had grown up in this part of West Texas. The thought of being right smack-dab in the middle of it once again didn't quite fit in with his vacation plans. Nor, for that matter, did Richmond, his ne'er-do-well brother-in-law. Edgar's wife, Leota, had had this idea of going to see the Carlsbad Caverns in New Mexico, and before you know it, as usual, Richmond and his wife Cora had invited themselves along.

There was always a catch when it came to Richmond and Cora. This time it was that they didn't have quite enough money saved up to make the trip. Cora came up with this plan that Richmond would come on over to Austin and work in Edgar's machine shop for a couple of weeks to earn enough for them to make the trip. It wasn't enough to just send Richmond over to get in his hair — with Richmond coming over from Odessa, Leota decided she'd just take a bus on out to Odessa and keep her sister Cora company while the two men worked in the shop. After all, it would work out just fine: the two men could leave Austin and pick up the women in Odessa because it was right on the way to New Mexico. Edgar had suggested that he simply lend Richmond the money for the trip and save a lot of bus fare in the process. Actually, it would have saved him the nuisance of tripping over Richmond's dead ass for two weeks, but Cora wouldn't hear of such a thing as Richmond taking out a loan from Edgar.

"Richmond, I think I'll just sit this one out. Why don't you just go on in and get yourself a little something to eat while I finish this nap? Oh, and while you're at it, bring me back a cup of coffee when you come back."

Edgar had never really taken a good hard look at Richmond in profile. In fact, he tried not to look at Richmond at all. But here in the heat of late afternoon, with a brown haze settling in, he noticed that Richmond had the roundest head he'd ever seen. It wasn't sort of egg-shaped like everyone else's, it was just round; just a bit on the piggish side of round. Richmond didn't really have a neck; his big ole round head just practically sat right on his shoulders, which didn't amount to much either.

"Well, don't 'cha want somethin' to eat?" Richmond asked. "I mean, after all, I could get somethin' to go for ya."

"I told you, Richmond. I just want a cup of coffee: black, no sugar, no cream. Think you can manage that?" Edgar scoffed.

Richmond huffed his way out of the Dodge and Edgar gave a sigh of relief as he watched him lumber off toward the indoor dining area.

As Edgar was drifting back into sleep, he remembered Leota's last words as she was boarding the Greyhound for Odessa. She said, "Now I know you don't much care for this arrangement, but honestly, Edgar, Richmond tries to do a good job and I bet once you get used to the situation, why, you'll hardly notice he's there."

He'd kissed her cheek and whispered "Fat chance" in her ear, which she promptly ignored. I mean, after all, it's just damn near impossible not to notice a six-feet-two, three-hundred-pound nitwit who daily raids your refrigerator and never buys his own cigarettes.

Disgusted with himself for even thinking about Richmond, Edgar slipped off into sleep, dreaming himself far away from the drive-in restaurant parking lot in San Angelo, Texas, and the dust storm creating an eerie glow to the drive-in's neon sign.

He was back on the Panhandle in 1922, working at a gas station just on the outskirts of Floydada. He'd met Leota there. She was the sister of his best friend's girl, Maggie. Maggie had fancied herself as some kind of flapper. She wore her hair bobbed and her dresses just barely touched her dimpled knees. He'd catch a glimpse of Leota now and then when Maggie would take her into town to go shopping. Sometimes they'd stop at the station for gasoline and he'd try to strike up a conversation with Leota. Each time she'd act as though she didn't have the faintest who she was talking to and he'd have to introduce himself again. He must've introduced himself to Leota at least fifteen different times before she finally acknowledged his acquaintance.

She was the smallest woman in her family, which consisted of five girls and two boys. Even with being the smallest, she was five-four. She was so thin that Edgar had been afraid to touch her on their wedding night. She had ash blond hair, which she kept in braids wrapped around her head, and eyes the color of fresh pine needles. It was those bright green eyes that had stolen Edgar's heart. The first time she turned her head and he caught sight of those eyes, he was in love. Leota's family was Dutch and her skin was like polished ivory. She had fine, high cheekbones and her hair would bleach to platinum around her face in the summer sun. Being as how all the other girls in the family were a bit on the stocky side, not a one of them under five feet ten, Leota, who could eat like a horse and still remain as frail as a whippoorwill, was considered the freak of the group and often took a good deal of ribbing about her size. His best friend, Harvey, could hardly believe his ears when Edgar persisted in nagging him into setting up a double date with him and Maggie.

Leota was sixteen then. She was just about to graduate from high school. Her father's name was Max, and every time Harvey and Edgar would come to the farm to pick up Maggie and Leota, Max would insist on calling Edgar aside to remind him that Leota was definitely going on to college in the fall. Every one of his kids, except for Maggie, had finished college, and Leota was not to be led astray.

He was dreaming about those summers when Leota was home from college. They were sitting on the edge of the water tank out on her daddy's farm, kicking their bare feet in the water and laughing; chuckling at the hot summer sun with their feet in the cool of the water tank. Leota was sporting her new bobbed haircut, which her father had blamed him for, and the sky was like parched cotton, leaving no distance between the land and the sky. Edgar had his hand on Leota's thigh and was just about to kiss her high, tanned cheek when Richmond slammed the car door, aborting any chance of finishing the dream.

It was almost dark outside. Even through the dust Edgar could tell that day was behind them and they were late. He was never late getting to Leota. He checked his watch at five after seven, which meant that Richmond had dawdled in that restaurant for two and a half hours.

"Richmond, now just what the hell have you been doing in there for all this time? Did they have to send to China for a chair your size? The girls are gonna have the state troopers out looking for us. Did you even get my coffee?" Edgar snapped as he straightened himself in the front seat.

"Well, I met this fellow from Longview. Ya know, one of those Pineywoods youngsters. He was wantin' to talk about the oil boom and the job prospects out in Odessa. I felt sorry for him, Edgar. His clothes were just like loose rags. Guess I just lost track of the time. It don't mean nothin' by Cora if I'm late anyhow. She's probably been cursin' me all day just for comin' home at all and Leota don't say nothin' sharp when Cora's around. I got your coffee, though. Black, no cream, extra sugar," Richmond babbled, holding out the coffee for Edgar in one hand and searching for the car keys in his pocket with the other.

Before Richmond could get the key in the ignition, Edgar jumped out of the car, headed for the driver's side. He said, "Richmond, you just scoot your fat self over and let me drive for a while. I don't blame Cora one iota for not carin' about your whereabouts, but Leota's a different story. You don't hear Leota say sharp words when Cora's 'round because she whispers, but she's bound to have a few of 'em to slap me with tonight. May you never hear one of her whispers. You know what the whisper usually is, Richmond? It's just one word: 'picklehead.' No, and I ain't seen Leota in two weeks. So, while you're a-thinking through this trouble you've gotten us into, sittin' in there gnawing the ears off some East Texas greenhorn about things you know nothin' about, I hope you wear yourself out and sleep on into Odessa. It's easier listenin' to you snore than to hear you talk, times like these. Good gosh, you can't even order a cup of coffee right and you ain't had anything to say worth listenin' to since Christ was in diapers. I'm no fool; we both know who started some conversation up in a drive-in. How else would the guy know you were even from Odessa? Two and a half hours . . . "

Edgar was ranting and raving, waving his right hand in Richmond's face as he pulled the Dodge back out onto the highway. All for naught: Richmond was asleep.

Edgar took the business route through Midland. He wanted to see all the construction going on in the downtown area. The cranes and buildings loomed up over the prairie through the darkness and the dust. It was a boomtown, preparing to open its modern doors to America.

His brother, Sam, owned a dry-cleaning chain in Lubbock and Midland. He also owned most of the liquor stores on the strips just outside both towns along the highway. He'd asked Edgar to go into business with him some years ago. Sam figured all those oil millionaires were gonna need clean clothes and plenty of drink if they were gonna live out in the middle of nowhere with nothing to look at but flatland, cotton, and oil wells. Sam had been right but Edgar had declined, saying you couldn't pay him enough to move back to godforsaken West Texas. He sometimes wished he hadn't been so hasty in making that decision — especially tonight, for Leota's sake.

The streets in Midland were all four lanes. Trees had been imported from all over the country to spiff the place up a bit. It was still early, only half past eight, yet the streets of Midland were deserted. They hadn't imported enough people yet to make the four-lane streets worthwhile.

It seemed to him there was a Baptist church on every street corner. If there was one thing Edgar disliked more than Republicans, it had to be bible-quotin', teetollin' Baptists. Three years ago, he'd ordered Richmond out of his house for wearing an I LIKE IKE button during the '52 elections.

As much as he disliked Richmond, he wished that old boy would wake up now and talk awhile. The streets of Midland were so quiet and still; it was enough to put any man into a coma.

Odessa was about twenty-five miles west of Midland. It was definitely considered the wrong side of the tracks. All the oil field workers and just plain riffraff lived over in Odessa.

Richmond and Cora managed a rundown apartment complex there. There wasn't much to running the place. All the tenants had jobs so the rents were paid on time. The grass hadn't grown in Odessa since the '20s so the upkeep on the grounds merely consisted of Richmond waltzing around with a garden hose two or three times a year, washing the dirt off the sidewalks. Edgar wondered how in the world a woman as nice as Cora could've gotten herself stuck way out here with nothing but Richmond and Odessa.

Cora had been a good friend and confidante to Edgar for the past few months. He told her all the things he couldn't bring himself to tell Leota. That's why he'd consented to taking this trip. He was hoping for a time of silence when the phone didn't ring or the washer didn't stop or dinner wasn't burning. He just wanted a few hours of grace because he knew he had to tell Leota. He knew they had to talk about her future. She'd be spending that future and all of his alone.

"CORA, I'M GOING to put this chicken back in the oven now. I've got a feelin' that those boys are gettin' close to home. I'll give 'em another fifteen minutes 'fore I get my dander up. After all, I know how that Richmond of yours can dillydally," Leota called out from the kitchen.

Cora was reading the newspaper in the living room of their small apartment. Leota thought to herself that they must eat out a lot down at that little steak place on the corner because the kitchen in their apartment was the size of her pantry at home. Cora had been telling her earlier that apartments like these were the wave of the future. Leota couldn't make any sense out of folks in West Texas cramming themselves all together in these ugly cinderblock boxes when they were surrounded by miles of flat, open space where they could build nice brick houses.

She leaned against the kitchen sink toying with the pocket of her apron and wishing she'd never come out here to Odessa. Edgar had been just too darned agreeable of late and she'd spent the entire two weeks pondering his new disposition. Each night she'd gone to sleep picturing the waves in Edgar's hair and wishing for the touch of his calloused hands. She couldn't recall ever missing him so much. They had a bond between them, and even though by circumstance they'd been separated before for longer periods of time than two weeks, this time apart had been a difficult one.

She'd acquired this impatience with time that she couldn't understand. Every movement was to the clock on the wall, and the time, or the stopping of it, was all she could think about. She had just turned fifty in August. For the first time in her life the passage of the days from hour to hour seemed to be flying by so quickly now.

All of her life she'd wanted to speed things up a bit. During her courtship to Edgar she'd wanted college to go by in a day so they could marry, so she could be a woman and know all those secret things her sister Maggie had told her she would find with her husband. With their daughter, Julie, she'd been so anxious for Julie to grow up and start a life of her own so that she and Edgar could be alone again. Of late, she'd actually begun to miss Julie's presence. It all seemed so peculiar that she should miss her now, because Julie had married and moved away some nine years ago.

She heard a honk out in the parking lot and knew by its flat roar in the dusty night that it was the Dodge and Edgar had finally arrived. She stationed herself just inside the front door, solidly intent on berating Edgar and Richmond for their tardiness before either of them could make themselves comfortable.

Richmond came barreling in first, leaving Edgar out in the parking lot to haul in the suitcases. By the time Leota had finished scowling at Richmond, she decided it wasn't much worth spoiling the evening by picking at Edgar. After all, the strangeness of his mood lately wouldn't make badgering him a challenge. He'd just say "yes, Leota" or "no, Leota." He wouldn't grin and crack jokes to try to change her mind on this night; he might find a grin, but there would be no jokes or laughter tonight.

Cora took on the responsibility of berating them. She accused Richmond of getting the two men lost, which Richmond doggedly denied with a grunt and a claim that even a post couldn't get lost out in the flatlands. He headed straight for the refrigerator, mouth agape, with Cora right on his heels.

By the time Edgar finished unloading the Dodge and cleaning out the trash Richmond had left behind on the floorboard, there was one drumstick and a half scoop of mashed potatoes left on the stove. There were plenty of turnip greens left, since Richmond didn't care much for greens; neither did Edgar for that matter, but with Richmond around you took what was left of the spoils and thanked the Lord he'd left you those.

It was nice just sitting across the table from Leota, watching her green eyes sparkle over his can of Falstaff beer. She hadn't aged a bit in his eyes. She still wore that same bobbed hairstyle, now sprinkled with gray. Still thin as a rail, she was, with that ivory skin carrying some fine lines of wisdom just around her eyes. You couldn't see those lines unless she wasn't smiling and, Lord, Leota almost always smiles.

CORA AND EDGAR washed up the supper dishes while Richmond and Leota watched a John Wayne movie, *Red River*, on television. Cora was a very large woman; given the size of the kitchen, Edgar spent most of his kitchen duty dodging Cora's elbows or keeping his feet tucked away from her path.

"Cora, you didn't tell Leota anything, did you?" Edgar asked.

"Nope, not a word — but you're gonna have to tell her soon. You know you can't keep a secret from Leota. She knows there's somethin' in the wind. I reckon you ain't been yourself lately. She's mentioned that a time or two. I'm hopin' she never knows that you told me first. She'd never forgive that, us being sisters and all. She'd always wonder why I didn't just come right out and tell her the truth. You should've told her months ago," Cora said in a whisper.

She studied the face of her brother-in-law. She felt she'd known him all her life, yet she'd never asked herself if she loved him. He was family, he was part of what they were together, he was a presence she accepted as tradition in the cycle of the familial. She was embarrassed now to ask herself if she'd ever really known the heart of the man, this member of her family who was as much a part of her being as her own right hand. To be without him would mean a loss of part of her own heart. They would all have to learn what it was he'd contributed to make their lives a complete entity in itself, and they would all have to join together to fill that void within their hearts as individuals.

RICHMOND AND CORA had a sofa bed in the living room for occasional guests. Leota now lay wide awake beside Edgar, listening to the dust tapping on the windowpane. In the morning, that dust would have worked its way in to rest on the windowsill. There was a mystery to the dust out here, she thought. She couldn't tolerate the dust when she'd lived on the Panhandle; now it intrigued her. It was a queer thing how the dust would creep into the house even with all the doors and windows shut tight. You couldn't build walls thick enough to keep God's earth from interfering with your life.

Edgar was asleep. They'd made love quietly with Edgar's gentle patience. In the darkness, when it was over and with the dust pounding at the window, she'd been reluctant to let Edgar withdraw from her body. It was as if holding him there inside of her, lost there inside of her warmth, could stop all notion of time and preserve all memories. There were so many nights of secret memories to recall between their two bodies. It was as though there was a capsule of two hearts safe and sheltered there within her body.

It was stuffy in that room, there in late September, in Odessa, Texas, with the dust rolling in around them and through them. Leota drifted off to sleep during the wee hours of morning, curled quietly into the shadow of the rhythm of Edgar's breathing.

THE SUN WAS SHINING through the blinds and squarely into Leota's eyes when she woke. She could hear the sound of Edgar and Richmond arguing in loud whispers in the kitchen.

"Well now, Richmond, it's just the simplest thing in the world. You put the coffee in the basket, one scoop per cup, then you put the little basket on this skinny little stand and the whole shebang goes right in the coffee pot filled with water right up to this little mark here on the side of the pot that says eight cups," Edgar ranted.

"Now, when I get back from filling up the Dodge with gas — which you ain't chipped in on yet — I'd like to have a cup of coffee, too, considering you drank the first pot I made while I was in the shower. You know, it's kinda funny, Leota sleepin' in like this. It's not like her," Edgar said, scratching his wavy hair and losing thought of the bantering he had going with Richmond.

Leota leaned against the doorjamb to the kitchen, watching Edgar's back. "Well, I'm up now, thanks to you two," she said, "and you might as well take Richmond with you to get that gas. I'd rather make the coffee myself than try to digest any brew either one of you could cook up. Go on now, it's gettin' on up in the morning and I'd like to see the mornin' colors on the countryside."

Edgar took one look at Leota and knew he was stuck with Richmond for a while. The two of them shuffled out the door in search of gasoline, with Richmond nagging along behind Edgar saying, "I knew you was gonna wake Leota up if you didn't quit talking so dadgum loud about that coffee. Hey, you know, Edgar, we oughta stop off at the icehouse and grab a couple of sixes for the cooler box while we're out . . . and I could use me one of those caps like you got to keep the sun outta my eyes."

Leota could hear Edgar's voice fading into the parking lot:

"Oh, Richmond, would you just shut the hell up? Even I know you can't buy beer in this town till noon and I ain't a-gonna spend all mornin' out shoppin' for a hat to fit your big ole head. Hey, did you see that look Leota gave you? Gonna be a hell of a day."

Leota heard the car doors slam on the Dodge, ending the chance to eavesdrop on the conversation.

Leota and Cora were packed and ready to hit the road when the men returned, Cora with her wing-tipped sunglasses on and Leota cartin' the road map. The four of them piled into the Dodge, women in the back seat, the men in the front, with Edgar balancing a coffee cup in one hand and Leota giving directions from the back. It was a dry, clear day with the temperature already pushing ninety-five degrees as they wheeled onto the highway heading north for Hobbs, New Mexico. They were a quartet of sorts, each one singing their own harmony lines, out looking at America together.

They arrived in Carlsbad just after one o'clock, where Edgar discovered that they had to wind around a mountain for forty-five minutes just to reach the entrance to the caverns. Edgar patted the dashboard of the Dodge every few minutes, hoping his affections would keep it from overheating.

The next tour through the caverns didn't start until three, so Edgar and Leota sat out on the hood of the Dodge while Richmond and Cora went in search of souvenirs. The air was cool of autumn there in the mountains, and since it was the tail end of the tourist season the whole place seemed to be theirs. It was Edgar's long-awaited time of grace, with Leota's hand nestled in his. The wind was a wall of silences he'd kept inside. The wind was steadfast and greedily tousling Leota's hair. It was an immortal whistling its own complaints in Edgar's ear.

"Let's talk for a spell, Leota," Edgar began. "We never seem to talk much anymore. Hell, I've never been good at bringing you bad news . . . most times I just kept the bad things to myself and they went away."

"Well, I s'pose I've always done the same. No sense to make somethin' outta what might be nothin'," Leota sighed, resting her head on Edgar's shoulder.

"But this time it is somethin', babe. It won't go away this time. For the past six months, I've been in and out of that Brackenridge hospital so many times that I've considered becoming a tour guide down there. All that time foolin' around with this treatment or that and thinking all would be well someday . . . but it ain't so, Leota. There ain't gonna be any more treatments. They say it's too late.

"What I'm saying to ya, babe, is that I'm dying here. You gotta understand that I've fought this thing, this cancer thing that I've dreamed of pulling out of my body with my own bare hands. I've fought it fair and square, but it doesn't play fair and I've lost now. Battle's over. Time to just take what's left.

"Shoot, I guess I always knew I didn't have a chance, but I didn't want to face that. It was a selfish thing, not facing the truth. But we've got to make these plans for you now. There's things I've done to make sure you're settled before I go. I wanna go in peace, knowing I did the best by you that I could. Hell, there ain't a thing I regret 'cept leavin' you here alone. Lovin' you was all that I ever wanted. God knows I'd like to see our Julie's kids grow . . . that little one, little Kerry. Looks just like her daddy, acts just like my own Leota . . . but they're bonuses to this life 'cuz my life was the two of us, lovin' you. God, I hope I loved you well."

There was silence then. Leota couldn't find words when she was crying, and for her there was just too much silence everywhere. There had always been Edgar. That was all to life; just Edgar.

WHEN THE TOUR started up Edgar and Leota decided they'd rather stay topside to look at the mountains. They sent a puzzled Richmond on his way, with Cora clamped to his arm, down into the caverns. The thought of seeing Edgar underground had made Leota's stomach queasy; he would be there soon enough. There was no need to send him there alive.

Richmond and Cora returned from the tour with Richmond babbling on about stalactites and stalagmites and Cora correcting him on which one grew up from the ground and which one grew down from the ceiling of the cavern. Both of them had forgotten the correct answer by the time they'd driven back to Hobbs, where the four of them spent the night.

Edgar spent the better part of the next day in Midland visiting his brother, Sam, while Leota sat on Cora's sofa, crying herself into hysterics.

Richmond was beside himself trying to calm Leota. He'd always thought her such a tough little woman and never in his lifetime did he expect to see her shed a tear. Cora finally sent him out to wash the sidewalks down with the garden hose, but he merely stood in one spot spraying the water into the dirt until he stood ankle-deep in a mud puddle.

It was their last waltz across the prairies of West Texas together as a quartet. In every way it had been the same as every other adventure they'd had, except this was to be the last one, and it's always that last waltz you recall the best when the music stops and the harmony ends.

IT WAS HALLOWEEN NIGHT, a month later, when Leota and Edgar stood watching the dusk on their screened-in porch at the back of the house. Julie's birthday was tomorrow, and Leota and Edgar had a special dinner that night to celebrate. Julie and her husband, Jeff, had gone off to the picture show downtown, leaving the children with Leota and Edgar.

An old black cat had shown up at their house last week and the kids had named it Spooky since it had arrived so close to Halloween. Leota stood there holding the cat in her arms and listening for the children inside playing Monopoly. The little one wasn't old enough to play and Leota fretted over her getting caught between the older boy and girl, who would inevitably end up in a wrestling match. Those two could get into the damnedest fights over Monopoly.

"Edgar, next year we ought to take those kids up to see Yellowstone Park. 'Member when we went up there with Richmond and Cora back in '50? Julie and Jeff never take those kids anywhere, and that'd be a trip they'd never forget," Leota said, stroking the fur of Spooky.

"Now, Leota, I don't see any point to humoring you with these plans you keep making for us in the future. We've just got these times here in our home to hold onto now. Let's not dream it away; let's enjoy these times we have here now. If you spend these last months busy makin' plans for things that ain't never gonna happen then you're gonna wonder what they were for when I'm gone," Edgar replied.

Leota couldn't cry anymore. The time had taken the will away and she shuddered in the early moonlight, with anger and contempt for her own frailties.

"You listen to me, Edgar. God can take you, life itself can leave you, but you cannot kill my dreams of you; you can't have my dreams. I will always dream and plan for you, even when you're gone, so don't tell me not to dream. Life itself will deny me enough and I'll have nothing without the shelter of those dreams of you. They may not be real, but they're mine," Leota said, letting the cat slip from her arms.

The first blue norther had blown in that day. Edgar's hands were cold as ice on Leota's cheeks, but his lips were the warmth she had always known. They were the only lips she had ever embraced other than her own. Their taste was as individual as the years they'd spent in unity. They were just two people forever to be single in existence as they stood in that cold night air, listening to the screams of their grandchildren in the throes of some heated wrestling match inside.

"I love you, Leota."

"I love you, too, Edgar — but it's still your turn to go in there an' knock heads," Leota said.

Edgar entered the dining room just in time to rescue States Avenue from the floor furnace. He promptly sent three bawling kids scrambling off to bed. The little one, Kerry, tiptoed back into the living room to crawl up in Edgar's lap while Leota washed dishes in the kitchen. Leota found them both sound asleep when she finished. She left them there and went to bed alone. Edgar woke in the darkness and gently carried the child back to her pallet on the floor. Leota felt him slide into bed beside her just before dawn. She meant to speak. There was so much she wanted to say, but fear had taken hold of her and she had always thought that only fear can speak before the heart, and the heart should always be the first to speak for itself. So it was in silence that they both drifted into sleep, with the cold of a gray morning surrounding them.

THERE WERE DAYS when Leota would forget that Edgar was dying. She would carry on her daily business in her usual ways. These were Edgar's favorite days, though he himself was never free from remembrance. His thoughts became frantic and his movements slowed as each objective became a task too consuming of his time. The future became a longing for one day without pain and the future was never so close to him as the life within Leota's green eyes.

He lived on through the winter, surprising everyone by holding out till the middle of March. It snowed twice that year, in January. It was an unheard-of occurrence for Austin, Texas.

Julie and Jeff had moved back to Austin in December. Edgar took the children down to the capitol grounds to build snowmen when it snowed. The oldest girl, Ethel, was afraid of him, and it disturbed him that she would cry and carry on whenever he came near her. Leota thought the child could sense that he was dying and was afraid to get close to death. Edgar simply thought the child odd and kept his distance.

Richmond and Cora came to visit around the first of February, with Richmond behind the wheel of a brand-new 1956 Chevrolet. He took Edgar out for a drive the second day of the visit and they'd hardly left the driveway before Edgar struck the conversation.

"Richmond, ya know, I've sort of mistreated you all these years. Hell, if it came right down to it, I guess you're prob'ly the best darn friend I've ever had. If I hadn't had you around to pick on all these years I might've gone crazy a long time ago. I hope you understand what I'm sayin' here now . . . it just wouldn't be right for me to drop dead with you never knowin' how I really felt," Edgar said.

Richmond began to cry. He hadn't cried in years. In fact, the last time he could recall crying had been over some argument with Edgar over the proper procedure for changing a tire. He'd known all along how Edgar felt toward him. Hell, you don't subject yourself to such ribbings for nothing, and he actually enjoyed being the dunce. It was just a game to Richmond, this day-to-day living where each person took a role and then played that same role against one another day in and day out until the game was over. Richmond knew that game was over but he couldn't seem to stop playing. He swallowed the lump in his throat and tried his best to continue listening as he shifted his eyes back and forth to the rearview mirror.

"Richmond, do you still have the rod and reel I gave you back in '48? You know that was my favorite rig. Caught many a bass out on the Perdernales with that rig. I only gave it to you 'cuz you'd always admired it so," Edgar said.

Richmond was too upset to be tactful and lie about the matter. He replied, "I lost that thing years ago. Back when we moved to Odessa it got lost in the shuffle. Hell, I never knew it was your favorite. Why didn't 'cha tell me then?"

"I figured. So, ya lost the goddamn thing. I give you my best rod and reel and you prob'ly just couldn't wait to go on off to Odessa and lose the damn thing. I hope you ain't plannin' on losing my Leota like you lost the best damn rig ever made," Edgar shouted.

"Edgar, come on now. It was just a dadgum fishin' pole. I promised Cora I wouldn't argue with you this visit. Hell, we ain't got that much time to spend together and I know you ain't feelin' so hot these days. I came to see you off. That's the argument now, ain't it? Comin' here to see you go. And I keep thinking it'd be better for everyone if it was me who was goin' 'stead of you. Hell, I ain't never done anything right in my whole life, 'cept maybe marryin' Cora and that ain't been right for her," Richmond cried, slapping at the steering wheel.

As they were pulling back into the driveway, Edgar grumbled under his breath, "You drove seven goddamn hours over here just to feel sorry for your nitwit self!"

"What'd ya say, Edgar?" Richmond asked.

"I said, I can't believe you lost that damn rig, Richmond."

EDGAR WOKE on the tenth of March knowing he couldn't get himself out of bed. The cancer had become so heavy inside of him and he was just plain tired of hauling it around. Leota called the hospital for an ambulance and sent the young granddaughter, Kerry, who'd come to spend the night with them, next door to the neighbor's house. The first thing Edgar did when he was set up in his hospital room was to call Richmond and ask him to come over from Odessa. Cora had to drive. Richmond had to have her stop the car every few miles for him to get out and throw up.

Then they had those final days, the hands to be held, the questions they let go unanswered. Edgar's time was spent in reflection, while Leota bathed in the image of the loss itself.

Edgar's spirits stayed amazingly high. Julie even managed to sneak that little Kerry up into the hospital room for a few moments before the nurse came in to send her out.

The morphine sent him places he'd never been before and would never go again. On the fifth day, Edgar forgot he was in a hospital bed and asked Leota if she'd like to go dancing, maybe catch a little Peck Kelley on piano and bebop the night away out at the Skyline Club.

He said, "Now, Leota, just close your eyes and we'll go. I can see us dancin' when I close my eyes."

Leota closed her eyes, and, sure enough, she could see the two of them out there dancin'. They would always be dancin' together like that whenever her eyes would close, just her and Edgar out on the dance floor together in her dreams.

When Leota opened her eyes, Edgar was gone. His hand was so still and the chill of it made her recall his icy touch back in October, when they stood on the porch in the cold of the first blue norther of the season.

Leota never would get to see the Carlsbad Caverns. Richmond and Cora went back once in '60 but Leota just couldn't bring herself to go. It was a long bus ride out to Odessa and she could waltz that prairie only once in her lifetime.

City of Austin, Summer 1962

IT WAS LATE JULY. Hard of sun in Central Texas. The mid-afternoon heat sizzled off the asphalt in waves and created the illusion that the pavement itself was dripping in sweat. Leota sat on the patio in the shade, alternately stroking her forehead with a tall, wet glass of iced tea in one hand and fanning herself with last week's Jehovah's Witnesses' brochure, frayed along the edges and never to be read, in the other hand. Her right foot, once her best foot, was propped up on two pillows and resting on the redwood bench, trapped inside its plaster cast, which extended halfway up the calf of her leg. Her ten-year-old granddaughter, Kerry, was spending the summer with her, though Kerry's own home was only a half mile away. Today was the first day out of the six days since Kerry had taken up residence at her house that Leota would have given anything to be mobile just long enough to chase that kid down and shake some sense into her head. Leota had not once in her fifteen years of grandmotherdom spanked a grandchild; she had, on the other hand, rattled a few teeth in her time.

Kerry's father, Jeff, had given her a sweet little yellow chick two years ago at Easter. Kerry had named it Janet, but as the months had gone by, they'd discovered it was definitely not a Janet. Leota had renamed it Jangles. This fully grown, no longer sweet, no longer yellow rooster had been sent to live at Leota's house. It was, without a doubt, the meanest rooster Leota had ever seen. She had permanent scars on her ankles from that bird taking swipes at her feet while she was hanging up clothes on the clothesline: he considered that area to be his territory. Kerry was the only human he was civil to and he would traipse along beside Kerry in the yard just like a puppy dog.

Leota looked on impatiently at Kerry and that no-good Jangles stood at the fence line, provoking the neighbor's dog to the point of creating a nonstop disturbance of barking from that side of the fence. The dog's name was Dodger. He was old and smelled bad, but normally he was a good-natured old hound. It was just this hot day, this one-hundred-and-one-in-the-shade day, the mischief of a ten year old who knew better, and an ugly little rooster who was totally mindless that brought about Dodger's continuous burst of loud barking.

"Kerry, I need some more ice for this tea."

Kerry was basically an obedient child and she did, after some lingering, come running to tend to her grandmother's needs. She was already in arm-reaching distance before she noticed that there was plenty of ice in Leota's tea. Ah, but Kerry was always just a little too late to noticing such things and Leota had a firm grip on her arm.

"Kerry, ya little dickens, if I've told you once I've told you a hundred times that Dodger is just too old for you to mess with. Why, you could cause old Dodger's heart to give out. Then how would you feel?"

Kerry was a wiggler and the more she wiggled the harder Leota shook. About the only asset Kerry possessed was talking and she could pretty well talk her way out of anything, even with her teeth a-rattling.

"Well, uh, Grandmother, I s'pose I'd be very sad if I caused Dodger's heart to give out. Jangles and I would be very sorry if that happened 'cause we'd miss old Dodger. We thought he was having fun with us, honest, Grandmother, we never meant to hurt Dodger's heart. I'll just run over there and tell him I'm sorry."

Kerry stood on one foot and then the other. She had a spike of her bangs dipping into her right eye, which caused Leota to be swayed from the issue at hand. Kerry had this stringy brown hair which she wore in long pigtails except for those bangs, and for some reason known only in the logic of Kerry's mind she refused to allow anyone to trim those bangs out of her eyes. It drove Leota crazy to see those bangs dangling in Kerry's eyes and obstructing the child's vision.

"Run along inside and bring back my scissors from on top of the dresser. Not the big ones, but the short, skinny ones. I can't stand another minute of watching that hair hang in your eyes," Leota said.

"But Grandmother, it's not in my eyes. I can see just fine. I won't bother Dodger anymore," Kerry whined.

It wasn't Kerry's whining that saved her this time but the clatter of a bicycle coming up the driveway, its wheels kicking the gravel into the spokes. Leota's only grandson and Kerry's brother, Raleigh, had a habit of pedaling that bike as fast as he could up that driveway so that when he reached the backyard he could jump off just before it hit the grass and see how far the bike would coast on its own before toppling over. This time the bike, seeming to take on Leota's sentiments, wobbled along at a good click right on the heels of a squalling Jangles before it smacked into the fence and set old Dodger to barking again.

Raleigh was rolling in the grass, balled up in laughter. He yelled, "Wow, Grandmother, did you see that? I mean, did you see that? That's got to be a world record right there, all the way to the fence, whew, I'll never do that again."

"Well, I certainly hope not, you like to scared me to death with that bicycle and I just scolded Kerry for bothering Dodger," Leota replied.

Raleigh was a big boy for twelve. His hands and feet seemed to have been made for someone twice his current size. Leota suspected he'd eventually make it to that size, what with the rate in which he was growing. Raleigh was doomed to live in high-water britches for the time being since he grew out of his Levi jeans so fast. He had what his mother referred to as his "summer cut" and the boys all called a "flat-top," though the actual style for a flat-top required that the hair stand straight up at a perfect point in the front. Raleigh had a cowlick right smack-dab in the middle, so his flat-top wasn't quite what the other boys considered to be the style. Raleigh could go through two to three jars of butch wax a week just trying to get that hair to stand up straight in the front like the other boys. Butch wax was this highly scented, jelly-type substance which Leota had banned from her house some time ago, and here was Raleigh bending down to hug her, reeking of the stuff and leaving quite a greasy glob of it on Leota's cheek.

"Grandmother, can Kerry go to the park this afternoon?" Raleigh asked. "They're gonna have a tetherball championship day after tomorrow and Kerry's just about the best player we have in our neighborhood. I thought maybe she should go down there and practice today!"

"Raleigh, I just don't know about this park business. Kerry's already been down there once today for swimming lessons and she was an hour late coming home. I can't be up running around looking for Kerry all the time. She's supposed to be helping me and all I do is sit out here a-wondering what she's into," Leota said.

Raleigh sat down in the grass and plucked one of the cool green blades from the ground to chew on. The heat of the day caused the butch wax to melt a bit and run down onto his forehead. With his hair cut so closely to his head on the sides, his ears gave the impression that at any moment the child could take flight and sail away into the clear blue sky, free from the boredom of a hot summer day in Austin, Texas, 1962. It was a standoff here, this waiting game he could play so well with his grandmother. Raleigh was quite good at understanding the differences between adults, the limits they would go to, and just what pose to take to make them wish you would go on about your business that they'd already said "no" to in the first place.

Kerry sat on the stairs by the back door and stared at her grandmother. She didn't really want to go to the park, but the fact that Leota had said no made it seem much more appealing. This was her place for the summer, over here in Grandmother's way, playing with Jangles. What was ole Raleigh doing coming here, anyway? She was too small to win the tetherball championship. She wished she'd grow this summer so that when school started in the fall she could laugh at all those kids who made fun of her for being small for her age. Actually, this was the first year that she'd ever paid much attention to her size. It never bothered her till now. During the last year all of her girlfriends had gotten Barbie dolls, and they sat on back porches for hours playing these private little games with these adult dolls. Her mother had given her Barbie and Ken dolls for Christmas; they were still in the box, up on a shelf in her room at home. Her mother had tried to get Kerry excited about having the dolls, going through their little wardrobes, which in Kerry's mind had nothing to do with her day-to-day. There on Christmas morning with her mother pointing out that the little black trousers which went with Ken's tuxedo even had a real fly in them, which made no sense at all to Kerry, who couldn't understand why anyone would want to have a pesky ole fly in their pants.

Kerry pushed a strand of damp hair off her forehead and tapped her foot impatiently on the ground. Raleigh was playing his waiting game with Grandmother and she wasn't much good at that waiting game. There was too much to do to wait for anything, not when you could be doing something else just as fun. But Raleigh could wait; he was a master at waiting for the world to come his way. Life came his way by the truckload and all he had to do was wait for it to pass by. Like at dinnertime, Raleigh hated corn. The rule was that you had to eat at least three bites of everything on your plate. Raleigh never ate his corn, and their mother would say, "Raleigh, if you don't eat that corn, I'm going to save it till breakfast and by then you'll be so hungry you'll have to eat that corn." Raleigh never ate his corn, their mother would forget and he'd have a nice, big bowl of Cheerios for breakfast, while that corn sat in a saucer in the refrigerator all shriveled up and greasy with the margarine congealed on top.

Leota marveled at her grandchildren. If only her husband Edgar were still alive to see how beautiful they were. Leota was fifty-seven, still lovely in her own way. The children often asked her why she didn't look like other children's grandmothers. She was small and very thin with the most magical green eyes. She could see through all with those eyes. Just like right now she could see that Raleigh was trying to wear her down into saying they could go to the park. Oh, she'd let Kerry go for an hour or so, but right now she just wanted to watch them both, to have them still and totally in focus. Sitting still and observing others would not be an occupation of Leota's, if not for this cast on her foot, and Kerry was just like her. She would grow up in the image of that same impatience, always in a hurry and moving too quickly from one thing to another to ever lose her own naivety to anything.

Her oldest granddaughter, Ethel, was a different story from the other two. Yes, indeed, this had been some summer for Leota, and she looked away from Kerry's tapping foot now at her own foot with its yellowing cast and colorful signatures and pictures that Kerry had drawn there. Ethel was the only one who hadn't signed it, for good reason — if it wasn't for Ethel, she wouldn't have a broken foot.

On the Fourth of July all the children and her daughter Julie had come to her house to cook outdoors, and in the late afternoon they'd gathered together to play a nice game of croquet. Leota's yard was the only place large enough to set up the croquet set. Ethel usually won their croquet matches, but on this day, for the first time in family history, Leota was winning. It seemed that every time she swung her mallet at the ball it would go sailing straight across the ground and knock Ethel's ball far away from the wire hoops, and Leota's ball would go right on through the hoop. The tension had mounted as the game progressed and Ethel began to accuse Leota of deliberately sabotaging the game. When it became apparent that Leota would win the game on her next turn, Ethel fell silent and her small, dark eyes squinted to a glare; her short, bubble-cut, bleached-blond hair seemed to stand on its end. A thin-lipped smile seemed to come on Ethel's face as she stepped up to take her turn. Leota looked up just in time to see the intention in the young girl's eyes and the swing of the mallet to the ball, which was aimed directly at her feet. That ball had smacked Leota's ankle so hard that it had lifted her completely off the ground and when she'd landed squarely on her thin behind, she lost consciousness completely.

Yes, indeed, this was one heck of a summer. When all was brought to the surface, when every coat of paint on every wall of understanding was burned away by the heat of the sun, leaving only the bare wood to defend the hearts of the innocent — for the innocence itself was not long for this world.

Leota prayed for her fifteen-year-old granddaughter, Ethel. It wasn't so much that Ethel was a bad seed; she did have some wonderful redeeming qualities, but Ethel herself could never be convinced of this and she relied heavily on the dark side of her mind to achieve her goals. It was almost as if she enjoyed the mysteries of that dark side of herself, as though her very survival depended upon hurting others. It was difficult to keep this dark side of Ethel in mind when Leota was around her, for Ethel was the pretty child. The other two had always been a bit gangly and disheveled, Raleigh with his cowlick and his oversized hands and feet, and Kerry with her mousy brown hair, her freckled nose, and that wiry little body. No, Ethel had never been awkward. She stood in the light of American perfection as a child and now the peaches and cream of a Marilyn Monroe culture, heavy of thigh and light of integrity.

It was Raleigh who brought Leota back to the present from the depths of thought. "Grandmother, may I have a Coke? I sure am thirsty. It must be a 'hunard' and fifty degrees out here."

Leota replied, "I reckon you can have a soda, and Kerry, too. Since you rode all the way over here, I guess you can take Kerry to the park, only for an hour, and if you're late coming back, well, I guess that Kerry just can't go anymore and that would mean missing that 'titherball' championship day after tomorrow."

"It's tetherball, Leo, not 'titherball,'" Kerry cried out. Leo was a nickname that Kerry had given Leota some years back, though she rarely used it anymore; it was too personal in its connotation and Kerry was trying to become very formal this summer. Raleigh and Ethel possessed the gift of being formal, of keeping secrets, of being separate entities. Kerry would never be formal and she would never learn to keep her secrets.

"Well, whatever kind of ball it is, if you're not back to this house in one hour, you're not gonna be a-playin' it. Do you understand that, Miss Kerry?" Leota asked.

Kerry mumbled, "Yes, ma'am."

Raleigh returned from the house with two cold bottles of pop. Leota picked up her cane and followed the two up the driveway to the street. They waved goodbye in unison and Leota watched them fade into the haze of the pavement, the cheerful patter of their childhood conversations slipping farther and farther behind the roar of airplanes taking off and landing at the airport just behind Leota's property.

LEOTA THOUGHT that perhaps it had been a blessing in disguise that Edgar had passed on so young in his life. If he'd lived to see what had become of their only child, his pride and joy, Julie, it would've killed him anyway. Julie had divorced her husband Jeff some five years ago and now she was dating this wimpy real estate salesman who'd moved down here from Boston. He was just as worthless as most of the Easterners Leota had ever come across, always thinking he had the upper hand on the Texans, always talking about how stupid most Texans were. Why, he even made fun of the way Julie talked, saying that where he came from the word "yes" only had one syllable.

His name was Lester and as far as Leota was concerned, Lester was the one who talked funny. Half the time Leota couldn't understand what the man was saying and the other half of the time she wished she hadn't understood. Lester certainly was a spineless little weasel with a sharp tongue, always flapping his jaws about "niggers" and inflicting his views on the children, which is where Leota drew the line of decency. As far back as Leota could recall in their family, she couldn't remember even one family member who'd been that wrong and that opinionated. In fact, conversations on that subject of racial issues just didn't come up much. Oh, she knew it was there, surrounding her, the ghosts of ignorance rattling the closet doors in the community, but that word, that word "nigger" — its vileness seemed to catch in Leota's throat and leave a bad taste on her tongue, like some foreign language that she couldn't pronounce correctly and hoped she never would.

Julie, of course, was blind to all of the flaws in Lester's character. Jeff had married a short, little redheaded woman named Louise last February, and Julie's main interest in dating Lester was to prove to Jeff that, by God, she could start over again just as he had.

Leota hadn't gotten to know Louise yet. She and Jeff had had a rather large wedding in Austin and hadn't invited the children to attend. Kerry had cried for days and days about missing the wedding and refused to see her daddy for several weeks. Ethel was the only one of the three who spent much time getting to know Louise and the two of them were thick as fleas. Kerry remained aloof toward her daddy and Leota feared that the bond between the two of them was forever broken. Leota was sad over the dilemma, as Jeff was such a goodhearted man and Kerry was the only one of the three who had inherited his physical characteristics. As a wedding gift for Jeff and Louise, Raleigh and Ethel had put their allowances together and bought a nice little bud vase made of many bright colors of handblown glass. Kerry had refused to chip in on the enterprise and had, in fact, broken the very same bud vase just a few weeks later playing with a large rubber ball in the house. Ethel claimed that Kerry'd done it on purpose and for once in her life Leota suspected that Ethel was right. But in looking closely at the situation, Leota still couldn't fault Kerry for being vindictive and breaking the bud vase, even though Ethel had made much to-do about that vase. There's still a big difference between the breaking of a bud vase and assaulting your grandmother with a croquet ball.

Leota's house was located on East Fifty-first Street in northeast Austin. When she and Edgar had bought the property back in 1943 it had been considered a place in the country. They were the first family to move in on the street once the road was paved and were the only ones around for about six months. Then Thomas Evans moved in to the place next door. Their houses had looked mighty peculiar for several years, being the only two houses on the block and sitting side by side like they were. Thomas Evans was a Negro man who worked for the city electric company. He and Edgar had worked together year after year on each other's property. Thomas' wife's name was Effie. She was a very quiet woman and once a week she and Leota would get together in Leota's kitchen over a hot cup of coffee to play gin rummy.

Developers had bought up all the land around that area by 1949 and began throwing up these ugly tack houses and chopping down all the trees. They renamed the area Windsor Park and young couples, all with three to four children, a year or so apart in age, began moving in and setting up neighborhood beautification committees and petitioning the city to allow them to remove their roadside mailboxes and have their mail delivered right up to the front porch. Most of these folks came from up North and they were down here in Texas to start new lives for themselves. Most of them joined the First Baptist Church so that their being Yankees wouldn't be quite so conspicuous. Edgar, God rest his soul, who didn't give a hoot for the Baptists, just wished they'd all pack up and move back North, East, West, or wherever the hell else they'd come from. Leota and Effie pretty much ignored the entire bunch of them and the only socializing either of them participated in was still that once-a-week gin rummy game.

In 1954, while Edgar was ill and tired to the bone, one of the so-called neighborhood leaders named Arnold Davis began creating a stir about Thomas and Effie. He'd convinced most of the folks in the neighborhood that property value was gonna go straight to hell if Thomas and Effie didn't move out. Well, Edgar just figured that most of these folks went along with Arnold so they could be accepted into the neighborhood association, because any fool with eyes could see that he and Thomas had the only decent places in the whole area. One cold night in November, Arnold Davis called up Edgar and asked if he and some of the other folks could come by and have a chat with him. Edgar told 'em to come on and get it over with while Leota slipped next door and brought Thomas and Effie over to their place. Leota fixed some nice hot chocolate and the four of them waited patiently for the rap of Arnold's fat fingers on the door.

Leota counted ten of them lined up on the front porch, all of them men, all of them with their chests poked out, and all of them seeming pretty damn proud of themselves. Arnold had come up with a plan where they could take up a collection around the neighborhood, enough for a down payment, and they'd offer to buy Thomas' place from him. Well, Edgar let them finish their speeches (mostly Arnold's speeches), and then he told them how stupid they were — that if any one of them could make their places look half as good as Thomas' place he might be inclined to agree with them, but for the time being, Thomas Evans was the best neighbor he'd ever had. As an afterthought he added that if he caught any of them snooping around his property, or Thomas', they'd be pickin' rock salt out of their behinds.

When it was all over, they'd all hung their heads and shuffled off to their own houses, except for Arnold, who was left standing in the cold of Edgar's porch when the front door slammed in his face. Effie told Leota that she thought Edgar's speech was just as good as any Abraham Lincoln had ever given and definitely more to the point.

Effie was gone now; she'd caught pneumonia last fall and passed on soon after. Thomas lived alone now just as Leota now lived alone, and though they never spoke of their sorrow, they still shared this same loneliness.

"How'd do, Leota? How's that foot doin' today?" said Thomas Evans, standing at the gate leading to Leota's patio.

Leota answered, "Oh, hello, Thomas, I didn't hear your car pull in. Doctor says this foot's gonna be just fine when the cast comes off; I've only got two more weeks of this miserable thing left to go. As long as I can keep up with Kerry and keep a cold glass of iced tea in my hand it's not so bad. With all this heat that cast sure does itch like crazy. Raleigh fixed me up with this gadget that's s'posed to be a back scratcher but it works just fine as a foot scratcher, too. Are ya keepin' cool over there at your place?"

"Well, it's mighty hard to keep cool these days. You know it hasn't rained here in forty-two days. Weatherman gives the same forecast night after night. Say, Leota, you wouldn't happen to have another glass of that tea floatin' around, would you?" Thomas asked.

"Why certainly, Thomas. 'Long as you don't mind fixin' it for yourself. Kerry brewed up a big batch of tea this mornin.'"

Thomas came through the gate wrestling with Dodger, whose canine eyes were fixed on Jangles, now patrolling his territory beneath the clothesline. Thomas won this round with Dodger and the old dog flopped down just inside the gate to wait for Thomas' return. As Thomas climbed the steps to Leota's back door, he couldn't help but wonder when the day was gonna come that old Dodger would get his wish and catch that Jangles on the wrong side of the fence. The prospect of nabbing that mean little rooster seemed to be about the only highlight in Dodger's life nowadays.

After Thomas had fixed himself a tall glass of iced tea and added a nice sprig of mint from Leota's flower bed, he settled himself on the bottom step of the stairs. Thomas was a very tall man with a light complexion and short-cropped salt-and-pepper hair. He pulled off his sports coat and folded it neatly beside him, feeling much better there in the shade in his white short-sleeved shirt. Leota's black cat Spooky came up and sat beside his feet, waiting for attention.

"Where is that little joy in life, Kerry, this afternoon?" Thomas asked.

"Oh, Raleigh came by here just a while ago and carried her off to the park. Seems they're having some sort of ballgame down there day after tomorrow and Raleigh seems to think that Kerry's indispensable. They went down there to practice up for the big game. I was glad to see Kerry go, even if she was s'posed to take care of the garden this afternoon. That child's been nothing but a damned nuisance all day long, and it's just too bad that they don't allow roosters at the park or I'd have sent Jangles with 'em."

They sat in silence now, Thomas and Leota, not missing the sound of conversation and neither feeling uncomfortable with the loss for words. They were both accustomed to the quiet, both content with their solitude and neither in need of anything more than their cold, wet iced tea and the shade of Leota's sycamore tree. They had both loved and lost, both held and been held by the treasures of passion, and both would bathe in the loss of harmony for the rest of their lives.

THE AIRPLANES were thundering overhead as Raleigh and Kerry neared the park. Raleigh had his hand buried in his right pocket, jangling two dimes, a nickel, and a penny, which were the remains of his weekly two-dollar allowance.

"You know, Ethel got her driver's license day before yesterday and Mother says she's gonna leave her the car one day a week till school starts again. Ethel says she's not takin' me anywhere 'cause she wouldn't be caught dead with her jerky little brother in the car," Raleigh said.

"Who?" Kerry asked.

"Your sister, Ethel. Gee whiz, Kerry, you've only been gone a week. Did you forget your sister Ethel?" Raleigh screamed. He'd stopped there on the side of the road and put his hands on his hips, waiting for a reply from Kerry.

"No, I didn't forget my sister Ethel; I just couldn't hear you, that's all. It's the planes and your mumbling. What's this about Ethel?"

Raleigh fell back in step with Kerry again and the jangle of the coins automatically followed.

Raleigh began again, "As I was saying, Ethel got her driver's license day before yesterday and she says that even though Mother's gonna leave her the car one day a week for the rest of the summer, she's still not gonna take me anywhere."

Kerry replied, "Oh, Raleigh, who wants to ride in that dirty old Volkswagen with the heater stuck on in the middle of the summer anyway? All Ethel wants to do is go park it down at the Holiday House and pretend she's eating french fries while she flirts with those creepy guys that hang out down there. If ya asked me I'd say you'd get to where you're going a lot faster on your bicycle than you would a-riding in that silly old car with Ethel."

"Well, nobody asked you, ya little smart-ass. I got plenty of places I'd like to go this summer, you just wait and see, Mother'll make Ethel take me there and you're not gonna get to go! And by the way, the word's out on the playground that you ain't got a chance of winning that tetherball championship 'cause there's a new kid in the neighborhood who can play ten times better 'n you can."

The two of them stood facing one another on the edge of the playground, Raleigh kicking the dirt up on his sneakers and Kerry, who stood at least a foot and a half shorter than him, pushing the bangs out of her eyes so she could look up and glare at him. They had the same hands-on-hips posture, something they'd picked up from their mother, who'd inherited the same stance from Leota. Both had the same small pugged nose, though Kerry's was freckled and peeling and still carried just a tiny smudge of white zinc oxide left over from this morning's swimming lessons.

"Just who says so, Raleigh Foster?" Kerry asked.

"Why, he says so, that new kid, Fletcher, he says he can beat you. He told Buster Ferguson yesterday that he'd seen you play and you weren't big enough to last past the first serve in any match with him!"

Kerry stomped off toward the recreation office and yelled back over her shoulder at Raleigh:

"I'm gonna go sign up right now for the playoffs and we'll just see who wins this championship — and if you see that new kid Fletcher snoopin' around this playground, you come over and point him out to me. OK, Raleigh?"

President John F. Kennedy was very big on physical fitness, especially in organized fitness programs for young people. The City of Austin had followed up with his policies by developing park activities that included games and facilities for children of all ages. There were more parks located within the city of Austin than any other city in the nation, and with each park came the children with pride and sporting spirit to lick the socks off of everything in sight. The neighborhood park in which Raleigh and Kerry engaged themselves was named Bartholomew Park. It was nestled between two gently rolling hills with a creek running through the center, which created a dividing line between the playgrounds and the Olympic-size swimming pool. In the center of the playground there was a covered basketball court and just behind it a stone building which housed the recreation office. The park counselor for Bartholomew this year was a young University of Texas physical fitness major named Stanley Grant. The kids all called him Stan. He was a lean, darkly tanned, towheaded young man of twenty who doubled as the swimming coach in the mornings.

Stan took special interest in the activities of Kerry and Raleigh Foster, as their sister Ethel was about the prettiest peach at the park. Ethel and her best friend Wanda would come to the pool every morning and sashay around in their two-piece bathing suits. Ethel loved to get the goods on any trouble that Raleigh and Kerry were into, so Stan's keeping up with the two of them gave him a good excuse to get to talk to Ethel.

Kerry thought that Stan looked just like Troy Donahue and she occasionally fancied herself as looking like Sandra Dee. She was under the unfortunate impression that Stan paid so much attention to her because he had a crush on her. If she'd only known that it was her sister Ethel who Stan was interested in she could've saved herself a lot of daydreaming and a bushel full of embarrassment. All the other kids knew that Kerry was smitten with Stan; they snickered at her as she strolled past them to enter the recreation office.

One of Kerry's classmates from school, Missy Krandel, sat at the desk stapling some kind of park flyers together. Kerry didn't care for Missy Krandel, who was constantly combing her curly blond hair. Most of the time Missy and a few other little girls from the neighborhood sat out behind the recreation office playing with their Barbie dolls. They very rarely took part in any physical activities. So, here was Missy, sitting behind Stan's desk with her crisp little blue sundress and spotless white sandals.

Kerry asked, "What are you doin' in here? Do you know where I'm supposed to sign up for the tetherball championship?"

"In answer to your nosy question, I'm getting these flyers together for Stan. There's gonna be a sock hop here on the basketball court next Friday night and Stan's letting Sherry and me deliver these flyers that tell all about it to every house in the neighborhood. And I don't know a thing about any stupid tetherball championship. If you want to ask Stan about it, he's sitting down by the bridge at the creek with your sister Ethel and her ugly friend Wanda!"

Missy continued on with the stapling and Kerry replied on her way out the door, "Well, you know the only reason Stan asked you to do those flyers was because I wasn't here!"

Ethel was observing Stan as he examined her new driver's license. He'd just been explaining to her and Wanda how you could change the birthdate on your license by taking a razor blade and carefully cutting the numbers you needed out of the license and replacing them to make your birthdate, added up to look like you were over twenty-one. Then all you had to do was take it downtown to Woolworths and run it through a machine they had down there that coated it with plastic, that way no one could tell the difference, except your parents. The best way to avoid your parents finding it and taking it away from you was to tell them you lost it, then all you had to do was go down with your parents and get a new one with the right birthdate. Every kid who was under twenty-one knew that trick, but Ethel had sat quietly and listened to Stan, pretending that this was the most ingenious plan she'd ever heard. She looked up to see Kerry coming toward them.

Ethel said, "Oh, here comes that little twirpy sister of mine. Honestly, she follows me around like a shadow."

As Kerry came within hearing distance Ethel screamed out, "Kerry, does Grandmother know where you are?"

"She most certainly does. Raleigh came by her house and he walked me down here. It's none of your beeswax anyway," Kerry answered.

"Well, what do you want?" Ethel asked impatiently.

"I didn't come down here to talk to you; I came to ask Stan a question. Is that your new driver's license, Ethel?" Kerry asked.

"Well, it certainly isn't yours," Ethel said.

"Oh, go blow your nose, Ethel. Stan, do you know where I should sign up for the tetherball championship day after tomorrow?" Kerry asked.

Stan said, "That new boy Fletcher has the list. I told him he could be in charge of signing everyone up. He's over there in the tetherball area; he knows who you are, just tell him you want to sign up. If you were wanting to play today you're gonna have a long wait. Tetherball's been mighty popular today."

Kerry headed back toward the basketball court. She couldn't believe that Stan was enjoying the company of someone as stupid as her sister Ethel. The tetherball area was just on the other side of the basketball court and by the time Kerry got there, there were at least nine kids sitting on the grass waiting for their turn to play. There was a tall, dark-haired boy on the winner's side of the tetherball circle and Kerry figured this must be that new kid, Fletcher. There isn't really such a thing as the winner's side of the circle in tetherball; that was just a rule that they'd thought up there at Bartholomew. The winner got to have the side of the circle where the sun was behind them; the challenger took the side where the sun would be right in their eyes. It never seemed quite fair to Kerry, but then she was usually on the side where the sun was behind her.

There was something peculiar in the way that Fletcher played tetherball. Kerry couldn't quite figure it out, but while watching him play Kerry kept thinking he was facing the wrong direction. The challenger in this game was Buster Ferguson. Buster was Raleigh's best friend. He was a wiry little boy with red hair, thousands of freckles, and a space between his front teeth that you could've driven a fleet of trucks through. Buster had become known throughout the neighborhood as a troublemaker, so much so that Raleigh's mother had forbidden Raleigh to play with Buster, as the two of them together spelled double trouble.

"Fletcher's a lefty," Raleigh whispered to Kerry.

Kerry said, "I'm not stupid, Raleigh. Any moron can see that."

"I was just trying to give you some tips on how to beat him. You don't have to bite my head off," Raleigh said, straining to keep his voice at a whisper.

With one more loud thump of the ball the game was over and Fletcher had won again.

"Excuse me, I hate to interrupt, but Stan told me I could sign up for the tetherball playoff. Is your name Fletcher?" Kerry asked.

As Fletcher turned around to address Kerry, she became very self-conscious of the fact that her hair hadn't been combed since eight o'clock this morning, her left sneaker was untied, and her T-shirt had a red stain on it, which was all that remained of the cherry popsicle she'd had after lunch.

"You must be Raleigh's sister, Kerry. Raleigh was just telling me what a mean game of tetherball you play. I left the clipboard with the list of players over there, by the water fountain. Just sign anytime you want to," Fletcher said.

Fletcher turned to take on the next challenger in line while Kerry bent down to tie her shoelace. Something felt different here on the playground, something Kerry wasn't sure she liked. As she walked to the water fountain in search of the clipboard her steps felt heavy and awkward, like they didn't belong with the rest of her, as if she didn't belong with the rest of anyone.

When Kerry located the clipboard, she discovered that some stupid kid had splashed water on it and she could barely read the three names that were listed on the page: Fletcher Seibel, Buster Ferguson, and Raleigh Foster. There was a pencil tied by a string to the top of the clipboard and Kerry added her name below Raleigh's in as neat a script as she could. She'd decided she was going to tell Stan that Fletcher had left the clipboard by the water fountain and that it had gotten all wet, but not today — maybe tomorrow. Right now she just wanted to go home to Leo's house and watch *The Uncle Jay Show*. The clock on the side of the recreation office read 4:15; the program came on at four. The show had about fifteen or twenty minutes of Uncle Jay talking with the children who were on the show that day for their birthdays, and after that there'd be a half hour of cartoons. If Kerry left now she could still catch the last cartoon.

Kerry walked along, thinking about Fletcher. He had the nicest face. Kerry even supposed that he was handsome. His eyes reminded her of her grandmother's eyes, though his were brown. It was the way he looked right through her, as though he could read what she was thinking. She'd seen a picture of a dolphin in a book her daddy had given her about life in the ocean and that's exactly where she'd seen those eyes before. Yes, Fletcher had eyes like a dolphin: eyes that were full of kindness and knowledge, as though the whole world had passed before them once and this was the second time around.

"Wait up, Kerry," Raleigh yelled. "I'll walk you back, I gotta pick up my bicycle at Grandmother's. What's a-matter? Don't ya feel well?" Raleigh asked.

Kerry said, "I feel just fine. I'm just not in the mood for company."

"I'm not company, Kerry, I'm your brother," Raleigh remarked.

"Everybody's company!" Kerry said.

IT RAINED all day the next day. Leota and Kerry sat at the kitchen table and played Chinese checkers for most of the morning. At lunchtime Leota fixed Kerry a mayonnaise and pickle sandwich, which was her very favorite, and the two of them sat down together in the living room to watch *As the World Turns* on television. Kerry, who was prone to falling asleep after lunch, stuck by her normal routine, and with the gentle sound of the rain, slept through the entire afternoon. Leota used the quiet time to get some phone calls made; she hadn't had a decent phone conversation since Kerry had moved in. The phone line remained busy for three solid hours.

Outside the world was sleeping just like Kerry. The lives of those in Central Texas were simple and uncluttered. Thunder roared across the sky, and finding no ears listening hard enough to deaden its rumble, it echoed off the rooftops of a nation fast asleep. President Kennedy, acting upon the advice of his Cabinet members, was sending troops: young human beings with feelings and minds of their own, now dehumanized, sanitized, and stripped of their separate identities by being labeled simply as troops, far across the world to Southeast Asia. The younger brothers and sisters of these same "troops" would mindlessly, even jubilantly donate their youthful energies to the president's physical fitness programs, which in the end would prepare their bodies, never their minds, to becoming "troops" themselves.

This would be a summer not unlike any other summer, but it would be the last summer in which a nation and its citizens slept in innocence, undisturbed by the screams in the distance, not so very far from home. Not far enough to be totally ignored.

THE SKY CONTINUED to overcast the next morning but no more rain fell. Leota made Kerry stay home from swimming lessons that morning, as Leota was afraid for any child to be in the water when the sky was threatening rain. By noon the sun began burning the clouds away, much to Kerry's disappointment. The tetherball championship was scheduled to begin at one and Kerry felt doomed to lose before she ever set foot on the playground. Raleigh and Ethel both came by to have lunch. This was Ethel's day to have the car, and Leota winced in anxiety as Ethel backed the Volkswagen out of the drive with Raleigh in the passenger seat and Kerry in the back, leaning forward with her elbows resting on the backs of the front bucket seats. The sound of the radio came blasting forth from the windows of the car and Leota could hear Ethel screaming at Kerry at the top of her lungs.

"Kerry, just sit back and SHUT UP!" Ethel screamed.

Leota watched in dismay as they drove off. It was enough to make her cry, the way her grandchildren treated each other. It wasn't so much the way Kerry and Raleigh nagged at one another, but the hostility that Ethel could inspire between all of them. Ethel seemed to take great pride in keeping the entire family riled up. Leota herself hadn't been very close to any of her brothers and sisters for several years. Her sister Cora was the only member of her family who Leota would even bother to give the time of day, but Cora lived in Odessa and that seemed like a million miles away to Leota. Leota understood the tenderness in young hearts and the unwillingness of siblings to respect this in one another. The young would test their strengths against their siblings, they would tear at one another until the wounds they had created were too deep and mangled to repair. The scars they would leave behind within each other's hearts would heal in thin, jagged lines and would rip wide open again with only the slightest bit of provocation. Leota understood all of this.

After making two swings by the Holiday House drive-in, Ethel drove the children to the park. Kerry kept raising a ruckus in the back seat about Raleigh and her missing the tetherball championships while Ethel reminded her that she (Ethel) was the one wearing the watch. She was actually looking forward to watching the game, as Stan would be there supervising the little brats, making sure they didn't kill each other over some stupid tetherball game. Ethel wasn't about to sit through this game for nothing; she was hoping Stan would ask her to be his date for the sock hop next Friday. She'd told her mother about Stan last night and her mother had told her Stan was too old for her. Well, Ethel figured that what her mother didn't know wouldn't hurt her.

The playoff schedule was arranged so that each player got ample opportunity to face the others. Though the championships had been posted since the beginning of the week, only four contestants had signed up for the match. None of the other children who normally flocked around the tetherball area wanted to play against Fletcher or Kerry — especially Kerry, who was known for pulling some dirty tricks during tetherball games. Kerry and Buster were scheduled to play first. Stan had taken special care to avoid a game between Raleigh and Kerry until later in the day, as Raleigh had a tendency to lose his temper with Kerry, which usually led to a wrestling match, where Kerry didn't stand a chance. The whistle blew promptly at one P.M., with Kerry on the side facing the sun. A crowd of children gathered around the area and even though most of them didn't like Kerry, Buster was about the most unpopular kid in the whole neighborhood, so the majority of them were rooting for Kerry. Kerry had managed to get the rope the ball was attached to wrapped halfway down the pole on her very first serve. The object of the game was to get the rope wound around the pole all the way to the ball by slugging the ball in your assigned direction as hard as you could with your fist. The best tactic in doing this, in order to avoid your competitor from knocking the ball back before you could gain a wrap of the rope around the pole, was to aim the ball over their head. Kerry was a master at this; her only drawback was the rule stating that you must not step over the line dividing the circle in half. Kerry Foster had a difficult time keeping herself on her side of the circle. Buster managed to get two hits on the ball before Kerry belted it a good one and sent the ball flying around the pole all the way to the top of the ball.

Kerry walked away as the victor for the first match and proceeded to sit down in the grass to watch the next game, which was between Raleigh and Buster.

Their game went on and on, with the two of them occasionally stopping to double up in laughter over some mistake the other one had made. Kerry was exhausted by the time their game was finished, with Buster winning the match. The games went on in this order, with each player playing the others, regardless of who won or lost, until Kerry and Raleigh entered the circle to start their match. On the one hand, Raleigh, who had already lost that one bout with Buster, wanted to beat Kerry, who hadn't lost a match yet, so that they would be even, but on the other hand he was inclined to let Kerry win so she could have a chance at winning the entire match by playing Fletcher, who was also thus far undefeated. Raleigh took great pride in loving his sister sometimes and decided that though he was inclined to let Kerry win, she wouldn't appreciate the gesture, so he opted to play the best damn game of tetherball he'd ever played. It was a heated battle between Raleigh and Kerry, with Kerry actually getting penalized two whole wraps around the pole for tripping Raleigh, causing him to fall flat on his face in the dirt. The match between them lasted a full ten minutes and all the children in the crowd became bored, yelling out for Raleigh to "just go ahead and knock it down Kerry's throat." Kerry had lost the sympathies of the crowd earlier by tripping Raleigh. Kerry did come out the winner and the anticipation for the match the entire playground had been waiting for filled the air with excitement.

Stan called for a ten-minute break before the last playoff, figuring all of them could use some time to cool off a bit. After all, the games had gone so fast that he'd hardly had time to flirt with Ethel, who was standing by the water fountain helping Raleigh wash the dirt off of a scrape on his chin, which he'd acquired during his match with Kerry. Stan gradually worked his way over to Ethel, not wanting to appear too anxious about striking up a conversation with her. He decided to address Raleigh first.

"That was quite a spill you took there, Raleigh. Are you OK now?" Stan asked.

"Oh, he'll be alright, it's just a scratch. Honestly, Raleigh, you're such a baby sometimes. Uh, Stan, how are the plans coming for the sock hop?" Ethel asked.

Raleigh looked up with exasperation at his sister Ethel, thinking to himself that it was a wonder he'd ever learned to talk at all with Ethel always buttin' in and answering for him. Raleigh liked to give some thought to his answers when being spoken to; he liked to leave a short pause between each person's statements, but when he was around Ethel he never got the chance to open his mouth, as she was very quick to speak and very rarely had anything thoughtful at all to say. In fact, Ethel talked constantly when she wasn't flirting with the guys, and Raleigh couldn't think of much of anything she'd ever said that held any importance to him. With this in mind, Raleigh decided that this was a good time to go have a chat with Kerry about that tripping business.

Stan spoke up, "The plans for the sock hop are coming along just fine. One of the DJs from K-N-O-W radio is going to come spin the records from seven till nine. Are you planning to come?"

"You know I'd like to, but I'd just hate to come all by myself. Wanda has to go out of town that weekend," Ethel hinted.

"Why, Ethel, I'd just be glad for you to come sit with me, maybe dance a few dances together. I'd consider it an honor," Stan said.

"I'll just count on that then, Stan. Thank you for offering — it's so nice of you to offer!" Ethel said.

With her goal achieved, Ethel excused herself and headed straight for Wanda's house, who was not, by the way, scheduled to be out of town that weekend, but if Ethel had her way she would be now! Ethel continued to congratulate herself on her date with Stan all the way to Wanda's house, only pausing once to scold herself for having allowed Stan to get her so flustered that she'd stammered a bit during their conversation at the water fountain.

Kerry and Fletcher took their places in the tetherball circle, with Fletcher losing the coin toss and ending up on the side with the sun in his eyes. The whistle blew while Kerry was still reminding herself that any and all eye contact with Fletcher was to be avoided. Fletcher had first serve since he'd gotten the bad side of the circle. He sent the ball flying around the pole, thinking he'd get a good start with the first couple of wraps, but Kerry caught it with her feet just inside her center line and sent the ball back around the pole with a loud smack before it could go the second wrap. The game continued on in this fashion, with Fletcher being penalized once for stepping over the center line, which Kerry was being careful to avoid. They'd been at it for five minutes, with the rope now wrapped three-quarters of the way down the pole in Fletcher's favor, when Fletcher hit the ball exceptionally high in the air. Kerry ran to the center line and leaped into the air to retrieve it, while Fletcher also rushed for the center line, fearing she just might succeed in doing just that. He figured that if he got close enough, he could slam the ball over Kerry's short, little noggin, which would surely win the game for him. Sure enough, Kerry did jump high enough to hit the ball, but upon landing her feet found purchase not on the ground but on Fletcher' feet, knocking Kerry off balance and throwing her small body into the steel center pole. Fletcher went sprawling as well, smacking his head solidly on the hard dirt. The last thing he remembered hearing was the crack of Kerry's wrist as it landed sharply against the pole. The game was over.

Julie was called at her office in a downtown architectural firm where she was the bookkeeper. Leota had been so distraught while talking with Julie on the telephone that it took several attempts on Julie's part to find out exactly what was going on. Ethel, adding to Julie's confusion, had the car and was nowhere to be found. Julie had finally called a cab. She rode the distance from downtown Austin to Bartholomew chain-smoking Winston cigarettes, barking directions to the cab driver, and cursing herself for ever having been so stupid as to divorce a man like Jeff Foster.

When Julie arrived on the scene of the accident, Kerry was sitting up on a picnic table by the basketball court. Stan had gotten a bag of ice from a concerned mother in one of the houses nearby and Kerry was holding the ice on an already-swelling wrist. A dark-haired boy sat beside Kerry on the table, alternating between patting her on the back to console her and massaging the back of his own head. He introduced himself to Julie simply as Fletcher, while the small, delicate woman standing beside him introduced herself as being Fletcher's mother, Millie Seibel. Since Ethel was nowhere to be found, Millie offered to drive them all down to the emergency room at Brachenridge County Hospital.

Kerry was quite familiar with the emergency room — considering she was somewhat accident-prone, she'd had several opportunities to visit the place. She was fairly at ease sitting in the waiting area with Julie, Fletcher, and his mother Millie Seibel. Fletcher was most impressed with Kerry's knowledge of the whereabouts of such things as the Coke machine, the water fountain, and the restrooms.

While waiting for the arrival of the family physicians, Leota came hobbling in on the arm of Thomas Evans, which in itself seemed quite peculiar to Millie Seibel, since she had only become acquainted with Kerry and her mother, Julie, an hour ago and wasn't anticipating meeting the grandparents this afternoon. She had, in fact, been engaged in her weekly game of mahjong when the call had come in that Fletcher had had some sort of accident at the park. Millie Seibel was an extremely patient and unassuming woman in her early forties; Fletcher was her youngest child, she and her husband, Rubin, having decided six years after their second daughter was born to try again for a boy. She was accustomed to Fletcher's minor accidents as was Julie to Kerry's, so she sat calmly in the hard plastic chair of the waiting area, listening in while Leota berated Julie for not having called her back when she couldn't locate Ethel with the car. Thomas Evans eventually directed Leota to a chair beside Kerry, which freed him to go in search of the men's room. Leota had flagged him down just as he was pulling into his driveway after work, waving her cane in the air and hollering.

"Thomas, we got to get over to the park — just put that Buick in reverse. Lord, Kerry's had an accident and Julie's stuck downtown 'cause that no-good Ethel's out galavantin' in the car. I declare that child's gonna be the death of me yet . . . "

THE SUM TOTAL of injuries was actually very small considering the impact. Kerry had definitely broken her wrist and a cast was placed on her arm, which stopped just below the elbow. Fletcher was relatively unscathed, escaping with only a bump on the head and a bruised instep on his right foot. The accident did manage to open a few doors, with Millie and Julie becoming close friends, and Ethel's car privileges being revoked for two whole weeks. Kerry went back home with Julie for a few days before returning to Leota's. While she was at home, she discovered that the Seibels had moved in to the old Jackson house, which was only two doors down from the Fosters.

Fletcher and Kerry became inseparable. Fletcher would ride his bicycle to Leota's every afternoon, where he and Kerry would sit out in the shade and play card games. Kerry knew more card games and more ways to cheat in each of them than any other girl he'd ever met. Leota was becoming quite fond of Fletcher; she thought he had the finest manners of any eleven-year-old any of the grandchildren had brought around to her house.

In the evenings around dusk, Leota and Kerry would sit out on the front porch, Kerry with her arm in her cast and Leota with her foot in hers, propped up on the porch railing. Leota would be turning fifty-eight on August fifth, which was only a few days away. Her birthday would be on a Sunday this year; she'd always liked having her birthday fall on a nice, peaceful Sunday. Julie had made plans for all of them to go downtown that day to eat lunch at the Picadilly Cafeteria and afterwards to a movie at the State Theater there on Congress Avenue. Leota was especially looking forward to the movie, as it was a new Gregory Peck film called *To Kill a Mockingbird*. In the meantime, the children had planned to attend a sock hop down at the park tomorrow evening. Julie had made arrangements for Kerry to ride with Fletcher's family to the park. Leota was counting on having a nice, quiet evening alone.

THE BASKETBALL COURT was lit up like a carnival with colored patio lights when Kerry and Fletcher arrived at the park at seven. It was just beginning to get dark outside and a cool breeze was blowing in from the southeast. The DJ from the radio station was enthusiastically introducing each song he played, hoping to entice the boys and girls, who had segregated themselves to separate sides of the court, to dance with each other.

He was introducing an Everly Brothers' song, "Cathy's Clown," as Kerry and Fletcher approached the edge of the court. Fletcher located a place for him and Kerry to sit at one of the picnic tables under the lights and headed off to sign out a checkers set from the recreation office.

Some of the mothers had brought Kool-Aid and cookies for the children. Mr. Ferguson was the only father who had volunteered to chaperone the event.

He stood lurking in the shadows with a flashlight attached to his belt and a walkie-talkie in his hand. Kerry couldn't figure out what good that was going to do him since Mrs. Ferguson was supposed to be manning the other walkie-talkie and she was off chatting with Missy Krandel's mother over at the refreshment table, leaving the walkie-talkie with Mr. Ferguson's froggy voice barking out of it on the cement ledge just behind Kerry and Fletcher's table.

With Julie absent from the scene, Raleigh had taken the opportunity to team up with his pal Buster. They were betting against the odds that Ethel was too preoccupied with the date she wasn't supposed to have with Stan Grant to pay much mind to the two of them.

It was a wonderful summer's evening with laughter and music floating across the playground. The sounds of lighthearted conversations seemed to rent the air with excitement. Leota stepped out on her front porch and could hear the faint sound of the Everly Brothers' harmony drifting down from the park all the way to her house.

For Kerry and Fletcher it had been a most enjoyable evening under the stars. They had stayed at their table all evening playing checkers. It was the first time in recorded history that Kerry had been given a good report by the chaperones. The same could not be said of Raleigh and Ethel.

Raleigh and Buster had taken it upon themselves to harass the devil out of Stan and Ethel. First it was water balloons, then it was some firecrackers left over from the Fourth of July — Mr. Ferguson had confiscated those. Then it was spitballs, manufactured from the paper flyers at the park and delivered through the very straws the mothers had brought for the Kool-Aid.

Raleigh liked to aim his spitballs directly at the lobe of Stan's ear. For a while Stan and Ethel thought they were simply being pestered by the horse flies that always hovered over the creek — until Ethel took a direct hit by a spitball on the cheek. Stan had stashed a six-pack of beer in the cold water along the edge of the creek that afternoon. He struck a bargain with Raleigh and Buster, giving them one beer each and four cigarettes as a bribe to get them to leave him and Ethel alone.

Buster got caught showing off his ability to smoke a cigarette right off the bat by Missy Krandel's mother, and he in turn spilled the beans about Raleigh and the cans of beer.

Ethel and Stan were caught making out in the back seat of Stan's 1957 Chevrolet by Mr. Ferguson's flashlight, which in itself wouldn't have been such a bad offense, except for the fact that Ethel was naked from the waist up and Stan had forgotten to zip his fly.

Leota's phone was ringing once again, except this time, thank the Lord, Kerry was sound asleep in the front bedroom and had been for a good half hour.

SATURDAY HAD BEEN a quiet day around Julie's house, with Raleigh confined to his room and Ethel out for a conference with her father. Raleigh was grounded for the rest of the summer. Ethel was to be sent to an all-girls private school in the fall. Ethel had driven past the school many times and thanked her lucky stars that she didn't have to go there.

In addition to being condemned to an all-girls school, Ethel, who blamed this entire fiasco on Raleigh and his big mouth, was to take Kerry and the big mouth to the library once a week till Christmas. Those two loved to go to the library and they'd spend hours and hours dawdling in there.

Julie had been tempted to cancel their plans to celebrate Leota's birthday tomorrow, but this was really the last special event of the summer and she just couldn't do that to Kerry.

ON SUNDAY MORNING everyone woke early. There were arguments between Raleigh and Ethel over the bathroom, which Julie settled by allowing Ethel to use hers in the master bedroom. They all bathed, even Raleigh, who doused his head with a double dose of butch wax and actually wore a tie for the occasion. Julie had bought her mother a dozen roses, which were stored in the refrigerator. It was such a beautiful day outside that everyone forgot their angers and everyone put their selfishness aside.

Kerry and Leota woke around nine. Kerry had bought her grandmother a new pair of slippers for her birthday. She placed them tenderly under the edge of Leota's bed so that she would see them when she got up. Kerry knew very few of the details concerning the activities of Raleigh and Ethel on Friday night. Leota and Julie agreed it was best to keep it that way.

Kerry had chosen to wear a red and white-checked skirt that her mother had made her in June, a plain white blouse, white nylon ankle socks with the cuffs folded just so, and her red patent leather shoes. Kerry had washed her hair this morning and decided to leave it down so that it hung clear to her waist and sparkled in the sunlight. Leota came out on the front porch carrying her house keys and pocketbook. She felt as splendid on this fifty-eighth birthday as she had on her first. This summer had made all the difference in the world in Kerry, Leota could feel it. All things pass, all things go by; she was thankful that with this change in Kerry she had been allowed to observe. Her own youth had slipped past her unnoticed.

"Happy Birthday, Leo," Kerry said, holding a lovely buttercup out to Leota.

"Oh, thank you, Kerry," Leota said.

Julie pulled the Volkswagen up in her mother's driveway and honked the horn three beeps. Ethel jumped out of the car with the roses, which meant that Leota had to unlock the house again to take them inside and put them in water.

Everyone piled into the VW, Leota and Julie in the front seats, Raleigh and Ethel in the back with choice spots by the windows, and Kerry sandwiched between them in the middle. Julie hadn't had time to get the car into the shop last week so the heater was still stuck on. The heater vents for the back were on either side of Kerry's feet and before too long Kerry's feet were so hot in those patent leather shoes that she actually thought they'd melted together. She whined a bit and she cried a bit but finally realized that there was absolutely nothing anyone in the car could do to solve the problem. She took it upon herself to create a minor altercation with Raleigh by placing her feet on his side of the floorboard. Ethel, wishing to disassociate herself from the disturbance, asked Leota to turn the radio on.

The radio came on with a start. It was tuned to the local bubblegum rock-and-roll station, but the song that was playing was one which was very popular in Austin because it was recorded by a young Austinite named Carolyn Hester. Kerry and Ethel had the record at home; they knew every note and every word by heart. Jeff had taken Kerry and Ethel to hear Miss Hester in concert not long ago. Ethel had been so embarrassed because Kerry had insisted upon getting Miss Hester to sign her program, which had meant they'd had to stand in line for some fifteen minutes. The concert had been part of the Austin Boat Show. There had been popcorn, hot dogs, Coca-Cola, and cotton candy. Kerry had gotten her cotton candy tangled up in her pigtails. She had been one sticky mess while waiting in line to get Miss Hester's autograph. Jeff had been leery of allowing her to get close to Miss Hester, fearing Kerry would get that sticky cotton candy on Miss Hester's clothing. Kerry had sensed Jeff's anxieties and began to cry long, silent tears of sorrow for her father's disappointment in her. Carolyn Hester had mistaken these tears for shyness when Kerry stood before her and had reached down to Kerry to dry the tears away with her own handkerchief. Kerry thought this was absolutely the kindest thing anyone had ever done for her in her whole life.

The song was winding up with the last verse on the radio. Everyone in the car was singing along with Carolyn Hester.

> Oh, the water is wide, I cannot cross over
> And neither have I wings to fly.
> Give me a boat that can carry two
> And both shall row, my love and I.

The jingle for the station then began playing: "K-N-O-W fourteen-ninety. News on the hour every hour. Stay tuned for news at noon with Dave Jarret immediately following this word from our sponsors."

Then there was a commercial for Burger Chef Hamburgers. "Come to Burger Chef, just a nickel and a dime" went the jingle.

"This is Dave Jarret reporting for K-N-O-W news on the hour. Screen goddess Marilyn Monroe was found dead of an apparent overdose of barbiturates this morning in her Los Angeles home."

"Did you hear that, Mother?" Ethel said. "I can't believe it! Marilyn Monroe's dead."

Julie turned the radio off.

"That's such a shame about Marilyn Monroe. You know, she had just turned thirty-six in June. Remember when she sang 'Happy Birthday' to President Kennedy on television?" Leota said.

Kerry said, "She always seemed like such a nice lady."

"Oh, what do you know? Ya little moron, you never even met her," Ethel snapped.

Julie said, "OK, that's enough back there!"

The whole car fell silent as Julie searched for a parking space on Congress Avenue. Raleigh had fallen asleep with his head leaning against the window frame and his mouth hanging open. Kerry's feet were truly melted together in that summer heat in the back seat of the Volkswagen with the heater stuck on. Ethel was attempting to powder her nose, having a hard time holding the compact mirror steady with the grinding of gears in stop-and-go traffic.

The two sisters, Kerry and Ethel, who'd been bound together only moments ago, singing harmony to the angelic voice of Carolyn Hester on the radio, were now separated by a wall of indifference, and though it had been Ethel who had taken notice of the news about the death of Marilyn Monroe and promptly accusing Kerry of not knowing anything about her, it would also be Ethel who would promptly forget. It would be Kerry who would always remember, and it would be Kerry who would always sing that song.

For the Heart of the Jewel

JULIE WAS SIX YEARS OLD AGAIN. It was the spring of 1936; the New Deal was in full bloom in the Rio Grande Valley. Along with her parents, Edgar and Leota, she lived with her grandmother in a modest, white house on Kimball Avenue in Raymondville, Texas. The house was clean, everything was clean and fresh; the yard was full of orange trees; the house was sparsely furnished with furniture of oak made by her grandfather Max in the late 1800s. Grandfather Max had died while pushing his plow across the West Texas Panhandle in 1930. The dust had killed him, strangled the breath from his body; the dust and the land had reclaimed him as their own. Her grandmother, Kerry Pearl, sold the farm after Max's death. She chose to retire in the Rio Grande Valley near the Mexican border, where the dust never blew, where the rain fell softly each and every day, where all things grew in abundance, and the radio station in Weslaco carried baseball and *The Rudy Vallee Variety Hour* with Edgar Bergen and Charlie McCarthy.

Kerry Pearl was an impressive woman. She was delicately boned for her height of almost six feet; her hair was silver and she kept it bound loosely in a bun secured by tortoiseshell combs. Baseball was her passion; her prized possession was an autographed baseball signed by Waite Hoyt of the New York Yankees. Max had an old friend named Howard Bates who was an insurance salesman in New York City; he'd sent Kerry Pearl the autographed baseball back in 1927.

Julie's father, Edgar, had moved Julie and Leota to Kerry Pearl's home so he could take a job on the Willacy County roads project.

The workdays were long, the humidity made Edgar helplessly drowsy after lunch, and the mid-afternoon rains made the roadwork near impossible.

Kerry Pearl ran the household; Leota was not allowed in her kitchen. Julie took piano lessons from an eccentric elderly woman named Miss Demerick. Leota also played the piano. She spent her mornings trading songs with Julie. The two of them would sit together on the piano bench with the ivory keys before them. The laughter would ring in the melodies, the love between a mother and daughter would balance itself within the ease in which their hands could move across the ivory together, with only an occasional discord.

Julie was dreaming of a Saturday afternoon in that spring of 1936. Edgar and Leota had taken her across the border to Mexico to go shopping. It was mid-afternoon and like clockwork the gentle rain was washing clean the crowded streets outside the market of Matamoros. Julie walked between her mother and father, holding on to each of their hands. Edgar spoke Spanish. Occasionally they would stop to examine some article on the tables in the market. In the dream the tables contained medical supplies, syringes, bedpans, and miscellaneous stainless steel instruments. Only one table had brightly colored merchandise of Mexican origin. It was on this table that Julie found a set of sterling silver hair combs decorated in turquoise. She begged Edgar to buy the combs for her grandmother Kerry Pearl but Edgar said they were too expensive, that the vendor would not come down enough on his price. The market became dark, filled with voices speaking words she could not understand. Her mother and father let go of her hands and she could not find them in the dark. She ran into the light of the rain on the sidewalks outside the market, where she saw the Mexican children running barefoot in the streets with no sign of adult supervision, their feet splashing with no sound in puddles of filth in the gutters.

"Julie, I've put the water on for some coffee," Leota said. "The movers will be here any minute now."

The rain was still falling. There was silence in the house on Kimball Avenue. Kerry Pearl's radio was packed in a crate awaiting its move to Austin. Julie woke from her nap with the strange feeling that she was still within the dream. This was not 1936, it was 1971. She was no longer six years old. That innocence was long forgotten; it lingered in the shadow of the dream itself, searching for the hands of her mother and father somewhere in the streets of Mexico.

Kerry Pearl had broken her hip in a fall last autumn. Julie and Leota had thought it best that she be moved to Austin, as her health had gotten steadily worse since the accident. Kerry Pearl was ninety-two years old. Julie could hardly believe that she had lived that many years. Kerry Pearl had never been sick a day in her life, she had never complained, she had never been dependent on anyone. She had always been her own safe harbor.

Julie swung her legs over the edge of the daybed and headed toward the kitchen, where she could hear Leota preparing the coffee. The cabinets were bare. The bookshelves were empty. The house was as it had been on the day Kerry Pearl had moved here.

"Mother, did you find those silver hair combs that I gave to Kerry Pearl when you were packing her personal things?" Julie asked.

"They were still in the box, Julie. Black as coal with tarnish. You know it seems like Mama wore those combs when she married Howard Bates. Lord, but that was such a sad day in my life that I can't truly remember," Leota answered as the teakettle began to whistle and the sun sent its first afternoon rays through the kitchen window.

"I had an awful dream a while ago. I can't tell you how happy I'll be to get back to Austin. This house just isn't right without Kerry Pearl here. I feel as though we're invading her privacy by packing her things, as though she doesn't want her memories moved from this house. Is there any sugar around for this coffee?" Julie asked.

Leota answered, "No, ma'am, 'fraid you're gonna have to drink it black this time. The sugar had been here so long that I thought it best to throw it out. I was afraid it might make us sick. I know exactly how you feel about this house. I've half-expected Mama to step in here at any minute and demand that I get the heck out of her kitchen. In all my years, this is the first time I have ever worked in my mother's kitchen. If you were still planning to take some of Mama's aloe vera plants back to Austin then you'd best get a move-on. Her gardening tools are locked in the shed out back. And Julie, don't worry too much about this move for your grandmother. We both know it is for the best."

Julie took her cup of coffee with her to the backyard. The orange trees were just beginning to blossom and their scent was intoxicating. In one section of what had once been Kerry Pearl's garden there were several large aloe vera plants with hundreds of small plants surrounding them. Julie went to the shed to find the garden tools and some empty containers.

As she dug the plants up one by one in the garden, she thought of her grandmother. Julie was forty-two, a long distance from the image of Kerry Pearl. When you are a young woman of forty-two, it is hard to feature yourself as ever being old; it is hard to picture the youth of someone who is now ninety-two. It is as though they were never young, they were never your age, they were never within your reach of understanding.

Julie laughed out loud there in the garden when remembering what her mother had just said in the kitchen about how sad a day it had been for her when Kerry Pearl had married Howard Bates. She laughed so hard that Leota stuck her head out the screen door and yelled:

"Just what the hell's going on out here?"

"It's nothing, Mother. Really, I'm fine," Julie answered, still snickering under her breath.

"Well, just hurry yourself up out there. Those movers are not a-gonna wait around for the yard work to be finished," Leota called out to Julie as the screen door slammed behind her.

Kerry Pearl had married Howard Bates in 1956 at the tender age of seventy-seven to Howard's seventy-two. The courtship had begun in 1948. Howard had written to Kerry Pearl asking if she had a spare room she might be interested in renting out during the winter, as he was retiring from his insurance business and would like to escape the cold during the winter months. Kerry Pearl had written him back to accept his offer. Every winter after that Howard had arrived sometime in November to remain in the warmth of Raymondville until the last day of April, when he would pack up and move back to his summer home in Upstate New York.

Howard Bates was a small man, very trim, and extremely proper. He had always carried a true affection for Kerry Pearl, even when Max was still alive. Kerry Pearl and Howard were quite the pair when observed out walking together: this tall, slender woman with her mountain of silver hair and this short, thin man with his white handlebar mustache. On Sunday mornings during those winters they would stroll hand in hand down Kimball Avenue to Gem Street, where they would attend Mass at Saint Mary's. The winters went on this way for several years, with the spare room remaining empty after that first winter. Kerry Pearl and Howard shared more together in those tropical winters in Raymondville than any family member would ever understand. They wrote poetry to each other during the summer and fall when they were separated. Howard would write endless letters to Kerry Pearl about the baseball season. They would argue back and forth through the mail about the Dodgers and the Yankees and they would long for the end of the World Series and the first of November.

Each winter Howard would ask Kerry Pearl to marry him and each winter Kerry Pearl would decline the offer for fear that her children would not approve. Leota had somehow gotten wind of the fact that the relationship between her mother and Howard could no longer be classified as non-prurient. Kerry Pearl figured Leota had gotten wind of this by snooping into her box of letters from Howard on one of her visits. Leota persisted in nagging Kerry Pearl about Howard for two years; the nagging itself finally resulted in provoking Kerry Pearl into accepting Howard's proposal. Leota had been beside herself with grief over this choice on the day of the wedding. It was a simple ceremony at Saint Mary's with only Leota and her sisters, Cora and Maggie, attending as witnesses. Father Ellis had smiled approvingly at the couple as they exchanged vows. After all, Howard and Kerry Pearl were in love, they were true to their faith in God, and there would be no problem with this couple breaking their vow of "till death do us part." That was one promise they would probably not have time to reconsider.

The movers came knocking at the front door just as Leota was packing the last of the china. Leota supervised the hauling of boxes and furniture while feeling very insecure about giving orders to anyone in her mother's house.

When the house was cleared of all its contents, Leota stood at the kitchen sink staring outside at nothing in particular through the kitchen window. The years her mother had lived in this house remained a mystery to Leota. It was as if this house was brand-new, as though it were just yesterday that her mother had moved here. All around her were the markings of her mother's day-to-day existence. The linoleum floor was worn beneath her feet, the porcelain was chipped in the sink, the clotheslines dipped toward the center, and the garden, though now overgrown, was meticulously enclosed within a white picket fence. This was her mother's life without her; this was her mother's own identity, separate from the life of Leota, separate from being her mother. It was difficult for Leota to ponder what her mother's life had been here. It was impossible for Leota to understand that her mother had been many things to many people in her lifetime besides just being her mother.

They had shared so much of their lives, each to her own discretion, those lines of discretion becoming the majority of their relationship. Leota felt as though she was this person who Kerry Pearl had created, that Kerry Pearl had molded her character with great care; with the love of a mother, with the grace of a stranger. Kerry Pearl now existed to Leota as that stranger, and in being Kerry Pearl's own creation there could be no mystery to Leota in her mother's eyes. It made no difference that the world had flown by between them nor that their paths no longer crossed common ground. Leota knew nothing of her mother's thoughts; it was only the heart of her mother which she could recall with clarity.

Leota locked the house behind her. Julie was waiting in the car, impatiently tapping the steering wheel with her thumbnails. Leota stopped to straighten the For Sale sign in the yard before getting into the car with Julie. Her eyes traced every detail of her mother's home in just that fraction of a second between the opening of the car door and sliding into the front seat. The history of her mother's life within those walls would now be lost forever within Leota's own curiosity.

It would be an eight-hour drive to Austin from Raymondville. Julie and Leota spent the major part of the trip trading stories about Kerry Pearl. Leota commented several times during the trip that there was a lot more trust between she and Julie then she'd ever had with Kerry Pearl. Leota specified that Kerry Pearl had never allowed her to get too close and that she was so happy that she and Julie could openly discuss just about anything under the sun. Julie, on the other hand, felt it odd that her mother felt exactly the same way about Kerry Pearl as she felt about Leota. Julie, understandably, kept these opposing thoughts to herself.

Julie had named her youngest daughter after Kerry Pearl and her husband Jeff's mother, Ruth. She spent most of her academic time getting involved in political troubles on campus while claiming to be studying journalism. She dabbled at being a folk singer aside from attending college, but couldn't really be pinned down to having any particular goals in mind for her future.

Julie secretly admired this in her daughter, as she herself had had a two-year-old daughter by the time she was Kerry's age and her life had been planned with no drama before her youth had even begun to explore itself. Kerry was irresponsible with just about everything in her life, with the one exception of visiting her great-grandmother every day. The visits only lasted an hour, but nonetheless they were the highlight of Kerry Pearl's days. Some days they played checkers; on other days they would discuss the war in Vietnam and Kerry's involvement with the anti-war movement. Kerry Pearl explained to Kerry that she had had the very same sentiments during World

War I. Not only did the young Kerry and her great-grandmother share the same name but they were very much alike in nature. Both were idealists, both placed matters of the heart far above common sense on their lists of priorities. It was due to this common link between them that had caused Kerry Pearl to choose young Kerry to read her weekly letters from Howard Bates to her and young Kerry in turn would write letters dictated to her by Kerry Pearl back to Howard. Kerry Pearl's eyesight was becoming so poor these days that she could not read anymore without giving herself a headache, and her hands, once graceful with long, tapered fingers, were now crippled with arthritis.

On this particular day, Kerry sat in the waiting area of the nursing home reading the latest letter from Howard. She always read the letters first before reading them to her great-grandmother, as sometimes she had to study Howard's handwriting closely to be able to make out the words.

> *My Beautiful Pearl,*
>
> *It was so nice to receive your letter. Please tell young Kerry that I find it so endearing that she takes time out of her busy schedule to keep our correspondence intact. I am still secure in my belief that I will get to meet her someday.*
>
> *Did they deliver the television to you? I ordered it last Tuesday. I hope that it is the model you had in mind. Now you won't have to argue with your roommate over which channels to watch. I hope you will think of me when you are watching the baseball games this spring.*
>
> *I am feeling much better, thank you. Those kidney stones were the darndest thing I've ever been through. I have asked my doctor about the possibility of me moving to Austin soon. He has told me that though I am in great health for an eighty-seven-year-old man, I still need some time to recover from this kidney thing.*
>
> *I am so lonely here. We missed our winter this year. There is still snow on the ground here in Saratoga Springs. It has been*

a long, hard winter and I do not like this place. The nurses seldom stop to chat and there is no television in my room here.

I don't know what to advise you on this problem with Leota and Cora. If they are so opposed to my coming to live in the same nursing home with you in Austin now, then I doubt they are going to change their minds in the future. You must understand that I don't intentionally mean to offend you in saying this, but I think those two ladies are full of horse cookies! (Tell young Kerry that I've asked her to cover her ears while she's reading this.) Leota has never accepted the fact that you and I are husband and wife and it's just darned well time that she did so. As for Cora, well you'd think with that diddle-brained husband of hers to look after that she'd have very little time to pry into your affairs. We must simply forge ahead with our lives and stop fretting over these inconsequential matters. There is nothing for me here in the North, I don't know why I've kept up this silly ritual of returning here for all these years. All those summers that I spent here were a waste of time, they were a waste of precious time. I should have been there with you when you fell. I am now more determined than ever that we shall be reunited again.

I will await your reply in loving anticipation. Do not fear, my sweetest, for though we are far apart, you are always in my thoughts. We must never give up hope for tomorrow. I will continue to pray for your recovery.

Your faithful and devoted husband,
Howard

Kerry folded the letter neatly and placed it back in the envelope. She smiled to herself as she walked down the hall to Kerry Pearl's room, her loafers tapping out a happy click on the tile floor as she entered the room. She knew full well that this letter was exactly what

Kerry Pearl had needed for a long time; Howard's letter would be certain to cheer her up. Kerry Pearl had been waiting for years for Howard to take a stand on her daughters' conspiracy against them. The thought of having Howard here beside her would give her something to live for, even if it was just a wild dream with very little chance of becoming a reality.

Kerry entered her great-grandmother's room only to find it engulfed in darkness. The curtains were drawn tight and she could hear the sound of Kerry Pearl sobbing softly in the shadows. Kerry located a small lamp on a bed table next to the door. She stood still just long enough for her eyes to adjust to the dim light. The bed next to the lamp was empty. Normally Kerry Pearl's roommate, Mrs. Garcia, occupied that space. The linens had been stripped from the bed, leaving the bare mattress to stare back at Kerry. Kerry Pearl's bed was on the other side of the room. She had requested that her bed be moved to its present location so she and Mrs. Garcia could be facing each other. The two women had become very close during the six weeks they'd been roommates. Young Kerry approached her great-grandmother's bedside with reserve.

Kerry Pearl extended her hand to her great-granddaughter. Young Kerry was shocked at what she saw surrounding her. Her great-grandmother had not had her hair combed, her water pitcher was empty, the remote control for the television was clear across the room on Mrs. Garcia's nightstand, and there was a strange smell in the room which Kerry could not quite place in origin.

"Pearlie, why is this room so dark?" asked Kerry.

"It's been an awful day, Kerry. I think they've forgotten that I'm here. I'm so thirsty and they've hidden my glasses from me. I've pushed on that button for the nurse all day but no one ever comes. No one ever comes. Mrs. Garcia passed on late last night. Please, Kerry, dear, would you mind getting me some water?" Kerry Pearl spoke in a very soft voice; she was too weak to speak any louder than a whisper.

As Kerry reached for the water pitcher she noticed that the floor beneath her feet was wet, as well as the side of the mattress.

"I'll be right back, Pearlie, and don't worry we'll get you all fixed up here in a minute. Have you eaten today?" Kerry asked.

"No," said Kerry Pearl. "Don't leave me here alone again, Kerry."

Kerry could hear her great-grandmother begin sobbing again as she left the room and she wished she'd at least opened the curtains before she'd left.

When Kerry reached the glass-enclosed nurses' station she tapped hard on the window to get the nurse's attention inside. She recognized this particular nurse on duty as one who had filled in a few weeks ago when the regular day nurse was ill. The nurse was a large woman at least twice Kerry's weight. She sported a red beehive hairdo, bright orange lipstick, and black eyebrows drawn on with eyebrow pencil. She was talking on the phone and upon hearing Kerry's knock at the window she cradled the phone between her shoulder and double chin in order to free her hands to slide the window open.

She said, "I'll be with ya in just a second, hon." She smacked her gum at Kerry and slid the window shut.

Kerry sat down in a chair facing the nurses' station to wait. There was a large, round clock on the wall inside the station and she watched it intently as the hands clicked the minutes by. The nurse looked up occasionally from her phone conversation to smile at Kerry, but as the minutes passed and Kerry's expression melted into rage, the woman turned her back to the window completely.

Kerry lost her patience when ten minutes had passed. She went back to the window, and without knocking this time, opened the sliding glass, reached inside, and spun the nurse around to face her. The nurse was so flabbergasted at having this skinny little hippie girl with wire-rimmed glasses yank her around that Kerry had a firm grip on the lapels of her nurse's uniform before she could regain her senses.

"You have a patient in Room 112 who has not eaten today. It is now four o'clock in the afternoon. Her drapes are drawn, her water pitcher is empty, she can't walk and the controls to her television are way across the room. She has been paging this nurses' station for help all day long. Not only that but her catheter has come loose and she is drowning in her own urine. Now, you get off this stupid phone and off your dead ass and go help her!" Kerry hissed.

"Now, there's no need to be so nasty, sweetie," said the nurse.

Julie and Leota entered the lobby area at that moment. Leota couldn't help but notice the wrestling match taking place at the nurses' station, but it was Julie who realized that half that squabble involved her daughter, Kerry.

Leota had a tendency to mind her own business and was going to quietly walk past this scene, pretending not to notice anything out of the ordinary.

Julie screamed, "Kerry, what in heaven's name are you doing?"

Kerry did not respond to her mother's voice but instead continued shaking this stocky nurse around and maintained a firm grip on the woman's uniform. The nurse still grasped the phone in her hand and was threatening to knock Kerry in the head with the receiver. Julie then grabbed Kerry by the arm and began to tug with all her strength away from the nurses' station, but Kerry had secured such a firm grip on the nurse's uniform that Julie only succeeded in aiding Kerry's attempt to pull the nurse through the window. Leota had managed to stay a safe distance away from the dilemma at hand. Leota, now secure in the belief that her strategy would be successful, calmly approached the trio. Leota was, by far, the smallest member of the brawl, and with great courage she reached up between Julie and Kerry to remove the wire-rimmed glasses from Kerry's face. Having safely stored the glasses in her handbag, she again reached up between the mother and daughter and politely, quite deliberately, delivered one sharp slap across Kerry's face. The act in itself rendered the entangled three women motionless while Leota stepped back from the scene and clutched her handbag tightly to her breasts.

"Knock it off, Kerry! Let's sit down and talk about this like civilized folks. Let go of that woman this instant!" said Leota, who was still quite calm considering the circumstances.

Kerry released her hold on the nurse while Julie in turn let go of Kerry's arm. The husky nurse, who hadn't bargained for anything like this occurring today, then slammed the window shut to the nurses' station, resumed her conversation with her boyfriend who was on the other end of the phone line, and glared at Julie and Kerry through the glass, hoping above all else that this third woman would talk some sense into this nutcase hippie kid.

Leota, who had tired of the whole scene, took off down the hall to see her mother. "If y'all will excuse me, I'm gonna go on down to visit Mama," Leota called back over her shoulder.

Within five minutes Leota came bounding back down the hall to the nurses' station nearly colliding head-on with the beehived nurse. Julie had gotten the situation in hand and as it turned out the nurse hadn't known that Kerry Pearl was in her room. When Mrs. Garcia had passed on the night crew had shuffled the records around so that the day staff thought that room unoccupied.

Within the hour, Kerry Pearl was sitting up in bed drinking iced tea and listening to young Kerry read Howard's letter to her. She held the remote control to her new television in her hand and annoyingly flipped the channels back and forth while Kerry was trying to read her the letter.

"Pearlie, just how am I supposed to read this letter to you if you won't stop fiddling with the TV?" Kerry asked.

"I'm just afraid that your grandmother Leota might be listening outside the door. She's a known eavesdropper from way back. Now, don't get me wrong, Kerry, I do love her dearly, but when it comes to Howard, your grandmother Leota's a fanatic," Kerry Pearl replied.

"Well, Pearlie, I have to go soon. I promised Raleigh that I'd meet him for dinner, so would you stop long enough for me to finish this letter? If you don't then it's gonna have to be continued until tomorrow," Kerry said.

"Oh, all right, Kerry, but if Leota comes in here fuming about Howard then I'm gonna know that she was listening outside and I'm gonna hold you personally responsible for the mental anguish she inflicts upon me," Kerry Pearl said as she placed the remote control on the nightstand.

Kerry finished reading the letter from Howard to Kerry Pearl. She placed it under Kerry Pearl's pillow before leaving to meet her brother Raleigh. Raleigh was twenty-two. He'd just recently left his wife and six-month-old baby. He had called Kerry last night sounding a bit desperate for someone to talk to. It wasn't normal for Raleigh to come to Kerry with a problem, but with their mother out of town and not due back till late that night, Kerry figured she'd been the last resort. Their sister Ethel still lived in town with her husband, Rodney, but talking to Ethel was somewhat similar to talking to one of those gameshow hosts on TV: her solution was always behind a closed door and nine times out of ten involved changing the subject around to some problem of hers.

RALEIGH SAT at a window booth in the Frisco Cafe waiting for his sister to arrive. It was just beginning to get dark outside. He studied the cars passing by, turning on their headlights, changing lanes, and stopping at red lights. It was a very ordinary hometown street, so unquestionably familiar. He had flown down this street hundreds of times as a child on his bicycle, pretending to be a great motorcycle rider, pretending to be anything but plain old Raleigh Foster.

Raleigh was a big man, almost six-four, with a large frame. Though he had never been overweight he had always been clumsy and he had spent the majority of his life being teased for his awkwardness. It seemed to him that no one took his ambitions or his dreams seriously. He was simply 'good old Raleigh' to everyone — that is, to everyone but his sister, Kerry. He felt that Kerry never took anyone for granted. She looked at each person separately and judged them accordingly. She was, in general, a trusting sort of person, yet she was quick to draw conclusions from the mistakes of others. She made her own mistakes often enough; she had a knack for being in the wrong place at the wrong time and she could certainly bring out the worst in those around her. Raleigh had been witness to several mistakes his sister Kerry had made during their lives. As a child, her reluctance to walk away from trouble had been a constant nuisance to him, as he had always been obligated to rescue her from turmoil. Kerry was upfront, she was wide open to the world, yet she was a mystery in herself because she never closed her heart. The pain of youthful battle went inside her and it never came out again. That was the mystery of Kerry to Raleigh: the thought that all of their youth rested peacefully within her memories. His sister Ethel, though not as widely known for her mistakes, had settled into her adult years with quite a malevolent disposition.

Raleigh was leaving Austin. His life here had become too black and white to hold his interests. He thought of himself as being hopelessly average, with no special gifts to offer the world. His sisters each held their unique qualities.

Ethel had once been homecoming queen, a beauty to behold, and though she was now overweight and a tad bitter about being just a housewife, she still had her social status. Ethel had married well; her husband, Rodney, came from a very wealthy family in Houston. Ethel had never worked a day in her life; she had gone straight from one year of college to becoming the wife of Rodney Preston. She was now the mother of two very beautiful, extremely spoiled daughters who were very much like their mother. Ethel was also an alcoholic, which was a fact that Raleigh was unaware of. It was a well-kept secret within the Preston household. Like Raleigh, Ethel spent her days and nights wishing she had been something other than the simple day-to-day person she had become. She drank away the laughter of her lovely children; she had ceased to view them as treasures and in turn they no longer respected her as a mother. Still, to Raleigh, her home in the prestigious Northwest Hills of Austin and her name in the gossip columns left him feeling like a failure. Ethel longed for her vibrant youth; she ached for the excitement of the back seat of a 1957 Chevrolet and the anguished eyes of the suitors she had shunned haunted her dreams. She was nothing within herself, answerable to everyone, trusted by no one.

Kerry was her sister's opposite. Raleigh pictured her as having the potential to succeed in many things. He considered her to be talented in many things. Kerry herself got in the way of her own talents, as she wasn't yet capable of concentrating on any one thing long enough to make a go of it, but she would. Raleigh knew she would. Somewhere down the line Kerry would hit the jackpot because she was different. She had hope for humanity and that hope came through on the surface as a spark in her hazel eyes. Kerry was not as pretty as her sister had been, yet she had her own unique style which gave her an occasional hint of beauty. She was tall with a fragile appearance; she had long, chestnut brown hair, which was soft and fine, most often left uncurled and stringy. She had lovely hands. Raleigh thought her hands were like porcelain. In fact, she herself had the image of being a porcelain doll from some foreign land. She carried a pristine quality about her that did not quite fit in with the American ideal. She considered herself mediocre, which was why she became so easily bored with her own projects. Raleigh felt that Kerry would never have allowed herself to be trapped within this lifestyle he had adopted; not Kerry, she was never one to be average. But Kerry would understand. She would look into his eyes and say, "Raleigh, it's OK if you desert your wife and child. Time will take care of everything. You go on out there and find yourself." Kerry's understanding was all he wanted at this moment in time — just a smile on his little sister's face would ease all guilt.

KERRY WAS LATE to the Frisco. The darkness became Raleigh's own reflection in the window before him, the streets of a hometown no longer mingled with the image of his face, they were no longer related to each other. They were both now the essence of an unknown quantity. Raleigh was the gentle soul, believing there to be more than this city, more than his family; believing that everyone had more than he would ever hold. He was the last of the true believers, he held the wealth of a heart to lend. It was Raleigh who was the special one of the three children. He would search the world for that something out there that would set his heart on end and engulf him with mystery, for this city held no secrets. This was the mecca for the idealist. This city of Austin had buried itself with the illusion of being the center of a lifestyle Americana; it had closed its own doors to growth with this conceit. It offered nothing more than any other middle-class American ghetto, built and protected by individuals who were either too lazy or too afraid to venture from its boundaries.

"Raleigh, I'm sorry I'm a little late. Pearlie had some trouble this afternoon," Kerry said as she slid into the booth.

"That's alright. It was kind of nice just sitting here thinking for a while. What's up with Pearlie?"

"Well, it's a long story. I'm not sure you're up for hearing all about it, it's all taken care of now anyway. Mom and Leo are back from the Valley. You know, I told you a few weeks ago that I'd been helping Pearlie with her letters to Howard? Well, it seems that Howard really is intending to move down here. Pearlie got a letter from him today. He's such a romantic. Leo's not buying the whole thing, she can't stand the fact that her mother married Howard. I feel so sorry for Pearlie. She really does love Howard. Sure has made things difficult between Leo and me. We've always been so close and now it's so hard for me to understand her. I don't think it's fair that I should have to see my grandmother's bad side, I always thought Leo was just perfect. The whole thing is so ridiculous. Don't you think so?"

Raleigh opened his menu to study the dinner specials.

"I guess it's ridiculous, Kerry. To tell you the truth, I hadn't really thought about it too much. Grandmother Leota has always been very strong-willed. I guess she feels like Pearlie should've lived her life as a widow just like she has. I know you've always placed Grandmother Leota above having faults but you have to realize that she's just as human as the rest of us mortals. She graduated from a different era," Raleigh said.

"Raleigh, I know you didn't call me just to have dinner. I don't want to burden you with all the stuff about grandmothers. What's on your mind?" Kerry asked.

The waitress approached their table to take their orders.

"I'm leaving here, Kerry . . . I'll have a cheeseburger, no onions, a side order of fries, and a large Coke," Raleigh said.

The waitress impatiently tapped her order pad with her pencil, waiting for Kerry to order.

"Uh, I'll have a grilled cheese with pickles and a small iced tea, please," Kerry said.

"Where will you go, Raleigh? What about Missy and the baby? Have you told them yet? Gee, I think it's great that you're gonna get out of this town but I don't understand why," Kerry said.

Kerry had visions of her gentle brother Raleigh traveling incognito across the country: Raleigh the patient one, out gazing at America. Raleigh was the heart of the Foster family in Kerry's eyes. He was such a good guy.

"Well, I can't really say where I'll be going. I leave for Fort Polk, Louisiana, in three weeks for basic training. I joined the army, Kerry," Raleigh replied.

"Are you crazy? Tell me you didn't do this, tell me you're only joking! I won't believe you did this — they'll send your ass straight to Vietnam. How in the hell could you do this?" Kerry said in disbelief.

Raleigh reached across the table with his huge, clumsy hands to calm his sister. Kerry was screaming at him in this public place; everyone in the restaurant began to stare. Kerry had been the last person he would've expected to react this way. He took her small, oval face between his hands and gently brushed a tear from her cheek with his thumb.

"It's alright, Kerry. It's what I wanted to do. It was my only alternative to insanity. My old friend Buster joined at the same time that I did. We're both going to Fort Polk. It won't be so bad. Maybe they won't send me to Vietnam. After all, they could send me to Germany or Korea. Please try to understand. I just couldn't take it around here anymore. Missy calls to hassle me two or three times a day at work and her dad, Mr. Asshole Krandel, even came by the shop threatening me last week. That baby doesn't even know who I am yet. Probably never will if Missy gets her way. You know, that

Missy's already been out on a couple of dates with some jerk who's in the Coast Guard. She says she's in love with this guy. Can you believe that crap?" Raleigh asked.

"What I can't believe is that you married that dumbass cheerleader in the first place. She's been jerking you around on a string since junior high and when she couldn't get you to marry her honestly, she got pregnant so you'd have to. I'll never forgive her for what's she's done to you. You were always so afraid of violence; you've always been so sensitive. How will you survive in a place like Vietnam if they send you there? Don't you watch the news, Raleigh? Even war heroes are rallying against the war. I know you're mad at the world, you're angry with this person who you used to love and you feel that things'll never change for you but it isn't going to be better in the army. It won't be Missy shooting back at you from the other side of a rice field, Raleigh, it'll be some guy just like you, just as innocent as you with a family of his own, and there you'll be, trying to kill each other. Remember how afraid you used to be of war? Remember when we were children during the Cuban Missile Crisis? You were so afraid, you thought the world was coming to an end. You made us hide in a closet because you were so sure the big bomb was coming — 'duck and cover, duck and cover.' You were so afraid of war. You just can't do this, Raleigh. I'll fix it . . . I've got some friends at the university who can help you get to Canada. I'm not going to let you go get your ass shot off or your mind blown out," Kerry pleaded.

"No, Kerry, I'm not going to Canada. I've made a commitment to my country and I'm going to stick by it. Jesus, look at that wimp, Rodney. Do you want me to be like him? I gotta do this for myself. I know it's kinda crazy. The only time I've ever been away from home was to go to camp. I think I want to be a paratrooper. I've always wanted to fly free like that."

"Raleigh, I hate to tell you this, but they'll never let you in the paratroopers. You've broken both ankles at least twice playing football in high school. You're always limping around with an Ace bandage on one or the other ankle and that just won't cut it in the paratroopers.

Besides, you'd be a sitting duck, flying around with no protection but a nylon parachute. I still say that we gotta find some way to get you out of this. If you ask me I'd say this was just a damn stupid thing to do," Kerry said.

"Well, nobody asked you what you thought about it. This time I'm simply telling you what's gonna be. Not everybody thinks like you, Kerry. Dad's been trying to get that through your thick skull for years. We've all got to live our own lives. I don't know what I expected to hear from you. Maybe just that I'm not crazy, maybe just that you'd accept me as I am, maybe just that you'd think of me while I'm gone and look in now and then on Missy and the baby," Raleigh said as the last of his cheeseburger disappeared off of his plate. "I think I'll order another burger. You want somethin'?" Raleigh asked with his mouth full.

"No, I don't think so, but by all means go right ahead," Kerry said. Her eyes followed Raleigh's eyes; all those questions unanswered.

By the time Raleigh's second order arrived at the table, he and Kerry had settled their differences. Conversation had changed to include talk of the end of the spring semester for Kerry and the proposed moving of Howard to Austin. Kerry's boyfriend, Fletcher, attended school at North Texas State in Denton. Fletcher would be home for the summer. Raleigh would be gone by then.

"Say, uh, Kerry, aren't you going to eat that sandwich? I'll take it if you don't want it," Raleigh said.

"Good grief, Raleigh, you've already had two burgers, an order of french fries, and half a bottle of ketchup. What about those little children in India who have no food at all? Don't you feel just a little bit guilty?" Kerry teased.

"Alright, I'm guilty, I'm guilty of just about anything you want me to be guilty of, except wasting grilled cheese sandwiches. Now do you want that thing or not?" Raleigh asked.

Kerry pushed the half-eaten sandwich over to Raleigh. Throughout their childhood Raleigh had been known as a human garbage disposal for leftovers. There were few foods in his long list of culinary delights which he could not tolerate, corn being one item, onions another, and pickles being last but not least.

"Jesus Christ, Kerry, ya had 'em put pickles on this thing. Who ever heard of putting pickles on grilled cheese sandwiches?" Raleigh winced.

"Beggars can't be choosers. If ya don't like 'em then take the damn things off," Kerry giggled.

"It was a trap, these pickles, you're trying to get back at me for twenty years of aggravation. Well, it's not gonna work. I'm gonna eat it anyway. When we were kids, I used to think that you always wanted those mayonnaise sandwiches at Leo's just so you wouldn't have to worry about me taking it away from you. Do you remember those times, Kerry, all those summer days we spent loitering at her house? You were top dog over at her place. You and Fletcher and that ugly little rooster, Jangles," Raleigh said as the waitress cleared the table.

"Oh, yes, I remember. I have a heart full of memories, some of them I'd like to forget. I sometimes dream of a time when childhood would become only a handful of memories; that the fear and the wanderlust of youth would be only the dream and not the reality. You see, Raleigh, I don't find our childhood very pleasant to remember. The memories hurt me and the mistakes I've made lurk within the shadows of each new decision and each new emotion. We were rotten children, you and I. Fortunately for Ethel, she was never a child; she will never regret or repent. Whatever problems she may have now can certainly not be blamed on any childhood trauma, considering that she never truly had a childhood. She is unaccountable. You and I are guilty," Kerry sighed.

"Aw, you're always so serious, Kerry. You can't say that Ethel never had a childhood. You're just a lot younger than she is and you weren't around during her rotten years. You know, when you were first brought home from the hospital Ethel thought you were a new doll for her. She grabbed you by the hem of your nightgown, dragged you off of the couch and halfway across the living room floor before Dad could get to her. She thought you were the greatest gift in the world," Raleigh said.

"I have heard that story many times, Raleigh, and it has been recently brought to my attention by Ethel herself that her motive for dragging me off the couch was to drown me in the bathtub before anyone could get the chance to become attached to me. In case you don't recall, it has been stated in the story that the bathtub had already been mysteriously filled with water before Ethel approached the couch. To this day, Ethel swears that the whole family would have been much happier if she'd been allowed to terminate my existence."

"Well, as long as we're on the subject of Ethel: Why don't we go barge in on her? It's only eight-thirty. The girls'll still be up. I want to tell Rodney that I've joined the army," Raleigh said.

"I think I'll pass on that one, Raleigh. I mean, you know, Ethel'll be sitting around sippin' her vodka and orange juice and Rodney'll be nagging her not to have any more. The girls will be screaming around the house like a couple of fire engines, and to tell the truth, listening to Ethel's voice is not my idea of a good time. Rodney's not such a bad guy to visit but the noise level around their house is enough to deafen the ears of Mick Jagger. Know what I mean, Raleigh?" Kerry said with a giggle.

"Yeah, I guess so. Ethel can sometimes be a bit abrasive. I think I'll head on over there anyway, maybe Rodney'll have some pot. I could use a joint or two to settle these burgers down and cut the taste of those pickles," Raleigh said as he picked up the check.

"Raleigh, I wish you hadn't done this. I wish you hadn't been so desperate inside that you decided your only way out was to go fight a war," Kerry said.

Raleigh shuffled his toothpick to the side of his mouth and replied, "It's just as well that I've joined up, Kerry. Chances are I might have gotten drafted anyway."

In the Frisco parking lot Raleigh would lean against his Chevrolet Nova while Kerry tied a string around the cuff of her bell-bottom jeans so they wouldn't get tangled in the spokes of her bicycle. It was a clear spring night with the stars just beginning to come out in the sky. They would never be this close again, for though Raleigh would come to understand all too well his sister's anger over his joining the army in the months ahead, he would also cease to understand that he was loved. There would be this night and one other which would haunt his days and nights in Vietnam. He would return home capable of understanding the discontent of those around him, yet incapable and unwilling to be understood himself.

Kerry would drift from reality herself as her desires to become a journalist would gradually erase the memories of an unhappy childhood with distant observation. The warmth of memories with her brother would always end with this spring night, for up until this night she had innocently collected these images for future reference. In the future she would consciously observe all emotion in search of the perfect line and would therefore cloud their purity. There would never be words within her which could reconstruct this last farewell to the shared secrets between a brother and a sister. The communication between them, so much of it silent and so taken for granted, would slip away from their reach. Raleigh would become a silent man.

The porch light was still on at Ethel and Rodney's. Raleigh rang the doorbell and waited for the Prestons to respond. Rodney answered the door. Raleigh could smell a hint of dinner as the door swung open. Fried chicken, he thought. Yep, must've been fried chicken.

"Well, Raleigh, what a nice surprise. How's it goin'?" Rodney asked.

"Who is it, Rodney?" Ethel called out.

Rodney clasped Raleigh by the shoulder and nudged him back out on the porch, gently closing the front door behind them.

"Gee, it sure is good to see you, Raleigh. We haven't seen much of you lately. Unfortunately, Ethel's not feeling too good this evening. Maybe it would've been better if you'd called before you drove all the way out here," Rodney said.

Rodney was not a large man; in fact, Raleigh called him "slim pockets" behind his back. He wasn't exactly a short fellow, delicate was more accurate. He was quite handsome, with dark hair and angular features. He had that sort of thousand-dollar smile which could turn the ladies' heads. He did so frequently.

"What's she got, the flu or somethin'?" Raleigh asked.

"No, it's not exactly the flu. Don't rightly know what it is, but it might be contagious," Rodney said.

"Hey, ya know, Ethel's been sick an awful lot lately. Maybe she ought to see a doctor. Seems like just a couple of weeks ago she was feeling bad. She missed Dad's birthday party," Raleigh said, stuffing his hands in his front pockets and shifting his weight back and forth from one foot to the other. "What is it really, Rodney? Did I catch y'all in the middle of something?" Raleigh said and gently elbowed Rodney in the side.

"Nah, nothing like that," Rodney began as the front door flew open, sending the smell of fried chicken into Raleigh's nostrils. Ethel balanced herself against the edge of the door, wearing last night's makeup and tonight's cocktail of bitterness.

"Rodney, why didn't you tell me it was Raleigh at the door? What's so interesting out here on the damn front porch?" Ethel snapped.

"Rodney just said you weren't feeling well, Ethel. He said you might have something contagious," Raleigh said.

"Oh, he did, did he? Well, you know how Rodney loves to pull pranks on folks. Don't 'cha, dear? Let's come inside, shall we?" Ethel chuckled, taking Raleigh by the arm.

"Ethel, you don't look so good. Are you sure you're feeling OK? I mean, I wouldn't want you to feel like you had to pretend you're up for some company if you're sick or something. I just came by to tell y'all some news; I won't be staying long," Raleigh said, as the three of them made their way toward the living room, Ethel swerving into Rodney's path, entangling their feet with the end result of Ethel depositing a house slipper into the shag carpeting. Ethel was beyond the point of noticing a naked foot and continued bouncing against Rodney till she reached the couch, where she plopped her ample behind down so hard that the cushions jumped up and down as if they had a life of their own.

Raleigh had stopped to retrieve Ethel's slipper. He sat down quietly in a chair facing Ethel, fondling the slipper in his lap.

"Rodney, get Raleigh something to drink, please — and I could use a little refill myself," Ethel said.

"Really now, Ethel, don't you think you've had enough? How's about a beer, Raleigh?"

"Sure, that sounds good to me," Raleigh said as Ethel interrupted him.

"Rodney, sweetie, just one more itsy bitsy nightcap for me," Ethel said, pointing in the direction of an empty glass on the coffee table.

Rodney silently obliged Ethel in order to avoid one of Ethel's nasty scenes. He headed toward their kitchen cursing Raleigh under his breath for not calling before he came by. At least if the big oaf had called he'd have had the chance to put Ethel to bed.

Two years ago, when Ethel had gone off the deep end on her drinking, Rodney Preston had thought his marriage had hit the skids for good. But as time went by, things just seemed to slip into place for Rodney and Ethel and her drinking was now just another routine part of their everyday lives. In fact, Ethel's drinking was very convenient for Rodney. Oh, he'd taken the car keys away from her long ago and hired a housekeeper to look after the girls. It was Ethel's lack of interest in his comings and goings that made her drinking convenient to Rodney. Divorce could very well ruin his social standing while adultery seemed to enhance the respect he received from his male counterparts.

It hadn't always been this way. Rodney had once been in love with Ethel. She had been the envy of his fraternity brothers: beautiful Ethel Foster. Rodney had envisioned a loving and healthy marriage between the two of them back in 1966. Ethel, with her beauty and poise, would have been such an asset to his career as a CPA when it came to entertaining clients. He had actually been a devoted if not possessive husband until after the birth of their first daughter, Jessica. Ethel began to gain weight after Jessica was born and without that physical beauty to enchant him, Rodney had finally come to know who Ethel was as a person. He did not like what he saw within her eyes. He stopped trusting her then. He did not stop loving his memories of what he'd thought she would be. He understood her. She was a survivor. More than that, she was a desperate survivalist.

She put forth the image of being so secure and balanced yet inside she was lost. She was so afraid of losing that she saw every person as a threat to her. Ethel would do anything to discredit someone she felt was threatening her. Rodney had stood by and watched her totally destroy the reputations of women acquaintances just for the joy of removing those women from her path. Ethel was ruthless in these matters. Rodney had never interfered; it was Ethel's nature to do such things. After all, he would not have wanted Ethel to turn her fury on him — he was no match for Ethel and her fury. He had instead done his best through the years to protect Ethel from herself. He admired her lack of conscience. For Ethel's sake, he prayed she would never develop one.

He could still conjure up the image of Ethel before the birth of Jessica. At night in the dark he could still love her now and then. They could make love on these nights with the same passion they had once held. Rodney could touch her then as though she were velvet, as though her skin was the texture of the haze around the moon on a cloudy night. These nights were rare to Ethel and Rodney. Ethel was usually too drunk to consider such prurient matters on some nights and on others she fell asleep with the bitterness inside of her so strong that she would dream of all Rodney's young lovers during the night. She had never particularly loved him. He had represented security to her in the beginning of their relationship but Ethel had never really known what she wanted from life. It was only those things that she felt she could manipulate that she insisted on holding on to. She knew within herself that it was only a matter of time before Rodney would fall in love with one of his lovers. He would find someone who could openly give him warmth without fear of becoming cold herself and he would realize that his years with Ethel had been wrong. Ethel knew that she and Rodney would always understand each other, they would always know the reason behind every action and every breath; yet two people cannot live on understanding alone. This was why Ethel drank: she understood him too well, she understood why he had married her and why she had married him. They were both for all the wrong reasons, and though she could live her life with many wrongs, with the spirits of restless mistakes surrounding her, she could not love wrong. No one can love wrong forever.

Rodney could hear the conversation between Ethel and Raleigh as he approached the living room with Raleigh's beer and Ethel's orange juice laced with vodka in hand.

"Well, how will Missy and Lisa get by without your support while you're in the army?" Ethel was saying.

"Ethel, Missy doesn't need my support. She makes good money these days. Besides, we've been separated for a while now. Don't you remember?" Raleigh said.

"What's this about the army?" Rodney asked.

"Raleigh's joined up. Now isn't that just the silliest thing you've ever heard of, Rodney?" Ethel chimed with the hand movements of a church choir director.

"Well, silly is not quite the word I'd chose for it," Rodney said.

"You must come tell Jessie. She'll be so surprised," Ethel said and she lifted herself up off the couch with great difficulty to steer Raleigh in the direction of her daughter Jessica.

Jessica was in the bathtub taking a bubble bath with the bubbles and her bath toys arranged just so by her five-year-old hands when her mother disrupted her kingdom. It was humiliating enough to have your mother barging in on your quiet moments, but here she was dragging her uncle Raleigh in behind her.

"Mother, I'm bathing. Can't you see that?" Jessica said with a huff.

"Yes, dear, but your uncle Raleigh has joined the army and I wanted you to be able to say goodbye to him. You may never get to see Uncle Raleigh again," Ethel said.

"Hi, Uncle Raleigh," Jessica groaned.

"Hi there, Jessie. Uh, I can see that you're busy now. We'll just step out here in the hall and wait till you're finished," Raleigh said in embarrassment.

"Now, Jessie, you really shouldn't be so rude to Uncle Raleigh," Ethel said.

"I wasn't rude. I just said 'hi.' Did you really join the army, Uncle Raleigh? Will they give you a uniform to wear? What does the army do, Uncle Raleigh?" Jessica asked as she splashed some bubbles over her knees.

"Well, the army does a lot of things. Can't really think of any one thing that they do. You'll understand what they do someday," Raleigh said hesitantly. He was a bit bewildered with himself for not having a good solid answer for what the army actually did.

"Where will you go? Will you take baby Lisa with you?" Jessie asked.

"Babies can't join the army, silly," Ethel chirped.

"I leave in three weeks for a place in Louisiana called Fort Polk. I'll write you letters from there and your mother can read them to you," Raleigh said.

"Three weeks is a long time away, isn't it, Uncle Raleigh?" Jessica asked.

"I suppose it is to you, Jessie," Raleigh said.

"Mom, if Uncle Raleigh's not leaving for three weeks may I finish my bath now?" Jessica whined.

"Jessica!" Ethel screeched.

"I understand just how ya feel, kiddo," said Raleigh. "You finish up in here and I'll wait out in the living room with your dad."

When Ethel and Raleigh had returned to the living room the conversations began to drift from Raleigh's enlistment to Ethel's current problems, just as Kerry had predicted. Raleigh felt awkward in the Preston household; it contained a certain amount of pretension which Raleigh was unable to fathom. Raleigh had no pretensions of his own.

"Ethel, Mom wonders why you never bring the girls or yourself down to visit Pearlie. She gets so lonely there. Kerry goes by every day," Raleigh said.

"If I went to visit Pearlie, I'd have to take a cab because I don't drive anymore and besides it's so depressing at that nursing home," Ethel said.

Rodney became a bit uneasy in his chair with the mention of Ethel not driving anymore and proceeded to try and change the subject. "Raleigh, could I get you another beer?" Rodney blurted out.

"No thanks. I've still got some of this one," Raleigh said.

"Well, how's about a Coke or something?" Rodney asked.

Ethel rolled her small brown eyes at Rodney in disgust.

"For Pete's sake, Rodney, leave him alone. He just said he didn't want anything," Ethel snapped.

"Ethel, you used to love driving around town. How come you stopped?" Raleigh asked.

"She doesn't drive because she had a small accident last year in the car and she's scared it might happen again," Rodney interjected.

"You never told me about it. What kind of accident?" Raleigh asked, as he leaned forward to rest his elbows on his knees while still holding Ethel's lost house slipper.

"I ran over one of the neighbor's dogs. Poor thing; it shocked me so badly," Ethel winced.

"That's a shame, Ethel, but that sort of thing happens so often when people let their animals run loose like that," Raleigh sympathized. "It happens so often I can't see it as a cause for you not to drive anymore. I never knew you were that fond of dogs."

"The dog wasn't running loose," Ethel said.

"Ethel, Raleigh doesn't want to hear some sad story about the dog. Let's talk about something cheerful for a change," Rodney said, crossing the room to sit next to Ethel on the couch. He put his arm around her and gave her shoulder a slight squeeze.

"No, no, you've got my curiosity up now. Let's hear it, Ethel. If the dog wasn't running loose, then how the hell could you possibly run it down?" Raleigh asked.

"Well, you must understand, Raleigh, that it had been a very hard day. Jessica was late to her ballet lessons and I was in a hurry to get back home so Mrs. Lopez could leave for the afternoon. It always throws my schedule off when Mrs. Lopez takes the afternoon off because then I have to take care of April as well as run Jessica all over town. Anyway, I was late from dropping Jessie off at ballet class and the damn dog just ran right under the car," Ethel said, as she began sipping once again on the vodka and orange juice.

"But I thought you said the dog wasn't running loose. Was it in the driveway or on a leash? Where was it?" Raleigh said in confusion.

"The dog was at his house," Ethel said.

"What?" Raleigh said, scratching his head in amazement.

"Oh, Jesus Christ, Ethel, if you're going to tell this story, why don't you at least tell it so it makes some sense? You see, Raleigh, what Ethel can't bring herself to tell you is that the dog was actually asleep in his own garage three doors down from this house," Rodney said.

"You're tellin' me that Ethel ran down the neighbor's dog in his own garage? I don't believe it. What the heck was Ethel doin' driving her car in the neighbor's garage?" Raleigh asked with a snicker.

"Now you see why I never told anyone about it, Raleigh. I knew you'd all laugh at me. It was an accident; it could've happened to anyone. These houses all look the same out here. I was just in such a hurry that I drove into the wrong garage. You can't imagine how embarrassed I was," Ethel said vehemently.

"Oh, yes, I can," Raleigh said, still shaking with amusement.

Rodney was growing increasingly uneasy with the conversation and happened to notice Jessica and her three-year-old sister April peeking through the living room doors. Their little faces took up the two bottom windowpanes in the glass doors, with April grinning through the bottom pane.

"Jessica, aren't you supposed to be in bed?" Rodney asked, in hopes that talk of the deceased dog would end.

Jessica stood up and, taking her sister April's hand, pranced into the living room.

"Mother said I could say good night to Uncle Raleigh. He's going away, ya know," Jessica said.

Both girls climbed up in Raleigh's lap, where April immediately began sucking her thumb and fingering the buttons on Raleigh's shirt while Jessica took an interest in her mother's house slipper, which Raleigh was still holding.

"I've got a great idea, Raleigh. Why don't you go put the girls in bed? You probably miss doing that sort of thing these days," Ethel said, with an edge in her voice suggesting criticism.

"OK, yeah, that'd be nice," Raleigh said.

He carried both girls to their room. April clung to him as though she would never let go. After he had placed them in each of their beds and turned off the overhead light, he stood in the doorway to watch them arrange their blankets and stuffed toys, feeling as lonely as he'd ever felt in his life. He wondered if he would ever see his own daughter do these endearing things. He wondered if she would ever love him as these children loved him.

"Uncle Raleigh?" Jessica called after him.

"What is it, Jessie?" Raleigh asked.

"You didn't say 'sweet dreams.' Daddy always says 'sweet dreams,'" Jessica said.

"May you have the sweetest dream tonight, sweeter than any dream you've ever had," Raleigh said, as he choked back his own tears.

"Uncle Raleigh?" Jessica called out again.

"What is it this time, Jessie?" Raleigh asked.

"If you do write those letters to me, and Mother takes the time to read them, then I won't forget you while you're gone. It'll almost be like you're still here. Do you promise that you'll write me from 'Fort POKE'?" Jessica whispered.

"I promise, Jessie. I'll write you a letter or two. Now you'd better go visit the sandman," Raleigh said. He turned from the doorway and headed back toward the living room when he heard Jessica's voice calling out again.

"Uncle Raleigh?" she said.

"GOOD NIGHT, JESSIE," Raleigh bellowed; silence overtook him.

Ethel had fallen asleep on the couch when he returned to the living room. He had stuck the house slipper in his back pocket on the way down the hall. Rodney was tampering with the stereo as Raleigh entered the room.

"Guess I should be heading out now. Thanks for the beer. Tell Ethel that I'll stop by again before I leave," Raleigh said.

"Sure thing, Raleigh. Hey, sorry about that little lie out there on the porch. Ethel was just a little jazzed is all it was. I thought I might be able to spare you some embarrassment. She gets that way sometimes. She's alright though, she'll be fine tomorrow," Rodney said.

"Yeah, sure. If you say so," Raleigh said, as he headed out the front door.

He was cruising around Missy's parents' house ten minutes later, wondering if she was out with her "duck." He stopped at the 7-11 around the corner to buy a six-pack before going home and berated the cashier for teasing him about the house slipper sticking up out of his back pocket. He'd forgotten it was there. He popped the top on his second beer as he swung his Nova onto Ethel's street. "Three doors down," he thought to himself, and remembering the swing of the arm technique he had once used as a paper boy, he tossed the slipper into that yard three doors down from Ethel's house.

"Peculiar," he thought. "That Ethel's just damn peculiar."

JULIE FOSTER was single again. Her last husband, who had been her third since her divorce from Jeff Foster, she had divorced a year ago. She didn't need men, couldn't understand how she kept getting talked into marriage. They sure could come and go though, those men, how they could slip into her life so quietly and make themselves seem so important to her own existence. Her last husband had been a wonderful man: someone she had counted on, someone who had not lived up to her own standards of perfection. Jeff Foster was her standard for perfection.

Julie was a marketing analyst for an advertising firm in town. She had worked hard at having a career, nothing had interfered with that career, not children and certainly not a husband; they had come in second place. When she had divorced Jeff Foster her only skill had been bookkeeping. It hadn't been enough to satisfy her need for advancement, and the boredom of doing the same job day in and day out had driven her crazy.

Julie lived in an apartment just a few blocks from her mother's house in Northeast Austin. Her house was most often quiet. She had a love for fireplaces, and though this apartment was not exactly what she'd had in mind when she moved here, it did have a nice fireplace where she could sit and relax. She would sometimes sit before the fire for hours with a book in her hand and never even open its cover, but would instead gaze into the flames as though in a hypnotic trance. This was her home, this quiet place. Her children were grown now, all of them on their own, all of them had turned out OK. The turmoil she had created within her own life had not harmed them. They would all be survivors. They had all learned to cope with her failures, just as she had learned to cope with herself. They were too young to know of their own failures yet. In time they would see her life as having been very successful in comparing it to their own.

Jeff Foster seemed to have made a happy life for himself since their divorce. His wife Louise ran a very tight ship for a household. She was always around to pick up the odd chores normally delegated to the natural mother, which Julie did not have time to take care of. This was a thorn in Julie's side. She would have liked to have done all those things; she would like to have had the chance, but Louise was always first to think of the chore itself. Louise had planned Ethel's wedding, she had stayed with Ethel and Rodney for two weeks when Jessica was born, she had worn black to Raleigh's wedding to Missy (which did indeed turn some heads), and she did not work. Louise was not an attractive woman, just the opposite of Julie in fact. She was short and plump, with flaming red hair which turned a different shade of red once a month. Jeff was a handsome man, tall and thin, with intense brown eyes and a small, straight nose. He was a no-nonsense sort of person who never seemed to make mistakes as often as others.

Julie was a most attractive woman. She had hazel eyes and ash blond hair which she wore stylishly in a French twist. She carried not one ounce of fat on her lean frame and was seldom considered to be as old as her actual years by strangers. She had inherited the best features of her mother and father, though her mother, Leota, was an unusually beautiful woman. Leota was a one of a kind beauty. Her bright green eyes and platinum hair were so unique that anyone who had ever passed Leota on the street would still recall clearly, perhaps not the exact picture of Leota, but the intense rarity of her image itself.

It had been a week since Julie and Leota had returned from their trip to the Valley to close up Kerry Pearl's house. A lot had happened since then. Raleigh had joined the army, Kerry had announced quite abruptly that she was not going to summer school and in fact may not return to school at all after this spring semester, and Ethel had shown up at the nursing home in a taxi, with both girls in tow, drunk as a skunk and dressed in her nightgown of all things. Louise had had to deal with Ethel even though she had never even met Kerry Pearl. She had driven down to the nursing home and politely introduced herself to Kerry Pearl as she packed Ethel and the girls up and escorted them home to Mrs. Lopez. Mrs. Lopez had been the one to call Louise for help when she couldn't stop Ethel from leaving the house in the taxi. Julie had been more than just a little upset with the woman for not calling her instead. Ethel was, after all, her daughter and Kerry Pearl was her grandmother; it had been none of Louise's business.

Julie sat relaxing in front of her fire with her usual nightcap of scotch and water resting in one hand and a Winston cigarette in the other when the phone rang.

"Hello," Julie said.

"Julie, you just won't believe what that little ne'er-do-well's done now. I just can't believe it! I was sitting here having a nice conversation with Thomas Evans from next door and that little so-'n'-so called here long distance to spoil my evening . . . "

Julie interrupted her mother quite rudely to find out what was going on, as Leota had a tendency to ramble. "Mother, it's late. Now just what exactly did Howard do this time?" Julie groaned.

"The little rascal's flying in here tomorrow! He's booked himself a room at Mama's nursing home — and him calling me to see if I wouldn't mind having you come to the airport to pick him up and deliver him to Mama. Now, don't you dare go down there and pick him up because I'm gonna get me a cab and go down there and put him right back on a plane to Yankeeland," Leota snapped.

Julie set her drink down on the table and took a long drag of her cigarette. She was thinking to herself that she had never in her life seen anyone who could get her mother as ruffled as Howard Bates. A smile came to her lips and for just an instant she forgot that Leota was still on the phone waiting for a reply.

"Well, aren't you gonna say anything? I didn't just call you up out of the blue, you know. We've got to figure out what we're gonna do about this," Leota said anxiously.

"What time does his plane arrive, Mother?"

"Now, don't go askin' me what time that plane comes in 'cause you are not going to pick him up and that's all there is to it," Leota barked.

"Mother, Howard is a grown man and he is certainly free to come and go if he pleases. He's also free to take a room at the nursing home of his choice. I think it'll do Grandmother a world of good to see him. Now I want you to tell me what time that plane comes in so that there will be someone from this family at that airport to welcome him to his new home. Do I have to call Howard and wake him up to find out when his plane gets here, or are you going to tell me yourself like he asked you to?" Julie said.

"Oh, you're all against me. Mama's got all of you thinking that Howard's just the perfect little gentleman when in fact he's a sleazy, fast talkin', midget insurance salesman," Leota cried.

"Mother, Howard retired years ago from the insurance business and he is not a midget," Julie said impatiently.

"Papa would just die — " Leota began, as Julie once again interrupted her.

"Mother, Grandfather Max did die. This conversation is beginning to be a bit redundant. It's late, you know, and speaking of lateness, I can't believe that Howard would call you so late in the evening — not only that but what the hell is Thomas Evans doing over at your place at this time of night," Julie said, knowing full well that this approach would slow her mother down a bit on Howard.

"Oh, he didn't just call and don't you go insinuating anything about Thomas; he just came by here for a cup of coffee after work. No, Howard called here about six o'clock. I've just been tied up on the phone since then and I wanted to cool off before I called you," Leota said, with a bit more warmth in her voice than before.

Julie could easily visualize what had been happening at her mother's house for the past three hours. Leota had no doubt spent at least an hour and a half ranting and raving to Thomas about Howard. Thomas himself was a widower who had not considered remarrying after his wife Effie had died back in '61. He and Leota were the best of friends; they were, in fact, each other's only friends of the opposite sex. Julie had thought many times that if Leota and Thomas were living somewhere far in the future, then perhaps they would have married. Perhaps somewhere in the future it would not matter that Leota was white and Thomas Evans was a Black man, and more importantly, perhaps they themselves would not have clung to their loneliness after the death of their respective spouses.

Of course, after Thomas had had an earful, Julie imagined that her mother had probably phoned her friend Anita. That conversation had most likely swallowed the last hour and a half.

" . . . and I just didn't know what to do about all this . . . Julie, I'm talking to you. Are you listening to me?" Leota was saying.

"Yes, Mother, I'm listening," Julie replied.

"That plane comes in from Albany sometime in the afternoon. I'm so flustered right now I just don't know how you'd expect this old woman to remember an exact time after hearing news like this," Leota said.

"I'll handle it, Mother," Julie sighed.

"Well, I guess there's nothing I can do about this tonight. Dadgum him, anyway; just when we had Mama all settled in and all," Leota said.

"I'll talk to you in the morning, Mother. Good night now," Julie said.

"Well, good night, dear," Leota said, still fuming.

Leota replaced the receiver in its cradle for the first time in two hours. She wore her hair in pin curls around the neckline at night with a bandanna wrapped around her head to cushion it against the metal hair clips she used to hold the pin curls in place. She had tangled one of those clips in the phone cord earlier in the evening while talking to Anita and had had to remove the clip altogether to free herself from the phone. She got up from the rocking chair by the phone table and strolled to the mirror to replace the clip and retie the bandanna around her head. It was an old cotton bandanna which had belonged to her husband, Edgar, its texture as soft and worn as chamois leather. Seeing the bandanna in the mirror prompted her to think of Edgar. She was sure he would agree with her that her mother had had no business remarrying after her father had died. She was sure that Edgar was proud up there in heaven that she herself had not remarried; yes, Leota was certain that Edgar would be waiting for her with outstretched arms when her day came.

She sighed a gentle sigh of grief for Edgar as she turned to walk to her bed alone. She lingered for a moment by the window and noticed that Thomas Evans' lights were still on next door. The two of them shared such simple dreams, Thomas and Leota: they dreamed only for the well-being of their loved ones and they prayed each night for a morning which would bring a better day. A better day for Leota and for Thomas would be the day when they did not wake from the dream at all.

HOWARD CAUGHT a morning flight out of Albany. The young couple who had rented his house from him a year ago had driven him from Saratoga Springs to Albany. He was accustomed to flying, having flown many times down to South Texas to stay with Kerry Pearl, yet this trip was special. Howard felt that this was his last voyage south; it would be his last rendezvous with his beautiful Pearl.

He was receiving the red-carpet treatment from the stewardess. It wasn't often that she had an eighty-seven-year-old man in her section, which was first class. Howard sat primly in his seat, dressed in his best wool flannel suit with his overcoat folded neatly in his lap. He wore a red ascot around his neck to protect him against a chill. His snow-white hair was cropped close to the sides of his head, with thickly waved curls on top, which were combed back from his forehead. His handlebar mustache had been heavily waxed with great care this morning before departing from Saratoga Springs. He was indeed in great shape for a man of his years, with his trim physique and his full head of hair. He was the only man his age, that he knew, who still had to go for a haircut every three weeks; he was, in fact, the only man he knew who was his age.

He thought to himself that it would be so nice to be with Kerry Pearl again, even if this particular nursing home did have inflexible rules that would not allow him to share the same room with his wife. They would, after all, have their meals together and it was baseball season now. He pondered the arguments they would have over those televised games.

His house in Saratoga Springs was in good hands for a while. The young couple, the Wilsons, had a lease which ran through the month of July, and chances are they would stay on at the place for as long as Howard wanted them to. His only real concern was his 1967 Pontiac, which he had been reluctant to part with. He'd left it with the Wilsons in hopes that they would drive it now and then to keep the battery up. It was the only automobile that Howard had ever owned so it was quite the prized possession.

Howard had had to change planes in Chicago and he'd had a two-hour layover in Dallas before arriving in Austin. The stewardess escorted him off the plane. Julie stood anxiously by the ticket counter. He recognized her immediately from the photos Kerry Pearl had sent him, and after retrieving his cane from the arm of the stewardess he advanced toward Julie with the walk of a man with great dignity.

Julie was expecting him to be much smaller; from her mother's description of him, she had foreseen him as being only about five feet tall. He was certainly a small man but he was almost as tall as Julie, who was five-seven herself. There were many things about Howard Bates that didn't quite match up with Leota's description of Howard — and Leota was known for her colorful monologues describing him in great detail.

"You must be Julie. My dear, it's such a pleasure to finally get to meet you. You are twice the beauty that my Pearl pictured you to be," Howard said while extending his hand to Julie.

Julie took his hand in hers and placed her other hand on his thin shoulders; she kissed him lightly on the cheek.

"Howard, it's so good to have you with us here in Austin and thank you very much for such a nice compliment. We'd best head for the baggage area now. How many pieces of luggage did you bring?" Julie asked.

"Well now, let me see . . . I brought two suitcases and a large cardboard box tied up with string. Yes, that's all, just those three pieces. Shall we find a redcap to help us carry them?" Howard said.

"If you think we'll need one," said Julie, who was amazed at how polite and soft-spoken Howard was.

"Now, tell me, when do I get to meet young Kerry? She has been so kind to my Pearl and I do wish to see her as soon as she has the time," Howard said as they approached the baggage claim area.

"Oh, I don't think you'll have to wait long for that. Kerry is so excited about all of this that I wouldn't be surprised if she's not pacing the floor in Grandmother's room at this very moment," Julie said.

Howard raised his cane high in the air to signal a porter for help with the luggage. Julie didn't understand his need for the cane at all, as Howard kept it looped on his arm and he had a brisk step to his walk, which certainly did not call for the aid of a cane.

"Howard, it's so warm here. I don't think you'll need your heavy coat. Would you like me to carry it for you?" Julie asked.

"That would be nice, thank you. I'd like to carry the cardboard box myself. I hope that nothing has been broken in there," Howard said with a mysterious lilt to his voice.

Julie spent the majority of the ride from the airport to the nursing home warning Howard about Leota. He assured her that he had had many years of experience now in dealing with Leota and was well prepared for the worst.

———

KERRY LIVED in an attic room close to campus. The house itself was a
large, rambling three-story in great need of repair. There were currently
only five tenants in the house, though it was capable of housing eight.
On the first floor there were two bedrooms; a dining room with a large
mahogany dining table which had never been used by the current
tenants; a large living area; the kitchen, whose refrigerator resembled
some freshman's chemistry project; a breakfast nook located off to the
side of the kitchen; and three bathrooms. Wiley, the house "Gestapo"
as they called him due to his responsibility of collecting everyone's
rent and relaying complaints to the landlord, lived on this floor alone.
He was the night manager of a bar just around the corner where Kerry
played music on Sunday nights. He was a stout, dark-haired young
man who sometimes attended graduate school at the university; his
thesis was in philosophy. Though it was never obvious to Kerry, he
had made himself her guardian angel and had trained himself to stay
awake at night until he heard the scrape of her loafers on the bottom
rung of the ladder, which led straight up to the attic room.

Two tenants lived on the second floor. One of them was a fellow
who was a guitar player for a country-and-western band; he was on
the road most of the time with the band so Kerry had never gotten
to know him very well. His name was Alvin. The other tenant on this
floor was a young hippie named Beam-us, as in the television series
Star Trek. No one knew a whole lot about Beam-us except that he
came from a wealthy family in Tennessee and lived on some sort of
trust fund. His checks arrived in the mail on the fifth of each month
and since Beam-us had a passion for LSD, he could be counted on to
remain in his room for at least two weeks after each check arrived. The
hallway just outside his door held a permanent cloud of marijuana
smoke and his favorite phrase in passing another tenant in the hall
was, of course, "Beam-us up, Scotty." Kerry had an acute allergy to
marijuana so she had a tendency to avoid socializing with Beam-us
whenever possible.

The third floor had an atmosphere which was totally different
from that of the other floors. There were two bedrooms, a parlor,

and a bathroom on this floor. The whole floor had been rented to the head chef of a neighborhood French restaurant named Lensel. Lensel was a homosexual who was a very quiet and polite sort of fellow. He had redecorated the third floor as best he could, with carpets from India and exquisite watercolors which had been painted by one of his former lovers who now lived in England. Lensel was, by far, Kerry's favorite housemate and she spent hours in conversation with him.

It was, in fact, not Lensel that Wiley and the other tenants objected to, nor was it his homosexuality; it was the lovers who Lensel chose to parade through the house at all hours that bothered each and every soul in this household, for Lensel was not in the least bit discreet in his choice of partners; Lensel, in truth, had no taste whatsoever in men. Fortunately for Kerry, the ladder leading to her attic room was quite intimidating so only rarely did one of Lensel's houseguests venture into her isolated domain.

Lensel had this tendency to become obsessed with his lovers. His current obsession was a filthy young man with long, stringy blond hair who Wiley had nicknamed Mr. Two Pants, since this young man always wore two pairs of pants, one on top of the other, with the top pair just an inch or two shorter in the cuffs than the bottom pair. He was an extremely peculiar young man indeed, and Kerry had been awakened at six A.M. this morning by Mr. Two Pants' annoying wheezing — he had been standing at the foot of her bed.

She had yelled "What the hell are you doing in my room?", which had lifted Wiley straight up off the mattress and up the stairs to Kerry's ladder. When his feet found their purchase on the bottom rung, that same bottom rung that creaked beneath the scrape of Kerry's loafer each night, the wood snapped in two and sent him sprawling on one of Lensel's Indian carpets. Beam-us had actually been brought back to reality by Kerry's scream and upon rounding the landing on the third floor to find Wiley flat on his back on the floor, he replied, "Would you like me to beam you up now, Captain Kirk?"

"Oh, just shut the fuck up, Beam-us, and go on back to bed!" Wiley had said as he brushed himself off and remounted the ladder.

As it turned out, Mr. Two Pants claimed he had simply been searching for the bathroom and it was his understanding from Lensel that there was one up in the attic room. The whole incident had caused such an uproar in the house that Kerry had been unable to go back to sleep afterwards.

Her attic space actually contained two rooms: a bathroom with only a toilet and a sink, her bedroom, a sitting room, and a screened-in porch which opened out of the sitting room. The ceiling sloped in such a way that there was only a space about four feet wide in the center where one could stand fully erect. This space ran down the center of both rooms, which were arranged in the traditional shotgun style. She had spent the remainder of the morning pacing the length of the two rooms within that small space. "Today is the day that Howard is coming to make Pearlie well again," she thought to herself. What a way to start the day.

Her mother had insisted on going alone to the airport to pick up Howard. Kerry began preparing for her bike ride out to the nursing home at noon, though her mother and Howard were not expected to arrive there until two. Lensel had poked his head up above the ladder at least a dozen times to say he was sorry for this morning's disturbance but Kerry had been much too preoccupied with her thoughts of Pearlie and Howard to acknowledge him, which had wounded Lensel so deeply that he had retreated to the seldom-used living area on the first floor, where he proceeded to play Samuel Barber's *Adagio for Strings* over and over again on the stereo that had a blown speaker until Wiley stomped out of his room and demanded that he "TURN THAT SHIT OFF."

Kerry had been bent down before the sink in her bathroom brushing her teeth when she heard Wiley bellow at Lensel. She then experienced her only thought for the day not having to do with the plight of Pearlie and Howard. She thought of her boyfriend, Fletcher. Fletcher often came down to Austin to spend weekends with her and in looking around the cramped space in which even she had to stoop to keep from bumping her head, she recalled with amusement that on his last visit Fletcher had commented that this attic room must have been especially designed for a woman because it was damn near impossible for any male to stand and pee into the toilet. They had laughed about this for hours. They had made love a second time, the first time having been just prior to Fletcher's visit to the toilet.

Kerry wished that Fletcher could be here with her today to witness the reunion of Howard and Pearlie. She wished she could always share those brief yet magical moments with Fletcher. Kerry had an eye for such moments. She would feel their presence and she would savor such things as most people would savor a good glass of wine. At times she would think to herself, as the magic transpired, that she would save its image for Fletcher, as though she could capture that special emotion which had moved her and relay its beauty to him, but it never seemed to happen that way. She never quite chose the right words for her images and they were lost somewhere in the translation. Her reasons for trying to bring forth these images were the very reasons Fletcher was in love with her.

The love between Kerry and Fletcher was a love of innocence itself; it was the love of a different era, for their hearts reached out in total trust of the other's and the respect between the two of them basked itself in the rhythm of their strength. Yet, they were two individuals so totally devoted to their love that they created only an illusion of union, for they were two separate souls whose hearts held the capacity to move in different directions. They sought opposite goals, and still the love could live and breathe in unison. They were not lonely without one another. They had known each other for so many years that they had forgotten the meaning of the word lonely. Their youth had been spent together; they had not experienced the horrors of pubescent solitude. It was this lack of experience in loneliness that created a special bond between Fletcher and Kerry, for as individuals they were incapable of tolerating the loneliness in others.

———

LEOTA SAT in a straight-backed chair beside her mother's bed, pondering a crossword puzzle and waiting for the entrance of Howard Bates. Kerry Pearl was quite vexed with Leota, for though Leota had not said one word about Howard's arrival she had chosen this day to sport a gold locket around her neck, which Max had given her as a child. The locket contained photos of both Kerry Pearl and Max, which were taken on their tenth anniversary. Leota sat poised with the locket in full view, resting gently on the collar of her white cotton blouse as though she were prepared to spring the locket open in Howard's face the moment he entered the room.

"Leota, you haven't worn that locket in years. Why, in heaven's name, have you chosen to wear it today? This is such a special day for me. Can't you at least take that into consideration and put your own feelings aside?" Kerry Pearl asked quietly.

"It is only a locket, Mama. I just had the urge to wear it again. I'm not going to spoil your day here; I'll be going home when Howard and Julie get here. I've plenty of things to do this afternoon. Ethel isn't feeling well and I've promised Rodney that I would go out to their place to look after the girls. Seems that Mrs. Lopez needs the afternoon off," Leota replied, without looking up from her crossword puzzle.

"You know, Leota, Ethel was so peculiar when she was here the other day. She had on some sort of evening gown and was only wearing one shoe. Actually, it wasn't a shoe at all, it was a house slipper of some sort," Kerry Pearl said.

"There's no need to be kind here, Mama; Ethel was here in her nightgown and she was drunk as a skunk and that's all there is to it," Leota said, finally putting the crossword puzzle aside to talk with her mother.

"Well, drunk or not, she embarrassed that poor child, Jessica. April isn't old enough to know of such things. She had a great time pretending it was some sort of girls' slumber party," Kerry Pearl said, as she switched the television on with her remote control.

"What game show is this, Mama?" Leota asked, pretending to be interested in the television show now blaring from the small portable Howard had ordered for Kerry Pearl.

"It's *Password*, dear. Don't you just love it when they play the match with some mystery word and the TV audience has to guess what the word is?" Kerry Pearl asked, feigning enthusiasm.

"I'm usually busy at this time of day," Leota began.

Kerry Pearl snapped the television off with a sharp turn of her wrist and turned to stare Leota in the eye.

"Well, since you have instructed me not to be kind about Ethel's problem then I must tell you that I have been shocked that this family is simply ignoring her troubles. There is something deeply wrong with that young woman or she would not be drinking like she is. In the entire time that I've been up here, I have only seen Ethel three times and all three of those occasions she reeked of gin. Now you know how I feel about alcohol. Even your Edgar was forbidden to bring beer into my home. For the sake of those beautiful little girls, I think something should be done about this drinking problem of hers before she hurts someone," Kerry Pearl said.

"It's vodka, Mama. Julie says she drinks vodka, not gin," Leota snapped.

"What? Oh, Leota, will you never address an issue?" Kerry Pearl said in frustration just as Howard arrived in the doorway.

"And what issue would that be, my dear Pearl?" Howard said, cautiously.

Upon seeing Howard in the doorway, the age seemed to vanish from Kerry Pearl's face, for love knows not the limitations of age and their faces at that moment became ageless.

"Oh, Howard, I can't believe you're actually here," said Kerry Pearl.

Howard sat down in the chair opposite Leota. Their eyes met for only a fleeting moment. Leota thought to herself that she had let her guard slip during that brief eye contact with Howard. He was such a handsome little man and she had actually caught herself smiling back at him.

"Well, Mama, now that Howard's here I think I should be leaving. If Julie doesn't mind, I need her to stop off at my house before taking me to Ethel's, and I'm sure she has a lot of work to attend to; she can't be spending her whole day lollygaggin' around with us old folks," Leota said as she stood to leave.

"I'm in no hurry, Mother," Julie replied. "Really, let's just visit awhile."

"Come now, Leota, I've only just gotten here. We have so many things to discuss and it has been so many years since I've seen your lovely face. Please stay. I had hoped that you would assist me setting up my room. I'm an old man, you know, and I've never had much taste in decorating. Pearl has told me that you have quite a knack for brightening up a room. I must say that this room looks so cheerful with all the flower arrangements. They must be your doing, Leota," Howard said, as he gently squeezed Kerry Pearl's hand.

"Actually, Howard, these flowers are just something I picked up in the flower shop here at the home. You could go down there and pick some out for yourself; you see, the shop is run by volunteers among the residents here and the proceeds are used to purchase recreational equipment. I'll stay, though, for a little while, but I really must go soon, as I have an appointment later," Leota said as she lowered herself back into the chair. She would not, under any circumstances, allow Howard's flattery to sway her from believing that he had no business whatsoever moving to Austin.

Howard had been aware that the flowers came from the floral shop in the nursing home. When he had called for information about the home it had been mentioned as one of the high points in living here and he had been quite excited about the prospect of working in the flower shop himself.

Julie had carried Howard's cardboard box into the room and placed it on the foot of Kerry Pearl's bed. Howard got up from this chair and began opening the mysterious box. From the box he took a small jewelry case which was covered in burgundy velvet. With the case in hand, he walked around the bed to stand beside Leota.

"I've brought you a small memento, Leota. It is only a small reminder to you for the love I have of your beautiful mother. I hope you will accept this as a token of my affection, as you are dear to my heart," Howard said. His small hands fumbled with the box for an instant and when it was opened a royal blue lining was revealed; a small pearl drop on a gold chain sparkled against the satin lining.

"Though it is not as beautiful as your mother, it is nonetheless a jewel, just as she is the jewel of my life," Howard said.

Leota was rendered speechless with Howard's presentation of the gift. The pearl was so delicate that even she would not deny that it was a lovely reminder of her mother's name and beauty. Tears filled her eyes as she reluctantly took the small box from Howard's hands. The locket around her neck suddenly felt as though it were an anchor; as though it weighed a thousand pounds or more.

"It's just lovely, Howard. It's very thoughtful of you to think of me," Leota said, choking back tears.

"Oh, Mother, what a nice present. Try it on. Come on, let's see how it looks," Julie said, as she bent down to examine the pearl.

"Yes, Leota, try it on. Here, let me help you," Howard said, reaching for the jewel case.

Kerry Pearl in the meantime could not take her eyes off of the locket Leota was wearing; the pearl itself was only a blur resting in Leota's hand. "Perhaps Leota would rather wait until she gets home to try the necklace on. Wouldn't you, Leota?" Kerry Pearl said in a stern voice, determined that Howard's feelings be spared by his never knowing the contents of Leota's locket.

"Oh, nonsense, my Pearl. I want to see how it reflects the heather green in Leota's eyes," Howard said. He had already removed the fragile gold chain and pearl drop from the jewel box, and as he fumbled to fasten the necklace around Leota's neck, he accidently released the faulty latch to the chain which held the locket. The faulty latch was why Leota seldom wore the locket and she had never taken the time to have it fixed; it hadn't seemed all that important until today. The necklace holding the locket spilled onto the edge of Kerry Pearl's bed and the sound of the locket springing open was muffled by its impact on the mattress.

"Oh, dear, how clumsy of me, Leota. I'll just fix this right up," Howard began, as he reached for the locket. His hands stopped short of retrieving it when he saw the pictures inside. He paused for only a second or two; he exchanged glances with Kerry Pearl, which were enough to allow him to regain his composure. "Why, what a wonderful picture of Pearl, and such a handsome shot of Max," Howard said, as he closed the locket and placed it in Leota's trembling hand.

"Yes, that was taken on their tenth wedding anniversary," Leota said, still quite shaken.

"Well, Max would be so proud that you wear it so close to your heart. I would be so honored if you wore the pearl now and then. It complements this locket so nicely. Don't you think so, Pearl?" Howard said.

"Why, yes. They look just lovely together," Kerry Pearl sighed. She was relieved that Howard had handled the situation so carefully. It was one of his qualities which she found to be the most endearing: his ability to always survive difficult confrontations with her children and come out smelling like a rose; for that was Howard, he was a cautious yet thoughtful man and he was her jewel.

Leota had not been prepared for Howard to actually see the contents of her locket. She had worn it to remind her mother of her disapproval of Howard. She was embarrassed by the incident so badly that she lingered in the room for only a few tense minutes before excusing herself and asking Julie to drive her home.

The first moments there between Leota and Howard had gone poorly, Kerry Pearl thought, but they did improve during the following days. Leota did not wear the locket when visiting with Kerry Pearl and Howard; she did wear the pearl, and when questioned by Howard about the locket she replied that it was being repaired at the jeweler's, though in truth it was at home in her jewelry box. She still did not have the time to have its latch replaced.

Young Kerry spent most of her afternoons visiting with Kerry Pearl and Howard. Howard's room was located directly across a courtyard from Kerry Pearl's. Their rooms, in fact, faced one another, and Kerry would open the sliding glass door which faced Howard's room and wave at him each afternoon when she arrived. Howard was almost always sitting by his glass door reading at that time in the afternoon. On Mondays and Thursdays he worked in the floral shop from one to four in the afternoon. He brought Kerry Pearl a different arrangement of flowers each day that he worked. For young Kerry he became the great-grandfather she had never known, and as each day went by, she grew to treasure his presence more. She did a great deal of juggling with her time in order to prevent Leota from feeling that she was forsaking her, yet these were happy days for everyone, including Leota, who was so pleased with her mother's improved disposition that she put her dislike of Howard aside.

The rules of the nursing home did not allow Howard to remain in Kerry Pearl's room past ten o'clock at night. It became exceedingly difficult for Howard to leave Kerry Pearl in the evenings, and it was only a matter of days before the nurses began finding Howard curled up beside Kerry Pearl in the mornings. He would leave Kerry Pearl's sliding glass door open when he retired to his room at ten o'clock and wait until all the lights went out, then he would slip across the courtyard and climb into bed with Kerry Pearl.

The nurses would scold him each morning saying, "Now, Mr. Bates, you know you're not supposed to sleep in here. Mrs. Bates isn't well enough for such strain." At which point Howard would always reply that he'd only just arrived here and hadn't spent the entire night there in Kerry Pearl's bed at all. "Well, you're not allowed up on the bed, you know that," the nurses would reply to Howard's denial. Still, the nurses found Howard's devotion to Kerry Pearl so endearing that they did not bother to check her room during the night, for they considered this a violation of the elderly couple's privacy. They were also perceptive enough not to discuss the problem with Leota.

It was a joyous reunion for the Bates. Kerry Pearl was in such high spirits and the laughter rang from Room 112 each day. Their presence in the nursing home together brought a cheerful lift for all the residents. Yet, Kerry Pearl was not healing properly. She had developed an infection in her hip which had demanded heavy doses of antibiotics. Within a few days it became evident that she had contracted pneumonia. It wasn't so bad at first. The doctor had placed her under an oxygen tent and Howard was specifically requested to remain in his room at night. Though Kerry Pearl was gravely ill, she still remained deliriously happy because of Howard's presence. It was as if being with him this last time was the last goal she had waited to achieve in her life.

On the third day after being placed under the oxygen tent Kerry Pearl called Leota in alone for a conference. She handed Leota an envelope and upon removing the documents inside, she calmly went over all the arrangements for her funeral with Leota in detail. She and Howard had made these arrangements years ago; they had left nothing for her children to decide and they had thoughtfully made arrangements which none of the children could disagree with.

Just one week before Raleigh was due to leave for boot camp the family had a gathering in the early evening at the nursing home. Howard once again brought out his mysterious cardboard box and from the box he brought out a gift for each member of the family. Young Kerry was given a rare first edition of Carson McCullers' novel *The Heart Is a Lonely Hunter*. Ethel and Rodney were given a photograph of Howard and Kerry Pearl which was taken sometime during the fifties and showed the two of them walking on the beach on South Padre island, which was only a few miles from Raymondville. The sky was totally clear and the white caps in the gulf appeared to be of puffed cotton. They were captured in the photo holding hands and Kerry Pearl appeared to be as lithe and swift as the gulf's white caps. Howard's trousers were rolled up at the cuffs and Kerry Pearl wore a beautiful dress, gathered at the waist, with the hemline falling just below her knees, and she was barefoot. Raleigh was given a small pocket-size journal covered in brown leather. Ethel's two daughters both received baby dolls, which were almost life-size. The two girls retreated to the corner of the room to examine their new babies. Julie was given a gold ring with a simple pearl setting. Leota was wearing her pearl necklace. Each adult passed their gift around the room for the others to admire, with Ethel losing her grip on Kerry's book and dropping it to the floor with a loud bang. Raleigh stepped back from the circle around the bed and did not pass his journal around for inspection but carefully placed it in his shirt pocket. With the exception of Ethel's intoxication, which was distressing to Kerry Pearl and brought about an occasional exclamation from Leota of "Ethel, keep your voice down!" it was an enjoyable evening for all. It was their last evening together.

At six the next morning the nurses entered Kerry Pearl's room to find Howard sitting in the straight-backed chair next to Kerry Pearl's bed with his head down on the mattress and Kerry Pearl's hand held against his face. The nurses approached her bed and upon finding that Kerry Pearl had indeed passed on, one of them left to call the doctor while the other placed her arm around Howard in an attempt to escort him from the room.

He resisted her at first, then became resigned to her escorting him along, only stopping once as they left the room to turn and reply with a hoarse whisper, "Oh, my dear Pearl, you have left too soon, you were my heart, my Pearl, my jewel."

"KERRY! PHONE'S FOR YOU," Wiley called out from the third-floor landing just below the ladder leading to Kerry's attic room.

"OK," she called back, scrambling from her bed in search of a robe to throw on so she could answer the phone.

"Hello," she said sleepily into the phone.

"Kerry, this is Mom," Julie began.

"She's gone, isn't she, Pearlie's dead, isn't she? I knew it when the phone rang," Kerry cried.

"Yes, Kerry, she's gone. She died sometime during the night. Howard was with her. I wanted to catch you before you left the house this morning to tell you myself and also to tell you that the doctor has given Howard a sedative so he will sleep for the rest of the day. There's no need for you to go out there, he won't even know you're there," Julie said.

"Where is Leo?" Kerry asked.

"Leo's doing just fine. She is making the arrangements to take Grandmother's body to Floydada tomorrow morning. I've already called Raleigh and he is expecting you to ride to Floydada with him day after tomorrow for the funeral," Julie said.

"You can't take her there! What about Howard? You can't do this to him. You can't bury his wife way off in godforsaken West Texas a million miles away from him. It isn't fair. First you and Leo take her from her home in the Valley and stick her in that awful nursing home and now you're going to bury her body next to a husband who's been dead for forty years. What kind of a person are you?" Kerry screamed into the phone, still dazed from the news.

"Now, Kerry, you're just upset. Listen to me," Julie said. Kerry interrupted her.

"It's your fault she's dead, yours and Leo's. You stuck her in that lonely place so you wouldn't have to take care of her yourselves and you let her die there. You let her die there and if it hadn't been for Howard making all his own arrangements to come here to be with his wife, Leo would have made sure Pearlie never got to see him again. Why are you taking her to Floydada?" Kerry screamed in anger.

"Because it is what Grandmother requested. Leo is following your Pearlie's arrangements to the letter and I think you'd better just calm yourself down. We are all lost in sorrow today," Julie cried.

"I'm sorry, I'm sorry I said those things. It's just that I feel so bad for Howard," Kerry said.

"It's alright, I understand. I'd best go now; you call Raleigh later on today. I'll either be at Mother's or at home later on if you need me," Julie said.

The two of them exchanged goodbyes before hanging up the phone. Kerry immediately called Fletcher in Denton to tell him that her great-grandmother had died. She wept most of the day and did not call Leota until early evening, as she wanted to get all of her grief over this loss out of her system before speaking to her grandmother. Her main thought throughout the day was that she was very lucky to have had the honor of having her great-grandmother for all these years. There are very few people who have that pleasure of knowing their great-grandparents on into adulthood, there are very few who come to know those great-grandparents as friends. To most people their great-grandparents remain a mysterious shadow from their childhood, but to young Kerry her Pearlie had been a friend, a confidant, and someone she loved dearly, with respect and admiration. The solid stance in which Kerry Pearl had stood in her convictions was the same strength young Kerry sought for her own life. Leota possessed that same strength, as did Julie. They were a family of strong women who had learned to survive. Ethel was the only one of them who did not exercise this power; she did hold that very same link, yet she never chose to cultivate its qualities within herself. She would live her life entirely dependent on the weaknesses in others to strengthen herself.

Leota rode in the front seat of the hearse from Austin to Floydada. Her sister Cora was meeting her at the funeral home there. Cora's husband Richmond had made motel reservations for all of the family. Leota supposed that at this hour he was most likely propped up in the bed of one of those motel rooms drinking beer and watching television. They were only an hour away from Floydada now; Leota had barely noticed when they made the steep climb onto the caprock, which was the beginning of the Texas Panhandle. She had been lost in memories since passing through San Angelo. She remembered, as if it were yesterday, a bus trip she had taken to visit Cora in Odessa just months before Edgar had died. She hadn't known he was dying then; he hadn't told her yet. She had taken that bus out to Odessa and stayed with Cora for a week while Richmond had gone to Austin to work with Edgar in the machine shop. Richmond and Edgar had driven out to Odessa at the end of that week and they'd all piled into Edgar and Leota's Dodge for a trip to New Mexico to see the Carlsbad Caverns. Edgar had told her he was dying there, and it seemed to her now as she came back to the present in her thoughts that death was always in the West. Her mother had moved west to Austin and she had died; Edgar had gone west to New Mexico and had died. Leota vowed to herself that she would never return here once her mother was buried; she would never look west again.

The dust was flying when they reached the funeral home. It was a hazy, cool day with the temperature in the fifties. Cora sat in the entrance hall to the funeral parlor and beside her sat her napping husband, Richmond. Cora stood up to greet her smaller sister and gently nudged Richmond's leg with her foot to wake him.

"What is it now, Cora?" Richmond mumbled.

"Wake up, Leota's here," Cora whispered while reaching down with her heavy arm to straighten Richmond's lopsided bow tie. Richmond was holding a large, gray derby in his lap and his huge, meaty hands clasped the hat firmly in preparation for greeting Leota. He stood up as she approached them and lumbered toward her, still keeping a firm grip on his derby.

"Oh, Leota, we're so glad you're here safely. Did you have any problems finding the funeral parlor?" Richmond asked, as he relinquished his grip on the derby long enough to pat Leota on the shoulder.

"Well, of course not, Richmond. I wasn't driving, you know," Leota snapped in exhaustion.

"You must be tired," Cora said. "Let's get you over to the motel so you can rest up a bit. Maggie will be coming in from Lubbock this evening and Horace will drive down from Dumas in the morning. We really didn't see much point in him coming in tonight. His health is not so good," Cora said.

"Well, it doesn't matter to me one way or the other with Horace. I wouldn't be upset if that brother of ours didn't bother to come at all," Leota replied.

Leota was carrying a small overnight case in her hand and as she stood talking to Cora, Richmond repeatedly tried to take the case from her so he could put it in the car, but Leota was, as usual, being quite elaborate with her hand movements in speaking with Cora and each time Richmond would reach for the case, Leota would swing it high out in front of her.

"Richmond, just what in the hell do you want?" Leota asked.

"I just wanted to put your bag in the car. I was trying to be helpful. Besides, you really ought not use such language in a funeral home," Richmond hissed.

"Oh, for Pete's sake, Richmond, by all means take it," Leota said, shoving the case at Richmond. The three of them shuffled out to the car together; Leota and Cora sat in the back seat, leaving Richmond in the front alone. It was like old times for Leota and Cora, as they had always traveled this way; the two of them in the back and the men, Richmond and Edgar, in the front, except in the old days Edgar had always driven the car and Richmond either slept or nagged Edgar to pull over somewhere and find a restroom.

"NO WAY," said Raleigh into the telephone.

"Oh, come on, Raleigh. We've already talked to Mother about it and she says it sounds like the best thing to do for Howard," Kerry pleaded.

"I don't care what Mother said, I am not riding in a car for eight hours with an eighty-seven-year-old man nor will I take the responsibility for Grandmother Leota's heart attack when she finds out that I drove you and Howard to the airport to Lubbock to make your getaway. If Mother thinks this hare-brained scheme is such a good idea, then she can take the two of you to Floydada and she can drive you on in to the Lubbock airport after the funeral. I wouldn't touch this one on a bet, and besides, Kerry, I offered to drive you to Floydada, not you and Howard," Raleigh argued.

"Well, it's just too late for you to say no. Mother's already left for Floydada and she made the plane reservations for Howard and me to fly to Albany from Lubbock before she left. She can't take us to Lubbock because she's going to drive Leo to Austin, and she plans to tell Leo on the way home that I've taken Howard back to Saratoga Springs. Would you rather Mother take us to the airport, and you drive Leo home and tell her yourself?" Kerry urged.

"Uh, I think you just made a very good point there, Kerry. I personally do not want to be anywhere near Grandmother Leota when she hears about it. Are you sure that Howard's in good enough health to be riding in a car all the way up to Floydada?"

"Oh, Howard's in great shape, he's just depressed over Pearlie's death. He is all packed and ready to go in the morning," Kerry said.

"Kerry, you're going to lose a whole semester of school if you leave now. What does Fletcher think of this?" Raleigh said, still quite perplexed with the plans.

"Fletcher might come visit us this summer. He understands that it's something I feel I have to do. I haven't been that happy here in Austin lately. I need to take on some kind of responsibility sometime and I can't think of any better way to do it. Can you? I love Howard and I know he'll be happier in his own environment. Can't you imagine how alone he feels right now? He doesn't have any family of his own; Pearlie was all he had and she's gone now," Kerry said.

"I understand all of that, I really do; it's just that I don't want to see you throw your life to the wind. Responsibility does not mean trading away your own talents for the well-being of an eighty-seven-year-old man whom you hardly know. I wish like hell that Mother had taken Howard to Floydada with her. What if something happens to him on the way up there?" Raleigh asked.

"In the first place, Raleigh, I'm not trading away my talents. I've learned more from Howard in the past week and a half than I ever learned in school, and in the second place, it made more sense for Howard to spend one more night resting before the trip than for him to jump in the car with Mother today and drive up to Floydada where he'd have to spend the night in a strange motel," Kerry said.

"OK, I guess you're right. One saving grace about this trip is that no one will have to look after Ethel. She and Rodney aren't going," Raleigh sighed.

"Yeah, Mother told me," Kerry said, as she looked up to see Wiley standing at the top of the stairs, signaling her to get off the phone. His signal consisted of a gesture in which he drew his index finger across his neck just below his chin. "I gotta go, Raleigh, Wiley needs to use the phone. I'll see you at five A.M. in the morning. Pick me up first, OK?" Kerry said.

"Well, what's it to Wiley that you need to use the phone? Tell that asshole to hold his horses, I'm not through talking with you, Kerry," Raleigh barked.

Wiley repeated his gesture from the top of the stairs.

"I gotta go *now*, Raleigh. I'll see you in the morning," said Kerry and she hung up the phone without saying goodbye to her brother, nor did she wait for a reply from him.

Raleigh held the phone out from his ear in disbelief and mumbled to himself, "What a jerk that guy is." He placed the phone back on his desk and went back to work packing up his belongings for storage. He thought to himself that this was one hell of a way to spend his last few days at home: packing up all his stuff, which he considered to be worthless, attending his great-grandmother's funeral, finalizing his divorce from Missy, and sending his sister off with Howard to Upstate New York. "Yes, indeed," Raleigh thought, "this is one hell of a send-off."

Kerry stood on the landing facing Wiley with her hands on her hips and her foot tapping loudly on the hardwood floor. "This better be important, Wiley," she snapped. "I was involved in a very important conversation with my brother Raleigh."

"You've been on that damn phone for hours, Kerry. Lensel has to go to the cafe to prepare for the dinner crowd and we all wanted you to come downstairs for a minute," Wiley said defensively.

"OK," Kerry said, feeling a bit ashamed of her treatment of Wiley.

They climbed down the stairs together. As they entered the living area on the first floor, Beam-us, Mr. Two Pants, and Lensel all rose to their feet to greet her. In the center of the room was a large, round coffee table. The table had been cleared of debris (it was normally the catchall for junk mail and phone messages) and in the center sat a metal bucket containing a chilled, tilted bottle of champagne. Kerry thought to herself that this must be Lensel's doing, as he was the only one of her housemates who she felt would know the difference between a bottle of champagne and a bottle of Thunderbird wine with a screw-on cap.

"We wanted to show you our appreciation for putting up with us for the past year," Wiley said with a grin.

"Hey, really man, ya been just like one of the crew," Beam-us added.

"This is so sweet of all of you," Kerry said.

Lensel gathered the paper cups around the champagne bucket while Wiley began opening the bottle; the cork went flying in the direction of Mr. Two Pants' head. Wiley poured the bubbling liquid into cups and they all toasted to Kerry's future in the North.

"We have a little surprise for you, Kerry," Lensel began. "We all talked it over this morning and we've decided that we'll each pay a little more on our rents for the next couple of months so we can save your room for you. It's just in case things don't work out up there. Wiley says the landlord wouldn't hold your room for you if he knew you'd moved so we're not going to tell him. Not for a while, anyway."

The news brought tears to her eyes. She realized for the first time that her housemates had become like members of her own family; they were like brothers; well, almost brothers. Lensel was more like the loving sister she'd always wanted to have.

Lensel walked to the bookshelves and withdrew his most treasured copy of the New York Philharmonic's recording of *Adagio for Strings*.

"Lensel, don't put that on, that left speaker is blown and it'll sound like hell," Wiley exclaimed.

"Oh no, Wiley, I wasn't going to play it. I wanted to give it to Kerry as a going-away present. It's a little something to remember me by," Lensel said haughtily as he handed the record to Kerry.

Beam-us reached in his shirt pocket and pulled out a joint with a small red ribbon tied around it. "This is just in case you want to 'beam' yourself home for a while. You never know when it might come in handy," Beam-us chuckled.

Much to Kerry's surprise, Wiley proudly interjected, "The champagne's on me!"

"Here's to ya, kid," Wiley said, lifting his cup in a toast.

"Thanks," Kerry said, "I'll never forget this. You've all been so important to me and I'll miss you, each and every one of you."

Mr. Two Pants gathered the empty cups when the party came to a close. Lensel hugged Kerry and kissed her on the cheek while making her promise to write him. He then turned and scurried out the door for work.

"Guess it's time to beam me up, Captain Kirk," Beam-us said to Wiley.

"Consider yourself beamed, Beam-us," Wiley said.

Kerry and Wiley sat in the living area alone. They were facing each other across the coffee table.

"Are you sure you want to do this?" Wiley asked.

"Yeah, I'm sure," Kerry said.

"Well, take care of yourself, then. Don't forget your room'll still be vacant for the next two months," Wiley said. He then shuffled out of the living room and Kerry heard his bedroom door close softly behind him. So much was unsaid, so much seemed incomplete, just as many things would remain incomplete in Kerry's life.

"You, too," Kerry said softly into the growing darkness in the empty living room. "You take good care of that sleeping heart of yours, Wiley."

Kerry returned to her room to finish packing her suitcase. Her father would be coming by at seven to pick up her boxes of books and her record collection. Kerry was prepared for the worst in confronting her father with her decision to move. She went through her record collection carefully, placing all but one of the records in a wooden crate to be stored at her father's house. It was an old album; she and Ethel had been given the album by their father in 1962. The recording artist was a woman named Carolyn Hester and the album itself remained, even after all these years, Kerry's favorite. She placed the record on the turntable and stretched out across the bed to listen.

She was lost in thoughts of her housemates and the boyfriend she would not see for a long while. She sang along with the last refrain on one of the traditional songs on the record. For just those fleeting moments, she actually missed Ethel's voice joining her in harmony as she had so often done in 1962.

> *Oh, the water is wide, I cannot cross over*
> *And neither have I wings to fly.*
> *Give me a boat that can carry two*
> *And both shall row, my love and I.*

Kerry fell asleep after this song and did not wake until she heard Wiley calling to her from the direction of the ladder.

"Kerry, your dad's downstairs!" Wiley yelled.

"Well, tell him to come on up here!" Kerry said sleepily. There was a pause of a few seconds before Wiley called back up to her.

"He says he lost a pound and a half of flesh off his shins last time he tried to climb that ladder and you're going to have to bring your stuff downstairs if you want him to store it for you," Wiley called back. "I gotta go to work now. Have a safe trip."

"OK," Kerry said as she walked toward the ladder to go downstairs to face her father.

Jeff Foster was pacing the floor in the living area, jingling the coins and his car keys in his pocket. He gave Wiley a hard stare as he left through the front door for work at the bar.

"She'll be right down, Mr. Foster," Wiley said as he slammed the front door closed. Mr. Foster always appeared to be so overprotective of his daughter Kerry that, even though Wiley wasn't due down at the bar for another two hours, he'd decided to go on down there. More than likely, Jeff Foster wasn't too pleased about his daughter's decision to move in the middle of a school semester and Wiley'd just as soon not be around to absorb the tension.

"Hi there, Dad," Kerry said, bounding into the living room. Her arms were loaded with the wooden crate of record albums.

"Hello, Kerry. Here, let me help you with that," Jeff said, walking across the living room to retrieve the wooden crate. "Do you have many boxes to store?" he asked.

"Nah, just two more boxes of books and a box of linens and stuff. I thought I'd leave my old stereo here at the house for the guys," Kerry said, handing him the crate.

"I'll just stick these things in the car then and come back in for the rest," Jeff said, thinking to himself that Kerry could hardly be referring to the little homosexual fellow who lived here as a guy.

He walked out to the car, which he'd been forced to leave parked on the street since someone was blocking the driveway. In many ways he was sad that his daughter was moving away, especially since Raleigh was also leaving, and he was certainly disappointed in Kerry for not waiting until this semester was finished, but on the other hand he was so elated that she would finally be moving out of this broken-down house full of weird characters. Howard Bates had to at least be a better alternative to these folks as a roommate. He had high hopes that perhaps Kerry would be forced to pursue her music more seriously now that she would be far away from the economic shelter of her family. He had read her poetry and several of her essays and truthfully did not feel she had one ounce of talent in the field of writing; he did feel, however, that she was most talented as a vocalist. He had a wonderful tenor's voice himself and he had always dreamed that one of his children would pursue a musical career. He knew that having a musical career was second choice for Kerry, who would much rather devote her efforts to journalism. Kerry had a smooth, powerful voice; he had nursed her talents since childhood. He had a reel-to-reel tape recording rig set up in his study, and when Kerry came to visit him they would shut themselves off in the study for hours to record Kerry's songs and tinker with the recording equipment. Kerry had learned how to play the guitar when she was nine and just last year Jeff had gone against Louise's wishes and purchased for Kerry a D-28 Martin. He and Kerry had driven all the way to Houston to find just the right guitar for her; they'd found the D-28 at a warehouse-style music store after having spent hours walking through aisle after aisle of different brands of guitars. Kerry had fallen in love with the D-28 the moment she picked it up, but the price had been more than five hundred dollars so Jeff had told her he couldn't afford it. Kerry had been silent all the way back to Austin but she had not complained; little did she know that Jeff had made arrangements with the owner of the store to have the guitar shipped to Austin later in the week. He'd presented it to her the following weekend. Louise had been so ticked off that he'd spent that much money on Kerry, she'd sulked about the house the entire time Kerry was there.

"What 'cha thinkin'?" Kerry said to Jeff, who was standing by the open trunk of the car, lost in thought. Kerry had actually been standing on the sidewalk for several moments watching her father daydream. He'd been whistling; he always whistled when he was in a pensive mood, and he was jingling the coins in his pockets.

"Oh, I was just remembering what you were like when you were a little girl, or should I say a younger girl? You're still awfully little," Jeff sighed. "In fact, you're still my little girl and I'm proud that you're going out on your own."

"You are?" Kerry asked in amazement.

"Yep," Jeff replied, and he took the box Kerry was holding and placed it gently in the trunk of the car. "Let's go get those other two boxes. Louise has got dinner waiting at home."

Kerry walked hand in hand with her father to the house. She was a bit chafed that once again, Louise was putting a time limit on the time she spent with her father; yet it had always been that way and her main thought now was that he was happy and she was relieved he'd given her his blessing for this move. Nothing can ever replace that portion of a young girl's heart reserved for the blessings of her father, and no woman in the world can ever erase the memory in the heart of a father of his daughter's smile.

———

KERRY PEARL'S FUNERAL was scheduled to begin at two in the afternoon. It was the twelfth of March and the wind was still terribly brisk in Floydada. Raleigh had had a heck of a time driving once he'd ascended onto the caprock, as a dust storm was clouding the highway. They arrived at the Sacred Heart Church just as the bells in the church tower tolled two o'clock. Leota was frantic for them to come inside and be seated; she escorted Howard up the aisle appearing to be nonplussed that he had chosen to attend. Julie had warned her that he would be arriving with Kerry and Raleigh.

It was a small gathering of relatives and old friends. Leota's brother, Horace, had seated himself beside Leota on the first pew. Horace was extremely hard of hearing and since his wife, Della, was a Baptist he hadn't attended a Catholic Mass of any kind since 1930. He had long forgotten the rituals of the rosary and each time the priest would begin a decade and Leota would echo after him, "Our Father . . . " Horace would interrupt her by tilting his head toward her and exclaiming loudly, "What'd ya say there, Leota?" Leota tried to continue on with the rosary and would turn and put her finger against her lips whispering "shh" to Horace. Horace continued to interrupt her throughout the second decade of the rosary, never allowing her to complete even one Hail Mary. Leota finally came to the conclusion that Horace was not about to accept "shh" as an answer, and resigned herself to miming the remainder of the rosary. She made a note to herself that she would rattle the dentures right out of Horace's mouth when this service was finished. Howard, who was seated on the other side of Leota, reassuringly patted her hand, which held firmly to her rosary beads. At the closing of the service, he intuitively guided Leota away from Horace and whisked her into the waiting limousine between him and Maggie.

There had been few tears at the service. Everyone, except Leota and Horace, had spent that time reflecting on their own experiences with Kerry Pearl. She had lived too full a life for her passing to lend itself to sadness, and the service itself had been more of a celebration of her life rather than the mourning of her death.

The grave site was located just outside of town in a small cemetery which had been abandoned by the present community for a more modern memorial park on the other side of Floydada. The dust blew with a vengeance through the granite and marble headstones. The family members clutched their coats about their bodies and used handkerchiefs to protect their faces from the piercing dust.

Howard leaned his small frame against Leota as they stood over the grave. His knees were feeling a bit weak at the sight of the coffin being lowered into the ground beside Max's headstone. He shakily tossed one red rose onto the casket, as did Leota. The year could now be filled in below Kerry Pearl's name and the name of Bates would never be connected with his Pearl again.

Max stirred in his quarters underground as Kerry Pearl came to rest beside him. "How nice of you to come to visit. I'd wondered where you'd gone to," he said. Their matching wedding bands glistened there in the dust, for the dust was the home of their love and the dust was their future.

The Great White North

THE GREAT WHITE NORTH was a new world for Kerry Foster. She was securely nestled between the Catskill Mountains and the Adirondacks in her new home with Howard Bates. The cold of mid-March was an incredible shock to her system. Her thin body wrestled with the chill of the nights and she woke each morning curled into a tight, cramped ball, buried beneath a mountain of blankets. It was her first encounter with real snow: the sort of snow that engulfs you with its presence. Yet, it was not the weather which impressed young Kerry there in Saratoga Springs, New York; it was the intellectual climate that raced her mind to exhaustion and left her anxious at the end of each day for the beginning of the next. Saratoga was a resort community. It had also been a haven for artists and writers for many years, and Kerry found herself burdened with her own naivety.

Howard went to great lengths to assure Kerry that she was not "just plain stupid" during her first two weeks in Saratoga Springs. Regardless of his encouragement, she continued to refer to herself as such.

Since Howard had leased his house to the Wilsons until July, he and Kerry had moved into a boardinghouse in the center of town, which was owned by an old friend of Howard's named Clare Friedman. Clare was a tiny whisper of a woman, with dark, curly hair sprinkled with gray. She had exceptionally intense brown eyes. She was not the sort to smile without sincerity, and Kerry, who was accustomed to the constant tradition in Texas of smiling in salutation, felt intimidated by Clare. She was certain that Clare Friedman had no use for her whatsoever.

Clare was a published poet. She also published a popular weekly newspaper based around the arts and political issues. Her paper was aptly titled *The Avalanche*. Because of the newspaper, she housed a constant flow of musicians, poets, artists of all sorts, and political radicals within her huge, wandering house.

Howard had met Clare twenty-five years before in New York City; she had been a client of his insurance firm. They had become close friends shortly after meeting one another.

It had been Clare who'd inspired Howard to retire in Saratoga Springs. She was a strong-willed woman in her mid-fifties and as the years had passed, Howard had come to love her as an adopted daughter. Clare seemingly had no family of her own; Howard was her only link to familial graces and he provided an air of normality which, in truth, did not exist in her lifestyle.

Clare did not dislike Kerry. Quite the contrary, she was most impressed with this young woman from Texas who had devoted herself to Howard's welfare. Kerry mentioned in passing one day that she wrote poetry and prose. Clare had heard her sing and play guitar and she liked some of Kerry's original songs, so she asked Kerry if she could read her work.

Well, Clare thought her poetry was very weak. It seemed to lack its own melody, as though Kerry could not write poetry without placing it within a song. The prose was a different story altogether. Clare was impressed with the approach Kerry took in relating the subject matter, she left herself open for the reader in her essays, she was believable yet so vulnerable in her work that the pieces held a quality of charm to them that Clare had not expected. She held such a refreshing view of things that Clare decided to ask Kerry to write a record review for *The Avalanche*. It was a Phil Ochs album, *I Ain't Marching Anymore*, that Clare presented to Kerry during her second week at the boardinghouse. The album itself was actually several years old and Clare wasn't totally convinced that it would be appropriate for *The Avalanche* to run the article, but she was anxious to instill new social thoughts in Kerry's mind.

Kerry became obsessed with the album. She spent two days sitting in Clare's parlor listening to the record nonstop. The entire boardinghouse became quite familiar with Phil Ochs during those two days and Clare was almost to the point of calling the project off for the sake of her tenants when Kerry presented her with her review.

Clare ran the review; she edited one line, which was "Phil Ochs' lyrics punch injustice right smack in the nose!" Kerry didn't miss the line when the review ran in *The Avalanche*; she was too consumed with the pride of seeing her name as a byline in print.

It just so happened, in the way that things are bound to happen, that Clare was one of the organizers in New York State who were planning the massive march on Washington to be held on May Day against the war in Vietnam. One of the events included a free outdoor music festival, which would feature, among others, Phil Ochs and a Texas band that Kerry was fond of, Tracy Nelson and Mother Earth. Kerry decided she was going to Washington, DC, with Clare. They, in fact, planned on traveling in Howard's 1967 Pontiac.

Howard forbade it! He sulked around the boardinghouse with his cane looped on his arm for days before he gave his verbal opinion of the plan. Once he'd made his statement out in the open to Kerry and Clare he ceased to sulk and would in fact repeat the same statement each time he passed one of them anywhere in the house. Howard was quite concerned that he didn't have a chance of persuading Kerry not to attend the rallies; his only hope was to play upon Kerry's sympathies. He would corner Kerry and in his soft-spoken manner he would say, "Leota will chip the enamel right off her teeth chewing me out if I let you do this. Through all these years, I've come closer than a mosquito's whiskers to having a serious falling-out with your dear grandmother Leota, and now that I am finally out of her doghouse, I wish to heaven that you would not throw a log on the old fire, Kerry." Howard would then wink at Kerry and shuffle off in search of Clare.

Now, Howard could afford not to be so eloquent with Clare; once he'd located her in the house, he'd simply wave his cane at her and scold, "Oh, you ought to be ashamed of yourself and I'll just be damned if you're taking my Pontiac!"

"Really, Howard," Clare would reply, "don't you think you're being a bit selfish in this matter?" Clare would roll her eyes skyward and continue on with whatever chore Howard had interrupted, which aggravated Howard to no end. Seconds after each of these encounters Clare would hear the slamming of Howard's door and the gentle sound of his pacing back and forth in his room.

Kerry was determined to gain Howard's approval for the trip to Washington. She finally shocked Howard by simply saying, "Oh, Howard, who cares what Leo thinks anyway?"

Howard's eyes lit up like the Fourth of July fireworks display and he replied, "Now, don't you start that 'Oh, Howard' business with me, young Kerry. I get quite enough of that from Clare, thank you. You're not going on this adventure — period — and neither is my Pontiac. Clare's a grown woman and she can do as she pleases but you just don't have any idea what you're getting into. That is all I'm going to say on this subject and I'd appreciate it if you would improve your tone of voice next time you address me; you're almost as sassy as your grandmother Leota." Howard doggedly walked away from Kerry firmly tapping his cane of the floor and mumbling, " . . . closer than a mosquito's whiskers, by God . . . Leota's going to skin me alive . . . "

Kerry could see the curls of Howard's handlebar mustache twitching as he walked away from her. She was now certain that Howard had resigned himself to the fact that she was going to the rallies even if he wouldn't admit it to her. If only he'd change his mind about the Pontiac!

One of the tenants in Clare's boardinghouse was a young photographer named Puttnam. Puttnam was a Vietnam veteran who had come to live in Clare's house as one of the fringe benefits of being the staff photographer for *The Avalanche*. He had only been out of the army for a year and a half and still had a lot of demons to exorcise from his experiences in Vietnam. Puttnam was six-feet-five with strawberry blond hair and a lanky frame. His appearance was most often disheveled and he had a habit of pushing his long hair out of his face constantly. He had enormous sky-blue eyes which held such deep sorrow that, even though Puttnam was often given to fits of bellowing laughter, you could still feel the pain within him; you could even hear his anguish within that boisterous laughter.

Lunches at Clare's could be maddening. Clare served a plate lunch each day. Her dining room seated about twenty folks and had become a gathering place for pseudo-intellectuals. Afternoons were given to screaming matches among the customers. Howard was an excellent referee, as he was past the point in his life when he felt compelled to make an impression on anyone concerning his intellect. On days when the noise level became too much for Howard to tolerate, he would tap his cane on the floor sharply and say, "Sure is getting up in the day around here. Haven't you folks got some work you could be doing? The world's a-waitin.'"

Of course, most of the folks that hung around Clare's at lunchtime didn't have jobs of any kind but Howard's age made him the voice of authority and they would usually begin clearing out of Clare's once Howard had made it clear that they were wearing out their welcome.

Kerry spent a great deal of time with Puttnam. He was the only individual in the group around Clare's who did not try to intimidate Kerry. Puttnam was a history buff and could go on for hours about American history, which Kerry found to be fascinating. Kerry was an avid reader of contemporary American fiction which Puttnam hadn't yet discovered, so they had an even trade of information for each other. While the others sat around the dining room discussing Proust and Shelley in literature and plotted their plans to overthrow the world by quoting Lenin, Engels, and Marx, Kerry and Puttnam sat off in the corner at a small table greedily exchanging knowledge current to their own generation. The two of them made no plans to change the world situation; they were, in fact, a change in American society because they were doers rather than procrastinators.

Once a week Clare held a staff meeting for *The Avalanche* in the dining room after lunch. The meetings were a free-for-all, with Clare usually making all the final decisions herself since the staff could not bring themselves to agree on anything with each other. The staff had grown to eight members since the addition of Kerry as music columnist. She also contributed essays on various subjects, which Clare used when the space was available. Kerry's columns were becoming quite popular among the readers of *The Avalanche* and she began receiving mail soon after her first article on Phil Ochs. The rest of the staff members enjoyed their own particular niches in preparing the paper each week, except for Kerry, who was filling a double slot with a writer named Ernest Hinkle. Ernest was quite indignant about having to compete with Kerry for what had been his slot before her arrival.

Ernest was from Teaneck, New Jersey. He was a small man who bathed only once a week, wore the same wool sweater day in and day out, had an annoying habit of meddling in other people's business, and professed to be an expert on just about everything. He was particularly peeved that Clare had chosen to take Kerry to the Washington rallies as a music reviewer for the paper. Ernest felt that he had earned the right to go since he had been with the paper for almost three years, and underneath his intellectual rhetoric dwelled the heart of a hardcore male chauvinist. When Kerry began receiving favorable letters from the readers (he'd never received any letters), Ernest set about trying to discredit Kerry in any way he could at staff meetings and attempted to finagle an invitation to the rallies as a staff writer from Clare. By the third staff meeting in April it became clear to Ernest that he was not going to be included at the rallies. He was convinced that anyone from below the Mason-Dixon line was an absolute nitwit and this person who was stepping in on his territory was not only from Texas but was also, very obviously, a *girl*.

Clare was embarrassed by Ernest's attitude. She hoped that in time Ernest would accept Kerry as part of the staff and that their dual role could become a somewhat disjunctive asset to *The Avalanche*.

Clare felt that she could not intervene on Kerry's behalf since she was well aware of Ernest's attitude toward women. She instead was inclined to feel that sooner or later Kerry herself would catch Ernest at his own game, and she quietly sat back to wait for that moment to present itself.

Ernest was a sincere writer as a rule. His columns were very basic, yet they had served *The Avalanche* well in defining the format for the paper. He was a bit narrow in his choice of material to review and chose not to listen to anything which was not political in nature. Clare had been encouraging him for months to expand his interests, as there were many records being sent to them by women artists; she'd had little success, as Ernest left those albums stacked in a pile in the corner of Clare's office. Kerry filled a gap in the paper that Ernest himself had created with his closed mind. She listened to every record sent to her, plus going through that stack of records which Ernest had abandoned with a deaf ear.

Kerry had thus far written reviews of Carole King's *Tapestry* album, Rosalie Sorrels' *Travelin' Lady*, Townes Van Zandt's *Our Mother the Mountain*, and a review of a performance by Don McLean at the coffeehouse, Caffè Lena, there in Saratoga Springs. Kerry did not write unfavorable reviews; she instead adopted a system of singularizing the material which she felt was performed with subtle clarity by the artists. She was not particularly discriminating in terms of the quality of the musical production itself; she focused on the lyrical content and the emotion those lyrics could turn in the listener. This flaw in her technique became Ernest's legitimate bone of contention at weekly staff meetings.

Margaret English was a poet. She reviewed the new poetry submitted to the paper. She was a shy, thoughtful young woman from Auburn, New York. Margaret had never been a social person. She wrote her reviews and her poetry with the tender observation of one who longs to experience without bias.

Jack Simpson covered world events and wrote either a political commentary or submitted a political cartoon for each issue. Ty

Gallagher covered art and theatre; he kept an apartment in New York City and only traveled to Saratoga for staff meetings. He was beginning to move up in his field; several of his articles had been picked up by a larger daily newspaper in the Northeast. Marlin Stancell covered national events and the underground political scene, plus writing an occasional review of new fiction. Clare was editor; she collected articles on health and the growing ecology movement.

The Avalanche was still a small production. It had about three thousand subscribers in the North and sold about the same amount on the newsstands. Though it was small by any standards in distribution, it was still a highly respected publication and more successful than most of the small magazines and newspapers which were attempting to follow the same format.

The staff meeting before the May Day rallies was a heated gathering. The staff was being forced to choose between an article Ernest had written on the collected works of Paul Robeson and a review Kerry had written about Jerry Jeff Walker's album, *Driftin' Way of Life*. The staff was voting in favor of Kerry's article — not for its merits, but because Ernest's piece on Paul Robeson hadn't quite come together on paper, and though it was more in line with the tone of that issue, Ernest had written it in haste and it rambled off the subject. It, in fact, focused more on the political stance of Ernest Hinkle and was a blatant attempt by Ernest to validate his own intelligence. Robeson lived in Philadelphia at that time, after spending many years abroad. Margaret had timidly suggested that Ernest arrange an interview with Robeson on the telephone, which would bring the article back to a more direct and personal level. This would mean postponing the article on Robeson for at least a month and Ernest was enraged over the possibility of being voted down by his colleagues, especially since the toss-up involved an article on some bimbo from Texas. Ernest had not done his homework — Jerry Jeff Walker was in fact from the northern regions of the country. Ernest pointed out vehemently that Kerry and Marlin already had a slot in this issue. They had collaborated on a review of Larry McMurtry's new novel, *Moving On*. He insisted that it was simply redundant to print two reviews in the same issue on Texas writers. The fact that he thought they were both from Texas doubled his rage. He considered Marlin a traitor.

"This is just outrageous that we're going to present two pieces in the same issue on Texas writers. Our readers know there are no *real* writers in Texas. They'll think we have Katherine Anne Porter on the brain. We'll be the laughing stock of the Northeast. This article on Paul Robeson is much more relevant to the interests of our readers. Texas writers have no credibility in this region of the country — they are a bad joke," Ernest proclaimed.

Kerry was sitting directly across the table from Ernest. She guessed that this must be the sixth day since he had last bathed, as the whole room reeked of damp wool and perspiration. The situation was not eased much by Ernest, who began to flap his arms wildly to make his point. Margaret sat on one side of him while Ty sat on the other side. Margaret excused herself from the table several times during the meeting. Kerry wondered if she was excusing herself to avoid contact with Ernest's body odor, for it was nauseating to everyone at the table.

"What you're saying is bullshit, Ernest. Maybe an article on Paul Robeson would be more in tune with this paper, but you just didn't pull it off," Kerry remarked.

Howard sat in a rocking chair across the room by the window, reading a magazine. Upon hearing Kerry's remarks, he closed the magazine and folded it gently in his lap, while his ears perked up in anticipation of Ernest's rebuttal.

Ernest slapped his hand flat down on the table, which woke Puttnam up from his daydreaming. "Just how would you know whether I pulled it off or not? You're not even old enough to know or value the work of Paul Robeson. Who is this scathing, gravel-voiced Jerry Jeff Walker anyway?" Ernest bellowed.

"You're missing the damn point here, Ernest. I do not agree with your attitude toward Texas writers, but I do agree that an article on Paul Robeson makes a hell of a lot more sense than a review of a Jerry

Jeff Walker album — but the Robeson thing just didn't come together and you're too hardheaded to admit it. Age has nothing to do with art. I know a good line when I read one and a decent score of music when I hear it. Robeson's work was and is more politically valuable to the arts than Walker's, but you did not do it justice; you didn't even come close. Walker is a good, solid artist. His lyrics are a bit light but the music is great. He's gathering a strong following up here. He's from up here, by the way. My article was simply intended to introduce our readers to something they might enjoy," Kerry replied.

"Your choice of vocabulary is disgusting! It's a prime example of your Texas no-talents. If you can't find any words to express yourself that aren't laced with profanity, then would you mind just keeping silent? You have absolutely no taste whatsoever in literature, music, or art," Ernest hissed. He then leaned back in his chair and began tapping a pencil on the edge of the table. He was extremely smug, deciding he'd finally put Kerry in her place, and his beady gray eyes gleamed with satisfaction beneath his thick horn-rimmed glasses.

Kerry stood up from the table while collecting her papers in front of her. She fumbled with the papers just long enough to get them in order before clutching them tightly to her chest. "You're a fucking snob, Ernest. You wouldn't know a good line or a decent song if it reached out and slapped you right in the face. You sit here each week claiming to know more about art than any of us, yet you leave a stack of artistic endeavors two feet high piled in Clare's office, untouched by your filthy fingers. You don't know art! You can't even make a solid decision of your own without reading the reviews of other writers first. You use the lyrics of the performers you do review to pat yourself on the back. When was the last time you took a chance on an unknown artist; when was the last time you even listened to one? You're not interested in finding out what made Paul Robeson's work so heartfelt — you're interested in the prestige of writing about Paul Robeson. Ya better get your ass on the phone to Philadelphia if you want that piece to work. I think it would be quite interesting to have a conversation with him, you might learn something. Perhaps he could lend you an ounce or two of credibility," Kerry said through clenched teeth.

She strolled to the door, leaving her chair in the middle of the floor. She turned around just before making her exit to address Ernest once more. "Ya know, Ernest, I'd enjoy these meetings a lot more if you'd take a bath now and then. It's no wonder that you're called chauvinist pig behind your back, considering that you actually do smell like one!"

"Bravo!" Puttnam exclaimed, jumping to his feet and beginning a round of applause that spread to each staff member around the table.

"Oh, grow up, Puttnam. This is an absolute outrage," Ernest shouted, but his voice was barely audible over the clapping hands of his fellow staff members.

Kerry could hear Puttnam's bellowing laughter from her room and before too long she also heard the front door slam shut. She walked to the window which faced the street just in time to see Ernest stomping down the sidewalk with a swift click. Papers were flying in all directions from his briefcase, as he'd forgotten in his haste to close the latch. Kerry opened the window and shouted out to Ernest, "Ernest, you're losing your papers. Hey, Ernest, pay attention to what you're doin', man!"

Ernest looked back at Kerry and shouted, "Fuck you, Foster, you little creep!"

An older woman who lived down the street happened to be passing by at the time and she stopped alongside Ernest, gave him a shove on the arm, and replied, "You just watch your language, young man. There are children in this neighborhood."

Ernest scrambled around the sidewalk and street to retrieve his scattered papers while Kerry stood in the window and giggled over her triumph. She had won this round with Ernest and somewhere within the squabble she had also won his respect. That was evident in the fact that he had just bestowed the greatest honor possible on Kerry by addressing her by her last name; that was a ritual normally reserved by men like Ernest for situations involving men among men.

Kerry returned to the dining room to find the entire staff still discussing the incident. Puttnam was still standing; he was in the process of delivering an impersonation of Ernest's indignant reaction to the rest of the staff after Kerry had left the room. Clare was trying to calm Howard down; he was shaking his cane in the air and shouting, "That young man should be banned from these procedures! If he ever talks to my Kerry like that again he's going to be picking rosewood out of his teeth!"

Even Margaret was laughing; Kerry had never seen her laugh before. She was normally such an intensely serious young woman. But at this moment she sat at the table with a delicate, slender hand poised over her mouth, giggling uncontrollably. She reached out with her other hand upon seeing Kerry enter the room and motioned for her to come stand beside her at the table. She wrapped her arm around Kerry's waist and hugged her tightly.

"Oh, but he's had that coming for so long," Margaret began. "I'm so proud of you for not letting him intimidate you. It's something I've been waiting for since the first day you joined us."

"But he's such a good writer, Margaret. He really does have a lot more on the ball than I do. He's so dedicated to keeping his columns pure. I feel terrible that he's walked out on the paper. I can't possibly fill the empty space it'll leave in *The Avalanche*," Kerry said.

"Oh, he'll be back, Kerry. When he comes back, he'll have that piece on Robeson honed down to the edge of perfection. This has happened before with Ernest. We've all had to humiliate him in public in order to get his attention. It was obvious that he wrote that article to spite you and now he'll have to write that article to defend his art and the journalistic integrity of the paper. We can all relax now as Ernest will go back to writing for this paper with the dedication he had before he began this campaign to oust you from the staff. It is the understanding that matters, and it's hard for Ernest to understand anything except his own narrow view. We are a family here at this paper; Ernest is part of us and we'll love him in spite of himself and regardless of his faults, for in many ways he is simply the bad side of all of us and it's impossible to dismiss a portion of one's self," Clare said as she helped Howard to his feet.

"Well, I think that a swift kick in the old rear-end is what that young man needs," Howard said. He placed the magazine he'd been reading in the rocking chair and followed Clare out of the dining room with his cane securely looped on one arm and his other hand nervously twiddling the curls in his mustache.

Kerry had earned a place in this family. In a sense, all of the staff members had put her through a probationary period; Ernest had simply been more vocal about it. In any family, whether it is by birth or one that is created out of loneliness for the lack of a natural family, there will always be a role that each individual is expected to fill; for each member of a family must be productive and contribute to the definition of that unity.

Many truths had been revealed about these peculiar individuals with Kerry's outburst. Margaret had shown a side of herself that the others had never considered her to have: a sense of humor. She and Kerry began a friendship that would last throughout their lives. It was a friendship which would open up new worlds for both of them, for in the same manner in which Margaret had never opened her life to the shared bonds of friendship, Kerry had never known the unspoken trust of having a woman friend and it created an awareness in Kerry that all women face a difficult and painful task in tackling an occupation controlled by men. Many of their female contemporaries would refuse to compete with the male world and would instead band together to form their own empires separate from the mainstream — in fact, separate from reality — with the end result of only reaching each other and reinforcing their own beliefs, which had already been established. Kerry and Margaret were so far removed from their contemporaries that they would unconsciously dive headfirst into the male establishment, and while neither would ever be considered serious artists by the "women's movement," they would survive and function within the media as proof that women could be equals in a male-dominated society. They would be more successful in changing the attitudes of chauvinistic men than their contemporaries who simply circulate among themselves, yet it would always be their contemporaries who would receive the credit for having changed the structure of the establishment itself. They had a grand example to follow in Clare. Margaret would one day devote herself to writing the biography of Clare Friedman, and it would be accepted in the literary world not simply as a book by a woman author about a woman author, but as a definitive classic about the life of a gifted and dedicated artist and publisher.

Clare, as a living example to Kerry and Margaret, taught them both that they could not simply produce their works and demand that they be accepted because they were women and thus deserved to be acknowledged; she instead instilled within the two of them the reality that their work had to be equal if not better than that of their male counterparts, and that they themselves were the only individuals who could make their work succeed or fail.

A LOVE AFFAIR began between Margaret and Puttnam. Her lovely laughter during the staff meeting had stolen his heart. Howard's room in the boardinghouse was situated between Margaret and Puttnam's and the sound of Margaret's cautious footsteps passing his room began waking him during the night, as well as the indiscreet thunder of Puttnam's visits to Margaret's room, which could shake the whole house.

No one was supposed to know about the affair except for Kerry, but the entire household was well aware of this blooming spring romance. Howard simply wanted a good night's sleep and one night when he'd been awakened twice by the pitter-patter of Margaret's feet in the hallway outside his door he decided it was time to address this problem. It was about three in the morning when he heard Margaret's door creak open and the crash of Puttnam's footsteps heading toward his room. Howard, who was dressed in his flannel nightshirt, yanked his bedroom door open, which startled the hell out of Puttnam, who was clad only in his boxer shorts; he immediately began his ritual of pushing the hair out of his face.

"Puttnam!" Howard barked.

"Yes, sir," Puttnam replied, wishing he could melt into the woodwork.

"By God I wish you'd stop this nonsense and simply retire with Miss English at bedtime. It's all this sneaking about from room to room that's keeping me awake at night, not the creaking of the bedsprings. Just what in the hell is the intrigue of shuffling back and forth all night long?" Howard asked. He only stood as tall as Puttnam's chest and he had to lean his head back uncomfortably to address Puttnam eye to eye.

"Well, nothing, sir," Puttnam said shakily.

"Well, then, by God, choose whose room you're going to horse around in and stay there," Howard bellowed.

"Yes, sir," Puttnam said, while Howard swiveled around on the toes of his bare feet and retreated to his room, loudly banging the door shut behind him.

Howard settled back into bed that night and the sound of shuffling feet ceased to wake him after that. On some nights the creak of the bedsprings or Puttnam's boisterous laughter would jolt him to an upright position and his eyes would snap open in confusion, but the sounds were so joyous in nature that Howard never complained and he would fall back to sleep almost immediately. He'd sometimes dream he was snuggled in the nape of Kerry Pearl's neck and during those dreams he could actually smell her sweetness, which had always been the scent of lilac. "Sweet dreams, my dear," he would mumble in his sleep, and a contented smile would rest upon his face as he slumbered, as though Kerry Pearl had actually been there to return his affections.

THE STAFF MEMBERS who were to attend the rallies included Kerry, Clare, and Puttnam. On Friday at six A.M. they met in the dining hall only to find Howard seated stubbornly on his suitcase, tapping the floor with his cane. He'd reluctantly consented to allowing them the use of his Pontiac. They were all three now aware of the one condition he'd forgotten to mention.

"Good morning, Howard," Clare said nonchalantly as she strolled by Howard, clutching her large straw handbag in both hands. "You're up awfully early this morning. Going somewhere?" she asked.

"You bet I am," Howard replied, shaking his cane at Clare. "I'm going to Washington, DC, and you'd best not argue with me because I hold the keys to the Pontiac and it's not leaving the driveway without me in it."

"Howard, this is not a vacation. This trip would be too hard on you. We'll be sleeping on the floor of a dorm at the university there. That's no place for an eighty-seven-year-old man," Clare said. Kerry and Puttnam had decided to stay out of the conversation completely and had withdrawn to the doorway to wait for Clare to settle the argument and send Howard back to bed.

"My dear, I was not in the outhouse when you were making plans for the housing arrangements and since I can afford to do so I have taken the liberty to reserve rooms at the Holiday Inn in Arlington. I intend to pay for the rooms out of my own pocket, as I won't have young Kerry sleeping on the floor of some dorm with strangers, and as I've already stated THE PONTIAC IS NOT BUDGING WITHOUT ME!"

"Howard, you're impossible," Clare replied in exasperation. They stared one another in the eye for several tense moments in an attempt to dissuade the other's intentions. Howard broke the silence; it was his victory.

"We're history in the making, by God. Puttnam, put these bags in the old buggy and let's get rollin'," Howard boasted in triumph. He gently pulled Clare aside at the front door and whispered, "I'll stay in the hotel room if I feel I can't handle the activities. I know my own limits, Clare, so don't fret over my health. I'd like to feel useful and at my age, the days of feeling useful are few and far between. I just wanted to see these young people speak up for their rights, for

I surely agree with their cause and what better way is there for an old man like me to show his support than to join them? I'll be serving my own generation by going to our nation's capital. You see, it isn't just the young or the radical left who are opposed to the war, and I have the same right to voice my opinion as they do. I promise to behave myself," Howard said with a grin.

They settled into the Pontiac for the long drive to Washington, with Clare driving first. Puttnam sat in the front with Clare and carried on a hushed conversation with Kerry, who was seated in the back seat behind Clare. Howard fell asleep almost immediately after they turned onto the highway; his mustache twitched in the morning glow and his hand, which clutched the worn handle of his cane, would jump occasionally when Clare would pass over a dip in the road. He snored quietly with his head resting on the window of the Pontiac and the car was engulfed with the smell of fresh coffee, which Puttnam poured for Clare out of the thermos she'd packed in early dawn. They were out to defend America; they were soldiers of peace and none of them knew better than Puttnam how important it was to bring peace.

After lunch Clare switched places with Kerry and Puttnam drove. It was mid-afternoon and Puttnam was cruising down the interstate going eighty miles per hour when Howard was awakened by the sound of loose gravel hitting the side of the car. He looked out the window just in time to witness a small foreign car swerving onto the shoulder to his right.

"Puttnam, I hate to be a back-seat driver, but do you realize that you've just run someone off the road?" Howard remarked.

"Where's that?" Putnam asked, somewhat in a daze.

"Back there, that little sports car — you nearly ran over those folks," Howard said.

"Oh, that. They'd been driving along for miles with their blinker on. I just sort of helped 'em make up their minds. They're OK. Look back there: see, they've finally turned that blinker off."

Howard turned to look out the rear windshield and sure enough, the little sports car had managed to veer back onto the highway.

"Well, that's one heck of a way to get somebody's attention. Let's slow down a bit ... I mean, after all, I don't really have insurance for you as a driver and we should proceed as carefully as possible," Howard pleaded.

"Ah, I'm a good driver, Mr. Bates. I'm just trying to get us into DC before rush-hour traffic starts," Puttnam said, pushing his hair back from his face with an exaggerated gesture.

"Puttnam," Clare barked, aggravated at having been wakened from her short nap. "Slow this vehicle down and don't argue with Howard; it's his car."

"Yes, ma'am," Puttnam replied cheerfully.

They did indeed pull into Washington at rush hour and Puttnam managed to get in the wrong lane several times, therefore placing them on the wrong freeways. It was dark when they finally pulled into the parking lot at the Holiday Inn, and after Howard and Clare had registered at the office and Puttnam had deposited their gear into the adjoining rooms, they all ordered sandwiches from room service and soon after collapsed from exhaustion. Howard was the last to fall asleep; he'd slept for most of the trip and he always had a difficult time falling asleep in a new environment. Puttnam, who slept in the other bed in their room, snored so loudly that Howard finally coaxed himself to sleep by placing a pillow over his head.

CLARE WAS the first one up the next morning. She was scheduled to speak at an organization meeting for the New York delegation at St. Edward's church. She took Kerry with her to the meeting, leaving Puttnam in charge of getting Howard up out of bed.

Howard was quite cranky that morning. He spent his first waking moments berating Puttnam for snoring all night.

"Puttnam, I do hope that you will try to fall asleep on your side tonight. Your snoring is so loud that I would not have been surprised had the management called to complain. Have you ever considered consulting your physician about this problem?" Howard asked.

"Well, if I ever decide to have a physician, Mr. Bates, I'll certainly consult them about it," Puttnam replied. He had settled into a chair by the window and was in the midst of trying to read the morning paper. It was a daily ritual for Puttnam to read the paper cover to cover without interruption. Having Howard as a roommate did not lend itself to this end.

Howard sat on the edge of the unmade bed still in his nightshirt, the tails of which he had tucked snuggly between his clenched knees.

"Where did you say Clare was gone off to?" Howard asked while straightening the curls in his mustache.

"Aw, she and Kerry went down to some church for a meeting. Each state is going to be assigned to different locations for the rallies. She said she'd be back 'round lunchtime," Puttnam said with a crack of the spine of the newspaper and a hard stare at Howard.

Howard pushed his feet into his slippers, which he'd left tucked neatly under the side of his bed. He stood up slowly and began to stretch his small, wiry limbs with a hearty groan, followed by two sets of knee bends.

"You don't think there's a possibility of Clare getting lost out there in the Pontiac, do you, Puttnam?" Howard asked shyly.

"Naw, fact is, she didn't take the Pontiac. Some gal came by here to pick her and Kerry up," Puttnam said in amusement. He folded the newspaper in his lap and watched as Howard performed his morning exercises. It wasn't the type of performance one would normally expect of an eighty-seven-year-old man.

Howard had positioned himself on his back on the floor with his hands folded across his chest; he counted his sit-ups out loud as he did them; sometimes he counted without actually performing the sit-up.

"Do you do this every morning, Mr. Bates?" Puttnam asked.

"Only when I want to nowadays. I'm too old to make myself do anything I don't want to do. It's good for the old ticker now and then. My dear departed wife was a firm believer in keeping the body pure. She was a walker, you know. I used to exercise like this every day for her benefit; I only do it every now and then these days, when I get to feeling guilty," Howard puffed.

Watching Howard exercise caused Puttnam's stomach to growl. He proposed to Howard that the two of them grab a bite of breakfast. Howard was a slow dresser. Puttnam paced the floor for a good half hour while Howard waxed his mustache and combed his hair just so.

Howard wore a white long-sleeved shirt and gray pleated trousers while Puttnam had chosen yesterday's blue jeans and a clean, navy blue T-shirt. The two of them strolled briskly to the coffee shop with Puttnam continually pushing his unruly hair back off of his forehead and Howard gingerly tapping his cane on the asphalt. Puttnam kept his free hand stuffed snugly in the front pocket of his jeans, as he had this irresistible urge to reach over and unbutton the top button of Howard's crisp, white shirt, which Howard had meticulously fastened. It had always bothered him to see any man with his top button fastened. He viewed it as a sure sign of fastidiousness and he did not wish to think Howard fastidious, for he had grown to respect this old gentleman.

Decidedly, he did not relish the thought of sharing a motel room with Howard for the next few days, but he lingered in thought on each sentence Howard spoke in conversation, for Howard did not speak without importance. He waited for truths to come from Howard as though the old fellow held the key to all truths within him. The truth for Puttnam Burley would not come from Howard Bates. It would rest in the clear, blue eyes of Margaret English. Her heart would connect him with the rarity of contentment, and contentment was the exact truth Puttnam sought.

The two men chose to sit at the counter in the coffee shop.

"So, tell me, Puttnam, what are your plans for the future?" Howard asked as the waitress poured their first cup of coffee.

"Can't say as I have any, Mr. Bates," Puttnam sighed.

Howard interrupted him gracefully. "Please call me Howard; it seems so formal with you always addressing me as Mr. Bates. You're the only one around Clare's who does so."

"It's a habit, I suppose. I was taught to treat my elders with a certain amount of respect," Puttnam said.

"Oh, I quite understand, I had that same habit in my youth. Pounded into me, it was, by my father. He had high hopes that all his children would rise above their humble beginnings in Plainview, Texas . . . none of us did, of course; we simply moved away," Howard responded. "Now, let's hear more about your plans. All young people have them. Surely you must have some goals in mind for the coming years," Howard continued.

"Well, my main goal for the immediate future is to survive these rallies with my camera equipment intact. There's been quite a bit of scuttlebutt going around that this ain't gonna be no picnic here in DC," Puttnam said as he winked at Howard. He bellowed with laughter then and Howard thought it odd that Puttnam could laugh at such serious matters. Puttnam chose the most peculiar situations in which to find humor. It was a desperate sense of humor; Howard hoped that years would ease the desperation for this young man who had seen too much for his age.

The waitress served them breakfast soon after Puttnam's burst of laughter. They ate in silence. Howard ate his food slowly, cleaning his mustache periodically with his paper napkin, while Puttnam attacked his scrambled eggs voraciously. When they had finished their meals and the waitress had cleared the counter Howard resumed the conversation.

"What about Miss English? I hope you don't mind my asking such a personal question," Howard said while pouring cream into his second cup of coffee.

"She wants to move to the South sometime soon. She doesn't want to spend another winter here in the North. She's good, ya know, she really doesn't belong at *The Avalanche*. Not that it's a bad publication or anything like that; she'd just be a lot happier in some sort of academic setting. Maybe teaching at some college somewhere," Puttnam said.

"What about you, Puttnam? What'll you do if Miss English moves away from Saratoga? Will you stay at *The Avalanche*?" Howard asked.

"No sir, I expect I'll go with her when she goes. If she'll have me," Puttnam replied with a tone of gentleness, somewhat hesitant; somewhat unsure of his own position in Margaret English's heart.

BACK IN THE motel room Puttnam spread his camera equipment out on his bed and began the task of getting organized for tonight's concerts. Howard pulled a chair up in front of the television to watch an old movie, in anticipation of a baseball game set to air at noon. The thundering sound of trucks rolling along Highway 395 could be heard clearly in their room as they silently went about their individual tasks, awaiting the return of Clare and Kerry.

Clare and Kerry arrived at the motel in a cab. Howard strolled to the window to watch them. Kerry was carrying a bundle of flyers in one hand and her notebook in the other; Clare held only a road map of some sort and her large straw handbag, which she balanced awkwardly on her hip as she fumbled to close her coin purse within the tangled belongings inside her bag.

She pulled a hairbrush from the bag, which had several paper clips, an ink pen, and the keys to Howard's Pontiac trailing after it.

"Kerry, how did this get in my purse? I do wish that you would carry your own things with you," Clare bellowed at Kerry, who was slipping quietly into their room.

Puttnam was waiting impatiently inside the door to their connecting rooms. He was ready to get on with their mission of covering the activities around the city.

"The boss is not in a good mood this afternoon, Puttnam. I advise you to step lightly in her path," Kerry whispered as she passed Puttnam in the doorway and proceeded on into Puttnam and Howard's room to visit with Howard. Puttnam turned and followed her back into his own room.

"Whatta ya mean she's not in a good mood, Kerry?" Puttnam tried to whisper. Puttnam didn't quite have the knack for whispering.

"My mood is just fine; thank you, Puttnam. So nice of you to be concerned," Clare said, slamming the door closed between the two rooms, leaving Puttnam staring at a blank wooden door which had barely escaped smacking him in the nose when it closed. He turned to face Kerry with a bewildered look on his face.

"What's up with Clare?" he asked.

"Oh, she's just upset because she doesn't feel that the rallies are going to have much of an impact with the way they've been organized. She's not really getting a chance to have much say-so about anything. Not that she wants to. But the rest of the organizers just sort of treated her like a hostile member of the press," Kerry said as she sat down on the end of Howard's bed. Howard was pretending to watch the television; he did not feel it was appropriate for him to get involved.

"Well, what's she planning to do?" Puttnam asked, dropping himself down beside Kerry on the end of the bed.

"She wants to go home. I don't think she will. Maybe she just needs a nap or something. She's mad at me because I said I didn't want to leave until after the concerts tonight; said she wished she'd brought Ernest instead of me because he was more interested in the politics of the whole thing," Kerry said with a sigh of discouragement.

"Aw, don't take it personally, Kerry. She's just very intense about her beliefs. She'll get over it. If Ernest was here, he'd be driving her crazy by now," Puttnam replied, placing a comforting arm around Kerry's shoulders.

"It's a long way home for me, Puttnam. I'm not used to this sort of thing," Kerry cried.

"It's a long way home for all of us, darlin'. Welcome to reality," Puttnam replied. "Clare can be a tough old bitch sometimes, Kerry; she's got a business to run and a group of misfits for employees to direct. If you're gonna be a journalist ya can't be getting upset each time things go a little haywire. It is the nature of such things to go haywire."

"I beg your pardon," Howard interrupted.

"Oh, sorry, Howard, no disrespect intended there about Clare," Puttnam winced, realizing his slip of the tongue belatedly.

Howard cleared his throat loudly and gave Puttnam a stern stare before turning back to the television, placing his elbows on his knees and cupping his head in his hands.

"So, what's the agenda here?" Puttnam asked, withdrawing his arm from around Kerry's shoulders.

Kerry removed her glasses and brushed the tears from her cheeks before answering Puttnam's question. "Well, there are the concerts tonight. Clare says we need plenty of pictures of that. There are a couple of meetings tomorrow at Georgetown University. The whole intention of the rallies is to shut this city down come Monday morning by blocking the bridges with marchers. Clare says it isn't going to work because organizing starts at six A.M. on Monday and she says John Mitchell will make damn sure we're all in jail before rush-hour traffic gets underway. Anyway, we're assigned to Dupont Circle," Kerry said.

"Sometimes Clare knows what she's talking about. She's a pretty sharp cookie," Howard said, not looking up from the television.

"Well, I think I'll take my camera gear and go on downtown and get some sightseeing in before the concerts. Tell Clare that I'll be back here by five to meet up with you guys," Puttnam said, collecting his gear on his bed.

"I think I'll watch the baseball game with Howard," Kerry said.

"Puttnam, why don't you take the old Pontiac? It's not gonna do any of us any good just sitting out there in the parking lot," Howard said over his shoulder.

"Thanks, Howard. Kerry, would you ask Clare for the keys?" Puttnam said. Kerry and Howard gave him one brief glance, then they both turned back to the television; neither could believe that Puttnam had asked such an obviously foolish question. They then turned to face one another; Kerry began to snicker, Howard just grinned.

"Never mind," Puttnam said as he knocked softly on Clare's door.

"What is it?" Howard and Kerry heard Clare bellow. Puttnam disappeared into Clare and Kerry's room; soon they heard the room door to the outside close and the sound of the engine starting up in the Pontiac.

PUTTNAM DROVE SLOWLY into the city. He had been in Washington many times yet still found it difficult to navigate in the traffic. He caught himself wondering, "Just what the hell am I doing in this city with an eighty-seven-year-old man, a middle-aged lady editor, and a vulnerable kid from Texas?" He'd read an article in the paper that morning about a protest march earlier in the month by Vietnam veterans and felt that he should have been here then, not now; not with all these misfits. He headed for the National Zoo in hopes of clearing his thoughts.

The traffic was heavy in Georgetown. It seemed to him that every long-haired hippie in the country had decided to sightsee today. He found a place to park the Pontiac several blocks from the zoo on Connecticut Avenue.

It was a clear, sunny day in the nation's capital. Puttnam ambled along the avenue with his camera bag swinging slowly by his side. Once inside the stone gates of the zoo his nerves began to calm and he whistled softly to himself.

He sat quietly on a bench near the seals' pool with his camera ready to shoot interesting passersby. He noticed a short, slender young man with oily brown hair tied back into a ponytail with a leather strap and a bright-red headband around the top of his head. He was wearing blue jeans littered with paisley patches, the denim faded to a pale blue, and an army fatigue shirt with the sleeves cut off just above his bony elbows, the edges of the sleeves ragged with loose threads. Puttnam had put in his time wearing fatigue clothing; he was quite perplexed that this clothing had become a fad here at home. The young man came closer to Puttnam and eventually sat down on the bench next to him. In close observation Puttnam noted the peculiar shape of the young man's nose, which was extremely pointed and off-center on the boy's face; it cast an unusual shadow on his right cheekbone, and the bridge of the nose was sunburned while the rest of the young man was tanned to a light bronze. The air around them smelled of springtime and the voices of birds and small children mingled into one cacophonous symphony, a sound unique to zoos and recognizable to anyone who had ever visited such a place.

"Hey, man, how's it goin'?" the young man slurred. He reached into a pocket of his shirt and pulled out a pack of Marlboros, generously shaking the pack in front of Puttnam in a gesture of offering.

"Can't complain," Puttnam said in an effort to discourage conversation with the stranger. He declined the offer of a cigarette with a waving motion of his left hand.

"Beautiful day, ain't it?" the young man replied. He lit his cigarette by cupping his hands around the flame of the match against the wind. He held the match awkwardly between his first two fingers of his right hand while shuffling his sandal-clad feet, which were caked with dust, in the gravel beneath the bench. Once the cigarette was lit he bent forward, placing his elbows on his knees and letting the cigarette dangle in his hand; he held it loosely between his thumb and forefinger with the lit end pointing toward his palm. He blew his first puff of smoke, which he'd inhaled deeply, out into the atmosphere, then turned to face Puttnam, resting his head in the palm of his left hand. He had small, brown eyes, which seemed not to focus on any one object and shifted back and forth with a constant flurry. The presence of the stranger made Puttnam uneasy and he directed his attention to the seals in hopes that the kid would go away.

"You do that for a living?" the strange kid asked.

"Do what for a living?" Puttnam asked suspiciously, forgetting his camera gear.

"Shutterbug stuff, you know, man, takin' pictures," the kid replied with an odd chuckle while miming the movements of holding a camera and making a clicking noise with his tongue as though he were taking pictures with his invisible camera.

"Yeah, I do this for a living," Puttnam mumbled. He pushed his hair back off his forehead and moved his large frame a couple of inches farther down the bench from the stranger in an exaggerated movement.

"Well, hey, man, I got some great pot here. You wanna buy half a lid? I got myself stuck here in this city with no scratch; I just wanna round up a few bucks to get back home," the kid whispered to Puttnam.

Puttnam turned to glare at the strange young man beside him on the bench. He was surprised to find a hint of sincerity in the kid's eyes. A sudden curiosity for the disheveled young stranger overcame him. He wondered if perhaps this kid was as lost as he was in the world. "That's dangerous stuff, fella: asking a total stranger if he wants to buy some pot. Where's your head? What if I had been a narc? Ain't you got no sense? Besides, only a fool would be walkin' around DC right now holdin' any drugs. Haven't you seen all the cops loitering around this city? They're just looking for a reason, any reason, to throw hippies in jail. Where you from, anyway?" Puttnam asked sternly.

Ignoring Puttnam's lecture the kid replied, "Atlanta, Georgia. I came up here with some pals of mine for the V.M.V. march earlier in the month and those fuckers left me here."

"You're a vet?" Puttnam asked in disbelief.

"Naw. My brother would've been 'cept he didn't make it home, if you get my drift," the kid said.

"So, I guess you decided to come here in his place?" Puttnam asked, receiving a nod of confirmation from the kid, who took a drag from his cigarette and tilted his head back to exhale the smoke.

"What's your name, kid?" Puttnam asked.

"Chuck Renfro. What's yours?" the kid asked, extending his hand to Puttnam.

"Burley. Puttnam Burley," Puttnam replied, shaking the kid's hand firmly. "So, Chuck, what'd you do back there in Atlanta?" Puttnam asked in a friendly tone.

"I play the bass. Electric bass, that is, in a soul band. We're pretty hot down there. I'm the only honky in the group," Chuck said with a grin.

He again put on a mime show for Puttnam, only this time he was pretending to play his electric bass: bouncing back and forth on the bench with one arm tucked in close to his belly and his other arm extended out to his left as though he were clutching the neck of his guitar. "Ya sure you don't wanna buy some pot, man, it's some good old homegrown stash, guaranteed to get 'cha off, man?" Chuck asked.

"Like I said, Chuck, this ain't exactly the most ideal setting in which to be holdin' anything. Thanks for the offer, though," Puttnam replied. He then let loose with his bellowing laughter, which startled the young man, who jumped a bit on the bench beside Puttnam.

"How 'bout some acid, then?" Chuck asked hesitantly. "I got some orange sunshine here," he added.

Puttnam pushed his hair back slowly, thinking of the concerts scheduled for that evening and the fact that Kerry had mentioned once that she and her boyfriend, Fletcher, had done quite a bit of acid together. He'd done a lot of acid himself, but not since he'd been stateside.

"How much ya sellin' that acid for?" Puttnam asked, fidgeting on the bench.

"Oh, to you, man, one hit for two-fifty, two for five, or five for ten bucks. How much do ya want?" Chuck asked, leaning close to Puttnam's ear.

"Gimme a couple of hits for five," Puttnam said as he pulled his billfold out of his back pocket and retrieved a five-dollar bill from its innards. He handed the five over to Chuck in the palm of his hand and Chuck in turn slipped him two small barrel-shaped tablets. Puttnam glanced quickly at the contents of his palm; the tablets were familiar to him from the past and he closed his hand around them gently before depositing the two tablets into his camera bag.

"Much obliged to ya, Puttnam Burley. This is gonna help me get back on the road south. You have a safe trip now, paisano," Chuck said as he stood to make his exit and stuffed the five-dollar bill in the pocket of his jeans.

"Yeah, same to ya, Chuck. Hey, now you be careful with yourself, kid," Puttnam said.

Puttnam packed up his camera as Chuck trotted away down the path. He left the zoo with the LSD stored neatly in an empty film can in his camera case and began searching for the closest pub on Connecticut Avenue where he might grab a cold beer before returning to the motel to meet Clare and Kerry. He strolled along the sidewalk, occasionally pushing his hair back, humming the melody to a Don McLean song, "American Pie," quietly to himself. Puttnam drew quite a few stares and turned the heads of many when he walked down the street, due to his great height. He often forgot how tall he was, which caused him to wonder why people looked at him so strangely. He was happy, though, feeling the sunshine warm upon his skin and daydreaming about Margaret.

He ducked into a pub just a few blocks from the zoo and perched himself on a barstool close to the television. It was a dark barroom, one of those places where the daytime did not exist; it was always nighttime in this bar; you could drink in good conscience. A person could be whoever they wanted to be in this bar, say whatever they pleased, stay as long as they wanted, as long as they paid their tab and left peaceably at closing time. Puttnam lifted his hand in a toast to the bartender when he was served his beer. He watched the tail end of the doubleheader on television and the announcer's voice boomed out across the barroom from the speaker in the TV set.

Puttnam chugged down three draft beers before leaving the bar. He stopped outside on the sidewalk long enough to let his eyes adjust to the bright sunlight. The Pontiac was parked just a few blocks up. A bright green Chevrolet had parallel parked so close to his back bumper that he had to maneuver the big Pontiac several minutes in order to free himself from the parking space. He headed back to the motel with a light heart, elated with his recent purchase for himself and Kerry, and anticipating an enjoyable evening at the concerts.

"WE ARE EVERYWHERE! POWER TO THE PEOPLE!" screamed a young woman standing next to Kerry, close to the front of the stage. The crowd swayed together with the beat of the music. The Beach Boys were playing "Good Vibrations" and Kerry was high, having taken half of a hit of the orange sunshine two hours earlier. Puttnam rushed in and out of the crowd in front of the stage, taking pictures of the band for *The Avalanche*. Kerry had been able to spot him by the flash of light from his camera when the concerts had first started, but now there were so many flashes of cameras within the crowd that Kerry had a hard time keeping up with Puttnam.

Clare and Howard had stayed behind at the motel to rest. Clare had been fearful of losing Howard in the dark and the turnout for the concerts was expected to be large, which meant that it would be virtually impossible to locate the small gentleman in the crowds.

Kerry wore a permanent smile upon her face. She'd left her glasses at the motel and her eyes seemed to sparkle in the dark. She wore a soft cotton Mexican dress of light lavender with bright-colored embroidery stitched in the yoke. Kerry had pulled the long hair around her face back and braided it into a long, flowing braid. Several wisps of hair had fallen loose from the braid and they curled slightly around her face. The rest of her hair, caught in the gentle breeze, danced around her waist. Puttnam had caught her unaware of his camera many times and had quickly snapped some animated shots of Kerry dancing to the music. He hoped he had captured her light heart on film, to preserve it for Margaret. It was so rare to see Kerry abandoning herself to such gaiety; she seemed intent on carrying the burdens of the world on her slender young shoulders, so lost in the seriousness of it all was she that her youth lay guarded within her, unexplored. Never had he known a person so withdrawn as Kerry. Outwardly she projected the carefully constructed image of one who is involved with the actions around her, yet it was a thin disguise, for Puttnam could see that she was merely observing; that participation was impossible for her; the giving of one's self to the emotion of fleeting moments was beyond her realm of understanding. She thrived on the emotions of others; she sampled those emotions within her own heart and savored their effects just as a wine connoisseur would retain the drops of a fine wine on the tongue. She sought to palliate the intensity of emotion within herself, for she could not forget pain once it was felt and she could not forgive its origins.

Puttnam pushed through the crowd to find Kerry. She was quite easy to spot in her lavender dress. They both laughed loudly as they collided into each other amidst the throng of people dancing wildly with their hands high in the air.

"Did you get the interview with Phil Ochs?" Puttnam yelled to Kerry.

"What?" Kerry yelled back, the music pounding in her ears.

"I said, did you get your interview with Phil Ochs?" Puttnam repeated, leaning closer to Kerry's ear.

"Oh. No, I couldn't find him. It's a madhouse backstage," Kerry screamed. "Seems that every musician in the country has gathered here to get a chance to go on stage. What about the photographs? How'd you do?" Kerry asked with a grin and poked Puttnam sharply in the side with her elbow, in reference to their partnership in being high on the acid.

"I think I did OK. It's so crowded around here that there hasn't really been much room to navigate. Hey, a couple of times I got so spaced out that I forgot to reload the camera. What a dumbass, out here running around snapping shots with no film in the damn thing," Puttnam replied, straining to be heard over the music, then throwing his head back, shaking with massive spurts of laughter. "Let's move back so we can hear each other," Puttnam screamed, reaching out to grasp Kerry's arm in order to lead her away from the front of the stage and the maddening crowd.

As they walked along through the crowd Kerry ducked just in time to miss being smacked on the head with a large picket sign topped with a poster of Gandhi sporting a clenched fist. The young man holding the sign was waving it wildly over his head, completely unaware of those standing close beside him. Puttnam recognized him immediately as being none other than the notorious Chuck from the zoo.

Puttnam tapped him lightly on the shoulder and upon getting his attention he said, "Hey man, how's it goin'?"

"Hey, this is somethin', ain't it? Makes me glad those guys went off and left me here," Chuck replied, nodding his head at Puttnam. "Oh and hey man, I even got a ride back to Atlanta day after tomorrow with some cats from Mobile, Alabama. I'm crashin' out in some dorm at American University. How's that stuff, man. You get off?" Chuck added, with a wink to Puttnam.

"Sure thing, kid. It's pretty tame stuff, though, compared to some of the trips I had over in 'Nam," Puttnam said. Kerry was growing impatient; she tugged at Puttnam's arm and motioned for the two of them to move farther back in the crowd.

"Puttnam, who is that guy? Come on, let's go sit down somewhere," Kerry said impatiently. Puttnam opened his mouth and pointed at his tongue, then motioned toward Chuck in an effort to make Kerry understand why he'd stopped to talk with the guy. Kerry caught on immediately and released her grip on Puttnam's arm, turning her attention temporarily back to the music.

"That your old lady, man? She's a fine-looking mama. Did alright for yourself there, didn't 'cha, dude?" Chuck asked, pointing toward Kerry.

"No, she's a friend. I mean, we work together. Nah, she's not 'my old lady.' Hey Kerry, this is Chuck, he's that fellow I met at the zoo today," Puttnam said, gaining Kerry's attention and grinning from ear to ear.

"Pleasure to meet you, Chuck," Kerry replied while trying to focus on the young man's eyes, which didn't seem to see her at all.

"Hey, likewise, doll," Chuck remarked and he stood up on his tiptoes to whisper in Puttnam's ear. "Man, if she ain't your date, what 'cha think? Maybe she might be interested in this old boy from Georgia?"

"No way, man. She's got a boyfriend back in Texas. Nah, she wouldn't be interested, Chuck," Puttnam said, shaking his head in amusement. He hoped that Kerry hadn't overheard Chuck's inquiry. She had, of course. She moved closer to Puttnam, wishing that the conversation would come to a halt, as situations such as this one were difficult to deal with when she was stoned.

"Well, I, man, hey man, like they say, 'outta sight outta mind.' Know what I mean? I could sure show her a good time," Chuck said in a snicker to Puttnam.

"What'd he say?" Kerry yelped. Puttnam began shuffling them away from Chuck and Kerry reluctantly followed Puttnam's sharp tugs on her arm.

"Well, we gotta split now, Chuck. We'll check ya later," Puttnam called back over his shoulder while pulling Kerry along beside him. Kerry kept looking back at Chuck with an irritated grimace on her face.

"Sure thing, man, hey; be seein' y'all down the road, man," Chuck called back as Kerry and Puttnam disappeared into the crowd.

"The nerve of that guy," Kerry said. "Where does he get off thinkin' he could pick me up like that?"

"It's just that you're so damned irresistible, Miss Kerry, ya little heartbreaker. Poor old Chuck'll probably never get over your rejection," Puttnam said, beside himself in amusement over the incident. Margaret would get a kick out of the story.

"Yeah sure, Puttnam," Kerry groaned. They turned to face each other in the crowd, there beneath the stars with the floodlights casting a surreal glow and the sound of lighthearted rock and roll crashing into their ears. The atmosphere was charged with the electricity of thousands of souls gathered together for a common cause. Kerry and Puttnam gazed into each other's eyes for a second or two before both doubled over in laughter from the effects of the acid, which made all things humorous to an extreme degree and any diversion well worth investigating.

"I'll race ya over to those benches," Kerry said once she'd recovered from the spasms of laughter. She turned flippantly on her heels and dashed off toward the east at a fast clip.

Kerry was no match for Puttnam's long legs. He stood back, watching her slender shape dart into the night with her hair flowing out behind her before breaking into a run himself. He pushed his hair back from his face as he ran, the sweetness of the humid night air lingering on his breath. He threw his head back, beckoning the May moon with laughter while thinking to himself, "Forgive me, dear Margaret, for I have sinned by thinking such lecherous thoughts about Kerry." He slowed his pace as he approached the bench where Kerry had collapsed in laughter, thoughtfully reminding himself, "It's only the acid, Puttnam old boy. Remember dear Margaret, and it's only the acid."

"It's a wonderful night, isn't it, Puttnam?" Kerry asked. Her hands were clasped firmly in her lap as she gazed up at the stars. She had kicked her sandals off and was running her feet through the grass.

"It's a welcomed distraction indeed," Puttnam replied. "I met this freelance photographer a couple of hours ago who invited us over to his apartment for a pickin' party later on. I've been thinking that that might be a good idea since we're both so stoned. Can't see the two of us going back to the motel this way. Can you imagine me trying to carry on a straight conversation with Howard? He's a far-out guy for such an old fella but I don't think he's gonna understand LSD like we do and the way I'm feeling right now, I know I'm not going to come down for a while," Puttnam said.

He pushed his hair back from his face, crossed his legs, and placed his other arm on the back of the bench behind Kerry, gently patting her on the head as he did so. Her hair was fine in texture; he had grown accustomed to the coarse fullness of Margaret's shoulder-length auburn mane. The softness of Kerry's chestnut hair took him by surprise and he rolled his large blue eyes skyward, berating himself once again for his prurient thoughts.

"Howard?" Kerry began with a snicker. "He'll probably be asleep when we get back. It's Clare I'm worried about. Nothing gets by her. She'll probably give me another one of her lectures about social reforms and journalistic responsibilities. Frankly, I don't think I could sit through one of those with a straight face; Clare seems to think I'm not dealing with a full deck as it is," Kerry said with a sigh.

Puttnam noticed that Kerry's accent seemed to become more severe with her current high. Her Texas accent was quite refreshing to his ears and the slowness of her speech created a suspenseful quality to their conversations.

"Aw, Clare's a piece of cake. She's been around lots of kids who were stoned on acid there at the boardinghouse. She probably wouldn't even say anything to ya about it. Whatcha think about going over to this party for a while, though? Guy's name is Hank, he's got a little darkroom set up at his place. I'd like to see how some of his stuff from tonight came out," Puttnam said.

Kerry was so stoned that the low resonance in Puttnam's voice seemed to take on the sound of an echo and she had to reflect on the context of their conversation in order to comprehend his questions. "Well, dadgum, Puttnam, I just don't know about going over to this guy Hank's. I mean, if he's anything like that character you scored from in the zoo, I don't think I'd be interested," Kerry giggled.

"Oh, get off my case about that jerk, Kerry. How was I to know that the little weasel would show up down here?" Puttnam replied lightheartedly and let loose with his side-splitting laughter.

"Oh, weasel, my ass. That guy was just a plain old weirdo, one of those loud-mouthed Southern boys whose mother probably raised him on paregoric," Kerry cackled. They both shook with laughter from Kerry's joke as the crowd began going wild over the last encore from the Beach Boys.

"Anybody ever tell you ya gotta smart mouth for such an innocent-looking broad?" Puttnam asked as Kerry stood up to watch the end of the concert.

Kerry hadn't heard his question above the roar of the crowd. Most of the band and musicians who'd performed earlier in the evening were coming out on stage for the last encore. Kerry stood on her tiptoes, straining to get another look at her new hero, Phil Ochs.

Puttnam got up slowly from the bench. He stretched his muscular arms high in the air then moved close to Kerry's side.

"I told that fellow, Hank, that we'd meet up with him down in front of the stage. He said we could walk to his apartment from here. We'd better get down there pretty soon. Guess I should get a few shots of everyone out on stage together," Puttnam said, bending down close to Kerry's ear.

"What about Clare and Howard?" Kerry replied. "They'll worry if we don't come back."

"We can give Clare a call from Hank's place," Puttnam said, digging into his camera bag for a new roll of film. Once his camera was reloaded, they strolled side by side back into the tightly knit crowd of thousands whose voices had joined together in unison to chant, "WE ARE EVERYWHERE! POWER TO THE PEOPLE!"

Puttnam reached out for Kerry's hand as they worked their way through the crowd. Kerry imagined that the whole world could hear the chants and they chanted along with them in all languages in harmony.

Kerry and Puttnam began to dance as they neared the front of the stage. The Beach Boys were closing up with their song "Wouldn't It Be Nice" and for a fleeting moment Kerry thought of Fletcher. This was a song they had sung to each other when they were younger, before they'd trusted their hearts to each other by making love, back when making love was a wicked temptation in their young minds. She remembered long Texas nights when they'd sit out on the curb at Kerry's house and dream for their future. They would kiss until their lips were sore and their hearts were stilled in the musky night air. Sometimes they could hardly breath for the longing they shared for each other's touch. She missed Fletcher then and she missed her home, where the seasons barely changed, where practically everything remained the same forever.

Puttnam studied the pensive look on Kerry's face for a few seconds. She had stopped dancing and he reached out to touch her softly on her cheek, which brought her back to reality. She glanced up into Puttnam's sorrowful blue eyes and winked candidly at her companion.

> *. . . Wouldn't it be nice if we were older*
> *then we wouldn't have to wait so long . . .*

ERNEST WAS WORKING LATE in Clare's office. His typewriter was on the blink and he'd had to swallow his pride and return to the fold at *The Avalanche* so he could get some work finished. The phone out in the main hall had been ringing off and on for several hours. He refused to answer it and Margaret was upstairs reading, also refusing to respond to the nagging peal of the phone. He heard her padding downstairs just as the phone began ringing again.

"Margaret, answer that phone, for Chrissakes!" Ernest bellowed through clenched lips nervously clinging to a lit cigarette, the ash of which measured at least an inch long. He squinted his eyes at the page in the typewriter and continued pounding away on its keys as Margaret reached for the phone out in the hall.

She gave a nasty look to the door of Clare's office as she tucked her thick auburn hair behind her ears, straightened the collar of her flannel robe where it had fallen open from her descent down the stairs, and picked up the receiver on the third ring.

"Hello," Margaret said in her shy tone of voice.

"Hello, is Kerry there? Kerry Foster, is she 'round?" Fletcher asked cautiously. It was late, almost eleven o'clock in Denton, Texas, which meant it was close to midnight in Saratoga Springs, and he was afraid he might have woken someone up at the boardinghouse. He'd been trying to reach Kerry all night; he had to talk to her tonight.

"She's in DC for the march on the Capitol. Is this by any chance Fletcher Seibel?" Margaret asked. She sat down quietly on the first step of the stairs to await his reply.

"Yes, ma'am, this is Fletcher. Sorry to be calling so late. May I ask who this is?" Fletcher asked, gaining a bit more confidence at the recognition of his name. He was sitting in an old, wooden cane-backed chair at his desk with only his study lamp on for light. Kerry's picture sat in front of him on the desk; he pondered her smile, the dimples on either side, her high, rosy cheekbones, and the hint of passion in her hazel eyes. He scratched his full brownish-black beard as he cupped the phone to his ear.

His dark brown hair was tousled on top and it waved thickly just an inch or two below the break in the collar of his short-sleeved denim work shirt. Fletcher was a breathtakingly handsome man of twenty-two. He was six-foot-one with a medium build; squared, broad shoulders; penetrating dark eyes; and an air of gentleness about him which made him most attractive.

"This is Margaret English, Fletcher. Kerry talks about you constantly. I'm sorry you've missed her," Margaret replied.

"Me, too," Fletcher began. "She's written to me about you so often. It's nice to finally make your acquaintance, even if it is over the phone. I almost feel like I know you from the way Kerry talks about you and your friend Puttnam in her letters. You know, I knew she was going to those Washington rallies but I guess it just slipped my mind. When's she due back to Saratoga?" Fletcher asked.

Margaret sensed a tone of urgency in Fletcher's voice. He had a smooth, southern drawl somewhat like Kerry's, but his voice flowed more smoothly with a quiet eloquence more akin to Louisiana rather than Texas. Fletcher's voice held the mysteries of bayous and pine trees, cool, green moss, and old families dating back for generations in the South, while Kerry's voice brought forth images of wide, dusty streets, Ford pickup trucks, tumbleweed, and short, spiked cactus plants. "She won't be back until Tuesday, Fletcher. It sounds like this is some sort of emergency. Is there anything I can help you with?" Margaret asked.

"I don't know . . . well, maybe. You see, I really needed to talk to Kerry tonight. I hate to just write her a letter with what I have to say. Just wouldn't be right," Fletcher said quietly.

"Tell you what, Fletcher. I have the phone number for the motel in DC upstairs. Hold on a second and I'll run up there and get it for you. She's sharing a room with Clare; they both keep pretty late hours, so you shouldn't have to worry about waking one of them up," Margaret said thoughtfully.

She laid the phone down on the step and, lifting her robe up at the knees to avoid tripping over its hem, she ran up the stairs to her room to retrieve the phone number for Fletcher, wondering what could be wrong with him.

"Here's the number, Fletcher. They're at the Holiday Inn in Arlington, Room one-forty-seven, area code seven-zero-three-five-five-two-four-four-nine-nine," Margaret said into the phone, gasping for breath.

"Thanks, Margaret. You know, on second thought, I think it would be a good idea to fill you in on what's going on down here. Kerry's not likely to talk about it. She sorta keeps things to herself . . ."

and I feel she's going to need a lot of understanding from her friends up there for a while once she hears my news," Fletcher said somberly.

"Well, I don't want to pry, Fletcher, but I'd be glad to help in any way I can," Margaret said as she settled back down on the bottom step of the stairs. She glanced off toward the door to Clare's office and began listening to Fletcher's urgent news, wishing that Ernest would just drop dead as the sound of the pounding typewriter became more and more irritating as Fletcher went on with his story.

Fifteen minutes later, the door opened to Clare's office just as Margaret was replacing the phone in its cradle. Ernest poked his head out into the hall, and finding Margaret there he asked, "Who in God's name has been calling here all night long? It's late and I'm trying to get some work finished in here."

"Oh, why don't you just go crawl back under a rock somewhere, Ernest? The world doesn't revolve around you, Buster," Margaret snapped.

Ernest stared at Margaret in disbelief for her outburst. Margaret was normally so docile that he could hardly believe what he was hearing. He pushed his heavy glasses back up the bridge of his nose, made an attempt at taming his hair, which was freshly shampooed for a change in honor of his return to *The Avalanche*, and stepped out in the hall, curious about Margaret's behavior.

"What's wrong, Margaret?" Ernest inquired in genuine concern.

Margaret stood with her hand still on the receiver of the phone and her other hand clutching the collar of her robe. "It's absolutely none of your business, Ernest," Margaret said, advancing toward the dining hall to her left. She was contemplating making a pot of coffee in the kitchen and the last company she desired right now was that of Ernest Hinkle.

Ernest seemed to read her thoughts exactly and he called after her, "Hey Margaret, if you're making coffee, would you mind throwing in a couple of cups for me? I really do have to get this work done tonight."

Margaret stopped in the center of the dining room, turned on her heels, seething in anger over Ernest's thoughtless request, and strolled right back past Ernest in the hallway. She stopped as she was halfway back up the stairs and replied, "Make your own damn coffee, Ernest Hinkle."

Ernest was bewildered by her reaction. Margaret had always been kind to him and he did not relish the thought of having another enemy at *The Avalanche*. He reluctantly mounted the first step on the stairs after her.

"Ernest, by God, you'd better be nice to Kerry when she gets back here," Margaret said out of the blue. She turned to face Ernest on the stairway. She had an intense look on her face and Ernest was confused in trying to figure out what any of this had to do with Kerry Foster. He was intent on finding out what the problem was. Ernest prided himself on having the scoop on everyone. Ernest sighed deeply in frustration. He had never understood women and this one was a poet, a very beautiful poet at that.

"How about this, Margaret? I'll make the coffee. I was ready for a break anyway. We can talk about it . . . whatever's bothering you. I'm not such a bad guy sometimes. Come on in the kitchen," Ernest said. He reached a hand out to Margaret, which she promptly refused. She did, however, follow him reluctantly through the dining hall.

Ernest's offer to make coffee was a shock to Margaret. She pushed a loose strand of her wavy hair back into place behind her ear and, studying the back of Ernest's head as they entered the kitchen, she replied, "I'm anxious to see if you really know how to make coffee, Ernest, but I'm warning you — no funny stuff!"

"Scout's honor, Margaret. Coffee, no funny stuff," Ernest said jokingly, waving his hand in the air without looking back at her.

"Promise?" Margaret asked hesitantly.

"Oh, good grief, Margaret. I promise not to lay one hand on your lily-white flesh. I'd have to have a death wish to do something that radical, now wouldn't I? Puttnam Burley would break every bone in my body for an offense such as that," Ernest scoffed as Margaret sat down at the small breakfast table in the corner of the kitchen. She watched in curiosity as Ernest fumbled with the Melitta coffee maker over the sink. It was a scene she could not have imagined, even in her wildest dreams.

"EVERYTHING'S FINE on this end, Puttnam. Howard's been asleep for hours. I don't think he'll even notice your absence as long as you're back by morning. I do have messages for both you and Kerry," Clare said quietly. She was propped up in her bed reading some notes for Kerry's next article in *The Avalanche*.

"Let's have 'em," Puttnam said jovially.

Kerry was kneeling down in front of Hank's record collection. Hank had excused himself to his darkroom, leaving Kerry and Puttnam out in the living room to greet the other guests he'd invited over to his place during the course of the evening.

"First of all," Clare began, "Fletcher called from Denton and requested that I have Kerry get in touch with him tonight, no matter how late. He'll be waiting up. And second, Margaret called, oddly enough, in reference to Fletcher's phone call and she asked that I have you call her at the house before I let Kerry call Fletcher. Sounds pretty important to me but Margaret assured me that it has nothing to do with death or illness in the family; it's just some sort of personal crisis," Clare said. She noticed an unusual tone of high spirits in Puttnam's voice. She could not resist the temptation to make note of it. "By the way, Puttnam, are you high on some sort of controlled substance?" she asked.

Puttnam never bothered to lie to Clare and he smiled to himself as he replied, "Yes, ma'am, I certainly am." He shook with laughter as he spoke, as did Clare on the other end of the line.

"Shame on you — and be careful," Clare said before hanging up the telephone. She overheard the music starting up in the background at Hank's apartment as she replaced the receiver on its cradle and began going over the notes again. During her reading, she fretted over the reasons for Fletcher's insistence on having Kerry call him, though they remained a mystery to her. She was in no way pleased that the young man was disturbing her reporter while on assignment — a point she had contemplated expressing during her conversation with the young man, but he had sounded so despondent that she had neglected to bring it up. "Reporters," she thought to herself. "Puttnam and Kerry are out there lollygagging around, stoned on

something or another, and I still call them reporters . . . some staff
I have here." Clare pulled a pencil from behind her ear and began
correcting Kerry's spelling, which was atrocious. Her glasses rested
on the tip of her nose and she'd pulled the blanket up over her chest.
Clare was a small woman with such a youthful face that, had it not
been for the streaks of gray in her close-cropped, curly dark hair, any
onlooker could have mistaken her for a child, curled up on a sleepless
night reading a storybook.

"Well, I suppose this is why this magazine sells," Clare mumbled to
the empty room, surprising herself by actually speaking out loud; her
voice had broken the silence in the room like a heavy clap of thunder.

PUTTNAM WAITED for the operator to clear the collect charges with
Margaret, noting how wonderful Margaret's voice sounded on the
other end of the line.

"Puttnam, where's Kerry?" Margaret asked immediately.

"She's right here, darlin', what seems to be the trouble?" Puttnam
replied as he leafed through the pages of a photography magazine
Hank had left out on the coffee table, waiting for Margaret's reply.
It was a long reply, and he glanced up occasionally at Kerry, still
pulling records out of the record bin. Kerry was unaware of his phone
conversation and the attention directed toward her. She was listening
attentively to the Janis Joplin record she had played on the stereo.

"He can't tell her that tonight, Margaret. She's stoned on acid.
That's a terrible thing to tell somebody who's stoned," Puttnam said.
His smile had quickly faded from his face. "Yes, I'm stoned, too," he
added a moment later. There was a pause in Puttnam's end of the
conversation. Kerry turned to address Puttnam just in time to hear
Puttnam close the conversation with, "No, I won't leave her alone
tonight . . . I love you, too, babe." Puttnam hung up the phone and
looked up at Kerry, who now stood in front of him as he sat on
the sofa.

"Kerry, Margaret says that you're supposed to call Fletcher
tonight," Puttnam said.

"Oh, I'll wait till tomorrow; it's after midnight already," Kerry replied cheerfully.

"He's waitin' up for ya to call, darlin', better go ahead and call him now. Here, take my place by the phone," Puttnam said sadly.

He stood up and walked to the stereo as Kerry sat down in his place on the sofa and began giving the required information to the operator for her collect call to Fletcher. He could only speculate Fletcher's end of the conversation from Kerry's responses; she seemed quite calm considering the circumstances.

"Hi, Kerry, I'm glad you got my message," Fletcher said. Their connection was a weak one and he strained to hear her voice on the other end.

"It's nice to hear your voice," Kerry said loudly.

"How are things in Washington? Have you gotten an interview with Richard Nixon yet?" Fletcher teased. He toyed with the phone cord, prolonging breaking his news to Kerry as long as he could.

"Oh, he's called several times but I just told him my schedule was full and he'd have to get in line, just like everybody else," Kerri giggled. "Why'd you call Fletcher, is something wrong?" Kerry added, not falling for Fletcher's attempts to beat around the bush.

"Hey, my mom had lunch with your mom last week. She says your dad's moving to Houston; his company is opening up an office down there. I wondered if you knew since you haven't mentioned it in any of your letters," Fletcher said, still stalling for time.

"That's interesting. No, he hasn't mentioned it, but I haven't talked to him in almost a month. I'm not surprised, though; he's been wanting to move out of Austin for a long time now," Kerry said, a bit surprised at the news. She couldn't help but notice that Puttnam was staring at her, though he was pretending to look over an album jacket for a Simon and Garfunkel record.

"Kerry, that's not why I called. I gotta tell you something and I know this is not the right time but there will never be another time and I had to tell you myself," Fletcher began.

"What is it, Fletcher?" Kerry asked, realizing that this was no ordinary phone conversation with Fletcher.

"Kerry, ya know, we've had this understanding between us that we should both date other people while we're so far apart . . . Kerry, I'm getting married next week," Fletcher said reluctantly. The muscles in his throat became tight and he could barely get the words out of his mouth.

"You're *what*?" Kerry replied in shock. "I don't think I heard you right; I don't understand," Kerry said in disbelief. "You can't do that. You're supposed to come up here after exams in a couple of weeks," she added.

"I won't be coming, Kerry," he replied, pausing briefly to regain his composure. "Remember a few weeks ago, I mentioned that girl who's the daughter of an old classmate of my dad's? Her name's Denise; she's a freshman and I took her out to The Office Club to hear Dee Moeller," Fletcher said.

"Yeah, I remember. That was before I moved to Saratoga. You said you didn't really want to take her out but you did it as a favor for your dad, since she didn't really know anyone up there. I remember you said she turned out to be pretty nice and you hoped I got to meet her sometime. You even suggested that we fix her up with Wiley and the two of you could come down to Austin for a weekend. Yeah, I remember. I thought that was a great idea 'cause Wiley was always such a hermit," Kerry said.

"She's pregnant, Kerry. I don't know how it happened, but she is and we have to get married — she doesn't believe in abortion," Fletcher said in agony.

"Well, hell's bells, Fletcher, you know damn well how it happened! That's stupidity at its max," Kerry said sarcastically. The news was just beginning to sink in and the acid caused her state of mind to turn to anger rather than tears. "How could you, of all people, make such a negligent mistake? You, who used to watch my calendar like a hawk. How could you do this to us — to our future?" Kerry winced.

"Kerry, let me explain. I know it was a stupid mistake, but — " Fletcher began before Kerry interrupted him.

"Who went to the 'free clinic' last year, took a number, and sat sandwiched between some freak with crabs and a female heroin addict waiting for methadone treatment for four hours just to get the Pill so we wouldn't have to worry about accidents anymore? You asshole. Who loved you, man? Who's loved you for almost nine years? What makes her exempt from abortion, Fletcher? It was your first choice for me a couple of years ago when we had that little scare," Kerry cried.

"We were too young then, Kerry. Besides, it was a false alarm. We're adults now and I have to take on the responsibility for my actions. She told her folks; they told mine. There's just no way around it," Fletcher pleaded.

"We had it all mapped out, Fletcher, you and I. We had those all-American dreams, we would live our lives together and we would change the world. What a crock of shit that turned out to be. Nothing lasts forever. The last person in the world I ever expected to break my heart was you . . . " Kerry said, trailing off with a soft shudder of anguish.

"Kerry, I'll always love you. It isn't that I love Denise; it's just my responsibility," Fletcher tried to explain. His head rested in his hand and the tears began to roll down into his beard.

Kerry blurted out in anger, "Don't you tell me that, Fletcher Seibel! I don't want to hear you tell me you don't love this person you've decided to throw away our future for! I don't want to have to live with that. It's you who has to reconcile that little dose of pain, not me, so don't try to pass that guilt on to my shoulders. I can tell you this: I'll always feel the same about what we had; it'll always be sacred. It was the first love; it'll probably be the last. I'm gonna hang up now, Fletcher. I'm about as stoned as one can get. I don't want to deal with this now — not now, maybe not ever," Kerry said calmly.

"Oh, Kerry, don't say that. You sound like your Leo when she talks about old Edgar: so defeated. We'll get over this. Tell me you won't become as bitter as your grandmother, Kerry. I'm not dying, not dead. Our relationship will just take on a new meaning now, as friends. I want us to be friends," Fletcher replied. In all his life, he never thought he would be saying farewell to the one who'd shared his dreams, to the one who held his heart.

"Well, maybe I'm just like my grandmother Leo, Fletcher, maybe we're just two peas in a pod. Maybe all people who hurt inside are alike in that regard. Maybe just two of a kind heart, we are. Not sharing the same mind, just sharing the same pain," Kerry said softly into the phone as Puttnam watched on.

"Kerry, we started out as friends. We'll always have that special bond between us," Fletcher said in response to her statement. "I don't want to live without that friendship," he added.

"We didn't start out as friends, Fletcher. We started out as adversaries, cursing one another across a tetherball pole — no, we didn't start out as friends. That came later; that was something we gave to each other when we learned to trust one another. We had secrets; we had trust — something you should have thought about two months ago or whenever the hell little Denise got pregnant. I have to go now. Congratulations — sorry I won't be able to attend the wedding," Kerry cried as she hung the phone up on Fletcher, who sat for several minutes with the dead receiver in his hand.

When he finally composed himself enough to get up from his chair and stretch out in his bed, sleep did not come to him; it eluded him that night just as it would for many nights to come. The peacefulness he had once held in sleep, in his dreams of Kerry and their future, would not return for many years, for the happy-go-lucky days of his youth were spent now for both of them and the first real trials of adulthood and disillusionment lay before him, wrestled firmly to the ground, the hard, cold earth, in his nightmares: the most dreaded nightmare of all, the loss of the love of Kerry Foster.

PUTTNAM KNEELED DOWN in front of Kerry, where she sat on the sofa with her elbows on her knees and her face buried in her hands.

"You knew, didn't you, Putts?" Kerry said in a muffled tone.

Puttnam reached out to stroke her hair in a comforting gesture. "Yeah, I knew, darlin'. I'm awfully sorry. Life's a drag sometimes, ain't it, babe?" Puttnam said.

"It's so humiliating, Putts, that you know; that Margaret knows and probably Clare. What's it all for, anyway? What good does it do to love someone if they'll never love you back?" Kerry said tearfully. The doorbell rang at Hank's and Puttnam feared that they would soon be surrounded by an apartment full of strangers.

"Let's get out of here, Kerry," Puttnam said as he got up to answer the door for Hank.

"But Hank said that the cops are everywhere tonight. We can't be walking the streets this late stoned on acid," Kerry replied.

"We've got a motel, remember? We can cruise on over there and sit out in the parking lot till we come down. Cops can't bust us there. Don't you worry, doll, it'll all work out. I know he was special and I won't try to convince you that he wasn't, but you're special, too, and you'll survive. Hell, you might even be happy again someday," Puttnam said, trying to add some humor to the subject as he reached for the doorknob to let in Hank's guests.

"You're right, Puttnam," Kerry called out. "Just screw old Fletcher. God knows everybody else has."

Puttnam and Kerry lingered at Hank's just long enough to say their farewells to him. Hank tossed a six-pack of beer at Puttnam as they were walking out the door. He sensed that they were both troubled about something, and remembering that Kerry was from Texas, he winked at her as she slipped past him and said, "Y'all come back, now."

Kerry and Puttnam sat together on a lounger out by the pool at the motel. Kerry quietly recounted many humorous tales of her years with Fletcher. She would burst out with wild laughter occasionally during the telling of such stories and Puttnam held her close to him, comforting her as only a friend or a brother could do; all thought of prurience vanished from Puttnam's heart.

They came down slowly from the effects of the LSD. Both felt Kerry's pain, both became enchanted by the early morning glow in the heavens. They were hypnotized by the sound of the water slapping against the side of the pool and they fell into a deep sleep in each other's arms as dawn came to greet them. The sound of the water gently stroking the edge of the pool created a healing force during her sleep; so far from home was she, so far from her true course in life's travels and so young to be wounded so deeply.

They had playfully tossed the six-pack back and forth across the pool to one another when they'd first arrived back at the motel; neither one had been interested in the drinking of any alcohol. The six-pack rested on its side beneath the lounger where they slept, unopened. Its contents were shaken and lukewarm, just waiting for the first sucker to come along and pop one of its tops.

SUNDAY SEEMED to fly by for Puttnam, Howard, Kerry, and Clare. Clare spent the better part of the morning at organizational meetings at St. Edward's church and the afternoon driving around the city just to get familiar with the streets. Slogans had been painted on all the bridges and on some of the federal buildings. Clare was most disappointed in the rallies. She felt the whole thing was been infiltrated by the FBI and that they were in control.

She had committed herself to staying for the duration. She was even proud of Howard for coming with them to Washington to throw in his own two cents for the anti-war movement, though she still did not think that he had any idea what lay in store for them over the next two days.

Clare was livid in her beliefs that the citizens had a right to march on their Capitol in protest against American involvement in Vietnam. The war was wrong; though all wars were wrong in Clare's heart. She was fearful that the Nixon administration was intent on making these rallies into a mockery of the movement.

Puttnam and Kerry, understandably, napped off and on throughout the day. They took turns playing cards with Howard; he won every hand and was extremely pleased with himself until he realized that Kerry and Puttnam weren't really giving the cards their full attention.

During one hand of Go Fish Howard became so frustrated with Puttnam that he threw his cards down on the table to gain Puttnam's attention and asked, "By God, Puttnam, are you playing this game or not?"

Howard's outburst had barely rattled Puttnam, who was lost in his own thoughts, and he answered, "Yeah, sure. Now what game is this we're playing here?"

Needless to say, they all retired early that evening in anticipation of the long day they had waiting for them on Monday.

Kerry's youth was her saving grace in the face of such hurt she felt over Fletcher's abandonment of their relationship. Her outward appearance of resilience deeply touched Puttnam and he admired her courage. Yet, the impression she purposely gave to Puttnam was a false one, for in her heart she was bleeding from the open wound of rejection. Her dreams were restless ones, full of conversations with Fletcher for all those things she had not told him on the phone, all those secrets she did not recite to him. She would share her pain with no one for the time being; she would now be one who gathered strength from suffering alone, for in the end, only she could heal herself. She had been luckier than most, for she had had the warmth of company during the desolation of adolescence and young adulthood; she had had a hand to hold and a hand to give. She would have to learn the meaning of the word loneliness now, and in doing so she would gain a better sense of compassion for those around her who were lonely. Though Fletcher would not be alone in physical terms he would also learn of loneliness with the vast, empty space in his own heart.

MONDAY MORNING was frantic for Clare. Howard insisted on carrying a small camp stool with them to Dupont Circle; he and Clare faced one another in the doorway to their adjoining rooms arguing over the matter for several minutes. Puttnam finally solved the problem by simply snatching the camp stool from Howard's hands, stomping out of the motel room, and literally giving the camp stool a swift toss out on the sidewalk in front of their rooms. The act in itself shocked Howard and Clare back to reality and they went about their business of preparing for the day in silence.

It was early in the morning, not quite five A.M., when they spun out of the parking lot in Howard's Pontiac with Puttnam behind the wheel, Clare snapping directions, Howard dozing in the back seat, and Kerry braiding her hair next to him. Unbeknownst to Clare, Howard had stashed the notorious camp stool in the trunk of the car, still insisting to himself that it would come in handy to someone later in the day.

The streets were still quiet in the twilight of predawn. Streetlights glowed with hazy halos reluctantly casting their last hour of illumination on the pavement. Puttnam drove north on Twenty-second Street; he couldn't help but notice the abundance of police vehicles, and in nearing Washington Circle he was shocked to see military police scattered throughout the area.

At Clare's request, Puttnam parked the car just a few blocks from Dupont Circle in a lot on Twenty-first Street. They walked the remaining distance to the circle with Puttnam toting Howard's camp stool on his arm, his camera gear resting on top of it. It was actually more of a good-luck charm for Howard; small and compact, it was made of two wooden frames which folded together, sandwiching a brightly striped strip of canvas which served as the seat of the stool when the wooden frames were unfolded. Howard has used it countless times on fishing trips and it had always brought him luck. The canvas in the center was worn from years of use. Howard strolled alongside Puttnam, tapping his cane on the pavement, occasionally catching Puttnam's eye by tilting his head to the side and shooting him an exaggerated wink while his mustache twitched from the bounce in his walk. Howard had worn his gray flannel suit, a white shirt, his blue bow tie, and a metal pin clasped to his lapel of the American flag, whose colors had become quite faded. Kerry Pearl had gotten the pin at the Fourth of July picnic in Raymondville back in 1960 and she'd sent it to Howard in payment of a bet they'd made over an all-star baseball game. He sported the pin proudly on this day in her memory.

Clare and Kerry walked side by side as they approached the small crowd of protesters already gathering around the traffic circle. Clare wore a green-and-white-striped seersucker dress belted at the waist and navy blue tennis shoes. She carried a small portable tape recorder for interviews and her large straw handbag, which she regretted bringing as it did not have a shoulder strap and made her load a bit too awkward to juggle. Kerry had braided her long hair into one long braid down her back; she wore Levi jeans, a yellow tank top, and her leather sandals. She carried only her notebook, with a ballpoint pen clipped to its front cover.

As six A.M. drew closer, the protesters began to take their positions around the circle, with the intention of blocking morning traffic from all directions. Policemen also converged on the circle with the marines following behind them, with orders for the crowd to disperse peacefully. Network television crews arrived on the scene as the protesters stubbornly stood their ground. It was still too early for the traffic to start backing up, but the few cars whose route had been blocked by the protesters began to honk their horns in angry protest. Puttnam became separated from his companions as the crowd grew to chaotic proportions. He weaved in and out of the masses, snapping photos and occasionally stopping to join in the chants of his fellow marchers.

"WE ARE EVERYWHERE! POWER TO THE PEOPLE!"

Clare was in the process of trying to interview an elderly grandmother who, like Howard, had come to represent her age group in protest against the war. She had a difficult time working her tape recorder and juggling the straw handbag. In frustration she returned to where she'd left Howard sitting on his camp stool and reluctantly asked if he would hold the handbag while she went back to conduct the interview.

Kerry stood just off the curb in the street next to where Howard sat on his camp stool. He delighted in chanting the slogan and was

totally immersed in the emotion of the crowd. He had never seen
so many people gathered together in disobedience in his entire life
and the thrill of it all filled him with sentiment for their cause. He
could hardly sit still on his stool. Each time the police ordered the
crowd to disperse peacefully Howard would jump up from his seat
and shake his cane in the air, barking, "You just come right here and
make me, BY GOD! I know my rights!" Howard would occasionally
forget which hand held his cane and instead he would wave Clare's
large straw handbag high in the air.

Howard's shouts of protest directed toward the rows of policemen
and the occasional waving of Clare's handbag caught the eye of a
network news correspondent who eventually worked his way through
the crowd to approach Howard for an interview. The camera crew
followed and the next thing Howard knew, a microphone was being
jammed into his face. The crowd was becoming restless and police
were beginning to make arrests just across the intersection from them.

"And what is your name, sir?" the commentator asked Howard.

Howard rose to his feet for the momentous occasion, blurting
out proudly, "My name is Howard Bates and I'm from Saratoga
Springs, New York," and reaching out to grab Kerry's arm, pulling
her alongside of him, he added, "This is my step-great-granddaughter,
Miss Kerry Foster." The reporter smiled at Kerry briefly, then turned
his attention back to Howard.

"How old are you, sir, and what made you decide to take part in
these marches here in the Capitol?" he asked bluntly.

Howard stood fully erect, clutching his cane and Clare's handbag
firmly in front of him, and replied, "I turned eighty-seven years old in
July. I have come to our nation's capital with my dear Kerry here to
protest the abominable war our country is waging in Vietnam. Too
many lives of our young are being spent there for a cause which is not
in the best interest of our nation's people."

"Do you feel you will be arrested today and will you go peacefully?"
the reporter asked, somewhat taken aback by Howard's responses.

"If it is against the law in our country for the masses to ban
together to protest against the wrongdoings of our government,

then I shall go to jail alongside these young people when the time comes, but, by God, it will be a sad day in our nation's history and will certainly be a reflection of the poor administration in our White House," Howard stated, shaking his head adamantly.

"Do you consider yourself a radical, politically speaking, Mr. Bates, or do you feel representative of the opinions of other people across the country in your age group?" the reporter asked, jabbing the microphone close to Howard's face while the camera crew zoomed in for a close-up of the elderly man.

"First of all, young man, I don't know any other people in my age group. I would say that we are very few indeed. And second of all I am not any sort of radical, I am simply one of the millions within that so-called 'silent majority' who was fed up with being seen but not heard. My mission in coming here was to prove with my presence that all Americans, regardless of age, sex, or social status, do have a say-so in the actions of their government. That's all I have to say, by God," Howard replied, sitting back down on his camp stool. The camera crew and the correspondent moved away from Howard, eventually being swallowed by the crowd.

Clare came bounding up to Howard and Kerry just as the interview was ending. Once the network crew departed she reached down and grabbed Howard by the arm anxiously and said, "Howard, fold that silly camp stool up right now. We have to get back to the car before we get arrested. Kerry, you carry that stool for Howard."

"I can carry it myself, Clare," Howard boasted in a huff.

"Where's Puttnam?" Clare shouted over the crowd. "Anybody seen Puttnam?"

"I haven't seen him for the past half hour," Kerry shouted back. She was engaged in a tug-of-war over the camp stool with Howard, who finally gave in and loosened his grasp on his side of the wooden frame, which almost sent Kerry sprawling out onto the pavement. He turned sheepishly to follow Clare through the crowd of protesters, mumbling his apologies to Kerry while suppressing a snicker over the tussle.

"I want to get over to Georgetown University to record the reactions of students to the marches. We can't worry about Puttnam now. He knows where the motel is and he's certainly capable of taking care of himself," Clare shouted to Kerry as they slipped past the edge of the marchers and headed toward the Pontiac on Twenty-first Street. Police sirens and paddy wagons swept past them as they hurried along. They had the good fortune of escorting Howard to the car, which more than likely was a blessing in disguise and aided them in making a clean getaway without the threat of arrest. Puttnam would not be so blessed.

Clare fished the keys out of her straw handbag and slid into the driver's seat of the Pontiac. Howard and Kerry both jumped into the front seat beside her and the three of them headed down Twenty-first Street in search of a diner where they could stop and have breakfast and wait for the streets to be cleared. Kerry and Howard were elated over Howard's being interviewed for network news and were discussing whether or not it would actually be used in that evening's telecast. Clare could not resist the temptation to tease Howard about the interview. She turned her head slightly and said, "Howard, didn't your mother ever tell you not to talk to strangers?"

"By God, maybe she did, but it had to have been so long ago that I plum forgot," Howard said with a burst of laughter and a relaxed Texas accent so long out of use and so uncharacteristic of Howard that all three of them shook with laughter until Clare pulled into the parking lot of a Toddle House restaurant.

All three returned to somber moods as they sat in a booth at the restaurant. They worried quietly over the absence of Puttnam, each hoping that Puttnam had managed to get out of Dupont Circle without being arrested, but the chances of that now seemed very slim, as Puttnam was not the sort to simply walk away peacefully.

THE POLICE were closing in from all directions on the protestors. Puttnam was weaving in and out, still snapping pictures of the chaos, when he noticed a lone protester being chased by a policeman on P Street. The man turned his head slightly and Puttnam, thinking he recognize the profile of the protester as being that of an army buddy of his, broke into a run behind the policeman to help the man. The wind slapped him in the face as he closed in on the cop; he remembered an instance in Vietnam when he had been running full tilt across a rice field. He was under fire then, running wild through the field with his boots sinking into the mud on each step and the sensation that his feet weighed a ton. Bullets had whistled by his ears and his breath had come in short, shallow puffs, so shallow that he'd felt he was hardly breathing at all. He remembered not caring about the other men falling around him in the field; their screams upon being wounded did not slow him down. He'd just wanted to survive, not to fight, as though running were the essence of survival. Someone had fallen behind him and as he fell he brought Puttnam down with him. He clearly recalled the face now, silent in death, that he'd turned to see resting on his boot. It was the same face that he thought he'd seen on the protester he was racing to aid. He stopped running then and veered off to the right, ducking into an alleyway. He walked cautiously through the maze of alleys surrounding Dupont Circle, knowing that somehow he had to get back to the other side in order to meet up with Clare.

Police were everywhere and Puttnam had about given up hopes of not being arrested when he came through an alley and saw that it was relatively clear on that side of the circle. Puttnam sucked in his breath in anxiety over his predicament as he turned the corner. Just in front of him, five cops stood leaning against a squad car and he realized he would have to get past them. He decided to simply display his press badge and take his chances by nonchalantly strolling past. It was impossible for a man of Puttnam's size to stroll nonchalantly: his hair was too long and his clothing too reminiscent of the other protesters for the police to let him pass. Puttnam was just about to step off the curb, having come side by side with the policemen and thinking himself safe from arrest, when a sturdy, dark-haired cop grabbed him by the arm.

"Step back on the curb, sir. Place your hands on top of the vehicle, feet apart," the policeman barked.

Puttnam did as he was told, turning his head to make one final protest as they searched him for weapons. "I'm a member of the press. Here, man, check out the badge. I work for *The Avalanche* in — " Puttnam shouted, but was not allowed to finish as the handcuffs were slapped onto his wrists.

"Just get in the car, sir. Don't talk; just get in the car," the dark-haired cop replied.

"Jesus Christ," Puttnam roared as the squad car in which he was riding turned on its sirens and spun out into the traffic as though it held in its back seat the world's most sought-after criminal. Canisters of tear gas began exploding in the streets behind them. Puttnam stared in disgust at the policeman sitting next to him in the back seat. The policeman in the back kept making jokes about the arrests of the protesters and boasting about the numbers they themselves had taken in.

"Either of you fellas ever served in 'Nam?" Puttnam asked.

"Nah," the cops replied in unison.

"Well, I did and let me tell you, if you had gone you'd be right out there in the streets demanding that Nixon get our asses out of there. You'd be right out there with the rest of us," Puttnam said. He tried hard to control his anger, realizing that basically the cops were just doing their jobs.

"Oh yeah?" said the cop next to Puttnam. "Well, maybe that's so, who can tell, but it ain't gonna help you any right now and that's for sure." The two cops laughed loudly at the smart remark.

"All of this is gonna come to somethin' someday," Puttnam began. "Wait and see. Ya can't just go 'round arrestin' innocent people and throwin' their asses in jail just because you disagree with their point of view. When all is said and done it's gonna be you guys who come out with mud on your face and those of us you hauled to jail who'll be the heroes."

It was the dark-haired cop who'd initially grabbed Puttnam to arrest him who sat in the back seat. He snickered at Puttnam's statement and, leaning forward in the seat, he replied to the driver,

"How about this guy, thinks he's some sort of hero. Maybe we oughta get his autograph before we book 'im."

Puttnam interrupted his laughter to ask, "Just what are you going to book me for?"

"We gotta nice list of choices, buddy. Most likely we'll stick ya with 'conducting yourself in a manner which might lead to a breach of peace,' so be quiet back there 'cause it could be worse. You're lucky, you're goin' in by ya-self; you'll be out in a few hours. Those guys goin' in in the paddy wagons is gonna be there awhile," said the cop driving. He didn't like the thought of arresting a vet. In his opinion, the whole situation stunk.

Puttnam was placed in a small holding cell with ten other men. The cell was only about five by seven feet in dimensions, forcing everyone to stand, except for one old codger who was slumped against a far wall with his feet sprawled out in front of him. Nine of the cellmates were protesters from American University and the old man was a drunk who'd been carted in long before dawn to sleep it off.

People were shouting at the guards and at each other up and down the long row of holding cells. Most of the protesters were trading accounts of their arrests, giving descriptions of friends whose whereabouts were unknown in hopes of finding out if they, too, had been arrested. Puttnam overheard one fellow down the hallway telling of an elderly woman who was a diabetic and had been arrested in Dupont Circle. He yelled out a description of Howard to the guy but the man hadn't seen any old men being hauled in. Puttnam came to the conclusion that if Clare, Kerry, and Howard had indeed been arrested, he'd hear about it soon enough. He resigned himself to leaning against the bars of the cell, listening to the stories of the students and wishing like hell that he'd eaten breakfast. He had a long, hungry wait ahead of him, as it would be almost five o'clock before he saw daylight again.

CLARE, KERRY, AND HOWARD spent the morning dodging cops and interviewing students on the campus of Georgetown University. Clare had had to park the car a considerable distance from the campus and Howard was worn out before they ever got there. Kerry fretted constantly over Puttnam's whereabouts, causing Clare to seriously contemplate ditching them both. Ten A.M. found the three of them resting on the steps of one of the buildings. Though the campus was in a state of panic, classes were apparently still being held and those students who were not involved in the protests traveled cautiously to and from their classes, avoiding any and all eye contact. A hint of tear gas still lingered in the air.

"Clare, it really looks like it's over for today. You've got plenty of interviews. Can't we work our way back to the motel now?" Kerry pleaded, thumbing the notebook resting in her lap. "Puttnam might call the motel for us to come get him and we won't be there," she added.

"The only interviews I've gotten so far have been from sympathizers. I want to get one solid counterpoint before I leave this campus. Besides, Puttnam isn't going to be able to call the motel if he's in jail — too many have been arrested. I just don't think he'd call there, anyway," Clare said with a sigh.

At that moment Clare spotted a young woman, loaded down with books, scurrying toward them. Clare took note of the fact that the woman was several months pregnant, very middle class in appearance, and dressed in normal maternity clothes consisting of a long tunic and skirt. Her hair was light brown and she wore it neatly tied back into a ponytail with a colorful scarf, which matched the colors in her tunic. She was a pretty, young woman, very thin aside from her bulging middle. Clare thought her the perfect candidate for her last interview. She stood up on the steps to intercept the young woman.

"Excuse me, my name is Clare Freidman from *The Avalanche*. Do you have a few moments to give us your opinion of the May Day rallies and the massive arrests that took place this morning?" Clare asked as she switched on her tape recorder.

The woman gave Clare a puzzled look as she stood in front of her. She thought for a moment before replying, "I don't think I've ever read your paper. I've seen it around campus, though. I don't know. You see, I'm late for a biology exam and as you can see I may never get another crack at it." She started to bypass Clare and noticed Howard and Kerry sitting on the steps behind her.

"Please, I could use your opinion," Clare said. "I promise not to take up too much of your time."

"OK," the woman replied reluctantly and slowly lowered herself onto the steps to sit down.

"How do you feel about the war in Vietnam?" Clare asked.

"Well, I'm not sure that it's right for us to be over there. You should've seen the Vietnam vets who were here last week. Even they are against it," the woman replied thoughtfully.

"What's your name, dear?" Howard butted in. Clare looked over her shoulder to give him a nasty glare of reprimand.

"Can I just give you my first name? My folks would be unhappy if they knew I was doing this," the woman asked.

"Yes," Clare replied.

"My name is Ann and to tell you the truth I've been too busy trying to finish school and solving my own problems to get involved with the anti-war movement. My husband works here at the university. We're both just trying to get our educations and our careers started. I should graduate at the end of this semester. Working part-time, going to school, and carrying a child hasn't left much time for politics," Ann answered.

"How did you feel about the protest marches around the city this morning? Did you have a difficult time driving to campus?" Clare asked.

"Well, I don't drive to campus, I walk. We live close to here. Not to sound cruel or anything, but I was glad that the police had the streets and bridges cleared before rush hour began. The radicals had been boasting around campus for days that they were going to close the entire city down and frankly it didn't work. You see, this is a city, not much different from any other city, not everyone works for the government here. It wasn't fair to the innocent people for the marches to disrupt their lives. It would've been like punishing the civilians for the actions of the government and the military. I really do have to go now — I can't miss this exam," Ann said as she clumsily tried to lift herself up off the step. Kerry and Howard stood up to help her while Clare held her books.

They watched her climb the steps and enter the building, hurrying as best as she could.

"She seemed very special to me," Clare said breaking the silence between them. "She didn't have to stop and talk to me, but she did. She certainly has a long road ahead of her in balancing a career and raising a child — it's a road I never had the courage to travel. In my day, you either had a career or you had children, never both," Clare added.

"Indeed," Howard replied. The three of them turned to walk off in the direction of the Pontiac, with Clare and Kerry stationing themselves on either side of Howard. Howard did not truly need their support; they in fact needed the support of one another. In their exhaustion they borrowed on each other's strengths to carry them the distance to the car.

LEOTA HAD HAD a wonderful day. She had her windows open to the spring air and the breeze blew into the house from the south with such a gentle, easy cross-flow. Her yard was in full bloom; she'd spend most of the afternoon out puttering in the flower beds. The day had started off on a wonderful note when the postman had delivered to her door not only a postcard from Raleigh, but a three-page letter from Kerry as well.

She leaned back on the kitchen counter, sipping on a large frosty glass of iced tea. Her television was blasting the last few minutes of a *Leave It to Beaver* episode which Leota wasn't much interested in watching. She'd turned the television on only a moment ago in anticipation of watching the evening news.

Thomas Evans watched Leota daydreaming, with her feet crossed in front of her as she leaned on the counter. He hesitated for a short while before interrupting her with a sharp knock on the wooden doorframe. Leota jumped at the sound of Thomas' knocking, but after all these years she knew simply by the number of knocks who it was.

"Howdy do, Leota. How's things with you today?" Thomas asked in his deep baritone voice as Leota pushed the screen door open to let him in. He held an envelope in his hand as he entered the kitchen.

"Oh, it's just been a lovely day, Thomas. I got two letters today, one from each of my wayward grandkids. How's things with you?" Leota asked, fussing with a few dishes she'd left in the sink after lunch.

"Fair to middlin', I s'pose. The postman delivered your gas bill over to my place. I thought I'd drop it by and see if you might have some of that special iced tea for this tired old man," Thomas replied with a grin.

"Sure thing, Thomas, but there isn't anything special about my iced tea. It's just plain old Lipton. Matter of fact, you're just in time for Mr. Cronkite. Why don't you grab yourself a seat in the living room and I'll bring your tea to ya?" Leota said, bustling around the kitchen preparing Thomas his glass of tea.

Leave It to Beaver was still playing when Leota seated herself in the easy chair across the room from Thomas. They both leaned back in their overstuffed chairs with their feet propped up on matching footstools, waiting for the evening news.

"How's that lovely daughter of yours doing out in Los Angeles, Thomas?" Leota asked. She dipped a finger into her glass of iced tea and swirled the ice around as she waited for Thomas' reply.

"Oh, she's doin' just fine, Leota. You know how Camile is; she's a lot like Effie. I think she could just about be happy anywhere long as she's got a good home and a decent job," Thomas said cheerfully. "It sure is lonely 'round my place nowadays without her droppin' by from time to time," he added.

"Well, Lord knows I can sympathize with that, Thomas. I thought I'd miss the daylights outta Kerry and Raleigh. Matter of fact I did for the first week or so after they left, but Anita and I go down to the church every Wednesday evening now to play bingo and we've started going to the picture show on Mondays, it's half-price for the six o'clock feature, ya know. Maybe you might like to join us sometime? You'd be surprised at how good it makes you feel just to get outta the house every now and then. Gives ya something to look forward to," Leota remarked.

"Well, that sounds just fine, Leota. I'll just plan on joining you two ladies on Wednesday for bingo. Are you goin' to the picture show this evening?" Thomas asked.

"Anita's got a late doctor's appointment today; I don't think we're gonna get to go today. Sometimes she gets stuck in that damned doctor's waiting room for hours," Leota sighed.

The news was just coming on and Leota glanced over at Thomas. She noticed that his glass was already empty and jumped up from her seat to refill it. "Here, let me get you some more of that Lipton's, Thomas," she said, hurrying off to the kitchen.

"Just a half a glass'll be fine for me, Leota," Thomas called after her. Leota returned to the living room with Thomas' tea just in time to see Kerry and Howard loom up on the screen.

"An estimated thirteen hundred arrests were made in the streets of Washington, DC, this morning just before morning rush hour. Our correspondent in Washington was able to catch an interview with eighty-seven-year-old Howard Bates from Saratoga Springs, New York, as Mr. Bates marched in the streets in what's been termed 'the May Day rallies' early this morning," the commentator said.

Thomas jumped from his seat, his feet barely finding their purchase on the floor just in time to grab the glass of iced tea from Leota as it slipped from her fingers. "Oh, dear God in heaven, what's that Howard gotten my Kerry mixed up in now?" Leota screamed.

"This is my step-great-granddaughter, Kerry Foster," Leota heard Howard say to the correspondent.

Thomas helped Leota over to her easy chair, where she plopped down mumbling. "Why, there ain't no such thing as a step-great-granddaughter, Howard Bates!" Leota shouted at the television in disbelief.

"Now, Leota, calm down. Let's just listen to what they have to say. Lord, I sure hope they wouldn't throw that Howard in jail at his age and let's just pray they didn't get our Kerry," Thomas said in a calming tone of voice.

Thomas returned to his chair, loosening his tie a bit as he lowered himself down on the cushion. He and Leota both sat transfixed to the television screen for the remainder of Howard's interview.

"He seems like a very intelligent man, Leota. I just bet you he's taken good care of young Kerry up there in the capital," Thomas remarked.

"Well, he did look pretty spiffy at that, out there amongst the unwashed generation in his flannel suit and bow tie . . . guess what he had to say made a whole lot of sense, too. But, that's no excuse for him draggin' our Kerry out into the streets. Lord have mercy, what if they're both in jail up there? Good Lord, Howard's too old to go to jail, just might kill the little ne'er-do-well, and Kerry — she doesn't know the first thing about real life. What if they've thrown her in jail with a bunch of prostitutes and drug pushers? Oh, dear me, those two are like the blind leading the blind. Thomas, get me that little princess phone off the table in there. I've got to reach Julie and I think my legs are too weak to even walk across this room," Leota said, pulling a Kleenex out of the cuff of her blouse and swabbing her nose. "Lord, and the little dickens was even carryin' a purse. What in God's name is this world comin' to?" Leota mumbled to herself as Thomas placed the princess phone on the arm of her chair.

Thomas rested his hand on the receiver of the telephone. He looked down at Leota, reflecting on their years of friendship. He thought to himself that she had one of the kindest hearts he had ever known. Her total honesty was her best trait, her lack of common sense in times of crisis, her worst.

"Now, Leota, I want you to think about this for just a minute or two. I love young Kerry just as though she were my very own granddaughter, and especially since Camile has never seen fit to bless me with any grandchildren of my own, and I would never in my life say anything bad about young Kerry. But you and I both know that she's been involved with this anti-war movement for a long time now. Maybe it wasn't Howard Bates who dragged her down to Washington. Maybe he just went along, you know, kind of as a chaperone. Now I know there's been some bad blood betwixt you and the old fellow, but I thought you worked all of that out. You just gotta remember that he can't be all that bad if Kerry loves him so. She's grown now, Leota, and if you can't stop bein' angry with her for movin' way up north there with Howard then you ought to at least be proud that she's out there speaking up for what she believes in. That old gent's probably never had such a time in his life as he's having right now up there in Washington, DC. It's only been a week or so ago since you told me that he'd helped our Kerry gain a position on some sort of newspaper up there. You got to put things in their proper perspective now and then, Leota. God knows your Edgar certainly did. He stood up for Effie and me right here in our own neighborhood way back when. Now that wasn't a popular thing to be doing in those times just like Kerry's activities aren't so popular to plain old folks like you and me in these times. Now, ain't that so, Leota?" Thomas asked, patiently awaiting Leota's reply.

"It's not quite the same thing, Thomas. Back then it was a matter of moral conscience and obligation to humanity to put an end to that ugliness in our country. Edgar was a loyal follower of Lyndon Johnson's campaign against the discrimination that was going on against your people back then. Yep, it was simply a moral issue and even though Mr. Cronkite keeps a-tellin' us that his war has become a moral issue, it just ain't the same. Why, what if Raleigh has to go over there? It'll almost be like the civil war again, with his sister out in the streets tellin' the world that he's wrong to be there," Leota said. She broke off her sentence to swab her nose again with the tissue. Thomas reached down to hold her hand, for he knew that she hurt inside, not because Kerry was out marching in the streets or because

Raleigh may end up in the war, but simply because they were grown now and they were gone.

"She won't be out there saying he's wrong for bein' there, Leota. She'll just be saying that the government's wrong for sendin' him there," Thomas said.

There was a long silence then between the two old friends. Thomas stood beside Leota's chair very gently holding her hand. He hadn't seen Leota cry since just before Edgar died. She'd been out in her garden then, hoeing the ground for spring planting, something Edgar had always done for her. She would hoe the ground furiously for a few moments, then she would lean back on the hoe, shake her fist at the sky, and weep loudly, as though she was cussing God directly to his face. It was on a Saturday and Effie had gone out shopping with Camile. Thomas remembered it so well, just as if it were yesterday. He'd walked quietly through the gate that separated their two properties, taken the hoe out of Leota's hands, and finished tilling the entire garden while Leota slumped against the clothesline pole watching him. He remembered it every year, as he'd been the one to ready her garden for spring planting every year since then, and Leota never failed to come out and lean against the clothesline pole while he worked. He stopped planting a garden of his own when Effie passed away; Leota shared hers with him.

"She's never comin' home again, is she, Thomas?" Leota asked, looking up into Thomas' dark eyes.

"She'll be back, Leota. She'll be a-walkin' through that front door before you know it. That little Kerry has always done exactly as she pleased and there ain't nothin' in this world that pleases her more than pickin' at you," Thomas said, smiling down at Leota.

Thomas' smile brought a lightness to Leota's heart. She reached for the princess telephone, freeing herself from Thomas' grip on her hand. "Well, let's just call Anita and see if she saw the evenin' news. Won't she be surprised that our Kerry was seen across the nation? And Howard, too," Leota said with a grin.

MILLIE SEIBEL was in her kitchen fixing supper and watching the television she kept on the kitchen counter. There was a sad atmosphere around the Seibel household since the announcement that Denise was pregnant. Ruben had hardly spoken a word all week long. If not for Denise's pregnancy, this would have been the happiest month of their lives, with their youngest child graduating from college and going to start his own life away from the shelter of their parental scrutiny.

There had been the fear of an accidental pregnancy between Kerry and Fletcher for years. Julie and Millie had talked it over several times, always agreeing with one another that should the situation arise they would both recommend abortion as the best solution.

They'd lived in curiosity during Kerry and Fletcher's high school years as to whether or not the two young people were sexually active. The question had not been answered until Kerry's senior year of high school and Fletcher's sophomore year of college.

Millie and Ruben had gone to visit their older daughter in Victoria while Fletcher had come down from Denton to stay at their house and take care of their small poodle dog, Jacques. Millie and Ruben had always trusted Fletcher to take care of the house when they left for vacations; this was no exception. They had returned on Sunday afternoon to find the house in fine order and Fletcher took off shortly after their arrival for his drive back to Denton.

Millie had invited Julie and her boyfriend, Bill Sanger, over for dinner. They'd just finished up the dishes and settled in at the dining room table for a game of bridge when Jacques came wagging into the room chewing on something, and with his tail all a-twitter, he'd padded over to Ruben's chair, plopped himself down, and much to Ruben's horror, deposited a well-chewed used condom right on top of Ruben's brown suede Hush Puppies. Ruben, as a rule, was a very quiet, unemotional sort of man, very easygoing in his manner, but on this particular occasion he had jumped from the table, grabbed the poodle dog by the scruff of the neck, and scurried from the dining room, screaming, "Bad dog, you bad little dog, you!"

The four adults had laughed about the incident later over coffee, especially over the fact that Ruben had been so shook up over the matter that he'd returned to the dining room after tossing Jacques outside, still wearing the condom on top of his shoe. Their curiosity about Kerry and Fletcher had been quenched that night and they'd all been thankful that there had been only the four of them around when the answer to their question was revealed.

Millie smiled to herself as she stood at the kitchen counter chopping onions. Tears rolled down her face from the fumes of the vegetable. The phone began to ring in a sharp peal and she wiped her tears away with the edge of her apron as she reached for the receiver. The phone sat next to the television on Millie's counter. She stared aimlessly at the picture on the screen as she answered the phone. Fletcher was on the other end of the line. They began discussing the time of his arrival from Denton on Thursday and the dinner plans for after the wedding ceremony. Millie was in the middle of describing the dress she had bought to wear for the wedding when she was silenced by the sight of Kerry Foster staring back at her from the television set. She had turned the sound down in order to hear Fletcher and she reached over now to turn it back up.

"Hey, Mom, are you still there? What is that noise in the background?" Fletcher asked in the confusion.

"It's Kerry!" Millie said in astonishment.

"Kerry!" Fletcher said. "But how — what's she doing there?"

"Oh, I'm sorry, son. She's on the news, the national news. Go turn on your television. Call me back later," Millie said as she placed the receiver back in its cradle without looking down from the screen.

PUTTNAM DID NOT CATCH Kerry and Howard's national debut on the evening news. He was in the process of doing an inventory of his camera equipment as it aired. Nothing had been taken from his camera bag, much to Puttnam's relief. Just as the policeman had told him, he was released before his cellmates, even though they'd been incarcerated hours before he had.

Luckily, Howard had slipped him a twenty-dollar bill that morning before leaving for Dupont Circle. It has cost him ten of that to get out of jail, which left him just enough for cab fare back to the motel.

He had not eaten all day and he slumped in the back seat of the cab with his stomach growling all the way back to the Holiday Inn. It was just beginning to get dark as they pulled into the parking lot. After paying the cab driver, Puttnam knocked softly on Clare's door. She answered it sleepily, tugging her blue, nylon robe around her small frame. Puttnam towered above her in the doorway and she stepped aside to let him in, then closed the door gently behind them.

"Where have you been all this time, Puttnam? Howard's worried himself sick about you," Clare whispered. Kerry was sleeping in the bed on the far side of the room. She was curled up in a tight ball on the edge of the bed with her back to them.

Puttnam dropped down into a chair by the door and replied, "I've been in jail, Clare. Where the heck did ya think I'd been?"

"Oh, dear. That's what I thought had happened. Puttnam, I'm so sorry, this never should have happened. After all, you are basically a member of the press. Did you by any chance get to see Howard's interview on the news?" Clare asked.

"Now, just how the hell was I supposed to watch the news in jail? They don't serve pretzels and beer in that joint, ya know," Puttnam said, trying to whisper. He pushed his hair back from his face in a huff.

"Shh, you'll wake Kerry up. I wish you'd gotten to see him on the news. He's so proud and throughout the broadcast he kept saying that he wished you'd been there to watch it with us. You know how he can puff out his chest and fiddle with his mustache when he's pleased with himself? Well, he'd do that, and then say, 'By God, I wish that Puttnam was here to see this. My one chance at stardom in eighty-seven years and he's a-missin' it,'" Clare whispered in an exaggerated impersonation of Howard.

"Well, I'm sorry I snapped at you, Clare. I wish I'd been here to see it, too. I wish I'd been anywhere but where I've been for the past ten hours. I'm about to starve to death. Got anything to eat around here?" Puttnam asked, his nerves beginning to calm.

"No, but I think your friend Howard has some pretzels and beer in his room," Clare said with a wink to Puttnam. They both chuckled loudly over Clare's remark as Kerry stirred from her deep sleep.

"Hey, Puttnam," Kerry said groggily, sitting up in bed and rubbing the sleep out of her eyes.

"Hey, little Texas," Puttnam said with a burst of his outrageous laughter while giving Kerry a thumbs-up sign.

Howard had heard the riotous roar of Puttnam's laughter and he came strolling into the room, pulling his flannel robe on over his nightshirt. He was relieved to see Puttnam back in one piece and he stood between Kerry and Clare's beds nonchalantly tying a knot in the belt of his robe. "By God, it's good to have you back with us again, Puttnam. I was beginning to get a little worried about you. They're predicting on the news that anywhere from seven to ten thousand people were arrested in the streets today and expecting most of those in jail to stay incarcerated until tomorrow morning. How did you keep from being arrested?" Howard asked.

"Well, I did go to jail. Guess by some fluke I got lucky and was taken in by myself instead of in one of the wagons. Anyway, I got out about five-thirty," Puttnam said as his stomach growled a loud reminder of his hunger. Howard heard the growl and raised one finger high in the air to gain the attention of his companions.

"I've got a splendid idea," he said. "Let's all get dressed and go on down to the restaurant for a bite to eat and celebrate our last night in this city, our nation's capital."

"That sounds like a winner to me here, Howard," Puttnam said. He lifted himself out of the chair and headed toward his and Howard's room with Howard following on his heels.

"You'll have to tell me all about it while we get dressed, old boy. We wouldn't want to offend our dear ladies' delicate ears," Howard said.

"Sure thing, Howard," Puttnam replied as they slipped into their room.

Kerry and Clare looked at one another in amusement over Howard's old-fashioned chivalry.

They stopped in the bar on the way back to the rooms. Kerry and Clare had red wine, Puttnam a scotch and soda, and Howard a ginger ale. They toasted each other in boisterous laughter and each of them felt they held a special part of each other within their memories of the hectic day they had just been through.

Kerry and Puttnam stayed up late watching old movies on television while Howard retired to bed and Clare reviewed the tapes of her interviews. The last rally was scheduled for the following morning at the Capitol steps and Clare was looking forward to hearing Bella Abzug speak, along with the many others who'd promised to take the podium. She remained wide awake long after the lights were turned off, worrying about the possibility of one or all of them getting arrested at the Capitol steps, especially Howard. This trip had obviously meant so much to him that she did not regret allowing him to accompany them to Washington, DC, yet she knew he must be exhausted, as she herself was tired to the bone.

Clare had many things on her mind that evening. Before leaving Saratoga she had pondered selling *The Avalanche* to a prospective buyer from New York City. She'd had many offers during the past few years to sell; she'd turned them down flatly, as most had been made from large corporations owning many small magazines and newspapers around the country whose format was totally incongruous with that of *The Avalanche*. She had spent too many years building the paper to simply have it reduced to trash by any large corporation. This latest offer had come from an old friend of Clare's who'd worked on *The Avalanche* a few years earlier as a political columnist, and Clare was seriously considering accepting. He had asked her to stay on as editor, but the load of responsibilities for the paper itself would be lifted from her shoulders. She finally drifted off to sleep contemplating the freedom of partial retirement from journalism. This trip out into the field had just about convinced her that she was ready for that difficult choice. It was time to pass the paper on to new energy, and the young, whom she'd provided with a training ground, would continue on in her path, which was now clearly marked, thanks to Clare, for obstacles. She knew they would not stumble there and they would not fail her with lack of journalistic integrity.

The next morning they left the Pontiac at St. Edward's church and rode to the Capitol in a church bus. Howard reluctantly watched the Pontiac grow smaller as they rode down the street. He was afraid he would never see his prized possession again. He and Puttnam sat side by side in the bus; Clare and Kerry sat behind them.

"Howard, are you sure you want to do this? They're saying it might get kinda sticky down there at the Capitol. It's surrounded by marines and the National Guard," Puttnam said, folding the daily newspaper up in his lap.

"Well, now, the way I figure it is this: if that nice little old woman who's diabetic can come all the way from Atlanta, spend a night in jail, and still be ready to go back out in the streets this morning, then by God, I ought to be able to do the same myself," Howard said impatiently. Every one of his companions had tried to persuade him to stay behind at the church this morning and he was determined not to let them get the best of him.

Thousands of people were gathered in the Mall when they arrived. It was just before noon and confusion reigned within the crowd. They all pushed forward to the Capitol steps where Bella Abzug was expected to speak. National guardsmen lined the steps and no one was being allowed to pass. Across the street many onlookers gathered to watch the spectacle; it was lunchtime and most of the spectators were federal employees on their lunch hours. Clare insisted that they try to stay together. She hooked her arm in Howard's as the throng of the crowd pushed forward to the steps. The National Guard began moving in from the rear and with the exception of protest signs being waved high in the air and the chanting of anti-war slogans, the crowd was peaceful under the circumstances.

Bella Abzug began mounting the steps despite repeated warnings from the loudspeakers not to. She was accompanied by Representative Ron Dellums of California. They were the first to be arrested on the steps as others followed behind them. Puttnam was snapping pictures right and left of the crowd while Clare did her best to interview the people around them and occasionally held her recorder up over her head in an attempt at catching some of the dialogue coming from the steps. Kerry was in awe of the whole gathering. She stood on the other side of Howard chanting with the core of the crowd: "WE ARE EVERYWHERE! POWER TO THE PEOPLE!"

Clare led the four of them to the edge of the crowd. A man dressed in a blue suit strolled up to stand beside them as people in front of them were being arrested and escorted to waiting military buses. Clare felt that they had somehow landed in the eye of the storm.

She turned to a dark-haired man, who appeared to be somewhere in his late thirties, for an interview: "What's your opinion of this rally here today, sir? Do you feel this is an unconstitutional action in arresting these people here on the Capitol steps?" Clare yelled above the shouts and chants in the madness surrounding them.

The man was holding a brown paper bag in one hand and a sandwich in the other, with its wrapper rolled halfway down. He took a bite of his sandwich and chewed it slowly for a moment or two, contemplating an answer for Clare's questions. He spoke with his mouth full of food. "I don't really know. I'm just on my lunch hour from the Library of Congress. Guess the police just don't want to take the chance that all these people might get inside the Capitol. Now that'd be somethin' — "

The man was interrupted by a guardsman and Clare looked around to find that they were blocked in. Kerry sat down and refused to budge when a policeman tried to arrest her; Howard simply looped his arm on a guardsman's elbow and went along peacefully. Clare followed while Puttnam stayed with Kerry. The policeman was tugging at Kerry and Puttnam was becoming aggravated that his toes were being stepped on and his camera was getting banged around by the chaos in the arrests being made.

"Kerry, get your ass up and go along with The Man. Jesus Christ, this ain't no fuckin' sit-in. We're going to jail and you might as well make it there in one piece," Puttnam shouted down to Kerry, who looked up at him sheepishly before allowing the policeman to lift her to her feet. The policeman gave her a sharp shove once she was on her feet.

Puttnam shook a finger in the scrawny cop's face. "Hey, watch it there, asshole," Puttnam shouted.

Kerry threw her long braid back over her shoulder as she and Puttnam joined hands. Howard had caught a glimpse of the policeman shoving Kerry through the arms and legs in motion around him. The same cop approached him and the guardsman escorting him along. The man who'd been on his lunch break from the Library of Congress was walking swiftly in front of him, trying to avoid arrest, when the cop reached out and grabbed the man's elbow.

"Hey, I'm just on my lunch hour — what is this?" the man screamed at the lunging cop.

Howard calmly pushed his cane out in front of him into the policeman's path. The policeman tripped on the rubber-tipped cane and went sprawling to the ground in front of Howard.

"Terribly sorry there, old man," Howard shouted down at the policeman as he and the guardsman stepped around him.

Puttnam could not see Howard in the crowd but he had seen the policeman disappear; he helped the skinny policeman to his feet when he and Kerry reached that point.

Howard turned to the guardsman walking beside him. He was a large, young man with short-cropped hair just barely visible under his helmet, big hands and feet, and a small pugged nose. His boots were polished to a mirrored shine and his uniform was clean and starched. Howard was reminded of Kerry's brother, Raleigh, now off to basic training himself. He looked up at the young man as they walked along and said, "It's been one hell of a morning, hasn't it, young man?"

"Yes, sir," the guardsman replied politely as he helped Howard mount the first step into the waiting bus. Clare ascended the steps behind Howard and nodded at the guardsman as he retreated back into the crowd. The man on his lunch hour did not escape arrest and he was pushed up the steps by the young, skinny cop just behind Kerry and Puttnam.

"By God, we're goin' to jail, Clare," Howard shouted from his seat in the back of the bus to Clare, who was seated just in front of him. "Power to the people," he added, which turned the heads of all the protesters around him and renewed their chants.

A stout MP standing in the aisle looked toward the back of the bus and without addressing Howard directly he waved his hand in the air and shouted above the chants, "Hey, PUT A LID ON IT BACK THERE!"

Howard could not begin to estimate how many protesters had been arrested in the area surrounding the Capitol. They were taken in buses to holding areas around the city. Clare, Puttnam, Howard, and Kerry were taken on their bus to an empty, cavernous National Armory building.

Several hundred protesters refused to give their names. They were segregated and moved to bleachers that had been erected against one wall inside the Armory, while the rest remained out in the center of the room.

Those who were on the floor stood in lines for hours without food or water, waiting to be processed. Howard longed for his camp stool, which Clare had solidly refused to allow him to carry to the Capitol.

During the course of the afternoon the nameless protesters on the bleachers tried to scramble down to the Armory floor and were escorted back into the seats. After a time, it became a game for them to see how far they could get. Those down on the floor would hoot and holler in mass support for the sprinting protesters. Howard was delighted with the game and he chimed right in with the rest of his compadres.

The guardsmen were fairly sympathetic with the protesters' cause. After all, many of the young men had joined the National Guard to avoid the draft and the possibility of going to Vietnam. There was very little hostility floating in the atmosphere in the Armory. Only an occasional outburst of anger occurred between those in charge and those being held against their will. In a sense, they were all there against their will.

Puttnam stood in line next to a fellow Vietnam veteran. They spent their time exchanging stories about the war. For Puttnam, it was an essential form of therapy to discuss the horror he had witnessed there. The United States government would only acknowledge the physical wounds of Vietnam veterans, ignoring the wounds of the heart and the soul. The emotional scars created by an undeclared war, with no right and no wrong, left the veterans alone in their own confusion. None of them could forget what they'd been through, yet no one could agree upon a reason for them having gone.

Puttnam was one of the few Vietnam veterans who had found avenues on his own for relieving his emotional anguish. He found that in talking to other vets about their turmoils since their return to the States, he was not alone in his nightmares and that situations such as the one he'd experienced in Dupont Circle were not uncommon to all of them. Though their stories of what they had seen in 'Nam varied uniquely to each individual, they all shared the same loss of innocence to the war. Their fathers who'd served in World War II and their grandfathers before them in World War I had shared that same loss of innocence, yet they had been celebrated for that loss, while the Vietnam veteran simply suffered the loss in frustration. He had performed a thankless job for a nation full of thankless Americans. Puttnam found great comfort in relating his emotions to other veterans. It eased his sorrow and loneliness, for they could not all be insane, they could not all be wrong. It was they who had been wronged by their own, a matter of flesh and blood.

There would be many veterans in future years who would not find that same avenue of release as did Puttnam. Raleigh Foster would be one of them. He would hide his tortured soul behind a wall of silence, which would be perceived by others as tranquility. His dreams would shout into the night and he would never again believe in his father's America.

During the late afternoon the guardsmen began passing out blankets to the protesters. Much was made of the passing out of blankets, since none of them had been fed; it was as though they were being sent to bed without any supper. A blanket toss followed across the floor, with some of the guardsmen joining in. Howard had a wonderful time watching the follies, though he did not participate himself. He was shocked to find Clare joining in on the fun. She was such a tiny woman that she had to leap high off the ground to catch the tails of the blankets as they flew by. Kerry sat cross-legged on the floor, sulking. She was such a private person that being locked in with such a close, boisterous crowd had brought on a touch of claustrophobia.

One of the guardsmen had been considerate enough to locate a folding chair for Howard and one for the elderly woman from Atlanta. Though the two of them sat on opposite sides of the Armory, they seemed to preside over the group as elder statesmen.

Food was finally delivered to the Armory in the early morning hours. It consisted of bologna sandwiches. Howard had fallen asleep in his chair. Clare woke him up by tugging gently on his mustache so he would eat.

With the food came news that since the beginning of the rallies the total number of arrests had been twelve thousand protesters. It had taken five thousand policemen, backed by a staggering amount of ten thousand troops, to round all of them up. Protesters were being charged with offenses ranging from civil disobedience to illegal entry.

They began transporting the protesters to the main Washington, DC, cell blocks at dawn. It was a long bus ride for Howard. Even the curls in his mustache began to droop from his exhaustion. He snapped at Clare several times during the ride downtown. She finally gave up trying to maintain a conversation with him and rode beside him in silence.

The men and women were separated once they got downtown. They were processed there for a second time and placed in holding cells. The American Civil Liberties Union had won a court order demanding that the protesters be fed. They were also pushing for a court order to force the authorities to place only two prisoners to a cell. That order hadn't come through yet; Puttnam and Howard were placed in a cell with seventeen other prisoners.

The cell was a bit larger than the one Puttnam had been in before, but it still only measured about five by twelve feet. No one had had any sleep except for Howard, and he had only catnapped during the night. The close quarters made all of them irritable. The air smelled heavily of perspiration and industrial cleaning solutions. Puttnam tried to coax Howard into leaning on him, since a clerk had taken his cane, but Howard stubbornly refused to do so.

They were served Big Mac hamburgers and peanut butter and jelly sandwiches. Howard was handed a Big Mac, which he immediately traded off for peanut butter and jelly. The aroma of the two foods mixed with the perspiration and cleaning fluids did not blend well in the stifling cell, so much so that Howard could not finish his sandwich. He felt so weak from nausea that he finally capitulated and moved closer to Puttnam's side to lean his small frame on Puttnam's sturdy arm.

Clare was not idle in her cell with Kerry. She shouted at the guards each time they passed by. The other women in their cell had joined in on her complaints about Howard's age and the fact that they were officially members of the press. The woman from Atlanta had been released earlier in the afternoon because she was a diabetic. Clare was deeply concerned for Howard's stamina. Her pleas were finally passed through the right channels and they were released late in the evening.

Howard was so drained that he could hardly walk. After an hour of bickering with a desk clerk over the whereabouts of both Howard's cane and Puttnam's camera bag, they were free to go. Howard's cane was located; Puttnam's camera equipment was lost forever in the Washington, DC, police department.

Years would go by before the legalities of the massive arrests would be examined in a court of law. The marchers vowed to launch another raid on the Capitol in the autumn. A class action suit would eventually be filed on behalf of all of them, but that case, *Dellums v. Powell*, would not be resolved until the next decade. Those who'd been arrested and held under such deplorable conditions would then be financially compensated for their discomfort; many of them would be held for another day and a half under the same conditions. Howard would not live long enough to see that case addressed in a court of law, but he did not need a check in the mail or the United States judicial system to convince him that he had had a right to be there on those Capitol steps. He knew in his heart that they were right to do what they'd done, and though the war would not suddenly come to an end because Howard Bates had gone to Washington, by God, he'd been there, and he was proud of his efforts.

Reporters snapped pictures of Howard as they left the building. He had become somewhat of a hero after his appearance on the evening news, along with the woman from Atlanta.

Howard balanced himself on Puttnam's arm. He smiled at the photographers with his mustache all a-twitter. Occasionally he'd wave his cane in the air, which came close to smacking Puttnam in the head. His presence there made it clear to a nation of onlookers that the anti-war movement was not simply a collection of misguided, unshaven youths, but the sentiments of patriots as well, who were in fact the heart of the "silent majority" and that majority would no longer be silent. Richard Nixon's rhetoric about Vietnamization, troop withdrawals, and peace talks would not be taken for granted by the people of America. They were no longer concerned with defeat; they simply wanted the pain to stop and it would not stop without their voices.

The Nixon administration may have succeeded in curbing the attempts by the marchers to close down the city of Washington, DC, but they had not made a mockery of those intentions and the beliefs of those who had participated were only strengthened by the fear they'd instilled within his administration for their numbers.

Hank was among the photographers outside. Puttnam hailed him over and asked for a ride for the four of them back to the Pontiac.

Howard squirmed in the back seat of Hank's car on the way. His eyes lit up when they rounded the corner by the church and lo and behold, there sat his baby blue Pontiac.

Puttnam stopped at a coffee shop to have Clare's thermos filled with coffee. They drove all the way back to Saratoga that night. Howard slept peacefully in the back seat, using Clare's straw handbag for a pillow. He was passing through the still of America, going home to rest.

THE LETTER FROM FLETCHER came in July, long after Howard's face had appeared on the front page of every major newspaper in the country and just on the eve of Raleigh Foster's arrival in South Vietnam.

The summer had been kind to Kerry. She'd spent her idle hours enjoying the concerts at Caffè Lena with Margaret and Puttnam. On some days, in the afternoon, Margaret and Kerry would walk over to the grounds of Yaddo, which was an artists' retreat located there in Saratoga. They would rest out on the lawn under the shade of a tree and speculate on the lives of those who'd come to work at Yaddo through the years. Many of Margaret and Kerry's favorite writers had come there to gather their lines; Carson McCullers had been one of them.

The fever that surrounded the horse races took over the city during the summertime. The beauty of the fever was that it made everyone feel like a winner. Everyone lost now and then at the tracks, so no one was considered a loser, and Kerry did not escape the optimism. There were cloudless days when all the world seemed calm in Kerry's heart. She floated through those days along with the tourists who flooded the streets. The heat was not as demanding as that of central Texas. For Kerry it seemed springlike, though Clare complained about the temperatures and the lack of air-conditioning each day.

Howard made many mysterious trips downtown during the month of June. He was at peace with himself by the time July rolled around. He spent most of his days in a rocking chair out on the front porch, drifting in and out of sleep during the late afternoons and chatting with the passersby.

Margaret had accepted a teaching position at a university in Houston. She would start in the fall, while Puttnam would remain in Saratoga Springs on the staff of *The Avalanche* until Clare could replace him.

Kerry had applied for writing positions in Dallas and Houston. She'd finally had an offer from a newspaper in Houston to work part-time on the weekly entertainment section. Clare was quite proud of her. If not for Clare's kindness in hiring Kerry at *The Avalanche*, Kerry would never have landed the job.

Howard was sad over the prospect of Kerry moving back to Texas. On that cloudy summer day, he sat on the porch holding Kerry's letter from Fletcher in his lap, waiting for Margaret and Kerry to return from a walk down to Congress Park. He watched the two women stroll side by side up the sidewalk. They were very close to being the same size, with Margaret standing just a tad taller than Kerry. They both wore sundresses, their hair flew wildly in the wind around their faces, and their voices bubbled in laughter. Margaret and Kerry both had a tendency to freckle in the summer sun just across the bridge of the nose. They both sported their freckled, pink noses as they climbed the steps to Clare's front porch.

"You've got a letter here, Miss Kerry, from London," Howard said, holding the letter up for Kerry to see.

"I don't know anyone in London," Kerry replied. She reached for the letter in Howard's hand and retreated to sit down on the top step to open the envelope.

"It's from Fletcher," Kerry said, looking at the return address.

"I'm going inside to see what Puttnam's up to, Kerry. See you at dinner," Margaret said, reaching down to pat Kerry on the shoulder. Kerry sat with her back to the front door. Margaret motioned to Howard for him to follow her inside so that Kerry could have some privacy, but Howard shrugged his shoulders at her, ignoring the request.

Kerry flipped her hair back over her shoulder then hesitantly opened the envelope. She recognized Fletcher's handwriting immediately.

Dear Kerry,

News from abroad! I've moved to London to study for a year. I wanted to call you before I left. I was in New York City for a few days visiting my cousin before I flew to London. It's so hard to explain things . . . they can never be explained away completely.

Denise lost the baby the first week in June. She moved back in with her folks a couple of weeks after that. I was not saddened for the loss but it hit me pretty hard to see such pain pass between all of us.

I know it is too soon to ask for any sort of reconciliation with you. Perhaps that will never be in the cards for us, but I can always hope. Perhaps the time apart will enable us to understand each other. Perhaps the time apart will create a need to be together someday.

I saw you on the news in May and your picture was in the paper with Howard. Your mother told my mom that you all went to jail. Hope Howard has recovered from the ordeal.

I won't assume that you'll respond to my letter. My address is on the back of this page if you want to write. Please give my regards to Margaret and to Puttnam.

I suppose it will be my punishment to have a full year of cloudy days here in London.

I love you.
Fletcher

Kerry looked up from the letter once she'd finished reading its contents. Her eyes were clouded with tears as a gentle rain began to fall. Howard was silent in his rocking chair. He wished he'd gone inside with Margaret, for the front porch seemed to grow smaller as the two of them sat facing the late afternoon. Kerry laid the letter down beside her. She folded her arms around her knees and rocked back and forth on the top step. Howard could feel her pain surging through his own heart.

"Kerry, is everything all right?" Howard asked, reluctant to pry. The rain began to fall harder in a steady rhythm around them. The air smelled sweetly of summer, holding the scent of freshly cut grass and roses.

"Oh, everything's just peachy. Guess Fletcher's already getting a divorce. He's moved over to London to study. He wants to be a great architect," Kerry mumbled, without looking back at Howard.

"Kerry," Howard said as she turned to face him. "You're such a lovely young woman to hurt so inside. There will be other love in your life. Love has many shapes and faces. Even if it's only him that you dream of till your last breath of life, there will be others who will waken your heart and still your memories. Put those thoughts of romance out of your head for a while and concentrate on your talents. They can cure what ails you. Why, you can spin a line better than most; the kind of lines that make us feel grateful for the written word. You work at that craft. One of these days love will come to you again. It'll be new and untouched; it'll make you strong and young again.

"My Pearl had a special place in her heart for you. She believed you could tame the world with the turn of your smile. Course, she was a little prejudiced, but she was excellent at choosing winners. Now, there's a great deal of propinquity between you and my Pearl. By God, she never lowered her jawbone for any man. She kept that chin up solid and firm. If things didn't work out just the way she planned them, then she'd just carry on and make the best of things the way they were. She'd be sittin' here telling you how much better off you are without that young man clipping your wings. I can't do that because I know you hurt too badly right now to believe something like that from this old fool. I'm always here if you need someone to talk to. The world's out there a-waitin' for ya," Howard said.

He tapped his cane on the porch, then standing to go inside, he shifted his weight on the cane, which he held firmly with both hands in front of him. Kerry noticed that he leaned more on that cane than he used to and he was cautious of his footing. He shuffled toward the screen door and Kerry jumped to her feet to open it for him. He turned to address her once more before entering.

"Now, don't you go writing that young man for a while. You just let him stew in his own troubles over there in London Town. I expect he has a heart of his own to mend. Forced solitude can do wonders for the heart," Howard said. He winked at her as he reached over to brush a tear from her cheek.

"I love you, Howard. You make my dilemmas in life tolerable, you give them perspective," Kerry cried. She bent forward to kiss him on the cheek and caught the familiar, spicy smell of the wax on his handlebar mustache; it carried the wealth of wisdom, the mystery of the love of the young for the old. The memory of Howard would always bring forth that particular smell in her senses, for it was an essential part of his person, as identifiable as his voice.

Howard produced a broad smile across his face as he turned on his heels to enter the house. "By God, Clare, it's starting to rain cats and dogs out here. We better get those upstairs windows closed," he shouted from the front hallway. Kerry stood watching him through the screen door, wondering how she could consider moving back to Texas and leaving Howard behind. He had given her so much in their short time together: he had taught her how to give unselfishly.

Clare kept a wastebasket on the front porch next to Howard's rocking chair. He liked to read the local sale circulars that came in the mail and he had had a tendency to leave them scattered on the porch before Clare had solved the problem by putting a wastebasket by his chair. Kerry held Fletcher's letter tightly in her hands and stared into the basket for a few moments before dropping the letter onto the pile of circulars. "By God, this one's for you, Howard," she said softly to herself before going inside to get ready for dinner.

Ernest was just coming out of Clare's office as Kerry came in; she flipped him her finger as she went up the stairs and he joyously reciprocated the gesture. It had become a ritual between the two of them and some things never change.

HOWARD IMAGINED that with the windows open in the house at night, the whole neighborhood must be listening in on the nightly lovemaking sessions between Margaret and Puttnam.

Howard had not felt well since returning from Washington. He often lay wide awake in his bed until the wee hours of the morning. A.M. would find him cranky, yawning his way through breakfast and anxious for a nap out on the porch in the fresh air. He went to the doctor several times but he could not find any physical reason for Howard's fatigue, except just plain old age.

His biggest fear in growing old had always been senility and the frustration of finding himself caught in its grips was most frightening to him. He found himself forgetting even simple things on a daily basis.

In mid-June, he'd sold his house to the Wilsons and tied all loose ends in his financial investments. Over the years he'd built a respectable estate. His lawyer drew up a new will for him. He left everything to Kerry and Clare.

By July, he'd forgotten that all of that was behind him and he called the Wilsons on the telephone to ask them if they would be interested in buying the house. Mrs. Wilson had been quite confused at first, but kind enough to realize the complexity of the problem.

"Why, Mr. Bates, it's so nice of you to inquire . . . but we've already drawn up the contracts on the house with your lawyer. How neglectful of him not to mention it to you. We so enjoy your fine little home here. It's our first real investment. Thank you so much for your kindness in extending our lease and for deciding to put the house up for sale. We just can't imagine ever living anywhere else. Please come visit us soon; we so enjoy your visits," Mrs. Wilson had said on the phone to Howard.

He'd remembered the meeting in his lawyer's office with the Wilsons back in June about halfway through her second sentence but was too embarrassed to interrupt her. His mustache had twitched across the receiver as he'd impatiently waded through the awkward conversation and had been quite relieved when he'd heard the familiar sound of the doorbell ringing on Mrs. Wilson's end of the line — it had given both of them a natural excuse to hang up.

Clare had made the final decision to sell *The Avalanche*. She and Howard shared the same lawyer, so she was well-informed about Howard's problem with his memory. She was quite patient with Howard and had made a point not to ask him embarrassing questions about his absences. Oftentimes he could not recall where he had been. Neighbors had seen him taking long walks through Congress Park with his shoulders uncharacteristically stooped against the heat of the sun. She heard him pace the floor late at night amidst the moans and laughter that came from Margaret's room.

It was a confusing time for Clare. The love affair between Margaret and Puttnam brought new life and joy to the household. The continuing saga of the battle between Kerry and Ernest had mellowed into habit and had become a source of humor and entertainment for them all, the two of them included. Ernest knew that Kerry was leaving in August along with Margaret, so he no longer felt genuinely threatened by her presence there. Clare was torn between these wild days of summer and the sorrow of watching Howard slip away from life before her very eyes. Each day he grew more distant and each day she saw less of the man who had served as a father to her for the past quarter of a century.

When she was alone, she would let herself cry. Her large, dark eyes would stare into a void and the tears would roll freely down her cheeks in great torrents. She could not bear the thought of losing him, yet she knew he was dying. She often hoped that he would go before the weather turned cold in the fall. She had visions of him going mad being forced to stay indoors.

In the evenings she would take a lawn chair out to the front porch and sit quietly next to Howard. Clare had never been a tactile person, having lived her life alone, but she found herself reaching out to touch Howard's arm or his shoulder now and then; it was the grip of dreaming, wishing he would always be there to reach out to. As long as she could feel his fragile bones beneath her fingers, she could ward off the fear of death itself. Clare understood that the greatest irony of death for those among the living is that you wait impatiently for your heart to recuperate from the loss; it never does, for all those who've died still walk beside your heart as though they were the living, and in your own reality, they are still living, still breathing out without breathing in. It's the breathing in which endeared you to them — as though they would always be a part of you and you could no longer be a part of them. The sorrow for the death of a loved one seemed to Clare a purely selfish emotion, for it was the loss of that gift of affection which humankind mourned. She was totally human, though she fought the pending sorrow with a grace uncommon to most.

THE LAST PICTURE SHOW opened in Saratoga Springs on a warm, clear day during the last week of July. The screenplay was written by Larry McMurtry and Kerry was anxious to see the film. The reviews for the movie had been tremendous throughout the country. Kerry flaunted them in Ernest's face for several days.

In honor of Kerry and Howard's Texas heritage, the whole staff decided to go to a matinee. Clare doubted that Howard could stay awake through the film but hoped that the air-conditioning in the theatre would at least keep him from snoring.

The Avalanche staff took up most of the row they chose to sit in, down close to the front of the theatre. Puttnam stood impatiently in the aisle waiting for everyone to be seated. Howard was clear-headed that day, though he was extremely cranky. The shuffling of popcorn boxes across him began to grate on his nerves and he startled the entire staff by barking out, "By God, I'm not going to tolerate a popcorn toss throughout this feature. Every one of you get up this instant and go buy your own damned box of popcorn before the movie starts."

The response of the staff was to pass all four boxes of popcorn, which had been floating between them, to Howard. The previews for upcoming movies were flashing on the screen. Howard chuckled softly, wrapped his arms around the boxes and declared, "I hope you young people don't expect me to ever venture out in public with the likes of you again." He stood up then and redistributed the popcorn down the row on either side of him, tossing one box in Puttnam's direction at the end of the row, which grazed the top of Puttnam's head and landed on the sticky carpet in the aisle. The theatre was only about a quarter full. A couple seated two rows back shushed Howard loudly and he turned to nod politely toward them before taking his seat again.

They were a motley crew indeed in that theatre that day. Kerry, Marlin, and Ernest slumped in their seats, draping their legs over the backs of the seats in front of them, while Puttnam rested in an almost horizontal position with his long lanky legs and big feet perched out into the aisle. Margaret sat in her normal position of perfect posture; Clare and Howard were so small that they could hardly be seen by the rows behind them.

Howard sat with his arms folded on his chest and his cane resting against his leg. He did not go to sleep as Clare had predicted and surprised all of them by responding to some of the scenes vocally. The dust-blown streets in the movie reminded him of his youth and through the film he relived a good portion of his young years in West Texas. The Baptist churches, the treeless landscapes which seemed to extend into the glaze of sunsets, the beer signs that laughed at the dry, parched land with high-pitched squeals as they swung in the never-ending wind, and the sight of naked cotton fields where the plants had no leaves in the fall, only yellow-stained cotton balls which appeared to have been placed there rather than having grown there: all came back to haunt Howard on that July afternoon in the theatre. In his heart he found beauty he'd never felt before for his birthplace; for his youth. Those who had endured that West Texas terrain were a sturdy lot and for the first time in his life he longed to return there.

Twilight was upon them as they left the theatre in search of the Pontiac. Jack Simpson walked along beside Howard, asking him questions about West Texas.

"Of course, this movie was set in a different time period than when I lived there. It doesn't seem to change much out there. For that matter, neither does New England. I hadn't set foot in West Texas since my best friend died back during the Depression, until my dear wife passed on in the spring. The buildings had changed and the churches all had neon signs, but the people were the same. There are good folks and bad folks everywhere, except in West Texas the ones with the money and power are usually the bad ones. You find me a fellow who survived the dust storms on a dry land farm during the thirties and forties and carved a living for his family out of almost nothing in terms of his skills and education, and I'd take his word over an Easterner any day. I liked that movie though; it'll make the rest of the country aware that the West is no longer full of John Wayne types and Indians. It's full of plain old folks with troubles similar to those of everyone else," Howard said as they walked along.

They all got into the Pontiac. Jack climbed in next to Howard so they could finish their conversation.

"Well, there was the movie *Giant*, Mr. Bates. What did you think of that one? Was it as authentic as *The Last Picture Show*?" Jack asked.

Howard twiddled with the tips of his mustache for a moment or two. "I recall that movie quite vividly. It reinforced my decision not to live in West Texas, but in reality, it was not true to real life. It did not focus on the middle class in Texas; it focused on the new elite and those on the bottom of the social structure. I didn't find myself or anyone I'd ever known in any of the characters, whereas with this one we saw today, I saw myself in some of those characters. A small part of me reached out to touch and embrace each one of them, like family," Howard said pensively.

"Oh, for God's sake. It was just a movie," Ernest remarked from the front seat. He was sitting next to Clare and she jabbed her elbow sharply into his side. Ernest darted her a disdainful look as they pulled up in front of the house.

Puttnam and Clare had decided to fix dinner that evening while Kerry and Margaret walked down to the park. Jack and Marlin departed for the bus station to catch the next bus into New York, where they were planning on spending the weekend at Ty's place in the Village.

The neighborhood was quiet as darkness began to fall. Howard sat on the front porch listening to the faint sounds of pans rattling in the kitchen and occasional outbursts of Puttnam's wild laughter. He took off his good shoes and replaced them with his slippers, which he'd left tucked under his rocking chair. He thought about his Pearl and he thought about his loneliness without her. The warm breeze engulfed him just as Pearl's body had once sheltered his frail soul from loneliness. He closed his eyes and began to dream in pleasant slumber of the touch of her small breasts. Her smile greeted him with its welcomed familiarity, and with his head tilted back, his hands crossed in his lap, the cane hanging on the arm of the rocking chair, and the wind stirring the curls in his mustache, he died peacefully in his sleep.

Kerry and Margaret strolled past him when they returned to the house. Kerry smiled at him, thinking he was merely taking a short nap. She placed her finger to her lips in a gesture to Margaret, motioning for silence so that they would not disturb his sleep. Neither bothered to turn the porch light on at the switch just inside the door for fear that the light would wake him.

Puttnam finished his work in the kitchen and carried the plates and silverware out to the dining room to set the table, leaving Clare behind in the kitchen to put the finishing touches on the salad. He placed all the utensils on the long oak table and went to the front door to notify Howard that dinner was almost ready.

He pushed the screen door open just a few inches, stuck his head out the door, and said, "Hey, Howard, it's gonna be chow-time in about five minutes." He didn't wait for a reply from Howard and since the light was off on the porch, didn't notice the odd angle in which Howard's head was resting. The screen door banged shut behind him and he scurried back into the dining room to finish setting the table. Ernest came out of Clare's office at about the same time. He'd been proofreading his next article for *The Avalanche*; Clare had been kind enough to invite him to stay for dinner.

Ernest reached out to grab Puttnam by the elbow as he hurried past. "Hey Burley, where's the old man? I ought to apologize for those untimely remarks in the car this afternoon," Ernest said.

"Oh, he's out there catching a few winks. Kerry and Margaret are upstairs getting cleaned up for dinner, so he's alone. He needs to get up, though, so he won't mind you waking him," Puttnam said, pointing toward the front door. He pushed his hair back from his face and rushed on past Ernest for the dining room.

Ernest walked to the screen door, straightened his shirt a bit, and pushed the door open briskly. The door banged shut behind him, bounced on the door jam, and slammed shut for a final loud crack. He heard Clare bellow out from the dining room inside: "I wish to heaven all of you would quit slamming that door! My nerves shatter every time it slams. Sounds like the roof is caving in!"

"Yes, ma'am," Ernest overheard Puttnam say, followed by one of his boisterous fits of laughter.

Ernest sat down on the top step of the porch with his profile to Howard. It was getting quite dark outside but he didn't seem to notice as he opened his conversation.

"I should apologize to you, Mr. Bates, for making that nasty comment in the car this evening about *The Last Picture Show* just being a movie. I mean, it was just a movie but it was also an art form and when any form of art touches the heart of the observer, that observer certainly deserves the right to be moved without criticism. To tell you the truth, I was quite moved myself by the film. There were times when I identified totally with that character, Sam the Lion. At any rate, I do hope you'll accept my apologies. I was way out of line. I know you've never had much regard for me as a person. Not too many people do — but hey, I respect you more than you'll ever know. You've been coming around *The Avalanche* since I came to work here. Maybe someday we can sit and have a good chat . . . you interested, Mr. Bates?" Ernest asked sheepishly.

He turned to face Howard in the gray shadow of the evening and when Howard did not reply to his statements, he added, "Well, I didn't really expect you to respond right away. I know you like to think things out quite a bit. I'm like that myself. It never pays to be hasty. Don't you think that's so, Mr. Bates?"

Silence greeted him and he began to squirm on the top step, wondering how he could possibly have offended the old man so badly that the guy wouldn't even accept his humble confessions.

"Well, don't you agree on the last statement, Mr. Bates?" Ernest asked again. He noticed that Howard had not moved since he'd been out there and he got up, walked over to the screen door, leaned inside, and flipped the porch light on.

The sight of Howard in death scared the dickens out of Ernest and he jumped a bit when he saw the angle of Howard's head, which was leaning in an awkward position to the side. He reluctantly reached out to feel Howard's pulse and, finding no life within the fragile wrist, he dropped Howard's arm, which landed in a dull thud in Howard's lap. Howard had been cradling his ticket stub from *The Last Picture Show* in his hands and the small piece of orange paper caught in the wind, blew off the porch, and came to rest in Clare's flower bed on the south side of the house.

Ernest rushed into the house, trying to regain his composure before confronting Puttnam with the problem at hand. He forgot about Clare's request regarding the screen door and he negligently let it slam with a loud bang behind him. Clare came bounding out of the kitchen into the dining room to confront the guilty party.

"Now just who in this household had the nerve to slam that frigging door again?" Clare bellowed, looking straight at Ernest and shaking a soup ladle in her hand.

"I did, I'm sorry, Clare. Uh . . . Burley, can you come outside with me for a moment?" Ernest replied, quite flustered. Puttnam sat a stack of paper napkins down on the end of the table and followed in curiosity after Ernest into the entrance hall.

"There's something wrong with the old guy. I think he's dead," Ernest said in a whisper.

Clare overheard his remarks to Puttnam and she ran outside to check on Howard. Puttnam followed after her in a state of semi-shock, with Ernest close on his heels.

"He was just sitting there. I swear I didn't touch him. He must've died in his sleep," Ernest said defensively.

Clare looked up at the two men, barking, "Oh, for God's sake, Ernest, shut your mouth and go call an ambulance. Have you no decency?" She was kneeling beside Howard, holding his wrist in her hand. "Puttnam, you go turn the fire off underneath the soup and keep Kerry inside," Clare added, turning to look up at Puttnam.

"Is he . . . ?" Puttnam began.

"I'm afraid Ernest was right," Clare said in a more controlled tone of voice.

Puttnam went back into the house, careful not to slam the screen door behind him. Kerry was halfway down the stairs, with Margaret close behind her. She took notice of Puttnam's confused behavior immediately. She stopped on the stairs, glanced at Ernest standing below her at the phone table, then made a dash for the front door. Puttnam caught her before she could reach the door, spun her around, and held her tightly as she struggled to get free.

"He's gone, Kerry. You don't want to see him like this," Puttnam cried. Kerry continued to struggle against him while Margaret and Ernest came to Puttnam's aid in restraining her. "Clare's out there with him. We should give her these few moments with him before the ambulance comes."

"Let her go, Puttnam. We all have to make our own choices in such matters," Margaret said softly. Kerry became more subdued with Margaret's support. Puttnam released her and she walked slowly out the door to join Clare on the porch.

Clare was still holding Howard's wrist. Kerry looked down at Howard's small person and his fragile appearance in death. He wore a white short-sleeved shirt, navy-blue cotton trousers, white socks, and his brown leather slippers. His good shoes were tucked neatly beneath the rocking chair.

Kerry knelt down beside Clare, placing her arm around the smaller woman's shoulders. They leaned heavily on one another with their heads bent together, sharing their final moments with their friend, Howard Bates, in silence. They remained still there on the porch; neither of them cried openly.

Clare jumped at the distant sound of the ambulance siren. She lifted her head and spoke softly into the summer night, "You were a good man, Howard Bates, my old friend."

Kerry helped Clare to her feet. They stood together on the top step waiting for the ambulance. The wind caught Kerry's long fine hair and the breeze blew it softly across Clare's face, tickling Clare's small pointed nose. She brushed Kerry's tresses from her face and smiled, saying, "Let's change sides here, shall we?"

Kerry smiled fondly down at Clare in respect for her composure and shifted to Clare's other side on the steps as the ambulance parked in front of the house.

Neighbors came out into their yards to gape in curiosity as Howard was placed on the stretcher. Margaret took Kerry upstairs while Clare gave the ambulance driver instructions for the destination of the body.

Kerry stretched out on her bed upstairs, listening to the muffled conversations below. Her bedroom windows were wide open and the lace curtains blew in and out with the rhythm of the warm summer breeze. She and Margaret had planned to leave for Texas in three days. Howard had given her the Pontiac last week as her going-away present. She lay awake deep into the night, driven by thoughts of going back to Texas where, as Howard had said, "the world awaited her." She longed to take Howard back to Texas, to join Pearlie. She longed to take him away from the winters he so hated in the great white North, back to the land of his birth.

The whole house could hear Kerry singing around midnight. She sat cross-legged on her bed with her guitar in her lap and her face wet with tears. She wrote a new song for Howard. Clare smiled at the lyrics. It eased her pain and brought the welcomed release of sleep. Kerry's high, clear voice bore a pristine quality and her song seemed to rent the air with the spirit of Howard Bates. Puttnam and Margaret lay side by side with their arms entwined, listening to the melody.

Oh, West Texas dream . . . I dream about the towers
    where the dust goes crazy in the summertime
We got this four-lane highway where the drivers all get sleepy
    Lord, don't they cuss our flatlands . . . New England-bound

Oh, the settlers who are lured to fight the caprock
    their wheat grows tall and the cotton fights for life
When the creeks run dry, they build no fences for their cattle
    Windmills tap those water wells . . . seldom on the rise

Build me a tower . . . high up on the plains
I wanna count the stars from Abilene to Amarillo
Waste my hours . . . prayin' for some rain
Just to watch the cold beer signs . . . be a-laughin' when
    the dust blows

Where the mountains meet the plains in far West Texas
    there are no rollin' hills or trees to block the sun
Oh, the callused hands that blessed the world with plenty
    left this land so hard . . . could break a heart of stone

Build me a tower . . . high up on the plains
I wanna count the stars from Abilene to Amarillo
Waste my hours . . . prayin' for some rain
Just to watch the cold beer signs . . . be a-laughin' when
    the dust blows

Oh, West Texas dream . . . I dream about the towers
    where the dust goes crazy in the summertime
We got this four-lane highway where the drivers all get sleepy
    Lord, don't they cuss our flatlands . . . all New England-bound.

———

HOWARD HAD REQUESTED that his body be cremated and that no services be held in his honor. Clare bought several bottles of champagne and they toasted Howard the next evening after dinner.

Premium Saltine Crackers were sold in decorative tins back in the 1950s. When Clare and Puttnam cleaned out Howard's drawers in his room they found an old cracker tin where he'd stored his letters from Kerry Pearl. Clare removed the letters carefully and tied them with ribbons. She gave the cracker tin to Puttnam and told him to take it to the funeral home so that Howard's ashes could be stored in it. Puttnam objected to Clare's choice of containers but did as he was told.

The cracker tin was of an ivory color with red and royal-blue lettering. This particular tin had obviously been purchased in Texas, most likely in Raymondville, as the lettering on the sides of the tin appeared in both Spanish and English. The mortician did not blink an eye when Puttnam dropped off the tin. Puttnam was curious about how normal this was in the mortician's line of work.

"Don't you think this a bit odd? I mean, putting some old gent's ashes in a cracker tin?" Puttnam asked, leaning on the desk in the mortician's office.

"Certainly not," the mortician replied. He was a short, plump man with rosy cheeks, contrary to what Puttnam had expected. "I've seen stranger things than this. Just between you and me, some of the requests we get from our clients are quite peculiar."

The mortician leaned across the desk and spoke almost in a whisper to Puttnam. His large belly prohibited him from leaning too far in Puttnam's direction. "Now, I'll just need for Miss Friedman to sign some forms as to the legal destination of the ashes and we'll be all taken care of here. You may pick up Mr. Bates'... cracker tin tomorrow," he said softly, and smiling up at Puttnam, he handed the legal forms to him.

Puttnam took the forms and left the funeral home. A chill had run up his spine as he passed through the parlor. Though it was a bright, sunny day outside, the parlor in the funeral home was dark and musky as though it were plunged eternally into winter. Puttnam's eyes stung as he stepped out into the sunlight, partially from the blinding effects of coming out of the shadowy gloom of the funeral parlor into the bright daylight, like being wakened during the night by someone flipping on an overhead light, and partly from the sorrow of losing his friend Howard.

He didn't go back to the boardinghouse right away. Instead, he folded the forms in half, stuffed them in the back pocket of his jeans, and ran all the way to Congress Park, which was almost a mile from the funeral home. Pedestrians on the sidewalks jumped out of his way as he tore along the streets with his hair blowing wild behind him. He collapsed on a park bench in the shade once inside the park. He could still hear the wind in his ears from his long flight from the funeral home. He buried his head in his hands, with his elbows resting on his widespread knees, and sobbed deeply for his loss.

Puttnam stayed in the park for more than an hour, trying to compose himself. On his way back to the boardinghouse he stopped off at one of the antique clothing stores along Caroline Street and purchased a lovely ivory-colored camisole made of silk and bordered with soft lace for Margaret. He drummed the fingers of one hand loudly on the counter and constantly pushed his hair back from his face with the other as he waited impatiently for the sales lady to wrap it for him.

Margaret and Kerry had postponed leaving for Texas for another week. Margaret was packed and ready to go, but Kerry seemed reluctant to leave Clare so soon after Howard's death.

Clare had interviewed several photographers to replace Puttnam, but none of them had struck her fancy and she seemed in no hurry to make a choice yet, which was OK with Margaret, as she was looking forward to the time alone in Houston.

Kerry and Clare had decided that it would be best if Kerry took Howard's ashes back to Texas with her. Kerry had plans of driving out to Floydada and leaving his ashes there.

The plan was for Kerry and Margaret to drive as far as Dallas together in the Pontiac, where Margaret would catch a plane for Houston. Kerry's father, Jeff, would pick her up in Houston, and Margaret would stay with him until she could find a house for herself and Puttnam.

Kerry had been astonished to discover from talking with her dad that Louise had not moved to Houston with him. They were, in fact, in the middle of a nasty divorce. Secretly, Kerry was pleased with the news about the pending divorce, as she'd never cared much for Louise, yet she inquired about Louise's emotional state in her conversations with her dad out of respect for the years she'd had Louise as her stepmother. It wasn't so much that she disliked the woman; it was just that Kerry had never really gotten to know her. Louise had kept a cool distance from Kerry throughout the years. Ethel, on the other hand, had grown quite attached to Louise, basically as a means to manipulate her father. She was sharp enough to realize that maintaining the close relationship with Louise had given her a direct line to her father's ear, which she filled daily.

The phone lines hummed between Austin, Texas, and Saratoga Springs, New York, all that week with gossip. Leota was the most fluent source of information. She claimed that Ethel had now deserted her friendship with Louise altogether and was bad-mouthing her soon-to-be former stepmother all over town. Leota also informed Kerry that Ethel was pregnant again and that Rodney had sent her off for two weeks at a health spa to celebrate. Kerry found out later from her mother that, in fact, they'd lied to Leota about where Ethel had been sent. She'd actually been placed in a hospital to dry out, as the consumption of alcohol could be devastating to an unborn child.

Kerry looked forward to the long three-day drive down to Dallas with Margaret. They studied the road maps carefully, planning to take the park road, the Blue Ridge Parkway, down through Virginia. She would drive on out to Floydada after she dropped Margaret off at Love Field in Dallas.

Her job was set to start in September at the Houston newspaper. Her final assignment for *The Avalanche* was to write a short obituary of Howard Buford Bates. It was unusual for Clare to print such personal articles but his was special, especially since Howard had made national headlines by attending the May Day rallies in Washington.

LATE ONE NIGHT, with the cracker tin resting on her desk, Clare pulled the bundled letters from Kerry Pearl out of her desk drawer and began to go through them. She hoped to find some interesting tidbits for Kerry's article in the letters and truly had no intentions of violating Howard's privacy. Through the years, Clare and Howard had shared their personal lives with one another so totally that she did not expect to find any surprises in Kerry Pearl's correspondence. She was quite wrong in her assumption.

Clare carefully arranged the letters in order of their postmarks. The earliest letter dated back to 1904 and the paper was yellowed with age, its texture crisp and fragile. Howard had been attending college at Princeton that year. Clare remembered from her conversations with Howard that he'd graduated from Princeton in 1906. Howard had had a difficult time completing his education. His family was fairly well-off for West Texas; they were a ranching family, and Howard's father had demanded that he drop out of school in the East twice to return home and help out around the ranch. Clare could recall that Howard had told her he'd met Kerry Pearl and Max sometime around 1900. His father bought his feed from Max's farm. The three of them had become the best of friends. Howard had even lived with them on both of his return trips from Princeton because he could not get along with his own father. It was most unusual for a West Texas rancher's son to go away to college. Most folks thought it a waste of time around those parts.

Max Schurgood was a strong-willed man. He was a huge, muscular Dutchman who spoke in broken English just a tad on the boisterous side. His cheeks would flush to crimson in the summer heat and in the dead of winter he could be seen out working his livestock in his shirtsleeves. Howard had often remarked that the love between Kerry Pearl and Max Schurgood was the greatest love affair he'd ever witnessed in his lifetime. They had a large family; one child came each year to their household. Max called them his "blessings" and they were indeed his blessings, as every one of them inherited Max's heavy bone structure and his boisterous qualities, except for Leota. Leota had been different and Max had always favored her.

Clare was not surprised to find Howard complaining of his father's ridicule in the letters in 1904. She read through them briefly and went on to a letter postmarked 1905.

July 6, 1905

Our dear Howard,

Max and I are indeed looking forward to your visit with us this fall. He's got that old mare you took a liking to last year all lined up for your transport back and forth to your daddy's place.

Max ran into your daddy in town a while back, by the way, and he gave our Max quite a talking-to about your staying with us on your visits home. Said it wasn't proper for you to be stayin' over here with us Catholics. He's an ornery old buzzard and it was all Max could do to keep from losing his temper. We realize that it's best for you that we try to stay on good terms with your daddy since he's paying your school fees out there in New Jersey.

The girls are all doing fine in school and the boys are already showing an interest in numbers. Horace is almost two now and he can hold up two fingers for his age just as pretty as you please.

Well, I've got some chores to attend to so I'll be saying so long for now. We'll see you in September.

Max says hello to you and for you to keep that scrappy mustache trimmed for the ladies. He's looking forward to you being around during harvesttime. He'll have to go to market down in Big Springs while you're here. Says it'll be a relief knowing you'll be lookin' out for me and his blessings while he's away.

Happy twenty-first birthday, by the way!

Love, Pearl

Clare smiled to herself as she replaced the letter into its tattered envelope. She went on to the next one from 1906.

January 20, 1906

Dear Howard,

I am writing this during the day while Max is out. He's gone to town for some supplies and won't be back until nightfall. We'll mail it next time we go into town for church services, which should be next Sunday.

I know now that I am with child again. I guess we'll never know if it is ours but there is that possibility.

I'm not ashamed of what happened between us while Max was away in Big Springs and he never has shown any anger over it himself. He says he loves us both too much to ever hold any grudges and we can't spend the rest of our lives crying over something that can't be changed. He is grateful that we never tried to cover up for what we'd done and that we told him right off what had happened.

You know that I love my Max with all of my heart. He's been a good husband to me and I will always remain totally devoted to his wishes.

He doesn't like to think that this baby might be yours. He says it's just another blessing for us and he won't allow me to talk about whether it's his or not. He intends to raise it as his own regardless of its heritage.

He said that if we lived in a city then maybe he'd be upset about you and me spending a night of physical pleasures together, but we're so isolated out here and when a man and a woman are placed in such situations then things just happen sometimes. Neither of us has forsaken your friendship. Max says if this baby is a boy, he's gonna name him Buford and if it's a girl, he's gonna name her Leota after his great aunt. He says we're all God's children.

I must be going now. Horace is out teasing those chickens again. I hope you can forgive me for my infidelity to Max. I do not regret it. The tornados and the big storm drove us together that night in November and had you been out in the barn in the loft you'd have been torn to pieces when that twister hit.

Max says our indiscretion saved your life and for that he thanks the good Lord.

Write us soon.

Your loving friend, Pearl

Clare dropped the letter on her desk. Its fragile pages made a crackling noise as they made contact with the hardwood surface. She took her glasses off and placed the end of one ear piece in her mouth as she contemplated what she'd just read. She leaned back into her chair and took a deep breath before reaching for the next letter with a 1906 postmark.

October 12, 1906

Dear friend Howard:

It is usually Pearl who writes you these endless letters but it is I this time who has the need to send my fond regards. Our daughter — I say ours because no one will ever know who is responsible for her birth — is a beautiful young baby.

Her eyes are turning from sky blue to blue-green and Pearl believes they will change again as she grows older. Horace is jealous of his pretty little sister, while my little Maggie carries her around like her own baby.

Your father helped at our barn raising last month. He
tells me you will finish your studies in economics in December.
Though he does not admit that it is so, Pearl and I can see he is
proud of his youngest son for finishing schooling. I intend to see
that all my blessings go to school as I did . . . though I could still
use lessons in English.

My crops were good this year. Pearl has been canning
from her garden for the past month. The woman is feeding the
whole county!

We wish to see you when you come home in the winter.
My hand of friendship reaches out to you in forgiveness and
understanding.

Sincerely,
Maxwell Schurgood

Clare continued reading through the letters until dawn. There was only the one letter from Max in the whole stack. From what Clare could gather with the one-sided correspondence, having nothing in the stack to indicate how Howard had felt about the situation, she assumed that the three friends had gone on to continue their friendship as though nothing had ever happened between Kerry Pearl and Howard.

She was astonished at how the three had handled the awkward situation. It must have been quite difficult for all of them, especially Max Schurgood, who had gone to his grave not knowing if his youngest daughter was his own flesh and blood. Howard had often made reference to the fact that Max had spoiled Leota shamelessly when she was a young girl. Clare had seen photos of Leota McFarland in Kerry's room and if ever there was a woman who could have the same features as Howard, Leota certainly was that woman. Of course, Clare had never seen any pictures of the other children so she felt she had no right to speculate that perhaps Leota was indeed Howard's daughter, and she was annoyed with herself for having read the letters at all.

There was a ten-year lag in the correspondence between Howard and Kerry Pearl. Clare assumed that Howard must have lost the letters. No more references were made in regards to Leota's parentage after the ten-year lag.

Clare removed the letters from the stack that contained the information about Howard's lifelong secret. She stood up in the early morning light of the gray dawn, searched her bookshelves, and finally pulled a thick volume of the collected works of John Keats. She opened the book to read the inscription on the front page: "To my lovely friend, Clare Friedman, I wish you a warm winter. — Howard Bates '52."

Clare turned the pages to "Ode to a Nightingale," placed the letters within, and closed the book. She climbed up on her chair and, standing on her tiptoes, made a space for the book on the top shelf.

Howard's secret would be safe with Clare for as long as she lived on the earth. The discovery of the letters would not take place until long after her death and that discovery would be made by Margaret English, who would in turn burn the letters and would not use that particular example of Clare's loyalty and character for her biography.

Margaret would come to know Leota quite well in the future years. Once she read the letters, there would be no doubt in her mind that Leota McFarland had indeed been the daughter of Howard Bates. She would share the secret with no one.

PUTTNAM LEANED his naked body against the window frame, pushing his hair out of his face with great sweeping movements and frowning at the morning sunshine coming in through the window. Margaret was just beginning to stir in the bed across the room. She rested on her elbow, gently brushing the sleep from her eyes, with her tussled auburn hair shadowing one side of her face.

"Good heavens, Putts, what are you doing standing butt-naked in front of the open window? You know that old lady next door would have a heart attack if she looked up and saw you," Margaret said, startling Puttnam. She reached out to him in a beckoning motion with her arm as he turned to face her. "What time is it, anyway?" she asked.

"It's almost seven. You better get movin' if you're hitting the road today. I'd rather you and Kerry not drive at night. It's hard to get a motel room after dark," Puttnam said, waving at someone out the window.

"Who are you waving at, Puttnam?" Margaret asked as she swung her legs over the side of the bed.

"That old lady next door. She's out hanging up her laundry. Come on over and give her a nice smile, Margaret," Puttnam said with a wink of mischief in his eyes. With two strides he was at Margaret's side, pulling her up and trying to make her go to the window naked.

"Puttnam, don't be silly. Stop this!" Margaret said in a loud whisper. Puttnam pulled her in front of the open window and when she finally stopped squirming long enough to look outside, she saw that the old woman's yard next door was empty, her clotheslines bare.

"Now see? Did you really think I would do something like that to that old woman? It's just another morning, babe," he whispered in her ear.

She felt him becoming aroused as he held her close. She was so miffed at the stunt he'd just played on her that she reached behind her and began to tickle him along his waist.

"Now, now, Margaret, it was just a little joke. You know I can't stand that!" Puttnam said as he backed away from her. He burst out with wild laughter as Margaret chased him around the room, threatening to tickle him again. When Margaret caught him, she reached out and pulled him close to her instead. She led him back to bed where they made love as though there would never be another time. The bedsprings cried out and the house shook from cellar to attic.

Clare was in the kitchen drinking coffee with Kerry. She still wore her bathrobe and slippers with her glasses balanced on the tip of her nose as she snapped the morning paper open. When the house began to rumble Clare rolled her eyes toward the ceiling and tapped Kerry on the arm. "Sounds like Puttnam's up and off to a good start this morning," Clare remarked in sarcasm.

Kerry wasn't quite awake yet; she hadn't noticed the house shaking at all. "Huh?" she asked, without looking up from her coffee.

"Oh, never mind. I've a feeling that comment was wasted on you this morning," Clare said, continuing to read the newspaper.

"Well, what were we talking about?" Kerry asked in a daze. She reached out and pushed the newspaper down in the center to get Clare's attention.

"I was referring to Margaret and Puttnam's morning escapades. You, my dear, hadn't yet chose to grace the world with words. How's your coffee?" Clare asked, smiling at Kerry.

"Oh, it's fine. I'm gonna miss your coffee," Kerry said as she stirred a spoon around and around in her cup.

"Well, I suppose you're all packed and ready to go?" Clare inquired, folding the newspaper in half. "Those bastards are bombing over there again," she added in reference to Vietnam.

"Yep, I'm all packed," Kerry said, worrying about her brother, Raleigh.

Clare got up from the table and walked to the sink to pour herself another cup of coffee. "I have some letters that your great-grandmother, Kerry Pearl, wrote to Howard over the years . . . I think you should take them back to your grandmother. That obit you wrote for *The Avalanche* was excellent. Perhaps you should take her a copy of that, or if you'd prefer, I'll send her one when the issue comes out next week," she said as she leaned into the refrigerator for the cream.

"Oh, that'd be great . . . she'd like that," Kerry said.

"Oh, good grief, Kerry. Which is it? Do you want me to send her the obit or do you want me to make a copy for you to take today?" Clare said, pouring the cream into her coffee, replacing the carton in the refrigerator, and kicking the door shut with her foot as she spun around to return to the table.

"I'm sorry, Clare. I guess I didn't answer you very well. I think it would be nice if you sent her the issue," Kerry replied just as Margaret came shuffling into the kitchen. Clare could hear the shower running upstairs.

"All packed, Miss English?" Clare asked, taking her seat beside Kerry.

"I've been packed for days. Puttnam's going to load the car when he gets out of the shower. Kerry, you should bring your things downstairs before he gets out. Are you ready to hit the trail?" Margaret asked cheerfully as she reached for a mug from the kitchen cabinet.

"Yep, I'm ready. I'll go up and get my stuff," Kerry said, pushing her chair back from the table.

"Kerry, I'm going to put those letters and Howard's cracker tin by the front door so you won't forget them. Margaret, don't you let her forget Howard," Clare called out.

Kerry smiled at Clare's good nature as she climbed the stairs to her room. She did not feel depressed about leaving until she passed the closed door to Howard's old room.

THE FIRST THING that Puttnam saw as he opened the trunk of the Pontiac was Howard's camp stool. His laughter burst out into the early morning stillness. He took the camp stool and placed it in the front seat so the two women would see it when they got in the car.

Kerry, Clare, and Margaret came out on the porch just as Puttnam was slamming the trunk lid closed. Kerry held the road atlas and wore clip-on sun shades over her glasses. Margaret carried the cracker tin and the small box of letters. Ernest came bounding up the sidewalk as they were preparing to get into the Pontiac. His head was tucked down toward the ground and his briefcase was swinging by his side. He was totally oblivious to what was happening in front of the house and he walked up to Clare, stopped in front of her, and shoved his glasses back up on the bridge of his nose.

A heat wave had taken over the normally mild weather for the past few days. They all stood by the Pontiac soaked with sweat. Ernest pointed to his briefcase and said, "Clare, we've got to get to work on these corrections. I just can't find the right angle for this story."

"You'll just have to wait a few minutes, Ernest. Can't you see that Margaret and Kerry are fixing to take off for Texas?" Clare said in response to his intrusion.

"Oh, hey, I didn't realize. So long, Foster! Margaret, you take care. Really, Clare, I do need to get to these things this morning. I want to take the afternoon off," Ernest said impatiently.

"Oh, Ernest, for God's sake, just go inside and wait in the office," Clare bellowed.

Ernest turned on his heels, seemingly nonplussed by Clare's outburst of anger. He grinned from ear to ear in joy over Kerry Foster's departure. He was surprised with himself for forgetting that it was today; he'd been looking forward to this for months. He knew he'd been right all along: she just couldn't hack it in the North. He stopped on the front porch and turned to wave goodbye to them.

Puttnam was leaning through the window on the driver's side kissing Margaret goodbye while Clare stood on the sidewalk with her arms folded across her chest. The engine started up with a roar and as they pulled away from the curb with Kerry's ponytail flying in the breeze out of the car window she yelled out, "Hey, Hinkle! Read a book someday!" and she flipped him her middle finger. Ernest laughed out loud, trotted down the sidewalk, and flipped his middle finger back at her. He stopped when he reached the street, opened his hand, and gave her a full, heartfelt wave goodbye.

Kerry watched Clare and Ernest turn to go back inside as they rounded the corner. Puttnam still stood in the street looking after them. His arm seemed to be in a permanent waving position over his head.

When the Pontiac disappeared from sight, Puttnam jammed his hands into the front pockets of his jeans and headed down to the main street to grab a beer. The sorrow in his blue eyes faded as the morning slipped by him, undisturbed by his laughter.

Kerry and Margaret had only been on the road for about ten minutes, both riding in silence with the hot breeze flowing into the car, when Kerry opened up the conversation.

"You know, Margaret, the only thing I regret about leaving is that

I never did get to go into New York. It's such a shame to have been so close for these past few months and to have never gone in to take a look around," Kerry said, resting her elbow on the window frame.

"Hey, that's right. I forgot that Puttnam, Howard, and I had planned to take you into the city sometime," Margaret said, turning onto the main highway.

"Have ya spent much time in the city?" Kerry asked.

"I went to school in the city and I lived there for a couple of years after I got my degree. My apartment was just a block away from where Ty's is now. I've gone in a few times since I've been at *The Avalanche* to stay over at Ty's on weekends. He's usually not there very much," Margaret said.

"Well, I guess I'll never get to see it. The city, I mean. Guess it'll just have to be one of those things I'll dream of getting to do someday. It's kind of weird to leave this neck of the woods without at least gettin' a glimpse of the lights," Kerry sighed as she pulled her elbow in and rolled the window up halfway.

"You've talked me into it," Margaret said, pulling off onto the shoulder.

"Talked you into what? I didn't know I was trying," Kerry said in confusion.

"We're going to the city! I'll find a phone and we'll call Ty and see if we can stay at his place tonight," Margaret said, turning to face Kerry and putting the car into park.

"You're crazy as hell. We can't go to the city! We've got to get on down to Dallas. We've only got three days, ya know. You've got plane reservations," Kerry said, surprised at Margaret's spontaneity.

"Reservations are changed day in and day out. How many chances will you and I get to do something like this? Pretty soon Puttnam and I will be lost to domesticity and you'll be off traveling the globe in search of the world's greatest story. Fuck it all, we're going," Margaret said with a chuckle, slapping the steering wheel with her hand.

"Oh, I don't know. It's so crazy. Isn't it dangerous to take the car into the city? It just won't seem right without Howard; he wanted to show me Manhattan," Kerry said.

"Well, your wish has come true: we've got Howard sitting right in the back seat," Margaret said as she made a U-turn in the highway and headed back to the last service station they'd passed. She pulled up in front of the phone booth and, slamming the car into park, she turned to Kerry. "I know a garage just around the corner from Ty's. It's expensive but we can afford it. You've got that pocketbook filled with dreams; you might as well spend some of them," she said in her soft voice and reached out to touch Kerry's cheek before she opened the car door.

Kerry watched her talking on the phone in the booth for several minutes. She couldn't believe the two of them were really going to New York City and could barely contain herself when Margaret climbed back into the Pontiac.

"Well, it's all set. Ty's planning to go hear a friend of his play and has invited us along. He's excited that he'll get to show you around," Margaret said as she headed down the highway, watching for the turnoff for 87.

The morning sky glistened above them in cloudless splendor. Margaret lit up a joint to celebrate as they flew down the highway doing seventy. The Catskill Mountains loomed around them and the trees shadowed the highway.

"There's lights beyond these woods, Margaret," Kerry cried out in happiness. She waved at every car they passed, grinning a broad, dimpled smile.

"You can bet your sweet ass there's lights out there," Margaret said, throwing her head back to laugh. "How you doing back there, Howard?" Margaret asked, then promptly gave an impersonation of Howard's reply: "It's a fine day to visit the city, by God." Her auburn hair flew around her face as they drove along.

Kerry giggled at Margaret's impersonation of Howard, rolled her window down, and screamed out into the air at the top of her lungs, "WAHOO!"

"GOD, I CAN'T BELIEVE we're here. Would ya look at all these people, all mashed up together, and the buildings? Good Lord, how did they build these places so close together like that? I always thought it was a lot more spread out than this. It looks much bigger in pictures. I guess I'm used to seeing Houston or Dallas," Kerry babbled on as they drove along the Hudson Parkway.

Margaret took them straight to Battery Park, found a place to park the Pontiac, and took Kerry by the hand, leading her to a place in the park filled with benches. It was the height of the tourist season and the park was filled with families and screaming children.

"Look over yonder," Kerry cried out in amazement. "It's the Statue of Liberty. I never knew it was green. Why is it green?" Kerry asked.

"Because it's made of copper. The elements cause it to do that," Margaret said, delighted with Kerry's reaction to the city.

> Not like the brazen giant of Greek fame,
> With conquering limbs astride from land to land;
> Here at our sea-washed, sunset gates shall stand
> A mighty woman with a torch, whose flame
> Is the imprisoned lightning, and her name
> Mother of Exiles. From her beacon-hand
> Glows world-wide welcome; her mild eyes command
> The air-bridged harbor that twin cities frame.
> "Keep, ancient lands, your storied pomp!" cries she
> With silent lips. "Give me your tired, your poor,
> Your huddled masses yearning to breathe free,
> The wretched refuse of your teeming shore.
> Send these, the homeless, tempest-tost to me,
> I lift my lamp beside the golden door!"

Kerry recited to Margaret as they stood looking out at the lady of the harbor.

"I can't believe you remember that whole sonnet, Kerry. Emma Lazarus would be proud," Margaret said. She was touched with Kerry's sentimental recital. "Let's go get a hot dog. It feels like the

Fourth of July around here," she said, turning to walk over to the hot dog stand.

The loudspeaker above them was announcing the time for the next ferry over to Liberty Island, first in English, then in several different languages. The families surrounding them in the park spoke in many different tongues. Kerry walked along beside Margaret in awe of the entire scene. She had hardly closed her mouth since they'd crossed the Tappan Zee Bridge.

It was getting late in the afternoon. Margaret had promised to meet Ty at the apartment around four. She and Kerry rushed back to the Pontiac, drove to the parking garage, and, strapping themselves with suitcases and Kerry's guitar, they headed over to Ty's apartment, which turned out to be on the sixth floor of the apartment building. The elevator was so small that Kerry got claustrophobic jammed into the small space with all their gear and a large sweaty man with a beagle dog, who proceeded to pee on Kerry's guitar case. The man merely cleared his throat and yanked the dog away from the guitar case while the beagle yelped as the tension on the leash yanked him off of the ground. The man got off on the third floor and as the door closed behind him, Margaret and Kerry burst out in laughter over the incident.

Margaret had buzzed Ty from downstairs and he was waiting in the doorway when they got off the elevator. The hallway was so dimly lit, Kerry felt like she was walking through an old movie set for a gangster film.

"You wouldn't believe what just happened to us, Ty. Some mutt just peed on my guitar case on the elevator," Kerry said as she stepped inside the apartment.

"So, you met our resident beagle, did ya?" Ty chuckled. "Just be glad it was your guitar case. How would you like to come in some morning sloshed to the gills and have that little mongrel pee on you? It has been known to happen more than once. You simply have to avoid boarding the elevator with him," Ty said, giving Margaret a hug and taking Kerry's guitar from her.

The apartment was a lot bigger than Kerry had imagined. She poked her head into the kitchen and then the living room, taking a look around. Ty was a slender man of about five feet eleven with soft, brown hair, blue eyes, and a heavy New York accent.

"Go ahead and make yourselves at home. I've got an appointment in about fifteen minutes. I'll leave the key to the front door downstairs and the key to the apartment on the kitchen counter. I'm gonna give ya my room tonight; I'll sleep out here on the sofa — that is, if any of us sleeps tonight," he said.

"Now, what's this fella's name we're going to hear tonight?" Kerry asked as Ty headed for the door. "Margaret here got so stoned in the car that she couldn't remember."

"Name's Phil Jesseps. I gave Ernest his last album to review in *The Avalanche*. Jerk never did write a review. You'll like him, he does sort of a country-blues-folk-type thing, writes his own stuff. Gotta go. See ya in a while, Tex. Welcome to the city," Ty said, kissing her cheek and hurrying out the door.

"I'd better call Puttnam and tell him where we are. Want to talk to him or Clare?" Margaret said as she picked up the wall phone in the kitchen.

"No thanks. I b'lieve I'll just sit here and listen to the city. It has so many sounds. It amazes me," Kerry said, sitting on the window seat in the living room. The windows were all open in the apartment and a hot breeze blew softly past her. The cacophonous roar of the street below drifted up to greet her ears. "Doesn't anyone have air-conditioning around here? How do they stand it?" Kerry asked, not really addressing anyone.

Margaret hung up the phone, walked quietly into the living room, and replied, "What did you say, Kerry? I didn't hear you. I was still on the phone."

"Oh, nothin'. Not really anything at all. You know, I think I'll just sit right here and watch the lights come on in the streets," Kerry said in a sigh.

"Well, if you don't mind, I think I'll take a short nap. Looks like it's going to be a long night. Puttnam said to tell you to live it up 'cuz there's only one first time in New York City. The next time you come it won't shine quite as bright," Margaret said gaily.

Kerry sat transfixed in the window until darkness overtook her. Her eyes had followed every movement in the street below and she had watched the streetlights come on. One of them on the corner had flickered briefly before coming to life. She turned to gaze into the darkened room, remembering that Fletcher had come to New York before leaving for London. She pondered the thought in sorrow that once again they had not shared one of life's greatest thrills. They had experienced it separately and she longed to know of his impressions — though, in truth, even if they had come here together they would still have had separate feelings.

"WELL, THIS IS CERTAINLY a refreshing way to spend an evening, watching two hearts mend," Ty said, stirring his drink with a plastic swizzle stick and winking at Margaret. Kerry stood talking with Phil Jesseps at the bar of the dimly lit nightclub.

"What do you mean, watching two hearts mend?" Margaret asked softly. She sipped her red wine and looked around the room. It was a small nightclub. Phil Jesseps had just finished his last set and loud rock and roll was blasting from the speakers mounted above the small stage. The bartender was barking last call to the patrons.

"I heard from Ernest that Kerry's boyfriend dumped her. Even if I hadn't heard that I woulda noticed the sparkle in her eye tonight. She's usually so dead serious and somber. Phil's been having hard times lately . . . his wife left 'im back in April," Ty said, motioning to the waitress for another round of drinks. "I was thinking of asking Phil and a couple of others over for a nightcap at my place. Little going-away present for the two a' ya," he added.

A heavy cloud of smoke lingered in the emptying club, the lighting cast a red glow on the hardwood floors, and the sound of clinking glasses as the tables were cleared surrounded the table where Margaret and Ty sat, both occasionally sneaking glances at Kerry and Phil.

"I don't know. Kerry might suspect that we're trying to play matchmaker here and I certainly never had that thought. Such matters are better left to take their own course," Margaret sighed. Her friendship with Ty had spanned many years and she understood that he would no doubt do as he pleased, regardless of her advice. "Who knows, Ty? Perhaps they have already made plans for the remainder of the evening," Margaret added with a chuckle.

"Yeah, well, I'm gonna ask 'em over anyway," Ty said, pushing his chair back from the table.

"Somehow, I knew you were going to say that, Ty Gallagher," Margaret mumbled, finishing off the last of her wine before starting in on the new glass Ty had ordered for her.

Ty turned around as he was leaving the table and flashed her a smile. The contrast of his brown hair and aqua-blue eyes was quite striking. Margaret recalled a time several years before when she and Ty had made an attempt at dating one another. Margaret had been the one to call it quits, claiming the relationship interfered with her work. It hadn't; it had actually been a welcome departure . . . it had simply been a time in her youth when courtship threatened her solitude and Margaret felt that a poet could not survive without that sacred wall of solitude between her and any lover. Ty had the uncanny ability of reading her innermost thoughts, which made him more appealing to her as a friend she could separate with distance, for she could not tolerate such a lack of privacy with a lover. She sipped her wine pensively, enjoying her thoughts alone and treasuring the love she now held for Puttnam, who could enter her solitude without disrupting the calm she found there. He had, in fact, become a part of her privacy.

Phil Jesseps and Kerry were the same height. He was slender of frame; had dark brown, wavy hair; a straight, prominent nose; and wore rimless gold-framed glasses shadowed by heavily expressive brows above them. He had a thick mustache, a pleasing smile, high cheekbones, and a squared chin. His hair, which was cut bluntly around his neckline and just to the top of his ears on the side, was full and disheveled on top as though he'd spent the evening running his fingers through it. It parted naturally on the side with a kick of a few stray strands standing on end in defiance. He was not exactly handsome but he had a wonderful sense of humor and a pleasingly gentle disposition. The combination of these added to the intensity of his heavily lashed dark eyes, the complexity of his music, and his finely sculptured hands made him most attractive.

He stood leaning against the bar with one sneaker-clad foot perched on the footrail. He wore a tweed sports coat with a pale-blue long-sleeve shirt underneath and a pair of loose-fitting faded Levi's blue jeans. He held a shot of whiskey in one hand and a cigarette in the other as Kerry bent close to him in conversation. Ty was disappointed to find them discussing trends in popular music as he extended his arms around the two of them, drawing them closer to his sides and knocking Kerry a little off-balance.

"Who wants to adjourn this gathering over to my place for a nightcap?" Ty asked, turning his head back and forth between Kerry and Phil. His blue eyes sparkled with gaiety.

"I gotta get paid first, Ty. Might be awhile before I can get over there," Phil said sharply, irritated with Ty for interrupting his conversation with Kerry, who chose to duck out from under Ty's arm and head back over to the table where Margaret still sat nursing her glass of wine. She glanced over her shoulder once to find the two men head-to-head in discussion.

She plopped herself down in the chair Ty had vacated next to Margaret, took a sip of Margaret's wine, and asked for a cigarette. "Boy, Ty's a little looped, don't 'cha think?" Kerry said, a little wobbly herself as she balanced the cigarette in her fingers. She was dressed in a faded jean skirt and white peasant blouse, blue opaque stockings, and her worn penny loafers. She'd started out the evening with her hair hanging loose to her waist, but as the evening had worn on and the wine had flowed, she had twisted the ends into a braid and tied it with a piece of red ribbon. The braid now draped over her shoulder, falling just below her small breast.

"I think I'm a bit looped myself, but I've had a wonderful time, just sitting here listening to the music. I wouldn't have traded this trip into the city for anything. Ty wants to have a few people over to celebrate our trip to Texas. I hope I can stay awake. The city, actually just this city, is so full of life, so full of energy and excitement. Do you feel it?" Margaret asked, seeking out Kerry's eyes in the smoky midnight air of the bar.

"What I think I feel is some sorta infatuation with the night: with Phil Jesseps' music, and the city . . . maybe the city just makes that more intense," Kerry whispered, taking a drag from the cigarette and grinning at Margaret. She reached out to push Margaret's heavy auburn hair away from her eyes, just as her grandmother Leo used to push her own bangs out of her eyes.

"Infatuation, is it? Looked a bit like lust to me," Margaret teased, the dimples in her ivory cheeks deepened with the flash of her smile. She wore the laced camisole Puttnam had given her beneath a soft, ruffle-sleeved cotton blouse tucked into a pair of corduroy jeans she'd borrowed from Kerry. The wine had tinted her full lips to a light red.

"Lust? What's lust? It's been so long that I've forgotten what it feels like," Kerry replied, briefly relaxing her smile.

"Let's go see if we can jog your memory, my dear. If you have forgotten the feeling, then it's been too long since you've felt it and it's high time you reacquainted yourself with life's greatest distraction," Margaret said, grabbing Kerry's hand as they both stood up from the table.

Kerry unsteadily clutched Margaret's arm as they approached the bar. She whispered softly into Margaret's ear, "I've never been with anyone but Fletcher. I don't think I've got the hang of this lust bizness. What would I say to this guy? I don't know him."

"Oh, that'll be the easy part, my dear. You'll find lots of things to talk about. You see, he doesn't know you either," Margaret answered, snatching her wineglass back from Kerry.

"Well, that's a helluv an answer," Kerry slurred, as she and Margaret stopped just behind Ty and Phil at the bar.

Ty had a plan worked out for Margaret to go back to his place with him and one of the waitresses while Kerry stayed behind to wait for

Phil to get paid. Kerry longed to see the clubs where her childhood hero, Carolyn Hester, had played, and Phil promised to take her by the clubs on the way over to Ty's.

Margaret reluctantly surrendered to the tug of her arm by Ty when he was ready to leave. She turned to wink at Kerry as she walked out the door.

Kerry felt so alone standing at the dark bar at closing time, waiting for Phil to emerge from the office door behind the bar. The barroom was empty except for the bartender, who was busy washing down the bar. The smoke was clearing and as she stared at the rows of alcohol lining the mirror in the back of the bar, she thought of Wiley. Of how he'd closed the bar where she'd played on Sunday nights: sweeping the broken glass from the floors; waking up old drunks and helping them to the door; changing the marquee outside; barking out at Kerry, who always sat at the end of the bar watching him work, to get off her ass and pack up a six for them to take back to the house. Those were known nights for Kerry, nights of no surprises, nights of endless conversation till dawn with Wiley and Lensel. She wondered if she would ever be that comfortable again, if she would ever be that open again, for she had felt so lost in the North and though she was returning to Texas, she would not be going home. Maturity was creeping up on her, building walls around her heart and extending caution into her actions.

Her thoughts were stilled and her heart began to pound as Phil Jesseps came out of the office carrying his guitar case. He waved goodbye to the club manager over his shoulder and nodded in Kerry's direction for her to follow him.

He shuffled the guitar case from between them as they stepped out onto the sidewalk and, taking her hand, they walked in silence along MacDougal Street. It was early for the city and the streets were full of life. Kerry glanced occasionally to her side at Phil's profile and he in turn would risk a look in her direction.

Phil took her by a few clubs, most of which had changed their names since the early sixties when Dylan and Hester had haunted their stages. Most no longer hosted folk music as entertainment. They rounded a corner on the narrow streets and Kerry's eyes lit up when she saw the marquee on Third Street for GERDE'S FOLK CITY. Kerry could hear the smooth sound of acoustic music coming from within and she stopped to look at their calendar, which was posted in the front window.

Phil broke their long silence. "You wanna go inside?" he asked.

"Yeah, let's go in," Kerry replied.

The doorman knew Phil and they slipped by him into the bar area, which was a narrow room that opened up to the concert hall in the rear of the club. It was much smaller than Kerry had ever imagined it to be, and probably the most famous of all the folk music clubs in New York City. The walls were lined with framed photos of performers who'd played to quiet, attentive crowds over the years. She became enchanted with examining the photographs on the walls in the bar area while Phil leaned his guitar case against the bar and spoke softly with the bartender.

Kerry located Carolyn Hester's photograph on the wall. It looked as though it had been taken sometime in the early sixties and Kerry smiled fondly at the picture, thinking of her chance meeting with Hester and of her sister Ethel. Phil strolled up beside her and cautiously placed his arm lightly around her shoulder.

"You've heard her before?" he asked, biting down on his lower lip.

"She's from Texas. I met her once, oh, it was a long time ago. She sings like an angel. In fact, my sister, Ethel, would trade her last pint of vodka to be a-standin' in my shoes right now. We idolized Carolyn Hester. Ethel taught me how to play her songs on the guitar and we used to sing along with the records. This is really somethin', being in this place. Must be a thousand ghosts in these walls . . . what stories they could tell," Kerry sighed, still staring at the photograph.

As they left Gerde's Folk City, Kerry reached out for Phil's hand. "How far is it back to Ty's place?" she asked, her voice startling Phil with its crisp Texas edge.

"It's several blocks from here. Think you can make it?" he asked, closing his hand around hers.

"Oh, it's not that I'm tired or anything. It's just that I've never been in a New York City cab before. I'd kinda like to give it a spin. Might never get another chance," Kerry said in excitement, as the warm summer breeze rustled the papers in the streets.

"You're kidding. You've never been in a cab before?" Phil asked, stopping on the sidewalk to face Kerry.

"Nope," she replied with a grin.

Phil hailed a cab for them, gave the driver Ty's address, and settled in next to Kerry with his guitar case resting between his knees and his arm secured around her shoulders. Kerry rested her head on his shoulder for a few moments and, feeling awkward, she jerked her head up and gazed out at the crowded streets of Greenwich Village.

Sensing her nervousness, Phil reached out to touch her hair and said softly, "Showing you around these streets has made all these joints seem new again. I've admired your columns in *The Avalanche* for quite some time . . . it's funny that you're here now, that I'm meeting you when you're on your way back to Texas. I felt as if I'd come to know you from your writing. I'd been wanting to meet you."

"That's a wonderful thing to say. Your music touched my heart. I wish Ty had brought your album to me to review. Don't 'cha ever play Caffè Lena's?" Kerry asked, turning to face Phil.

He smiled back at her as the flash of streetlamps lit their faces. "I'm booked up there next month," he said.

"Well, dadgummit it all, you make me wanna turn around and head right back to Saratoga Springs," Kerry said cheerfully, placing her head back on Phil's shoulder.

Phil laughed softly at her honesty. "As long as you're not goin' tonight," he mumbled.

"This it, buddy?" the cab driver barked out as they pulled up in front of Ty's building.

Phil fished the right amount out of his pocket as Kerry stood on the sidewalk holding his guitar case. They stopped by the mailboxes just inside the entrance of the building and Kerry buzzed Ty's apartment for him to open the front door to the building. Kerry was amused by Margaret's voice coming out of the speaker and when Margaret barked, "Who's there?" Kerry lightheartedly replied, "Howard!" at which Margaret chuckled loudly and the front door jumped open a crack with a loud buzz.

When the elevator doors opened up in the lobby, Kerry stuck her head inside and looked around before entering.

"What are you doing?" Phil asked.

"Makin' sure there's not any beagle dogs who pee on innocent guitar cases in this elevator," Kerry replied, stepping inside the empty elevator and extending her hand toward Phil, who shook his head and followed her in. Talk of someone named Howard and urinating beagle dogs had him somewhat confused.

Thoughts of confusion left him somewhere between the second and third floors as he chanced embracing Kerry and kissing her softly on the lips. Kerry could hear the soft echo of his voice in song in her mind as she returned his embrace before the elevator door opened and, to Kerry's embarrassment, the fat man with his beagle dog stood facing him. She jumped back from Phil's arms in alarm.

"Goin' down?" the man asked bluntly.

"Goin' up," Phil replied, reaching over to press the button for the door to close.

When the door had closed and they were in motion again, Phil laughed out loud in his light, easy voice. "How did you know we'd meet some goddamned beagle dog on the elevator?" he asked, bending down to grab his guitar.

"Some things are just downright inevitable," Kerry said, folding her hands in front of her and rolling back on her heels. The door opened on Ty's floor and as they came out of the elevator Margaret threw the door open to Ty's apartment to welcome them inside.

Ty greeted them with a glass of red wine for Kerry and a shot of whiskey for Phil. A Doc Watson album was playing on the stereo and a few people sat around Ty's living room smoking pot and listening to the music.

"Let's get some live music going around here," Ty said. He brought Kerry her guitar. She sat in the open window, away from the marijuana smoke which filled the living room. Margaret came to sit next to her while Phil unpacked his guitar from its case. Kerry cradled her guitar in her lap, tuning the strings.

"What did you want to hear, Margaret?" Kerry asked nervously. She hadn't played for strangers in several months and Phil's music had been so beautiful that Kerry suffered from a loss of self-confidence.

"Play that traditional song, 'I Never Will Marry,' and I'll sing with you," Margaret replied in response to Kerry's uneasiness.

Phil pulled up a chair next to Kerry and Margaret. He reached over and plucked one of Kerry's guitar strings in order to tune his guitar to hers. "What key ya doin' this in?" he asked her while tuning up.

"D," Kerry replied, dropping her eyes to the floor. Margaret jabbed her with an elbow and Kerry began to play the song. Phil was not far behind in joining her on guitar and Kerry watched in amazement as his fingers flew like lightning across the neck of his guitar. Margaret had an alto singing voice, which blended nicely in harmony with Kerry's soprano. Kerry sang the first traditional verse alone and Margaret joined in on the chorus. The three of them made up verses to the rest of the song as they went along.

One mornin' I rambled down by the seashore
The wind it did whistle, the water did roar
I heard some fair maiden give a pitiful cry
It sounded so lonely, as it swept off on high,

Kerry sang on the first verse while Phil and Margaret joined in on the chorus:

Oh, I never will marry, I'll be no man's wife
I intend to live single all the days of my life,

they sang. Margaret took the second verse in her deep, mellow voice:

No, I won't change my name, dear, I like it just fine
It's one of the few things that I can call mine,

Margaret sang, throwing her head back and giggling shyly when she'd finished. Kerry and Phil played an instrumental break after the chorus, then Phil took a verse.

> *Love is an anchor in rough rolling seas*
> *I dream of the harbor where the waters are stilled,*

his voice rang with a conversational tone, which carried a low resonance that tingled Kerry's spine. Ty, the waitress from the nightclub, and the other couple at the party boisterously joined in on the next chorus, gaily toasting each other with their drinks in praise of being single. Kerry took the last verse.

> *Though my life on the highway leaves me weary and pale*
> *It's the love of the music keeps the wind in my sails,*

Kerry sang in her high, clear voice. They all sang the last chorus with gusto while Kerry was lost in the beauty of the guitar leads Phil played. She watched his hands fly across the strings, in awe of the grace they held. He, in turn, had watched Kerry's hands and felt the same awe for her long, tapered fingers. He searched her voice for the heart within and found himself lost to its qualities, for it reached out to him with the warmth of outstretched arms or the kiss of warm lips upon his.

Kerry did not think of Fletcher when the song ended, and as she lifted her eyes to meet Phil's, she instead thought of Howard's words to her out on Clare's front porch. Sure enough, she did feel her heart waken and her memories of Fletcher stilled while her body began to stir. She was surprised, pleasantly so, by her response to this stranger, whose eyes were filled with questions and mystery. They were, after all, both writers, both seekers and observers. Neither was blessed with the art of completing a successful one-night stand; they were too obsessed with searching hearts for reason. Kerry lifted her wineglass to her lips and drained the glass of its contents. She excused herself and walked to the kitchen for more wine while Phil played a bluesy instrumental piece on guitar.

Margaret followed her into the kitchen. "What's wrong, Kerry? You seemed so sad there for a moment," Margaret asked, filling their glasses.

"Oh, I dunno. I just don't know how to be a date with someone I may never see again. I think I look too deeply into people's eyes . . . it makes it difficult to just have a passing acquaintance," Kerry whispered. "I mean, I just don't know how to lay down next to someone I've never touched before, someone who's never held me in the night. This is like some sort of maiden voyage and I'm lost at sea," she sighed, leaning against the kitchen counter, cradling her wineglass in both hands.

"Well, you just have to remember to keep all hands on deck," Margaret chuckled, reaching out to touch Kerry's cheek with warm fingertips.

"Oh, now that's a disgusting thing to say, Margaret. Haven't you ever had to face this fear of being with someone you don't know?" Kerry said with a grin.

Margaret replaced the cork in the wine bottle and, turning to face Kerry, she replied, "No, I haven't ever had to face this dilemma. I've always been too shy to reach out to strangers when they turn my head. I've probably missed a lot of nice things in life because of that."

"Well, then just why the hell am I standin' in here taking advice from you if you've never been through this torture before?" Kerry laughed.

"Because you love me, and you want me to tell you he's very nice and give you some sort of consent. I can tell you he is nice and he is handsome and he writes wonderful lines and plays guitar beautifully, but I can't give you consent. That's your choice," Margaret said softly.

Kerry and Margaret heard the front door close in the apartment and Ty stuck his head in the kitchen to announce his departure. "I'm gonna run Barb over to her place. With any luck at all, I won't be back tonight, but just in case I'm taking the keys. If I don't see ya in the morning, have a safe trip. Write me," he said, winking at the two women and, reaching out to touch Margaret's hand that cupped her wineglass, he added, "I'm gonna miss the hell outta ya."

Kerry and Margaret went back to the living room with their wine. Kerry brought the whiskey from the kitchen and filled Phil's glass. The couple who had been sitting on Ty's couch had left while they were in the kitchen.

The three of them sat in the living room discussing Ty's wild disposition and Kerry and Margaret's work at *The Avalanche*. Conversation shifted to Phil and his life in the music scene in New York. Kerry loved to hear him speak; he had a very soothing, soft voice in conversation.

They exchanged stories for an hour. Margaret got up to go to the kitchen at three A.M. hoping to find more wine. When Margaret left the room, silence fell between Kerry and Phil. He stood up, stretched his arms, and picked up his guitar, which was leaning against the edge of the sofa. He walked across the room, opened his guitar case, and placed the guitar gently inside. As he snapped the latches closed on the case he said, "Well, sure has been nice spending the evening with you . . . guess I'd better hit the road for home."

"Do you have to go?" Kerry asked nervously. She sat cross-legged on the couch with her hands clasped firmly in her lap, anchoring her skirt.

"No, not really. I'm used to greeting the morning light. I just live a block away." He gazed into Kerry's hazel eyes and sat down in the chair across the coffee table from her. He reached into his shirt pocket and pulled out a cigarette, lit it with his lighter, blew the smoke out slowly, and rested his elbows on his knees. He ducked his head down slightly and toyed with his lighter in his hand while scratching his head with the hand that held the lit cigarette. "You sure do sing pretty," he said shyly.

"Thanks. Ya don't do so bad yourself," Kerry replied. She reached up and untied the ribbon in her hair, placing it on the coffee table, and ran her fingers through the ends of her hair, untangling the braid.

Phil watched as she shook her head and her hair cascaded around her shoulders. "Um . . . you wanna make love?" Phil asked in a mumbled tone. He ducked his head back down and took a drag of his cigarette.

Kerry stopped untangling her hair, disbelieving what she thought she'd just heard him ask. "What?" she said softly. She looked across the table at Phil, watching him exhale the smoke from his cigarette.

"Um ... do you wanna make love? I mean, I know we just met, but I feel like I've known you for a while through your writing. I sorta got this feeling that you wanted to," Phil said quietly.

"Yep," Kerry said vibrantly, unscrambling her legs and placing both feet on the floor, resting the palms of her hands on her knees.

"What does 'yep' mean?" Phil grinned, looking over to Kerry.

Margaret was just about to come back into the living room when she overheard the conversation from the hallway. She rolled her blue eyes toward the ceiling and retreated back into the kitchen with her wine. She didn't want to intrude on their privacy but Ty's apartment left her only the choice of the bathroom or the kitchen in which to stay out of the way — she certainly didn't want to be in the bedroom at this point.

"Yep means I'd like to make love with you, although I have to warn you, I feel awfully clumsy at this. I'm liable to be quite a disappointment," Kerry said in a breathy voice. The excitement within her made it difficult for her to catch her breath. Her heart pounded so loudly within her breast that she thought Phil could probably hear its beat across the table.

"I seriously doubt that you could disappoint me. I'm a clumsy fool myself," Phil said, standing up and reaching for Kerry's hand across the table.

They walked into the hallway hand in hand. Kerry noticed Margaret leaning against the counter in the kitchen as they passed by. Margaret was nursing her glass of wine and trying to avoid eye contact with Kerry, who stopped in the doorway.

"Good grief, Margaret, you're getting as bad as my sister, Ethel. How much wine are you a-gonna drink tonight?" Kerry teased, shaking a finger at her friend and winking openly at her.

"I assume the sofa is up for grabs now," Margaret replied, toasting Kerry and Phil with her wineglass as she waltzed past them, heading for the living room.

The bedroom was lit only by the pale moonlight shining through the windows. Sounds drifted up from the streets as Phil lit a candle on Ty's dressing table. Kerry stood beside him with her hand resting softly on his sleeve as he withdrew the lighter from the flame of the candle.

"Smells like it might rain in a while," Phil whispered into Kerry's ear, which put chill bumps on her arms.

"With all these smells in this city, how can you tell if one of them is rain on the way?" Kerry asked, laughing softly.

"Oh, I dunno. I guess when you grow up here, you learn to separate such things," Phil said, helping Kerry pull her blouse over her head. She draped the blouse on the back of a chair and returned to Phil, reaching out to unbutton his shirt with nimble fingers. He grasped one of her hands lightly and lifted it to his lips. "You are very lovely," he said softly, racing Kerry's heart.

They separated for a few moments to finish undressing, occasionally glancing at one another. Kerry giggled quietly when once they happened to look back at each other at the same time.

Kerry folded the comforter back on the queen-size bed and slipped modestly between the cool sheets. Phil climbed in beside her and slipped his arm beneath her head, drawing her toward him. They talked softly for a while, gently touching each other and acquainting themselves with the texture of one another's skin. Kerry felt awkward holding his slender body close to her own, as she had only known the solid, muscular frame of Fletcher in her past. The newness of Phil's light touch upon her breasts, as skilled as his touch on the strings of his guitar, surprised and delighted her as she pressed her lips to the nape of his neck and ran her fingers over the fine hair on his chest. She met his lips with her own, taking comfort from the warmth of his breath and the feel of his moist tongue against her lips. The taste of his tongue was pleasingly tinged with whiskey and Kerry returned his kiss passionately.

Both were quiet lovers. Their lithe bodies fit together perfectly and the rhythm of their two bodies blended in harmony, yet Kerry became distracted in listening to Phil's breathing and the taste of his scented warmth to her lips. The sensations filled her heart as she moved beneath him and even though she did not achieve her own orgasm, she sighed deeply when Phil met his and stroked the soft, damp hair on the back of his head, feeling her own sense of ecstasy within the rise and fall of his chest against her breasts and the pounding of his heart above her, alternating beats with her own. She felt his velvet warmth within her and held him tightly against her.

Phil lifted himself up on one elbow, gazed down into her eyes, gently pushed her hair back from her face, and said, "I told you I was a clumsy fool. It was too soon for you, wasn't it?"

"No, I don't think it was too soon. It was just too new and I was enjoying just the warmth of your skin against mine. I think it takes a lot of practice for my body to take over and relax just to achieve an end," Kerry replied, looking up at Phil with her cheeks flushed to rose.

They held each other in the morning air, still laced in darkness, as rain began to fall outside. Phil fell asleep with his head buried in Kerry's long, fragrant hair. Kerry turned to face him, watching his eyes in slumber, wondering if he was dreaming as she reached out to pull the sheet up over his shoulders.

She carefully pulled her hair from beneath his head, slipped from the bed, and walked over to the open window where the rain fell softly outside. She felt a bit lonely for Fletcher as she watched the rain. The streetlights glowed, with the rain creating an artificial rainbow for a halo around them.

Half awake, Phil reached out for Kerry and finding her not there, he opened his eyes to see her silvered silhouette in the window. He admired her small waist, the soft curve of her hips, and her long, slender legs before speaking. His voice shattered the stillness of the early morning and Kerry jumped at the sound.

"Can't you sleep?" he asked, resting on his elbow.

"I just wanted to see the city streets in the rain. It's nice, sort of washes them clean. Makes them new again," Kerry said, turning to face him.

"Well, maybe we should get in a little more practice over here," Phil said, smiling at Kerry and reaching a hand out for her to join him.

Kerry laughed softly and went back to bed. They made love again, this time with a mutual ending. Dawn found them asleep with their limbs entwined and their faces close together on the same pillow.

THE LAST FULL BLOSSOMS of summer stood laughing along the Blue Ridge Parkway with their petals sheltered from the hot winds of August by cool green foliage as the miles slipped lazily beneath the fat treaded tires of the 1967 baby blue Pontiac, which seemed to float along on the haze above the black, two-laned asphalt on its first journey south. Kerry was behind the wheel with her snap-on shades clipped to her glasses while Margaret sat beside her studying the road map. The wind roared in through the open windows of the car, snapping the edges of the road map in loud, crackling noises. It was mid-morning and the shadows across the tree-lined parkway created the effects of late evening.

"So, you going to write him?" Margaret asked, folding the road map carefully and placing it in the glove compartment.

"Who?" Kerry asked, still lost to her own daydreams. "I promised Howard that I wouldn't write to Fletcher for a while. I'm still too hurt over the whole thing to write," Kerry said.

"I wasn't talking about Fletcher; I know you're not going to write to him. I was referring to Phil. He wouldn't have left his address with me when he left the apartment yesterday if he didn't want you to keep in touch," Margaret said, wiping off the lenses of her sunglasses with the tail of her blue denim work shirt.

"I dunno. I don't really feel like getting anything started up right now. Maybe," Kerry said.

"Well, I think he's a nice man. I wouldn't want him to think that I didn't give you that note with his address when you got up," Margaret said.

"He shouldn't have left like that. He should've woken me up

before he left. It scared me when I woke up alone in such a strange place," Kerry said, juggling a can of Coke in her hand against the steering wheel. She had not been driving for very long and it still felt strange to her to be behind the wheel.

"Oh, for Chrissakes, Kerry. It was nine in the morning. He had an appointment with his booking agent. You're so hard on people sometimes. I think it was most kind of him not to wake you. You slept till noon, ya know. Don't know why you would've been scared in broad daylight. Nope, I think you're just looking for excuses so you can stay all wrapped up in that little shell of yours," Margaret said, smiling a toothy smile at Kerry.

"Look who's talking about shells. Besides, it's comfortable in this shell. But, just to put your mind at ease, I think he's a nice man, too. He made me feel warm again. So, I'll write him. I'll tell him you gave me his note. I wouldn't want to be accused of being heartless," Kerry replied, with the beginning of a smile crossing her face.

Margaret toyed with the cuffs of her shorts, watching the scenery pass by. "Virginia is lovely, isn't it? Takes my breath away. I'm glad we took the parkway instead of the interstate, but I guess we'd better try to reconnect with 81 somewhere near Roanoke if we're going to get in some good mileage today," Margaret said over the roar of the wind.

"How far do you want to go today?" Kerry said.

"Oh, I don't know. I feel pretty good. Thought we might make it to Nashville tonight," Margaret replied.

"That's nine hours away, Margaret. Puttnam told me he asked you not to travel at night. Sure you want to try to get that far?" Kerry asked, glancing sideways at Margaret.

"Yeah, I'm sure. I don't see Puttnam anywhere in this car, do you?" Margaret chuckled.

"Nope. B'lieve I'd have noticed if he was. Looks like it's just you and me riding this southern road," Kerry laughed.

"I think I'll name my firstborn Virginia, for this beautiful state and the state of mind of Virginia Woolf. The sound of her name will always call forth remembrance," Margaret sighed.

"What if your firstborn's a boy?" Kerry giggled.

"Smart-ass. I'll name him Tennessee, since that's the next state down the road. He'll be a playwright like Tennessee Williams," Margaret said huskily.

"You're as silly as hell this mornin'," Kerry said, shaking her head. "I bet by the time your firstborn comes along, you'll have forgotten all about these names you've cooked up for 'em," she added.

"Never underestimate the memory of a poet, my dear. What's the bet?" Margaret asked, trying to tame her auburn hair while the wind whipped it from her fingers.

"Oh, I dunno. It's gonna be your ankle-biters running around with those names. You set the stakes," Kerry replied.

"I'll bet you one letter to Phil Jesseps," Margaret said, reaching over to tap Kerry on the shoulder.

"Oh, come on. Would you forget about that?" Kerry winced.

"One letter or no bet," Margaret said, leaning back in the seat and propping her feet up on the dashboard.

"One letter it is," Kerry sighed in defeat.

"So nice of you to agree on the stakes. You won't have too long to remember. Puttnam and I want to have a little one this year," Margaret said with a grin.

"This year? What about your job? What about Puttnam's job — the one he doesn't have yet?" Kerry asked, in surprise.

"It won't affect my job. Puttnam's going to raise the children. We've agreed. He's the one who wants to have children the most and I wouldn't make a good full-time parent. Loud noises bother me," Margaret replied.

"But, how will you support an entire family on your salary?" Kerry asked.

"Oh, we've got it worked out. I have this small inheritance from my grandmother. Puttnam wants to use it to open a music club in Houston. Nothing extravagant, just a small club with acoustic and blues acts," Margaret said. "He says it should go over well there — especially since he'll have your support at the newspaper," she chuckled.

"It's a good thing you're a poet. You'd never make it in the secretarial pool — you dream too much," Kerry said, clamping her hands firmly on the steering wheel with her can of Coke resting between her knees.

"We all dream. Even secretaries dream, even if it's just about who they're going to jump in the sack with at the next company picnic. Right now the only thing this poet dreams of is food. Let's get the hell off this scenic route, back to civilization. Let us weave to and fro amidst the crowded lanes of lonesome dreamers on the interstate and find a diner where we can indulge ourselves in the splendor of a juicy hamburger," Margaret said, waving her hands dramatically in the air.

"You've gone mad out here, Margaret," Kerry laughed, searching for road signs along the side of the road.

"I have never strapped myself into the binding chains of sanity. Sanity is boring," Margaret said with a soft laugh.

"Yep, it sure is. But then I don't think anyone's really sane. They just play the game to avoid a padded cell somewhere. You and I will never have to play that game," Kerry said.

The two women traveled across the south trading philosophies, exchanging laughter, and solving every problem in the universe, from urban traffic to world hunger. Margaret's smoking habit was passed on to Kerry during their trip. They drank wine late into the night, smoking cigarettes and watching all-night movies in their motel rooms.

Neither of them would ever forget their trip across the country. It would grow in their hearts like a child's memory of their first trip to the circus. They shared their last motel room in Texarkana. Margaret bought a bottle of champagne, which they drank out of the plastic cups provided by the motel for water. They toasted their travels with laughter, Margaret in her soft, deep chuckle and Kerry in her light, airy giggles. No mile was wasted between them, for they both had traveled those miles with their eyes wide open to the world.

Kerry's heart began to sink as she turned into the parking lot of Dallas Love Field. The temperature was up over a hundred degrees that day in Dallas. The two struggled with Margaret's suitcases as they worked their way through the crowds to the ticket counter.

Kerry stayed with Margaret until her plane was called over the loudspeakers. They sat in silence at that gate, Kerry pondering her long drive to Floydada and Margaret dreaming about her new life in Houston.

Kerry waved goodbye to Margaret as she filed into the corridor with the other passengers. Margaret turned to wink at her with a tear resting on her cheek.

"So long. Have a safe flight," Kerry called after her.

"See you in Houston," Margaret replied over her shoulder as she disappeared into the hallway leading to the plane.

Kerry walked back to the Pontiac brushing the tears from her face. She placed Howard's cracker tin in the front seat beside her, pretending he was her traveling companion, and drove west on Highway 287, picking up the smaller Highway 70 in the town of Vernon. It took her seven hours to get to Floydada. The flat land between was a harsh contrast from the terrain she had passed through with Margaret. The mesas stood alone on the prairies in undisturbed solitude. They were the towers Kerry had written about in her song for Howard. The colors at sunset cast an eerie glow across the flatland. Kerry pulled over to the side of the road to watch the highway turn into a ribbon of gold in the distance before her as the sun went down between the mesas. When twilight was upon her, she climbed back into the driver's seat of the Pontiac, tapped lightly on the top of the cracker tin, and whispered, "Bet you'll be glad to get home after all these years."

Kerry checked into the motel where her grandmother Leota had stayed during the funeral. She grabbed a quick grilled cheese sandwich at the diner down the street and fell asleep in her room almost before her head hit the pillow, while the television blasted the ten o'clock local news from Amarillo and the bedsprings creaked loudly from the activities of the couple occupying the room next to hers.

She did not dream that night. She had not dreamed since her night with Phil Jesseps. Her sleep was peaceful without the haunting dreams of Fletcher and when she awoke in the morning at six, she felt rested and calm. Traveling without Margaret had been lonely the day before but today she was glad for her solitude.

She got directions from the desk clerk at the motel and drove to a nearby florist, where she purchased a bouquet of daisies, carnations, and dandelions.

After parking the Pontiac at the cemetery, she took the bouquet and Howard's cracker tin and strolled in the still, hot silence of the graveyard in search of Kerry Pearl's grave. The grass had only just begun to cover the grave and the weeds were tall around her as she stood beside the headstone. She freed the flowers from the green tissue paper surrounding them and dropped them one by one across the grave. She opened the cracker tin, studied its gritty contents for only a moment in curiosity, and began to sprinkle Howard's ashes across the grave. They landed with a soft thud on the dry earth. Kerry got down on her knees and covered them gently with soil and flowers. With the stem of a carnation, she wrote the name BATES across the foot of the grave in the dirt. She cried no tears, she spoke no words, for Howard was home at last. The wind would catch his name and scatter its letters across the graves of Max and Kerry Pearl Schurgood.

She drove all the way to Austin that day, arriving in the city just before six in the evening. The familiar streets made her eyes light up with joy as she drove to Leota's house. Her body was so tired that she could hardly move from beneath the steering wheel after she'd parked in the driveway. Leota did not care much for air-conditioning and her windows were wide open. Kerry could hear the sound of the evening news on the television as she approached the front screen door. It mingled with the voice of Thomas Evans as he asked for another glass of iced tea. Kerry pounded on the screen door, her brow dripping with perspiration from the heat.

Thomas came to the door. He opened it wide to let Kerry in and placed his fingers on his lips.

"Who's a-knocking on that door now, Thomas?" Leota called from the kitchen.

"Why, I think you'd best come see for yourself, Leota," Thomas replied, giving Kerry a hug.

Leota pranced out of the kitchen carrying Thomas' glass of iced tea in her hand. Her mouth fell open when she saw Kerry. She sat the tea down on the coffee table and ran to hug her.

"My stars! Would you look at this? My girl's home at last. Why didn't you let me know you were comin'? How'd you get here?" Leota asked, holding Kerry out in front of her, tears brimming in her green eyes.

"I drove here, Leo, all the way from New York. I dropped my friend Margaret off in Dallas. She flew on down to Houston," Kerry said with a laugh. Thomas stood back watching the two of them embrace with a smile on his lips.

"Well, that is quite a surprise. I didn't know you even knew how to drive! And for you to come home today of all days," Leota said.

"Happy birthday, Leo," Kerry said, as her eyes met Leota's and the voices of home rang in her memories.

I Heard — Love Is Just a Four-Letter Word

"HEY, RALS. PLAY 'EM. It's your turn," Buster barked, snapping a couple of dominoes in Raleigh's face.

Raleigh knocked the row of dominoes in front of him over onto the table with the sweep of his large hand. "I ain't in the mood. I can't concentrate on this. What the hell are we doin', anyway?" Raleigh said in a sigh, running his fingers through his short-cropped hair.

"What-a ya think we're doin'? We're sittin' in a sleez-o bar in Saigon playin' dominoes. Let's go get some-a that shit from the old chick with the kids," Buster said, smiling a toothy smile that revealed his gapped front teeth. "That was some good shit. You MPs always got a line on the best shit."

"Let's get outta here. This fuckin' place gives me the creeps," Raleigh said, standing to leave. He'd lost thirty pounds during basic training in the spring and three inches in the waist. His figure was most imposing as he downed his shot of gin and stretched his arms over his head.

Buster had firmed up quite a bit himself during basic. Though he was still a small fellow, he was all muscle and bone. His face had trimmed down to a lean, oval gem, splattered with freckles and a bushy red mustache which draped over his upper lip. "It's fuckin' raining again. Wanna get a cab?" he said as they walked outside into the rain.

"I guess it's gonna rain whether we're walkin' or ridin'. I'd just as soon walk," Raleigh said, stuffing his hands in the pockets of his pants.

"Come on, Rals. You've hardly even spoken to me since we met up yesterday. What's the deal? I mean, shit, we ain't seen each other in months. How is it up there in Biên Hòa? Can't be any worse than Airborne. Christ, ya don't know how lucky you are," Buster said, lighting up a cigarette, cupping it in his hands against the slow drizzling rain.

"Luck! Don't talk to me about luck. Don't talk to me about this fucked-up place 'cuz it ain't my favorite subject. Understand?" Raleigh said, gripping Buster firmly by the arm.

It was mid-afternoon, the streets were crowded, and an unidentifiable stench clung to the damp air, filling their nostrils with disgust for the filth around them.

"All right. Whatever ya say. You just don't seem to be in much of a partying mood's all I was sayin'. Let's just go get some shit and forget about it," Buster said, trying to keep up with Raleigh's long strides.

"Ya already did all that we got yesterday? Man, you better slow down on it before it comes a-lookin' for you 'steada you lookin' for it, know what I'm sayin' to ya?" Raleigh said, never breaking his pace as they walked along the streets at a fast clip. "Goddamn, I hate these fucking streets. Musta had shitheads for city planners 'round this place. Fucking blind-ass corners," he added.

"City planners. Christ, you someplace else upstairs today," Buster snickered.

"What the hell you laughin' at? This was somebody's home, man, this place. This place ain't just a traffic jam, ya know. What's the use? You ain't got any common sense," Raleigh replied, shaking his head.

"Well, speakin' of home . . . I been thinkin'. Ya said Kerry and Seibel broke up. What's my chances? Think maybe she might take a shine to a fella like me? I always liked that Kerry. I was thinkin' 'bout writin' to her. Did ya say she's workin' at the *Houston Globe*? Man, that's sumpin'. Never thought she'd really be some big-time reporter," Buster said.

"Aw, she ain't no big-time reporter. She just writes a column for the entertainment section. It's no big deal. I'll give you her address. It ain't gonna do you any good, though, 'cuz she's already seeing some other guy. Hey, I bet she'd get a kick outta hearin' from you, but ya know, you can't really expect a girl who's seen your daddy bare your ass and swat 'cha with a belt two or three times a week out on the playground to harbor romantic thoughts about you, asshole," Raleigh laughed, slugging Buster in the arm.

"Why not? Hell, Missy took a shine to you, didn't she? I'm gonna write Kerry anyway. Tell her 'bout some-a these things I've seen here," Buster said seriously.

"Missy's got no shine for me now. Maybe I'd have been a lot better off had she seen my mama riding my ass around the house. She's married to that jerk in the Ducks. They're quack-quack-quackin' along somewhere in Louisiana," Raleigh said bitterly.

"Know what I hate 'bout this place the most, Rals? It's these kids. Man, look at these kids. When we were that age we didn't have a care in the world. We were out playin' four square and tetherball, just jivin' away. These kids, ya never see 'em laughin' less one of us is dyin' . . . and they're all so skinny," Buster said, throwing his cigarette butt into a puddle of gray water on the street.

"Look who's talkin', skinny. Don't talk about it, makes my skin crawl. All these assholes we're supposed to be fightin' for. It's like that fuckin' song. How's it go? 'One, two, three, what're we fightin' for? Don't ask me, I don't give a damn,'" Raleigh said, lighting up a cigarette and turning onto a side street filled with trash in the gutters and rags hanging out over balconies.

Raleigh pounded on the door of an upstairs apartment in a rundown wooden framed building. The paint was chipping away from the wood shingles and the gray stared back at them as they waited for someone to answer the door.

A young girl answered; she was maybe twelve years old, Raleigh guessed, from the look in her eyes. Her face was framed by the darkness within and the smoky air drifted out of the door as she stepped aside to let them pass. She scurried outside past them. Raleigh looked after her as she reached for a bicycle, which was leaning against the railing of the decaying balcony. The rain beaded in her black hair, cut short around her face, as she turned to look back at him. Buster pushed past Raleigh in the doorway, back out onto the porch. He took the bicycle from the girl and carried it down the stairs for her. Raleigh waited in the open doorway for him to return. He let his eyes adjust to the darkness inside.

"I couldn't let that little lady carry that bike all the way down those stairs, now, could I?" Buster said, walking inside, brushing his hands together.

"My heart bleeds," Raleigh said, closing the door behind him.

They walked through the dark front room bumping into one another as Raleigh growled at Buster to watch where the hell he was going. The front room had two windows facing the street, though their panes were cloudy. It was lighter in this room. Raleigh sat on the couch against the wall, facing the old woman who sat at a kitchen table much like the kitchen table he'd grown up with at home. It had a metal frame with curved corners and a linoleum top of green and yellow tangled in a swirling pattern beneath the old woman's folded arms. Four other American GIs sat against the far wall with their knees drawn up, their arms draped over their knees, and their eyes closed. The pot smoke clung heavily around them. One of them still had a strip of rubber dangling from his arm just above his elbow. Buster stood by the window watching the street, alternately shifting his weight from one foot to the other.

"Again, you back," the old woman snapped through rotting teeth. Her gray-streaked hair was tied back to the nape of her neck in a tight knot. Raleigh pulled a joint from his shirt pocket, lit it, inhaled deeply, and stood to pass it to the old woman. A radio was blasting from the other room, tuned to the Armed Forces Radio Network. Raleigh could hear Bob Dylan clearly singing, "How duz it feel/To be on your own ... a complete unknown ... with no direction home." He closed his eyes, hearing only the lyrics he wanted to hear and seeing only his old street back in Austin.

Buster came to sit beside him, nudged his arm, and handed him the joint. "How much ya wanna go in for, Rals?" Buster asked, exhaling a lungful of smoke.

"This is your deal; get what you want. I just wanna relax for a few minutes," Raleigh said, leaning back against the cushions of the couch, taking a long hit from the joint and holding it inside for a few moments. He sputtered and coughed as he exhaled the smoke. The radio continued to blast and he closed his eyes to drift for a while, vaguely aware of Buster leaning over the table where the old woman sat, fishing money out of his pocket, and slapping it down on the table. The woman handed him a vial the length of a cigarette. Buster shoved it in his shirt pocket and walked to the window to stare down at the street, tugging at the joint held between his lips beneath his thick mustache. The room spun around him as one of the other GIs stood to stretch his legs, scratching his nose as though mosquitoes had attacked it.

"Hey, Rals, would ya look at this? Some fuckhead ran over that little darlin's bike. Come look at this," Buster said, wiping off a cleaner spot on the window pane with the palm of his hand.

"Six to one, half dozen ta the other. Who cares? It ain't your beef," Raleigh said, shuffling his boots on the bare wood floor littered with cigarette butts.

"But, the fucker's manhandling that kid! Goddamn bike's ruined," Buster said impatiently, turning around to walk toward Raleigh with the joint in his hand. Raleigh took the joint from his fingers and placed it to his lips.

Buster went back to the window, cupped his hands around his face, and stared out through the clean spot in the window pane. "I can't stand it. I gotta go help that kid. That guy's slapping her around down there. Big fuckin' delivery truck he's drivin', thinks he's a big man!" Buster said, turning away from the window to face Raleigh.

"Oh, man, stay out of it. There's nothin' but trouble out there," Raleigh said, slipping to the edge of the couch, sitting upright now, trying to regain his senses.

"Hey, you! Southwit! Sit your ass down," one of the other GIs shouted from against the far wall. "Ya think I come here to listen to your jaws flap?" he added, shaking a fist at Buster.

"Sorry, man. Why don't 'cha mind your own?" Buster said, flipping the GI his middle finger. The GI slumped back against the wall, reciprocating the flip of the finger toward Buster.

"I can't help it, Rals. I gotta go down there. Like I said, it's these kids. Hell, ain't that what we're here for?" Buster said quietly, turning on his heels to leave through the darkened front room.

"Now, just hold your goddamn horses, asshole," Raleigh tried to interject, realizing that Buster was not listening to him as he heard the door to the apartment slam.

"You ought to take better care of your own," the GI mumbled to Raleigh.

"Hey, FUCK OFF," Raleigh barked as he walked to the window to look down at the street. They were three flights up in the building. The traffic was almost at a standstill outside, the cars and bicycles weaving in and out of the chaos. Raleigh couldn't hear the sounds of the streets. The radio blasted into the room. It was all he could relate to: that radio, the music, the English language, home. It was the sound of home.

The spot that Buster had cleaned on the window was too low for Raleigh. It made him dizzy to lean down to it, so he cleared a spot of his own with his shirtsleeve. He watched as Buster ran out into the street. The Vietnamese stepped back against the front bumper of his delivery truck as Buster approached. The bicycle was crumpled beneath the front tire of the truck as the girl tried to pull it free.

Raleigh couldn't hear the conversation between Buster and the truck driver above the sound of the radio, now blasting the Rolling Stones. "Take me down little Susie, take me down." He could see that tempers were high, and in his stoned state of mind he chuckled as Buster shook his fist in the man's face while the little girl tugged at Buster's shirttail and the traffic engulfed them as though they did not exist at all.

Buster pointed up at the building and turned his head to face Raleigh for a moment. During that moment, Raleigh saw the Vietnamese reach back into the rear waistband of his trousers and pull out a small handgun.

Raleigh drew in a sharp breath, pounded on the window, and shouted, "That sum-bitch's got a gun! Goddamn you, Buster, he's got a fucking gun!"

The young girl saw the gun before Buster and she dove for the side of the truck. Buster stood as if in shock, as Raleigh pushed at the window, trying desperately to get it open. It finally gave beneath the strength of his massive hands and flew open. Bearing down against its wooden frame he shouted, "Get back, you asshole! Bus, Bus — !" as the gun went off in Buster's chest. It was only a sharp popping sound to Raleigh's ears, one that lingered with the honking of horns and the fumes of automobile exhaust mixed with the rain. The gun fired again and again as Raleigh climbed out onto the window ledge. He forgot about his ankles, he forgot his apathy, his tolerance, his fears, and jumped from the window into the street.

He heard his ankles snap with a sharp crack as he hit the ground, along with the thud of his skull as it struck the pavement. He tried to struggle to his feet to lunge toward the truck driver as his legs collapsed beneath him.

The engine roared in the delivery truck. The child screamed, standing over him, and Buster's face lay close beside his in the street, his eyes wide open and the blood rushing from him in a pool around their bodies. If the delivery truck had not been parked where it stood in the street, Raleigh would have fallen on the hoods of cars instead of on the pavement . . . Buster would have had a needle in his arm upstairs . . . if only, Raleigh thought, as he began to black out.

"You stupid bastard! Ya ain't never gonna write Kerry those letters. GODDAMNIT all. You and your fucking children," Raleigh cried, as the world faded to darkness and the child weaved into the shadows above him.

The rain had stopped but not the traffic. The people barely noticed two Americans laying in the street in front of a delivery truck with its blinker on. No one saw. No one cared. It was a problem with America.

"WHAT DAY IS THIS?" Raleigh said, staring up at a MP with a clipboard in his hand.

"Thanksgiving. It's turkey day. Welcome back, Foster," the MP replied, tapping his clipboard with a ballpoint pen.

"I been out for three days. I only had a two-day pass," Raleigh said in the confusion swirling in his mind. His head throbbed and he reached up to feel a thick bandage on the right side of his head. His feet and ankles were both bound in heavy casts, poking out of the sheet at the end of his hospital bed. A radio blared from somewhere else in the ward. The bed next to him was empty; the MP stood on his other side. The walls were gray, so gray that the glare hurt his eyes.

"It's all taken care of. I need to ask you some questions about the incident. There was a witness, but we need a statement from you," the MP said patiently, still tapping the pen on the clipboard. He was a tall, blond-haired young man, as large as Raleigh, with an intimidating grimace on his face.

"What kinda questions? Where's Ferguson?" Raleigh responded, trying to sit up. The sharp pain in his temples made him collapse back onto the pillow beneath his head.

"Just take it easy, Foster. Were you depressed on the day of the accident?" the MP asked in a flat monotone.

"Whadda ya mean, was I depressed on the day of the accident? 'Course I was depressed. Ain't a soul in the country wearing an American uniform who's not depressed. You depressed, man?" Raleigh asked impatiently, suspicious of the motives of the MP.

"Your pal — he's dead, by the way — what was he doing down in the street when the kid shot him?" the MP asked.

"What kid? Wasn't the kid that shot old Bus, was some fucking delivery truck driver! Jerk ran over the kid's bike. Bus saw this creep slappin' that kid around and he went down to see if he could help — he had a thing for kids. Wanted to be a teacher when he got out of the army," Raleigh said, feeling a lump in his throat where his sorrow rested. The IV in his arm pinched the skin and he rubbed at the bandage covering the needle in his vein. "Who the hell said that kid shot him, anyway?" Raleigh asked.

"The witness, a GI who was in the room with you. Said he thought the kid shot him. He didn't see; he didn't make it over to the window till after you'd jumped out. What were you doing in the building?" the MP asked.

"We went looking for a friend of ours. Guy wasn't there. I just wanted to sit down and rest for a while and then Buster looked out the window and saw this kid getting jerked around down there. The kid, little girl — yeah, it was a little girl — anyway, she'd been upstairs at that place when we got there. Buster helped her carry her bike down to the street before we went inside," Raleigh mumbled, trying to avoid any further questions about why they'd been in the building.

"Well, enough of that for now. Foster, what are your duties at Biên Hòa?" the MP asked, raising one eyebrow.

"You oughta know. I'm a MP just like you, asshole. I walk a beat from four to midnight dodgin' snipers. I'm on the buddy system, usually have a medic walkin' with me. Keeps us from having to arrest guys who're just a little too stoned or drunk — well, you know 'bout that. Only thing I don't do: I don't go 'round trying to dig up some shit from guys in hospital beds," Raleigh barked, tired of the interrogation.

"That's only because you don't have a hospital to work," the MP replied in anger. He shook the ballpoint pen in Raleigh's face. Raleigh reached up and grabbed the pen from his hand. The MP snatched it back from him. "Don't try that shit again. Understand, Foster?" he said through clenched teeth.

Raleigh felt the blood rushing to his face. He sank down into the pillow, trying to keep his temper under control. "What else ya wanna know?" Raleigh said.

"Your friend: was he a heroin addict? He had a vial in his shirt pocket. That why you were in the building?" the MP said abruptly.

"Musta been planted on 'im. He loved the kids, man, like I said. He had a soft heart," Raleigh lied.

"Come on now, Foster. That's why you were there, to buy some shit. That was it, wasn't it?" the MP chuckled.

"I told you. We went there a-lookin' for some yahoo Bus knew. Why don't 'cha go fight the war or somethin'?" Raleigh said, turning his head to the side, away from the MP. The lump was larger in his throat and he gasped for air.

"Well, you ended up with two broken ankles and a head full of stitches for your efforts to find this guy. Now, your pal's dead. You got your own ass to think about. What's this guy's name you and your pal were looking for in the building?" he asked, raising his eyebrows again.

"Hey, I ain't talkin' to you. Now, get your fuckin' clipboard outta my face. I need a nurse; I gotta piss," Raleigh said.

"Sure thing, Foster. Have a safe trip home," the MP sneered. He reached down and tapped the wooden clipboard on the bandage on Raleigh's head before turning to leave. Raleigh let out a sharp cry of pain. He felt the blood begin to seep through his stitches into the bandage.

He fell back asleep after the MP left. He dreamed it was winter and clutched the bedsheet to his chest. He dreamed of Buster. He saw his face in death, the blankness in his eyes, and the gap between his front teeth.

He did not dream of home as he had in Biên Hòa. Home was a place long ago and home no longer existed for Raleigh.

The days and nights in the hospital passed in a fog for Raleigh. He began writing letters to Kerry and Leota the week after Thanksgiving. His letters were short and did not mention the details of his accident, only that Buster had died a hero, defending a child in the streets of Saigon.

He worried that the MP would return, or that his case would be turned over to the CID, but as the days passed his fears began to subside and the incident became a memory and the loss became a distance he refused to ponder.

The leather-bound journal Howard had given him in the spring became his favorite companion. He kept it under his pillow and would sometimes pull it out in the middle of the night, jotting down notes to himself within its crisp pages.

Jeff Foster sent his son a small cassette tape recorder and a case of cassettes. Raleigh took a few minutes each day to talk into the recorder, cracking jokes he'd heard around the ward and sending messages to friends. Once he just let the machine record on its own, allowing it to pick up all the sounds of the ward: the radios, the conversations. He wrote a note to his dad, identifying all the sounds. It was a game, the tape recorder. He enjoyed the game; it gave him something to do. The game made the time pass as the days stretched into weeks while he waited for his orders to come through. He knew he was going home; the MP had told him that much, but time was agony. Time was lost here.

The doctors told him his ankles were shattered, with his right foot being in worse shape than the left. He would need months of therapy once the casts were removed. He searched for patience within the gray walls of the hospital and found none. The hair had begun to grow back around the raw, red scar where his stitches had been in his head. Raleigh often brushed his hand across the rough texture of the new hair and it became a habit, one that he would still cling to long after the hair had grown out completely.

Kerry sent him copies of the *Houston Globe* which carried her column. Her picture was always above the reviews she wrote and sometimes she'd enclose a tape of the artist she'd reviewed in the column. Raleigh would tear out the columns and pass them around the ward for the rest of the guys to read. Her packages arrived regularly two or three times a week, and Raleigh never stopped being excited about their arrivals. He tore into the parcels like a child opening presents on Christmas morning.

Ethel did not write to her brother, her excuse being that her baby was due in mid-February and she didn't have time to write letters. Grandmother Leota sent him pictures that his niece, Jessica, had drawn for him, and he kept his promise to write to her, hoping Ethel would take the time to read them to her. He taped the pictures up on the wall behind his bed, treasuring the warmth of the bright colors and the love the child had expressed within them.

Julie wrote to her son often. Her notes were similar to the ones Raleigh wrote. The two of them shared a compact writing style, although Julie's notes were typed and usually on her business stationery, which never bothered Raleigh. He was used to her hurried lifestyle.

During the second week of December, he received a Christmas card from his ex-wife, Missy. She told him she was sorry to hear about Buster, and asked if he would sign some papers allowing her new husband to adopt their baby, Lisa. She wished him a merry Christmas and a speedy recovery in her tight script with circles above the i's instead of dots. Raleigh ripped the card into tiny shreds and left the scattered pieces on the floor beside his bed for the orderly to sweep up at the end of the day.

Christmas came. Leota sent him a box full of homemade candy, something she called idiot's delight, which she made each year at Christmastime. It was a praline candy filled with pecans and dried fruits, and each piece was meticulously wrapped in wax paper. She'd been thoughtful enough to send a double batch to Raleigh so that he could share the candy with the others in the ward. She had, in fact, fretted over the amount to send for days, and the fretting had involved calling Julie on the telephone two times a day until the package went in the mail.

Each time he unwrapped a piece of the sticky, caramel-colored candy, he would picture his grandmother Leota standing over her stove with the candy thermometer in her hand, cooking the candy while Thomas Evans sat at her kitchen table sipping coffee and wrapping the pieces she'd already cooled and sliced on the kitchen counter. He remembered the candy-making process quite vividly from his childhood. It was an activity he and Kerry had looked forward to each year, and the taste of the pecans made him long for the wink of Leota's pine-green eyes.

He gathered the courage to write to the Fergusons. He told them of Buster's love for the children in 'Nam, that he'd died for the love of the Vietnamese children. He told them about Buster's plans to become a teacher and that the loss of his good friend had left an empty space in his own heart which could never be filled again. It was a beautifully clumsy letter, shrouded with emotion. He ceased to feel that he'd stretched the truth in describing the death of his friend to the MP or to his family. Buster was his bona fide hero. He'd given him the greatest gift of all: a ticket out.

The new year came. Raleigh lay awake in the darkness at midnight. He hid his face in his pillow and wept for a new year of uncertainty. He wept through the night until the dawn crept up on him, painting the sheets the same color of gray as the walls, and the daylight dried his tears.

His acquaintances on the ward came and went as the weeks passed. They always exchanged addresses, promising to write one another once they got stateside, knowing full well they would never correspond. They knew it each time the slips of paper with the addresses and numbers scrawled across them crackled in their palms. They would never forget to write; it wasn't that simple. They would simply long to forget.

Toward the end of January, Kerry sent him a package of tapes and newspapers along with a long letter. One of the tapes was of her new heartthrob, some fellow in New York City named Phil Jesseps. It became his favorite tape and after a couple of days Raleigh had all the lyrics to the songs memorized. He came to know Kerry's friends Margaret and Puttnam through her letters, and looked forward to meeting them once he got back, especially since Kerry mentioned that Puttnam was a vet.

One of the newspaper columns Kerry had written for the *Globe* was about the opening of Puttnam's music hall in Houston. Kerry's article praised the club as being the new outlet for serious music lovers in the city. Raleigh could almost see the place from reading Kerry's article. It was called Burley Hall, and was a cross between a concert hall and a beer joint. The opening night had been a blues night with Lightnin' Hopkins, Mance Lipscomb, and Big Mama Thornton. Kerry wrote that her old housemate, Wiley, had moved down to Houston to run the bar for Puttnam. Raleigh never cared much for Wiley's abrupt personality, and he crinkled his nose when he read that part of Kerry's letter. He folded the article up and tucked it into his journal for safekeeping, wishing he could have been there for that opening night.

Kerry also sent him a picture of all of them standing out on their dad's front lawn in Houston. He was attracted to Margaret's wavy, auburn hair and her slender shape. She looked so small and fragile standing between Puttnam, with his sad blue eyes, and his dad, who stood pointing up at the clump of green miniature bananas in the tree behind them. Margaret had a full, rich smile that touched Raleigh's heart, and it looked as though the wind had been high because her hair had caught in the breeze and a strand had fallen across her cheek. Kerry had informed him that Margaret was a professor in the English department at a university there. He had daydreams about using his GI bill to enroll in college, where he'd take only English courses and sit in the back of the lecture hall gazing upon Margaret's beauty all day long — until Kerry wrote him that Margaret was pregnant. The daydreams stopped then.

Raleigh treasured each parcel that arrived for him from Austin or Houston. He saved them all, rereading the letters many times over and listening to the taped messages his dad sent until the tapes practically fell apart in his hands. He savored the feel of the words, wondering where he would fit in when he got back. It seemed that everyone in his family had found their own particular niche in life and he felt he had none.

February brought him news of his orders, although he'd actually been waiting that week to hear of the birth of Ethel's baby. Ethel was famous for her overdue pregnancies, and he had a bet going with his dad over when the baby would finally come. His orders raised his spirits considerably when he discovered that he would be sent to the veteran's hospital in Houston after a short layover in San Francisco. He smiled more as the days passed. He pondered the roads that stretched like webs before him. He grasped at choices for the future. He wanted choices, wanted reason. He embraced the news of his orders, suppressed his sorrow over the death of his oldest friend, and clung to his loneliness like his pillow in the night.

On the morning of the day he was scheduled to leave for the States, Raleigh sat in a wheelchair with a new walking cast on his left foot. He pressed his cheek to the window and watched the cloudy skies outside while balancing his tape recorder in his lap. He listened to a new tape Kerry had sent him of a live concert album called *Big Sur*, which had cuts by Mickey Newbury; Kris Kristofferson; Taj Mahal; Blood, Sweat & Tears; and Joan Baez.

He held back a tear in his eye as he listened to Baez's piercing voice sail through a Bob Dylan song. The refrain of the song went something like, "I heard . . . love is just a four-letter word," and Raleigh agreed.

ETHEL'S BABY came the last week in February, with Jeff winning the bet over the date it would be born. Ethel named the baby boy Justin and much to her chagrin, she found that it was the year for naming babies Justin, as there were four other boys in the hospital nursery bearing the same first name. The nurses joked about the confusion of having so many Justins in the nursery, which provoked Ethel into hysterics.

Rodney was quite proud to finally have a son, as was Jeff to have a grandson. Ethel . . . well, Ethel was just glad it was over with and was anxious to get home from the hospital to turn the baby over to their housekeeper, Mrs. Lopez.

Ethel had gained thirty pounds during her pregnancy. She lost ten after the delivery, and gained six back eating cookies in her hospital bed. She stayed sober for those first few months, watching the weather turn to a warm spring and making an honest attempt at curbing Rodney's extramarital affairs, which came close to bringing their marriage to an abrupt impasse.

She snooped around his office; she snooped through his pockets; questioned him endlessly about his whereabouts when she couldn't reach him by phone; and plowed through his crumpled bits of paper and matchbook covers hidden in the folds of his wallet. She even joined a health club in an attempt to trim down her bulging thighs, but she ended up spending more time lounging by the pool gossiping with her Northwest Hills neighbors than in her exercise classes. The Nautilus equipment could breathe a sigh of relief, as it would never have to bear the burden of Ethel Preston's ample rump.

Julie gave her daughter as much encouragement as she could. Her business was booming and she really didn't have much time for familial affairs. It was most difficult for her to understand Ethel's dilemma, since she'd never had a roving husband, or, for that matter, a weight problem. She did callously forget about Ethel's past difficulties with alcohol, and generously offered her daughter a drink each time she came to visit, which Ethel accepted with a dull nod of her head.

By May, Ethel was back on the bottle again, forsaking her pursuit of thin thighs and Rodney's private affairs. She turned the care of her children over to Mrs. Lopez completely. Rodney was relieved; Ethel forgot her woes in the vodka; the children clicked along at a healthy pace behind Mrs. Lopez; and the Preston household in general returned to normal — their normal now including a beautiful baby boy named Justin.

Ethel had learned the art of discretion in staying sober for those months of pregnancy and the few that followed the birth of her son. She now only drank in the privacy of her own home, and Lord could that woman drink. She was extremely careful when out in public, sipping on club soda and lime, hoping that her sobriety would be noticed by the ladies at social gatherings, and that they in turn would keep their paws off of Rodney.

In reality, Ethel had nothing to be afraid of. Though Rodney threatened her with divorce when she was sober and nagging him about his activities, he had no intention of ever leaving her. His happiness had become firmly anchored in the toothless smile of his son. He was delighted with the boy, and to Ethel's own amazement, he even changed the child's diapers without complaining.

Ethel could never have been convinced it was so, but Rodney hadn't been fooling around for months. After the baby was born, he pounded the steering wheel of his Mercedes in rush-hour traffic, anxious to get home to his boy and forsaking his past of lingering till dark in barroom happy hours. Grateful to Ethel for giving him a son, he tried to be more attentive to his wife at home, though Ethel often ignored his solicitations. He tried to make himself fall back in love with her, stroking her hair in the night after she'd fallen asleep. It had grown to her shoulders and was frosted in several shades of blond. He tried to remember what her natural hair color was and could not. He tried desperately to love her, tried to recall some warmth between them other than just the emptiness of occasional sex. Finding no memories there, he would fall asleep with only the love for his children to still his loneliness.

The girls, Jessica and April, took great pride in tending to their brother. They followed Mrs. Lopez around on tiptoes, studying the care of the baby. Each girl would take her turn sitting in the rocking chair holding the baby in her lap and they would giggle endlessly when Mrs. Lopez changed his diapers. Jessica was in charge of holding the diaper ready over Justin when the soiled one was removed. Mrs. Lopez instructed her to throw the extra diaper over him quickly in order to keep the baby from taking a squirting shot at her face, but Jessica was easily distracted and on those occasions Mrs. Lopez would swab her face with her handkerchief and scold fondly, "Oh, you naughty boy," while the two girls would roll around on the carpet squealing in laughter.

So, the Preston household carried on. It held its own rhythm and congruity. There was love in this household; though it was oftentimes hidden from the naked heart, it was nonetheless there. The children gave it laughter, which they created amongst themselves; Ethel provided the much-needed flaw, for nothing is perfect; and Rodney simply took from it, gathering strength from its vacuum.

HOUSTON WAS A VAST, tropical span of asphalt stretching its balmy arms for miles and miles in all directions across the coastal plains of southeast Texas. Suburban housing developments were sprouting up in the midst of the once-tranquil rice fields to the west of the city to accommodate the growth of a boomtown, while the petroleum industry littered the land to the south and east with refineries.

Margaret huffed her way through the summer, pregnant and weary from the heat. She spent her days shuffling from their screened front porch, where she was safe from mosquitoes, to the sofa in their living room.

Puttnam spent his nights at his music club, Burley Hall. He came to love the hall itself, which had once been a Polish community center. The hardwood floors were kept polished to a high shine on the stage and in the hall itself. Puttnam had installed theatrical lighting and a state-of-the-art sound system. He was the first to arrive at the hall in the afternoons. He would climb up to the sound booth at the back of the hall, place a tape in the cassette deck, bring up the stage lights, and, leaning back in his chair, he'd light up a joint and gaze out on his enterprise conceived from the heart. Wiley usually showed up for work at six. Puttnam was always in the process of stocking the bar by the time Wiley arrived, and he would immediately begin helping Puttnam. The music played nonstop in the hall, bouncing off the walls like thunder. The walls took on their own life; even when the hall was empty, the music could be felt and the warmth of applause lingered like a ghost within the wood.

Puttnam had opened the club at a good time for this type of format. Burley Hall was enjoying nights with sold-out shows and the heat of the summer made the bar sales skyrocket. Of course, there were always a few unruly drunks who had to be asked to leave by the bouncers; there were always the cabs to call for those too drunk to find their way to the exits unescorted; and then there were the fistfights to break up. Sometimes they developed over domestic squabbles, sometimes over waiting in line at the bar. They occurred three or four times a week and Puttnam eventually learned to spot a potential knuckle match from up in the sound booth.

Photographing the performers became a passion of Puttnam's, and he was developing quite a collection. He lined the walls by the bar with the photographs, which were autographed by the performers and framed in simple black, wooden frames. Kerry used Puttnam's photographs in the paper to accompany reviews of the shows at the club. His name became one of the most respected in the Houston music scene. Agencies from all over the country began calling him to try to book their acts at Burley Hall, and before too long, Puttnam found himself with fifty full-time employees on the payroll, including Wiley as manager and a middle-aged secretary who nagged Puttnam constantly about signing contracts and returning phone calls.

Despite the fact that he'd found the club to be more of a job than he'd planned on, Puttnam maintained a deep love for his empire and for the quality of music he presented six nights a week. The sound of delta blues ringing lonesome into the hall full of hungry souls always made the problems of keeping the place running smoothly worthwhile.

Margaret only visited the club on nights when Kerry was going down. The baby was due in August and she found it difficult to navigate in the crowds, considering that she could no longer see her feet, and the hardwood floors were slick. She found the same magic in the music as Puttnam, and understood his long hours at the club completely.

They lived in a small house in the Heights which was centrally located, close to the downtown area. Puttnam drove out to the veteran's hospital twice a week to visit Raleigh. Raleigh came to depend on Puttnam's friendship as his link to the outside world, and in late July, Puttnam picked him up at the hospital and drove him to their little house in the Heights to spend the weekend. Raleigh still had to use a cane to walk for long periods of time, but just being out of the hospital environment for two days created a salubrious effect in his spirits.

He went to the club with Puttnam that Friday night. He thoroughly enjoyed the lighthearted banter he exchanged with Wiley over the bar. They snapped at each other on and off throughout the evening, while Puttnam stayed up in the sound booth running the lights and sound.

Raleigh met a waitress at the bar named Amanda. She slipped Raleigh her phone number when the club was closing, and the next morning, after watching Margaret putter around the house for a couple of hours, Raleigh finally decided to give Amanda a call. Amanda had already driven over to pick him up by the time Puttnam woke up; Margaret and Puttnam didn't see him again until Monday morning when Amanda dropped him off at the house.

Puttnam berated Raleigh all the way back to the hospital for causing his waitress not to show up on a Saturday night. Raleigh winked at him, crossed his arms across his chest, and, grinning broadly, he slumped down into the seat, pretending to be asleep.

"Ya can't keep an old hound like me down for long," Raleigh said with his eyes still closed.

"Yeah, but it looks like Amanda sure tried," Puttnam bellowed in a fake Texas accent, reaching over to slug Raleigh in the arm.

The laughter faded as they drove into the hospital's driveway. Raleigh pulled his bag from the back seat and waved goodbye from the curb. Puttnam watched him turn and walk slowly toward the glass doors. Even though Raleigh had disappeared into the building, he found himself still staring into his rearview mirror, searching for his friend as he pulled out onto the highway.

THEY WERE BORN on Leota's birthday, two beautiful babies with soft tufts of red hair and unfocused aqua eyes. Their skin turned to milk-white hours after their birth. The girl child cried in a continuous wail, while the boy was a quiet, peaceful baby.

Margaret chuckled in her weakened post-delivery state as she named them: Callum Tennessee and Virginia Frost. Puttnam was so elated with the double birth that he hardly noticed the names she'd given their newborns. He, in fact, could not remember what their names were when he lumbered out to the waiting room to inform Kerry and Wiley that his babies were finally in the world.

Actually, it made no difference that he'd forgotten their names. The bet between Kerry and Margaret had been settled months before, as Kerry had indeed written to Phil Jesseps. She flew to New York often to visit him and he in turn booked into Burley Hall as an excuse to get to come down to Houston and visit her. They did not fall in love; they simply landed safely in its shelter, quietly there for the other in a friendship which sometimes disguised itself as a prurient relationship. The best part of their affair was that they both knew they weren't lost to this love, so neither one ever took too much or too little from the other.

Kerry ran to find a phone after Puttnam announced the news. He and Wiley went in search of breakfast and coffee, slapping each other on the back as they shuffled down the corridor of the hospital.

Kerry nervously dialed Clare's number in Saratoga. She waited anxiously for Clare to answer as she listened to the hollow ring on the other end of the line. It was eight in the morning in Saratoga and Kerry could picture Clare making coffee in the kitchen while Ernest drummed his fingers on the kitchen table in anticipation. Kerry flipped her braid back across her shoulder and toyed with the metal phone cord of the pay phone.

"*Avalanche!*" Ernest answered briskly.

"Ernest, what are you doing answerin' the phone?" Kerry asked impatiently as the connection crackled in her ear.

"Who is this?" Ernest demanded on the other end. He yanked his thick glasses off and slammed them down on the phone table there in the hallway.

"This is your old friend, Kerry. Where's Clare?" Kerry giggled.

"Oh, it's you, huh. Well, Clare hasn't come down yet. I came in to use the typewriter. What's it to ya?" Ernest barked into the phone.

"Well, go fetch her. I've got important headlines for her," Kerry said, enjoying the hell out of provoking Ernest's bad temper.

"I don't want to wake her. What's the headlines? I'll give her the message," Ernest replied in his sharp, biting manner.

"Nope. Can't wait, and this is long distance, so go roust her out," Kerry said, nonplussed by Ernest's belligerence.

"Oh, for God's sake. The world comes to a halt because Kerry Foster learned how to dial a telephone," Ernest bellowed into the receiver before dropping it on the phone table and padding up the stairs to wake Clare.

Clare was awake. She'd been enjoying those lazy moments of lingering in bed after waking when the phone had rung. She had her robe fastened and was just slipping her feet into her house slippers when Ernest knocked softly on her door.

"Foster's on the phone," Ernest called out. Clare wanted to tell him to inform Kerry she'd be right there, but she heard Ernest pounding back down the stairs. Clare shook her small fist at the door to her bedroom in response to Ernest's never-ending malevolence.

She walked softly down the stairs, giving Ernest a sharp look of reprimand as he glanced back at her before disappearing into her office.

"Kerry?" Clare said into the receiver.

"Yep, that's me. Guess what?" Kerry giggled.

"No guesses, just the what," Clare laughed.

"The babies came this mornin'," Kerry sang into the phone.

"BABIES! Two or three? What do you mean, BABIES?" Clare replied in surprise.

"Two little redheaded sweet peas: one boy, five pounds and four ounces, and a girl, five pounds, one ounce. TWINS!" Kerry squealed into the phone.

"Oh my, are they healthy? What about Margaret? Is she OK?" Clare asked, accidentally knocking Ernest's heavy glasses off onto the floor, where they landed with a thud.

"Margaret' s fine. She's sleeping. She went into labor yesterday mornin', and it's been a long day and night for her, but she'll be fine, and Puttnam's so proud he's about to burst at the seams. You'd think he had those babies himself. He came struttin' into the waiting room with his hair in a ponytail and cigars danglin' out of each side of his mouth. The boy's just beside himself," Kerry said, leaning in close to the pay phone.

"You tell them I send all my love, and have that Puttnam send me some photos," Clare said jubilantly.

"Knowin' Puttnam, you'll probably be getting a box of pictures the size of a Pennsylvania barn in the mail by next week," Kerry replied. "Y'all take care up there. We'll be seeing you soon. My regards to Marlin and Ty. Tell ole Ernest that I said 'read a book,'" Kerry added.

Clare replaced the receiver in its cradle and kneeled down to retrieve Ernest's fallen glasses from the floor. She padded softly over to the door of the office and yanked it open. Ernest was leaning back in her desk chair with his feet propped up against the typewriter on her desk. Clare startled him when she entered the room and he swung his feet to the floor as she approached him. She folded the glasses and pitched them to him flippantly.

"Margaret had twins: a boy and a girl," she said, and turning on her heels she walked back out of the office. "READ A BOOK, ERNEST," Clare bellowed in laughter as she slammed the door closed.

Clare strolled lazily to the kitchen, put the water on for coffee, and sat down at the kitchen table to read the newspaper. She smiled softly to herself, thinking of the birth of the twins. The morning slipped by her with business as usual at *The Avalanche*.

A New Year's Eve, 1975

JULIE FOSTER BENNETT could not recall a lonelier year in her family's history. The year of 1975 seemed to drag on for an eternity, not once promising a better year ahead in '76.

She was divorced again, clinging to her past marriages in memory. Such sad memories to bear for one who wished she'd lived her life single.

Cecil Bennett had been the last to come and go. He was an ad executive from New Hampshire. Julie did not miss him when he left. He had gone quietly, without argument or bitterness. She simply missed being part of something outside her office, now a thriving business of prosperity.

She had acquired a new condominium in the hills outside of town through this divorce. She practically hid within the walls of her new home, furnishing it with sparse, modern Scandinavian furniture and covering the large, spacious windows which looked out over the Texas hill country with colorful mini-blinds. The dividing wall between her formal living room and dining area housed a fireplace large enough to stretch out in, and it served both rooms nicely. She moved her own office into one of the extra bedrooms, turning her main offices over to Raleigh, who had come to work for her in October.

Raleigh lived on Twenty-fourth Street near the University of Texas campus. He had a small cottage with only one bedroom, a shaded front yard surrounded by a picket fence, and a large back yard with a neglected garden which he planned to bring back to life in the spring. His house sat farther back from the street than most of the houses on his block. He sometimes felt he was out in the country when he woke in the mornings, and it frightened him to feel so isolated.

He was adjusting to civilian life in his own way. He dated frequently — never the same woman for very long, but his telephone rang constantly with the voices of attractive young women greeting him when he answered "hello." Yet, he had become the impatient, discontented one who was quick to say "goodbye."

He was Uncle Raleigh to almost everyone these days. He spent at least two weekends a month in Houston with Margaret and Puttnam. He seemed only to communicate well with the children and occasionally Margaret, with whom he had admittedly fallen in love.

Puttnam was not threatened by Raleigh's love for Margaret. The friendship between the two men had strengthened into a lifelong bond. He knew that Raleigh would never act upon the love. He also knew that Raleigh knew that Margaret was going through a period in her life when she wished they would both vanish and leave her to her solitude, taking the twins, the noise, and the blank pages in her typewriter with them.

Jeff Foster lived alone in his modest house close to downtown Houston. He was only a few blocks away from Margaret and Puttnam, and just around the corner from Kerry, who lived in a garage apartment buried beneath a sprawling old pecan tree. He was driven by his work, rising each morning long before dawn to read the newspaper and perched at his desk at the office by seven, where he stayed until suppertime each evening. He, too, had come to depend on his grandchildren for warmth and contact with the outside world. Raleigh usually packed up April and Jessica and brought them down to spend the weekends there at Jeff's house. Rodney was grateful for the chance to send the girls away on the weekends. Times were not so good at the Preston household.

Ethel's years of drinking were killing her. The year of 1975 had sent her to the hospital on six separate occasions, all from complications of alcoholism. The children had grown quiet around the house when Ethel was at home. Rodney often found the three children huddled in one of their rooms together when he came home from work in the evenings. He had sent Ethel away to a treatment center in Arizona in September. She was home now for the holidays, tanned and overweight, and morbidly searching for any excuse at all to have a drink. New Year's Eve was coming. Everyone drank on New Year's Eve.

Richmond had died in August. It was quite unexpected for the family. He'd bought a new CB radio in July and he loved to cruise the highway between Midland and Odessa, just toying with the CB, talking with truckers and weary travelers. One late afternoon, as he drove into Odessa, he'd gotten so carried away talking on the CB that he hadn't noticed the red flashing lights at a railroad crossing and he'd driven head-on, full speed into the side of a cargo train. It had killed him instantly. Cora had been devastated by the loss of not having Richmond to look after. She did not like living alone, so, just before Thanksgiving, she'd packed up her household and moved in with Leota in Austin.

Leota hadn't made up her mind whether she liked the idea of having Cora as a housemate. Cora was such a large woman and they often collided in hallways, which left Leota at a disadvantage. She once scolded Cora so badly for knocking her down outside the bathroom door that Cora packed an overnight bag and went next door to Thomas Evans' house for two whole days. But Thomas was out in California now for the holidays and the two women were having to learn to adjust to one another without him as a referee.

Kerry seemed to be the only member of the family who was not going through a period of change and discontentment. Her column was syndicated now in fifteen papers nationwide, and her personal life was quiet and uncomplicated. She was not in love and that suited her just fine. She continued to visit Phil Jesseps in New York and he in turn relied upon her company as well. They were comfortable in this arrangement, though as the years had gone by, both of their careers had commanded more time, and as their popularity had grown, the time they had to spend together had become less frequent than it had in the past. Phil stayed on the road traveling the concert circuits most of the time, while Kerry continued to write her music column for the *Globe* and began to branch out by writing more freelance articles for other publications, including *The Avalanche*, which had grown into a national publication with a slick-paged left-wing format. The love between Kerry and Phil was a detached sort of love which held all the qualities of being in love without the demands. It was the sort of love many people live out their lives in hope of finding: a rare gift which Kerry held dear to her heart with distance and care.

Clare had remained as editor of *The Avalanche* after she sold the paper, and Ernest Hinkle was promoted to assistant editor. Kerry had just spent the last three weeks out in New Mexico researching the working conditions of the Indian miners in the uranium mines. She'd stopped off in Austin for Christmas and had decided to spend the week between Christmas and New Year's at her mother's, taking advantage of the IBM typewriter and the fireplace to gather her thoughts together while finishing the article. Clare was expecting her to finish the piece on the Indian miners by the first week in January. It was slated to be her first serious article and she wanted it to be a clean job in order to avoid Ernest's sharp criticisms.

Julie was planning a New Year's Eve party in her new home for the family and her close friends. Puttnam and Margaret had been invited, and Puttnam had finally been persuaded to turn over Burley Hall on the busiest night of the year to Wiley in order to load the twins and Margaret up in the car to come to Austin for the party.

Margaret was anxious over the trip up to Austin. She had longed to attend alone, but had not had the courage to ask Puttnam if he minded being alone as the new year came along. The twins were a joyful pair of redheads. Virginia carried the best of her mother's features; she was truly a lovely child who had inherited her father's personality and his boisterous laughter. She bounced and bubbled from room to room, bringing proud smiles to her father's face and driving her mother bananas. Tennessee, on the other hand, was a soft-spoken, quiet child, tall for his age, with his father's wide, blue eyes and facial structure; he held his mother's heart securely in the wink of those eyes.

Jeff Foster had also been invited to Julie's party. He had been invited to every party Julie had given for the family for the last fifteen years. He had never accepted any of the invitations. With Kerry out of town for the holidays, he had just about decided to accept an invite from Wiley to rent a tux and go down to Burley Hall, where he could help bartend and work the ticket booth. It was a secret fantasy of Jeff's to be a bartender. He'd even gone out and rented the tux. But, at five o'clock in the afternoon on New Year's Eve, he happened to glance down at Julie's party invitation still sitting on his coffee table with its familiar script, and something from long ago stirred within his heart. He picked up the invitation and examined it carefully, turning it over in his fingers. After pondering the invitation for a few short moments, he tossed it into the air, jumped up from the sofa, packed his shaving kit, an old pair of khaki pants, a polo shirt, and, of course, his rented tux. He threw his things in the back seat of the car, telling himself he would only stay at his ex-wife's party until midnight and that it was a wonderful opportunity to visit with both the Burley twins and his own grandkids.

MILLIE SEIBEL knocked softly on the guest room door. "Fletcher, are you just about ready, hon? Julie's invitation specifically said nine o'clock. Your father's getting restless."

"I'm ready," Fletcher replied, opening the door to the room and standing before his mother, straightening his bow tie.

"My, you do look so handsome in your suit. If you'd only shave that beard off. Such a handsome face," Millie said, reaching up to tug sharply on Fletcher's full beard. He shrugged his shoulders as Millie rearranged his bow tie.

"Where's Dad?" Fletcher asked as they walked down the hall of this once-familiar home, the home he'd grown up in.

"Oh, you know your father, dear. He's been waiting in the car. It's raining, you know," Millie said, grabbing her wrap from the living room sofa. Fletcher placed the silk shawl around her shoulders as they walked through the kitchen to the back door, which opened onto the garage.

"Are you sure I'm invited to this thing? I mean, maybe Julie wouldn't want me there because of what happened with Kerry and me," Fletcher said, holding the car door open for his mother on the passenger side, while his father drummed on the steering wheel with impatient fingers.

Millie stood beside the open door picking at the lapels of Fletcher's suit. "Oh, that's nonsense to think of that. That was ten years ago and Julie said I should definitely invite you to join us. This will be such a wonderful evening and Julie said her mother, Leota, would be so excited to see you. You were one of her favorite neighborhood children, you know. Now, isn't that right, Ruben?" Millie asked, leaning in to address her husband.

"Would ya just get in the car, please, Millie? We're late, you know," Ruben replied, scratching his chin and shaking his head.

"After all, you do both live in Houston now, and perhaps this will give you and Kerry a chance to get to know each other again," Millie said, standing again to face Fletcher, who still held the car door open for her. Millie winked up at her son in anticipation of his response.

"Millie, would ya just get in the car, please? We can discuss this on the way. Fletcher, help your mother into the car, please, or we may never leave our own garage on this New Year's Eve," Ruben barked good-naturedly.

"Oh, for goodness' sake, Ruben. You're always in a hurry," Millie said as she climbed in beside him and Fletcher closed the car door softly behind her.

"Well, you can't be late to a Julie Foster party. She might change husbands or boyfriends on you in the meantime and you'd never be able to remember the names of those fellows," Ruben joked as Fletcher climbed into the back seat, missing the bulk of the comment but too lost in his own thoughts to request a repeat.

Fletcher now was an aspiring young architect for a firm in Houston. He was aiding in the construction of the tall, glass skyscrapers sprouting from the swamp of downtown, as cold as the snow of Montana and lovelier than any buildings that had been built to date.

He'd seen Kerry a few times during the last few months. She had not seen him. She was always hidden in the shadows of Burley Hall, with her pad and pencil, reviewing the shows. He had seen her standing at the bar one night. She was laughing the same laugh he remembered from years before in their early youth as she stood talking with the musician who was playing that night.

Fletcher couldn't remember his name, but he searched for it in his mind now as they drove out into the hill country outside of Austin. He had been afraid to call her since he'd been in Houston. He'd thought about it a lot, even tried to look her up. Her phone number was unlisted; the operator didn't understand that he'd known her for more than half his life. Operators don't understand such things.

His father broke his train of thought. His words seemed to shatter the silence as the rain slipped down the rear windshield and the wipers slapped across the front pane. "Millie, I think I left my wallet in the glove box. Would you mind getting it out for me, please?" Ruben asked softly.

"Oh, for goodness' sake, Ruben. You never leave your wallet in the car," Millie said, opening the glove compartment despite her doubts.

The light came on inside the compartment and instead of a wallet, Millie found a clear plastic box from the florist with a lovely lavender orchid inside.

"Oh, Ruben! It's just beautiful. Look, Fletcher, isn't it lovely? And it matches my dress perfectly. Fletcher, help me pin it on, dear," Millie said, climbing up on her knees to lean over the back seat. "Ruben, turn on the overhead light so Fletcher can help me pin it on, dear."

"Millie, it's raining. Would ya wait till we get to Julie's, please?" Ruben said, smiling to himself.

"Yes, dear," Millie said coyly, as she slipped back down into the seat, turning her head slightly to wink at Fletcher.

"WELL, THIS IS IT, Mother. Your big party. Anything I can help you with?" Kerry asked, standing beside her mother with her arm draped around Julie's shoulders.

"I can't think of anything. The caterers have everything ready, and Raleigh has gone to pick up Mother and Aunt Cora. I've got my special recipe for hot-buttered rum ready, and Rodney is bringing the eggnog — something nonalcoholic for Ethel, I believe," Julie said, rolling her eyes at Kerry in mutual understanding of Ethel's drinking problem.

"Well, I think we ought to let up on Ethel for tonight. It is New Year's Eve and the children are all set up with games and television in your front room," Kerry said, reaching for a cup of coffee on the counter in the kitchen where they stood.

"Maybe you're right. I just get so cautious when I'm around her now. You can never tell what she's really thinking," Julie said.

"Oh, it'll be the same as always: Leo will snap at her all evening and I shall hide in your study to work on my article. I gave Phil your business number for the phone in there so he could call later," Kerry said, walking out into the dining area with her coffee mug cupped tightly between her hands.

"You don't know your sister very well anymore, do you, Kerry?" Julie asked. She followed Kerry into the dining area. She was dressed in a black strapless gown which was tight at the waist and she tugged at the waistband as she followed along behind her daughter. The dress had a short-waisted jacket of an ivory color which went with it and Julie had left it draped across the back of a chair in the dining room. She reached out for the jacket as she waited for her youngest daughter's reply.

"No, can't say as I do know Ethel very well. We've never been the best of buddies . . . can't really recall ever knowing that much about what goes on in her mind. She is a different sort than me. Someone I would not choose as a friend on a social level. I would have to say that Margaret has been more of the sister I always envisioned in my young years; she was the one who understood," Kerry said, cupping her coffee mug close to her lips.

"But, she's your sister, Kerry. And she is my daughter. We must try to understand her. We love her; we are a family," Julie said softly, as she pulled her jacket on and straightened the three-quarter-length sleeves just below her elbows.

"You never had brothers or sisters, Mother. You cannot understand the differences between siblings. I have tried to understand my sister and she remains the dark enigma that I cannot reach, and there comes a time in one's life when you cease to concern yourself with those differences, and simply take or leave that sibling just as you would any other person you might meet in life," Kerry sighed as she blew softly into her coffee out of habit to cool the mellow liquid which had become such a part of her presence.

"Oh, it just breaks my heart to hear you say such things. Ethel's been away for a while. You'll see the difference in her," Julie pleaded in her own reserved fashion.

"I just saw her at the Christmas Eve gathering, Mother. She was sober as a judge and the same damn Ethel who's been present in this family all of my life. She is simply Ethel. Let's not dwell on this subject too long; it's what I suspect she wants of us," Kerry said with a chuckle.

"I just wish you wouldn't talk that way about a member of the family. We've been through so much. We should share our lives in good and bad times," Julie said, lighting up a cigarette.

"Now you sound like Leo, Mother. She has the gospel truth and nothing but. We should all be kind to one another; it is in our blood — yet Leo was never kind to Howard and she made Kerry Pearl miserable with her petty grievances," Kerry said, turning to face her mother.

"And Leo has never been kind to Ethel, not since that croquet game when Ethel accidentally hit her with the ball," Julie said as the doorbell rang out, interrupting their conversation, which had grown too intense for Kerry.

"Can you blame Leo for that?" Kerry asked, standing face to face with her mother. Their faces were so different. Julie was rattled by how much Kerry resembled Jeff.

"Uh, no, I can't really blame your grandmother for harboring some bad feelings. She just sort of does that," Julie mumbled.

"Then I guess you'd better answer the door, Mother. It is your party, darlin'," Kerry said, knitting her brows together just as Julie had seen Jeff do on so many occasions in their years together, when he wished she would just go on about her business.

"It's probably the Seibels. Ruben likes to be punctual. Fletcher is coming with them — I forgot to tell you," Julie said, getting some sweet revenge in on her daughter for her harsh remarks about Ethel.

"You forgot to tell me! What the hell kinda thing is that to forget to tell me? I didn't even bring a decent dress to wear and you forgot to tell me," Kerry snapped with a smile on her face as she held a finger up in the air on one hand and her coffee mug in the other.

"It's my party, my dear," Julie laughed as she opened the front door of the apartment while Kerry rushed back to the guest room to change clothes.

"APRIL, YOU LOOK so pretty in your dress!" Kerry overheard her mother saying as she closed the door to the guest room softly behind her.

The Prestons had arrived and Ethel promptly headed for the bar to get a drink while Rodney escorted the children to Julie's front room to play. Justin was sleepy since it was past his bedtime and he toddled along behind his father with a corner of his blanket tucked into his palm, cupped around the thumb in his mouth, and the tail of the blanket dragging along beside him for April to trip on. Jessica was nine years old now, such a sophisticated young lady, and she remained behind in the living area to enjoy the party.

"Where's the party, Grandmother?" Jessica inquired, twisting a short curl in her dark hair. She'd worn a pink dress with puffy sleeves, her first pair of pantyhose, and a fancy new pair of pumps with straps around the ankles. "Will Uncle Raleigh be here, Mother?" she asked as she seated herself softly on the edge of the cushion on the sofa.

"Well, of course he'll be here, Jessie. Didn't I promise you he would be?" Ethel replied, pouring herself a drink at Julie's bar.

Julie had not gotten the chance to answer Jessica's question about when the party would begin; she was too busy monitoring Ethel's movements at the bar. She slipped into the kitchen to get the bartender she'd hired for the evening.

"That's the one I was telling you about," Julie whispered to him, tugging at the waist of her dress and straightening the black satin pleats in the full skirt. "No matter what she says, you are not to serve her large doses of alcohol. And if she objects to what you put in her drinks, then you just come and find me."

The bartender winked at Julie in reply. He was smaller than she was by a few inches and Julie was intimidated by his familiar wink. She hurried back to the bar to stand beside her daughter, who had poured herself a healthy portion of vodka with a touch of orange juice sprinkled in for good measure.

"Ethel, really. You know you're supposed to be careful, and Rodney brought that wonderful brew of eggnog he makes so well," Julie scolded, lightly placing her hand on Ethel's shoulder. Ethel flinched at her mother's touch. She did not like to be touched.

"Oh, Christmastime, eggnog: yes, I know it well. I've had so much eggnog in the past ten days that cholesterol is beginning to come through my eyeballs. Since when does this family drink eggnog, anyway? It's New Year's Eve. Time to put the eggnog away. Time for buttermilk or something," Ethel remarked, slipping away from her mother's hand on her shoulder.

"Well, if you want buttermilk, I'll send Raleigh out for some when he gets here with Grandmother," Julie said in unison with the doorbell.

"No, I fucking don't want any buttermilk," Ethel chided under her breath as her mother rushed to get to the front door. Julie looked back over her shoulder to throw Ethel a look of disgust over her comments, tucking her hands into the pockets of her satin gown.

The bartender slipped behind the bar, and, smiling, he glared back at Ethel, eyeball to eyeball.

"What's your name, barkeep?" Ethel asked, the slur of her voice betraying that this was not her first drink of the evening.

"It's Shelton, ma'am," the bartender said with a smile, shuffling his bottles to his side of the bar.

"And you're in on this, too, aren't you?" Ethel demanded, slamming her drink on the bar.

"Well, I don't quite know what you mean, ma'am," Shelton replied, still smiling the same calm smile.

"Oh, you asshole," Ethel barked at him, placing a beefy elbow on the counter of the bar.

"Well, yes, ma'am. I suppose sometimes I am," Shelton remarked as he wiped a crystal glass with his apron.

"Well, I've already got one. I can't imagine why I'd need another one," Ethel sneered at Shelton.

"Well, yes, ma'am, I suppose you have got one. We all do," Shelton said softly, never taking his eyes from the crystal he was polishing.

"Oh, you're just a barrel of laughs, Shelton," Ethel said over her shoulder as she carted her one stiff drink over to the sofa, where she plopped down next to Jessica, who immediately inched away from her.

The room began to fill with friends of Julie's: associates and clients from her business. The Fergusons came, arm in arm, in their everyday clothes. They clung to one another on the far end of Julie's sofa, waiting patiently for Raleigh to arrive so they could discuss old times about their son, Buster, with one who had known him so well before his death. They were the quiet couple now, where once they had been the go-getters of every party. They were the righteous ones of the past, now broken in spirit by the loss of purpose in their lives.

The Seibels arrived, with Ruben holding an umbrella high above Millie's head as she shivered from the chill of January in only her evening dress and silk shawl. Julie escorted her to the powder room, where she helped pin the orchid to the bodice of Millie's elegant lavender chiffon dress, which was a simple design with thin straps and gathered skirt, tied at the waist by a deep-purple ribbon. Fletcher sauntered in behind them with drops of rain nestled in his dark, wavy hair and beard. He went straight to the bar to order a drink, avoiding looking around the room for Kerry.

Raleigh pulled into the parking lot just behind his father. Leota and Cora had chosen to sit in the back seat and he glanced in the rearview mirror, catching a glimpse of his great-aunt patting down her white hair as he turned the engine off. He'd felt like a chauffeur all the way out here, with the two women carrying on their own conversations in the back seat without including him. It was something from another generation, he supposed, and he'd shrugged his shoulders and driven along in silence.

Jeff tapped lightly on Raleigh's car window and Raleigh jumped in surprise to see his father's face before him.

"You wanna show me where your mother's place is? This complex is like a maze. Sure am glad I saw you pull in," Jeff said, opening the door for Cora in the back seat. "It's so dadgum dark out here," he added, helping Cora from the car.

"Well, it's just up past the courtyard and the swimming pool and . . . man, it's such a surprise to see you," Raleigh said in a stutter, as he reached to grasp his father's hand.

"Sometimes I do some crazy things. I just couldn't see spending New Year's without family. I went to Mexico for Christmas, you know," Jeff said as Leota sprinted around the car to latch onto his arm. She held firmly to the only umbrella in the group and was the shortest amongst them. Jeff retrieved it from her hand as they walked briskly along behind Raleigh in search of Julie's condo.

"Why, it's been a month of Sundays since I've seen your handsome self, Jeff Foster," Leota said as her crisp cotton dress snapped in the cold, damp wind. She grasped her gray wool jacket by the lapels and held it tightly to her breast.

"It certainly has been, Leota. And how are you and Cora this evening?" Jeff said, trying to juggle the umbrella around over Cora.

"Oh, we're fair to middlin', I suppose," Cora replied as she stepped on the back of Leota's wedge-heeled shoes. "Oh, I'm sorry, Leota," she said softly.

"Quite all right, dear. This is a very small umbrella," Leota said good-naturedly as she stumbled along, trying to adjust her shoe and keep up with Jeff at the same time.

Jeff had gotten a hotel room for the night in downtown Austin, where he'd showered and changed into his tuxedo. A vendor had been selling carnations in the hotel lounge where he'd stopped to have a drink on his way out and he'd purchased a bright red one for his lapel. Leota reached up with her delicate hands to straighten the carnation as they stood on Julie's doorstep, waiting for the door to open.

Julie swung the door open to greet her mother, looking up at her with Cora to her right, Raleigh to her left, and her ex-husband, the man whose name she still held, standing just behind her mother.

"Well, it's about time! It's colder than Richard Nixon's nose out here," Leota snapped with a wink at Julie as she rushed past her into the warmth of the living area, with its warm fire burning in the fireplace and the room crowded with smoke and conversation.

Cora followed along behind her as Leota tugged at her arm and Raleigh running the race at a close third. Julie stood in shock at the door, looking into Jeff's eyes in surprise of his presence.

She gained her composure after a moment or two and stepped aside to usher him in. He bussed her on the cheek as he entered.

"Jeff, this is quite a surprise! So glad you decided to come," Julie said, as she closed the front door behind them.

Jeff smiled back at her with his familiar stance. "So nice of you to invite me," he said.

"Yes, well, I always invite you," Julie whispered, as the room seemed to become silent.

"Yep, you always do. I've been in Mexico, you know," Jeff answered as he looped his arm in hers and directed them toward the bar.

Ethel joined them at the bar, leaning her weight against her father as she pushed between them. "Hi, Dad," she said, controlled and poised. She tilted her frosted head to rest upon his shoulder briefly before pulling away sharply from his arm, which he'd draped lightly around her shoulders.

"So, where's my charming, skinny sister?" Ethel asked, addressing her mother. Jeff glanced at Julie, surprised by the smell of alcohol on Ethel's breath, considering that Rodney was spending a fortune to have her in a treatment center.

"Seems to me I saw your sister duck into the office. She has a deadline to meet on this article she's been working on and I think she intends to work on it until midnight," Julie said, trying to discourage Ethel from going in search of a sister who was not in the mood to banter with her.

Ethel gave Shelton a glare of contempt over the bar and barked sharply, "Well, since Shelton is rationing my drinks, I think I shall go in search of my dear, infamous sister."

Fletcher Seibel's ears had perked up during the conversation: he knew she was there now. He could wait; midnight was not far away — yet it was as far away as the moon in his heart, in his dreams.

MARGARET AND PUTTNAM were the last guests to arrive at the party, rushing in from the cold, each one supporting a redhead on their hips. Leota, who had cornered Fletcher at the bar, lit up upon seeing them, as the twins were her special little friends. Margaret lowered Tennessee on the ground, where he immediately took off in a run to cling to Leota's skirt, as did Virginia, who stood before her with outstretched arms.

Leota was finally beginning to look like someone's grandmother. Though her hairstyle and her clothing hadn't changed in some forty years, her face had begun to show the lines of wisdom she possessed in her beauty and her glasses were thicker now, magnifying her pine-green eyes to twice their true size and intensity.

Her high, rosy cheekbones had sharpened over the years, and her thin, petite form had become even smaller. She theorized that she was losing an inch in height every two years.

"Justin, Leo?" Virginia asked, looking into Leota's eyes.

"Oh, he's here, my little fireball," Leota said, extending a hand to each twin. She led them to the front room, where Justin was fighting off sleep on a pallet on the floor and April sat cross-legged in front of the television, watching a movie. Leota sat down on the daybed and Tennessee climbed up into her lap. She was happy being alone with the children, and even happier to be separated from her sister Cora for a while.

Virginia sat down on the pallet next to Justin. She tenderly put her arm around him in a clumsy, child-like attempt at a bear hug. Justin abandoned his blanket, and, grabbing Virginia's hand, he stood and beckoned her to the toy box. Mysteries, there were mysteries in his grandmother's toy box: toys that were ancient, made in the fifties, including Barbie and Ken dolls with a cigar box full of doll clothes. The children found the old-style dolls fascinating and they looked brand-new; they were, in fact, virtually untouched by their original owner.

"WHAT THE HECK are you doin' hiding away in here with your nose to the typewriter on New Year's Eve, dear Kerry?" Ethel slurred, balancing her near-empty glass in her hand as she leaned over Kerry's shoulder. Julie's office was dark except for the thin fluorescent light, which was mounted on the wall and extended out over the entire length of the teakwood desk.

"I'm working on an article for a magazine and it has to be sent off day after tomorrow. I'm also expecting a phone call — so, if you don't mind, I should get back to work," Kerry said, pushing her glasses up on the bridge of her nose. Ethel absent-mindedly let the condensation on the outside of her glass drip onto Kerry's shoulder. The cold seeped through her thin linen dress. "Damnit, Ethel, how would you like it if I came in to where you were working and dribbled all over you?" Kerry said, jumping back a bit in her chair.

"I don't work," Ethel chuckled. "Your old flame's out there, you know. And where did you get this tacky little dress? It's not quite right for New Year's Eve — so plain. Beige: what a dull color."

"It just so happens, Ethel, that this is the only dress I brought with me. I had to have a simple, conservative dress for an interview with some oil exec out in New Mexico. I mean, it's not as if I could have borrowed something formal to wear from you or Mother. We're not quite the same size. I suppose I could have borrowed something from Leo, but miniskirts went out of style some years back," Kerry said sarcastically, reaching over to turn her cassette player off and pulling the earplug from her ear.

"Touché, my dear sister. Oil executive . . . there isn't any oil in New Mexico, is there?" Ethel asked in curiosity.

"Not really, guess there isn't, but the oil companies own and operate most of the uranium mines out there. Let's just change the subject, OK?" Kerry said as Ethel seated herself in the chair to the side of Julie's desk.

"Well, I thought perhaps you might have interviewed this 'exec' person for personal reasons. I mean, you could do worse. Rodney did your taxes last year and he says you're broke all the time. 'Starving for art,' as he so mildly puts it." Ethel winced at the thought of poverty.

"Rodney should learn to keep his lip buttoned. I do just fine. I get by," Kerry said, annoyed with Ethel for prying into her finances. The two sisters had never been close and they had never had a personal conversation together in their lives.

"Since you seem to be taking a small break here, would you mind getting me a refill on this little drink of mine? That bartender out there, the one our dear mother hired, won't serve me anything but eggnog," Ethel asked, flashing the empty glass in Kerry's face.

"Ethel, you're supposed to be on the wagon. Can't 'cha do it this one time? Just straighten out your drinking problem before you throw your entire life into a bottle?" Kerry said bluntly.

"Who told you I was supposed to be 'on the wagon'?" Ethel demanded.

"Oh, for goodness' sake, Ethel, I didn't just roll off the back of a turnip truck, ya know. Ya been hittin' the sauce for years and it finally made you sick this year. The kind of physical problems you've had this year are the kind that usually happen to the geritol set. It's killin' you, you know," Kerry said, staring into Ethel's small, narrow eyes.

"Why should I quit? And don't you give me that shit about my three lovely reasons to quit. They have their own lives; this is mine. It's New Year's Eve, GODDAMNIT! I'd like a drink, just like a normal person. I'll quit next year — tomorrow!" Ethel blurted out in desperation. Kerry had never seen her so vulnerable and naked to the bone.

"Nope, wasn't gonna say you should do it for your kids. They're fine little folks, but I've never been one who felt that adults should have to live their lives in a different routine than what suits them just for the children. Wasn't going to say that to you at all, Ethel," Kerry said, shaking her head gingerly.

"Then what were you going to say?" Ethel asked, placing her empty glass on the edge of the desk.

"Well, I suppose I was about to say that you ought to do this thing for yourself. I'm inclined to believe that tackling a problem within ourselves is the hardest obstacle in life. Once that problem's gone, though, it makes better people out of us," Kerry said softly, never taking her eyes off of Ethel's.

"I just want a drink tonight, Kerry. I haven't had a drop in months. Just tonight. It's New Year's Eve. I'd do it for you," Ethel pleaded, risking leaning closer to her sister beneath the glow of the florescent lamp. Their eyes met as total strangers in the artificial light: two people who had no earthly concept of what the other thought.

"Let's not make promises you would never think of keepin', Ethel," Kerry said, cracking the corners of her mouth into a cynical smile as she reached out to grab the empty glass on the edge of the desk. "Only because it's New Year's Eve. No one should ever be without on the last day of the year," she added as she padded out of the room, leaving Ethel to slump back into her chair in triumph, waiting for the grand prize.

Kerry merged with the crowd in the living area, working her way over to the bar. She stopped to bid casual hellos to the Fergusons and the Seibels along the way. Raleigh stopped her as she passed him to ask her opinion of his new secretary, who was huddled in the corner with her cocktail, fending off the advances of Rodney Preston.

Margaret approached her before she could reach the bar. "Can we find a place to talk alone sometime this evening?" Margaret asked, her wavy, auburn hair dipping down over her left eye.

"Sure. I'm still working right now, but in a while. You OK?" Kerry inquired, pushing the hair back out of Margaret's eye.

"Yeah, I'm OK. I've just made a decision. Just need to talk to you and feel supported," Margaret replied, reaching out to touch Kerry on the arm.

"Man, it's a new year, ya know. We all ought to lighten up a bit around here," Kerry grinned. "We shall all survive these times, though we may never find humor within them," she added with a wink to Margaret as she pushed her way closer to the bar.

"What'll it be?" Shelton called out to Kerry as she neared the bar.

"One vodka and orange juice, heavy on the vodka, please, and one glass of Burgundy," Kerry replied, glancing to her side to find Fletcher's dolphin eyes at the end of the bar.

"This glass looks familiar. How 'bout some eggnog for this one?" Shelton winked.

"Just pour the damn vodka, Shelton, and mind your own, all right?" Kerry said. "I realize you're telepathic and all but clear your mind just this once," she added.

"My sentiments exactly," Shelton said, snapping a knowing smile at Kerry as he poured the vodka into Ethel's glass.

Fletcher worked his way over to Kerry in the crowd around the bar. He retrieved Ethel's drink for her while Kerry took a sip of her wine.

"Wanna sit by the fire for a minute?" Fletcher asked softly.

"Oh, only for a minute. I have a patient waiting," Kerry sighed.

They sat down on the brick hearth together. Fletcher placed Ethel's drink down between them.

"So, how was England?" Kerry asked, holding her wine between both hands and letting her eyes wander around the room; she was afraid to look into his eyes.

"I'm back now. I work in Houston," Fletcher answered as he stirred his drink. His elbows rested on his knees as he did so and he, too, was distracted by the bustling party.

"I live down there, too. I write for the *Globe*," Kerry said, surprised that no one had informed her that Fletcher was living in the same town.

"Yes, I know. I read your column. I just had a great conversation with Puttnam Burley. I found out about that place through your column. It's a great hall. Puttnam's really put a lot of heart into it. And Margaret, I finally got to meet Margaret. She's really something. All those things you wrote me about her and more. Lovely. She sort of takes your breath away," Fletcher said, searching for Kerry's hazel eyes.

"Yep, she is. She is my saving grace, my Margaret," Kerry sighed softly, searching for Margaret's agile shadow in the crowd.

"Wanna go play some tetherball?" Fletcher asked, snapping Kerry's attention back to his eyes. The ice in Ethel's drink was melting in front of the fire, as well as Kerry's cold shoulder.

"I think I've played enough tetherball for this evening, thank you," Kerry said, standing to leave.

"Oh, I'm sorry," Fletcher began, reaching up to grasp her arm. "Stay for a minute, just a minute or two," he added, as Kerry settled back in beside Ethel's melting screwdriver.

NEW YORK CITY was supposed to be all aglow on New Year's Eve. It was cold as hell in New York — one of those nights when the wind blew with a fury while people hurried about in formal evening gowns and such, not suitable for the cold.

Phil Jesseps sat at a large table of friends, including Ty and his dark, brooding date, Elizabeth. They were in a bar down in the Village where Phil had just played a guest set. It was warm in the bar; the friends around the table were a family of warmth, sharing stories and tales. Most of them were musicians, songwriters, and performers, so odd in their individuality that they all complemented each other like pieces in a jigsaw puzzle. There was no banter here, no hired bartender, just a family of friends sharing each other's lives.

Dave Van Ronk took the stage and the circle of friends turned their heads toward the aim of the spotlight on the stage. Phil swung his right leg up to rest his black-booted foot on his left knee, leaned back in his chair, and loosened his tie slightly before lighting up a cigarette as Van Ronk began singing the first verse of "He Was a Friend of Mine."

The family of friends at the table never spoke during performances. They listened to each other and learned; they grew from the heart in their own solitude. Elizabeth was a new member of the "family," and she insisted upon trying to engage Ty in conversation. Failing to do so, she turned her attentions to Phil, who sat on her other side.

"Later on, perhaps," Phil whispered to her. "I'm listening to the music now." He patted her knee in a friendly manner beneath the table and turned back to watch the stage.

The club was dimly lit and smoky as the music poured over them. The quiet of the audience was deceiving, since their minds roared in thunder and creativity while Dave Van Ronk's hands glided so smoothly across the frets of his guitar and his voice sung out into the late night of 1975.

When the set ended the room exploded in applause and conversation: a release of energy and gratitude. It was eleven-thirty in New York. Ty was restless, as was his date, Elizabeth. Phil still sat casually leaned back in his chair, lost in thought, tuning out the conversations at the table. He was drinking scotch and water and he reached to the table for his drink just as Ty and the rest of the group were standing to leave.

"So, ya comin' or not?" Ty inquired, his blue eyes flashing back at Phil as he helped Elizabeth with her coat.

"Where ya headed?" Phil asked, confused by the abrupt departure of the family of friends at the table.

"Where the hell else? Times Square. We thought we'd go see how the other half spends New Year's Eve at midnight," Ty replied before downing the last of his drink.

"Aw, come on, man, you're not goin' up there?" Phil said in surprise.

"Yeh, that's where we're goin'. Get your coat," Ty said, drawing Elizabeth close to his side.

"I have a phone call I need to make first," Phil said. He took a long drag from his cigarette and snubbed it out in the ashtray.

Ty stepped away from Elizabeth to stand next to Phil. "Where is she, anyway?" he asked.

"Austin, Texas. Working on an article for *The Avalanche* about the Indian miners in the uranium mines," Phil replied, sipping on his drink as Ty sat down on the edge of the chair next to him. He had already put on his coat and his ascot was wrapped securely around his neck. Phil was amused by his formal appearance.

"Hey, I remember. Margaret's in Austin, too, for Kerry's mother's party. She wrote me a letter, can ya beat that? A letter from Margaret English after two years of silence," Ty remarked. "So, ya miss her? New Year's Eve sure can be lonely — lots of lovelies on the street," Ty said, helping himself to Phil's drink while Elizabeth waited impatiently by his side.

"No, not particularly. Just something . . . something out there. Excuse me, it's been a night," Phil said cautiously. He took his drink away from Ty and gulped down a large portion of the liquid inside.

"Yeh, well, when you make that phone call, send my regards to Miss Margaret . . . might be out there somewhere," Ty said, leaning close to Phil while reaching into his pocket to bum a cigarette.

"Perhaps we'll cross paths later on," Phil said as Ty stood to leave.

"Not a chance," Ty said over his shoulder as he escorted Elizabeth to the waiting family of friends standing at the bar.

Phil finished his drink just as the next musician was about to come on stage. He fished in his pocket for a tip to leave for the waitress, and after dropping it loosely down on the table, he shuffled out to the pay phone by the bar. He had tucked Kerry's mother's phone number into his wallet and he reached into his back pocket to retrieve it. He placed the call, dealt with the operator swiftly, and waited for the phone to ring on the other end.

Ethel picked up the phone on the first ring. "Hello?" she slurred into the receiver.

The voice seemed so familiar in its timbre to Phil that he simply replied, "Kerry."

"Definitely not. Kerry is in the party, tending the flames, I suppose," Ethel said, as though she were having a casual conversation with an old friend. Phil was not one to speak so casually to strangers, even if they did sound a bit like someone he knew well.

"Excuse me. Perhaps I should try to reach her some other time," he said briskly.

"Wait a minute! She is here. This is her sister, Ethel. May I tell her who called?" Ethel said, a tad rattled by speaking on the telephone after so many months of isolation. She was sincere in wanting to take a message for Kerry. She was also nosy in nature when sober and she was only halfway to the borderline of intoxication.

"This is her friend, Phil, um, Phil Jesseps. Tell her I'll call again later at this number," he said into the receiver, trying to outshout the bar noise behind him.

"Phil, Phil who? I didn't catch your last name. You'll have to excuse me. I'm trying to find a pen to write this down," Ethel said, searching the desk for a pen and finally settling in front of the typewriter where Kerry had been working. She flipped the switch to on and hit the return button to jump to the next line.

"Phil Jesseps. Tell her I'll call later . . . New Year's . . . tell her, happy New Year," he said, and without saying goodbye he placed the receiver back into its cradle and grabbed his coat, which he had draped over the top of the pay phone.

He walked out into the street, lighting a cigarette and watching the people hurry past. It was almost midnight, almost the conclusion of this New Year's Eve in New York City, and after three years, Kerry Foster's own sister didn't even know who he was.

He ducked his head as he walked, long lost in thought, almost colliding with a clinging couple lost in idle chatter, bustling down the street with their breath clinging to the night air.

He turned the corner at midnight just a half block from his apartment. The streetlights and faces of passersby burned into his memory as he pulled his jacket collar up against the cold, straightened his glasses on the bridge of his nose, and climbed the steps to his apartment building. The new year rang in around him in total silence as he stood at his window, watching the moon with its thin, wispy clouds, laced in the chill of the night, sheltering its idle solitude.

KERRY FOSTER made her way back through the crowd at the party, glancing back over her shoulder a few times at Fletcher, who had joined Julie and Jeff at the bar. Julie had her favorite Frank Sinatra albums playing on the stereo and the whole atmosphere of the party seemed unreal to Kerry. She had freshened Ethel's drink with more ice and the contents sloshed out onto the carpet as she fended off elbows and juggled both Ethel's drink and her glass of wine. Raleigh was engaged in a conversation with Puttnam just in her path and Puttnam swung his arms out wildly to articulate some point or another, knocking both of Kerry's drinks and their contents to the carpet.

"Dammit, Puttnam, do you always have to talk with your hands?" Kerry snapped as both Raleigh and Puttnam kneeled down to help her retrieve ice cubes and contain the growing pool of red wine. Julie arrived with towels to help, and the four of them bumped heads and elbows cleaning up the mess.

Puttnam walked back to the bar with Kerry once the mess was in hand. He stood towering over her with his hair, which had grown to halfway down his back, tied back into a ponytail at the nape of his neck. He parted it on the side, revealing his high forehead, and streaks of gray were beginning to ease into his sideburns, with a few strands of gray mingling into the part in his shining strawberry-blond hair. He'd simply worn a white long-sleeved shirt, covered by a navy-blue wool sweater, and a pair of Levi's to the party.

"Have you had a chance to talk with Margaret?" Puttnam asked. "She was hoping to find some time to talk with you this evening."

"Nope. I can't seem to get away from Ethel long enough to get anything accomplished tonight — but I will. Ya doin' OK, Putts? I mean, this isn't the end or something serious of that nature, is it?" Kerry asked, leaning her cheek on her elbow, which rested on the bar as Shelton prepared her drinks.

"Nah, it's not the end of us. She's just not happy. God knows I want her to be happy. She can't seem to write. Guess it's a block of some sort. She's been offered tenure, ya know. I don't understand all of that, but she seems to have this fear that accepting it would be like nailing the nails into her coffin.

"The children hardly know her, especially Virginia. Virginia makes her so tense. She is always so formal with them. Of course, Tennessee just idolizes her. He's such a quiet child, but she's just so afraid to let them in, to get to know her, and Virginia is so loud. It doesn't bother me but ya know how Margaret is. She can't tolerate loud noises. It was difficult enough for her to get used to me," Puttnam said, pushing a stray strand of hair from his face.

"Well, I know she can't tolerate being discussed either, so I guess I'd better find some time here to sit and talk with her," Kerry said, throwing her hair back over her shoulder. Raleigh joined them at the bar and handed his empty glass to Shelton for a refill. Shelton had everyone's drinking habits memorized now and he silently mixed up a gin and tonic for Raleigh.

"So, what do ya think of Candice?" Raleigh asked Kerry.

"Oh, I think she's just fine, Raleigh — if you ever get her outta the grips of our brother-in-law," Kerry replied, walking away from the two men at the bar. Puttnam's roar of laughter followed her as she slipped into the crowd gathered by the fireplace.

"Hey, where's that Ethel, anyway?" Raleigh called after her.

"Waiting for heaven to arrive," Kerry volleyed over her shoulder, determined not to lose this set of drinks to the carpet.

"Well, send her out here, will ya?" Raleigh bellowed, lifting his drink in the air.

"Yep, be glad to, bro," Kerry yelled over the croon of Frank Sinatra and the conversation in the room.

"Sorry it took too long, Ethel. I got a little sidetracked out there," Kerry said, closing the door of the study with her foot. She walked over to the desk, placed the drinks down, and stood behind Ethel, who was still sitting in her chair in front of the typewriter. Kerry waited impatiently for Ethel to get the message and remove herself from her work space. Ethel was an expert at ignoring messages of any kind.

"Ethel, darlin', I need to sit there. Here's your drink. Raleigh's askin' about 'cha out there," Kerry said, pushing Ethel's drink closer to her sister's hand.

"I suppose that's the equivalent of 'your mother's callin' ya, kid.' Remember we used to say that to the Ferguson kid to get rid of him?" Ethel said, reaching for her glass as she pushed the chair back from the desk.

"No, I don't remember that, Ethel. Must've been somethin' you and Raleigh did. You didn't like me hanging around, as I recall," Kerry said, sliding into her chair, still warm from Ethel's presence, as Ethel walked over to the window and opened the mini-blinds slightly. She held her cocktail glass up to her forehead as though it were hot in the room, as though it were a summer day in late July when the cold chill of a glass could ease a troubled mind.

"You look like you did as a child since you've cut your bangs again. You never seem to change or grow older," Ethel sighed.

"Yes, well, I am older. I'm all grown up now, Ethel. You don't have to scold me for hanging around anymore; you made your point long ago," Kerry said, picking up her glasses from the edge of the desk and carefully putting them on, tucking the curved earpieces around her ears.

Ethel's rose-colored silk dress seemed to billow out around her as she stood with her back to her sister, watching the slow drizzle of rain blanket the outer edge of the sidewalk outside.

"You always hated me because I was homecoming queen and a cheerleader, and you were never pretty enough to be any of those things — that's why you don't like me now, isn't it, Kerry?" Ethel slurred, turning to face Kerry, who sighed deeply and shoved her bangs over to one side in nervous frustration.

"I never begrudged you those things, Ethel. I was proud of you; they were something you held that was all your own, a part of you that no one else could claim. I never cared about being pretty, Ethel. I had other things. I still have them, those other things," Kerry said softly, sipping her wine between sentences.

"So, you're saying that was all I had, being pretty? And now that that's gone, I have nothing," Ethel said, hesitantly. "I never told you that you grew out of being ugly. I always meant to," she added.

"I don't care, Ethel. It's only the heart and mind that matter," Kerry returned, somewhat taken aback by their conversation. It was the most tedious exchange she'd ever experienced. "And I never said that your beauty was gone. You said that. Beauty seems to be something you must feel within yourself before it can be seen by the general public," Kerry added.

"Well, I think I'll go find Raleigh — that is, if he's really looking for me," Ethel said, briskly walking past Kerry with her drink in hand as though they'd never spoken at all.

"Good idea, Ethel," Kerry said.

Margaret opened the door gently just in time to have Ethel sweep past her in a huff.

"Ethel," Margaret said in salutation.

"Margaret," Ethel snapped in response as she hurried back to the party.

"Honestly, Kerry. I don't think your sister has ever said more than two words to me," Margaret said, closing the door softly behind her. Kerry pushed her chair back from the desk and propped her feet up on the corner, letting her shoes drop to the floor in a soft thud.

"Oh, forget it. She's just like that: off in another world most of the time," Kerry chuckled, motioning to the chair by the side of the desk for Margaret. Margaret sat down gently on the edge of the chair, cupping her cigarettes and lighter in her hands.

"So, I've met Fletcher now," Margaret said, grinning at Kerry.

"So you have," Kerry said, taking her glasses off and setting them on top of the typewriter.

"He's quite handsome. Puttnam has invited him to dinner next week. Think you might like to join us?" Margaret said with a slight hint of mischief in her voice.

"You can't fool me, Margaret. We'll see. Next week: ask me then," Kerry said, reaching out to touch Margaret's cupped hands. "How about — let's smoke together?" Kerry snickered. Margaret shook her head from side to side.

"You never have your own cigarettes," she said, shaking the pack for Kerry, who reached out to retrieve a cigarette.

"Yeah, I know. I keep thinking I don't smoke," Kerry laughed. "So, what's this I hear about tenure?" she asked, blowing her smoke high into the air.

"Well, it was offered at the end of this last semester . . . I don't know, Kerry. I think I should go away for a while . . . maybe this summer to New York. It's a block I'm going through and I'm making the children and Puttnam so ill at ease in their own home," Margaret said, lighting up her own cigarette.

"It's your home, too, Margaret," Kerry said abruptly.

"No, I don't feel it is my home right now. I've lost something and I can't seem to find comfort or stimulation there. I love Puttnam so dearly but I can't live within the walls of a simple domestic routine. I need to breathe in and out among other productive writers. I watch my colleagues go through their day-to-day existence resigned to only teach what is written. Most of them feel they will never produce again themselves, and I must produce. I can't simply teach; I have to feel I'm contributing to the craft. I can't grow there. Their attitudes are so stifling," Margaret sighed.

"Can you wait until summer to go? That's months away," Kerry asked.

"I think I can. If I have that to hold on to, perhaps the time will pass more quickly and I can relax some. I wrote to Ty asking if I could stay at his place for the summer. God, Kerry, I need to fall in and out of love a few times. I need to see and hear all those things I have shut myself off from, things that don't happen at Burley Hall under Puttnam's scrutiny or at stuffy faculty parties. I need something old to feel new again," Margaret said, leaning close to Kerry and reaching out to touch her shoulder.

"We all need those things, Margaret. You and I, we just seem to need to reach out and touch them and hold them, their texture. We need to actually feel it beneath our fingers, whereas most people seem satisfied to merely admire it and treasure it as only part of their dreams. You and I only dream of making the dream a line, and the line a reality," Kerry said, smiling softly at Margaret, whose lips parted into a gentle smile, bringing her dimples to life.

"So we do, my friend," Margaret said, reaching out for her half-empty wineglass, which she'd left next to Kerry's. Kerry in turn reached for hers and they toasted one another in the glow of the fluorescent lamp.

"It always amazes me at how much you and I can say to one another in just a few sentences. We are medicine for each other, two kindred souls," Margaret said.

"Yeah, we're just two young fools — two permanently restless minds," Kerry returned.

"Not to mention hearts," Margaret chuckled.

"No, not to mention hearts. Sure is a hell of a night, isn't it?" Kerry said, walking over to the window to close the blinds. The rain had stopped outside and Kerry noticed Ethel staggering her way along the sidewalk, headed in the direction of the courtyard.

"Ya ready for New Year's, darlin'?" Kerry said, turning back to Margaret, who had stood up and was straightening her dress.

"Ready and better prepared, thanks to you," Margaret said, collecting her cigarettes and wine from the desktop.

Kerry reached over to turn off the lamp above the typewriter, failing to notice the message Ethel had typed there from Phil. Margaret had opened the door to the study and the light from the hallway combined with the big-band music and muffled voices came through to greet them softly in warmth.

"How's Phil doing these days? It's been so long since we've seen him," Margaret asked as they stood in the doorway, reluctant to rejoin the party.

"Oh, he's doin' fine, writin' a lot. We don't get to see each other very often nowadays. I thought he'd call tonight but you know how things can get on New Year's Eve. There's always a thousand people around to carry on with," Kerry said quietly as she closed the door to the study behind them and they walked hand in hand back into the haze of smoke and gaiety.

KERRY LEFT MARGARET sitting by the fire with Fletcher and Puttnam. She went to her mother's room and borrowed a coat from the closet. She glanced down at her bare feet and trotted back to the study to retrieve her shoes, feeling her way in the dark with only the dim light from the doorway to aid her in her search. She closed the door behind her, and with her mother's coat draped over her arm, she pushed her way to the front door to go out in search of Ethel. The phone began to ring in the study, greeting deaf ears. It rang for more than a minute before it finally fell silent in the darkness, as did Phil Jesseps, who sat alone in his apartment with his guitar perched in his lap as he replaced the receiver in its cradle.

Kerry rounded the corner past the courtyard just in time to see Ethel balanced on the edge of the swimming pool. She hadn't even bothered to put a coat on and her dress whipped around her in the light, cold breeze.

"Ethel," Kerry called out, "let's go back inside. You don't even have a coat on."

"Go away, Kerry!" Ethel shouted, kicking her shoe off and dipping her toe into the water. She had a fresh drink in her hand and she tilted it back to her lips.

"Now, goddamnit, Ethel, you've been tellin' me to go away for almost twenty-four years. One a-these days I'm really gonna do it," Kerry said as she stood on the opposite side of the pool from her heavyset sister. Ethel ignored her and jumped feetfirst into the water with a loud splash, which sent water shooting into the sky. Ethel struggled in the water, trying to catch her breath.

"Ethel, come outta there!" Kerry demanded as Ethel continued to thrash around in the water.

"I can't! I can't remember how to swim," Ethel cried out, flailing her arms in the water.

"Ethel, ya never knew how to swim very well. Ya spent too much time sauntering about in your bikini to learn," Kerry screamed through cupped hands.

"I'm drowning! Go get Rodney," Ethel wailed.

"He isn't going to save you, Ethel. Besides, for Chrissakes, you're in the shallow end. Put your goddamn feet down," Kerry coaxed, pacing the side of the pool and clutching her mother's coat around her.

"Go get Rodney! I'm drowning. If you love me at all you'll go get him," Ethel said, stabilizing herself in the water on tiptoe.

"Ethel, dadgum you. It's fucking forty-eight degrees out here. Get yourself outta there!" Kerry screamed as Ethel began thrashing around in the water again, with her ruined silk dress floating around her and her ample rear end occasionally bobbing to the surface.

"Rodney will save me," Ethel mumbled into the night, throwing her head back and coughing out water.

"Rodney is not going to save you, Ethel. You're gonna have to save yourself," Kerry cried out as Ethel began to struggle her way to the deep end, tangling herself in her dress.

"Well, if you're gonna be that way about it I guess I'm elected by lack of an opponent to drag your ass outta there," Kerry yelled, pulling her mother's coat off and kicking her shoes back into the grass. She jumped into the pool, surprised to find it was heated, and worked her way over to her sister. The water felt as warm as a bubble bath compared to the damp chill of the night air.

Kerry grabbed the back of Ethel's dress and swung her arm across Ethel's shoulders as Ethel proceeded to struggle against her hold on her. Kerry huffed her way to the side of the pool in the shallow end, where she and her sister both leaned against the tile, throwing their heads back to greet the moon, now peeking through the clouds.

"I wanted Rodney to save me," Ethel cried softly, tugging on her lower lip with her teeth.

"Well, he didn't. He never has, so far as I can tell. The son of a gun doesn't even have a personality, much less the backbone to save someone," Kerry said, sinking down into the warm water to avoid the cold. "And speaking of saving people, you've probably just given pneumonia the perfect opportunity to claim us both," Kerry snapped.

"I never asked you to jump in here," Ethel barked, climbing out of the pool far enough to reach her drink, which sat on the edge where she'd left it.

"Well, if I'd have known it was like a bathtub in here, I'd have gone on and left you to your misery," Kerry said, slapping at the water.

"I just want to die," Ethel sobbed, draining her glass.

"Well, ya didn't," Kerry said, turning her head away from Ethel.

"But, you don't understand. You have all those things that keep you company. I don't have anything. I'm just a nothing now, just an overweight alcoholic," Ethel cried. "I just wanted to die. Maybe I'd find something on the other side. Maybe I'd have something to do there."

"Well, you're breathin', Ethel. Man, that's somethin'," Kerry said, risking reaching out to stroke her sister's brow.

The two of them stumbled back to Julie's apartment dripping wet. Julie met them at the door and laughed, thinking they had simply had a wild notion to jump in the pool on New Year's Eve: two loving sisters concocting mischievous schemes together. Julie had always dreamed they would be such sisters.

Cora sat next to her sister, Leota, as the two wet women stood by the door waiting for Julie to return with towels. Cora turned to wink at Leota but instead found Leota with a stone gaze in her eyes directed toward her granddaughter, Ethel. Leota had noticed Ethel leaving earlier without a coat and Kerry following soon after. She suspected that this was just one more of Ethel's stunts.

Rodney walked up to Ethel as she stood with her dress clinging to her folds. She reached out to touch him and he pulled away from her, saying "Come on, now, sweetie, you're all wet," at which point Kerry shot him a sharp look armed with daggers.

Julie returned with the towels while Leota got up from the sofa to come help Kerry into the study where she'd left her suitcase.

"You can tell me all about it," Leota whispered to Kerry, with her arm draped over Kerry's towel-clad shoulders.

"I don't want to discuss it, Leo," Kerry whispered, looking back over her shoulder to see Julie leading Ethel into the guest room.

"Well, suit yourself, then. I'm just tryin' to help," Leota sighed, reaching up to brush a clinging, wet spike of Kerry's bangs from her eyes.

Jeff Foster sat next to Fletcher by the fire. They exchanged glances as the two women left the room.

"So, tell me, Fletcher: what firm are you working with down in Houston? It's been years since I've seen you," Jeff said, tugging at the knees of his trousers.

"YOU'RE SO THIN, Kerry. How much do you weigh these days?" Leota said, as she fingered the texture of Julie's leather couch in the office. She looked up at Kerry with her magnified green eyes, waiting for a response. Kerry stood a few feet away from her with her wet clothes at her feet as she toweled herself off.

"Oh, I dunno, Leo. Hundred 'n' five, hundred 'n' ten. Somewhere around there. Why?" Kerry asked, tilting her head in front of her and rubbing the towel briskly over her hair.

"Because you're too tall to weigh so little. Why, you must be five foot seven or so. You ought to weigh more, like your mother," Leota replied, folding her hands into her lap.

"Well, I'm not built like Mother. We have different bone structures and she's got the big boobs. They weigh a lot, ya know," Kerry grinned down at her grandmother as she pulled her sweater over her arms. She had replaced her wet linen dress with blue jeans, a white cotton turtleneck, and a pale blue V-neck sweater. She sat down next to Leota on the sofa to pull her socks on, turning the cuffs down just the way she wanted them before slipping her feet into her penny loafers.

"Well, I wouldn't know about that," Leota sighed after a long delay in conversation. Kerry turned to face her with a confused look on her face.

"Ya wouldn't know about what, Leo?" Kerry asked.

"Why, big boobs weighin' more and all," Leota answered with a grin.

"No, guess ya wouldn't," Kerry said with a snicker. "It's almost midnight, Leo. Maybe we should get back to the party. Guess I should dry my hair a little bit," Kerry said, hinting for her grandmother to return to the party without her.

"Oh, in a minute. It's just so nice to sit here with you; we so seldom get the chance to just sit and talk alone like we used to out on my patio in the summertime. You were the only one who always came by to see me on a daily basis. I just want you to know how much I treasure those days of your childhood. You and Raleigh were such special children, always had your little minds racin' like the wind in a hurricane," Leota said, reaching up to dab a tear from her eye with the tissue she kept in the cuff of her sleeve. She knocked her glasses slightly ajar on her nose in the process and Kerry reached over to straighten them.

"Thank you, dear," Leota said, readjusting her glasses even though Kerry had straightened them for her.

"Oh, you're welcome, Leo. And thank you for lovin' us so much, even though we don't deserve it," Kerry said, winking at her grandmother, who looked so small and fragile sitting beside her on the couch.

"It's such a treat getting to see young Fletcher. What a handsome young man he's grown into. And so polite. He was always my favorite, ya know. I used to include him in my prayers at night and I also asked the good Lord to bring the two of you back together someday," Leota said, coaxing a grin onto Kerry's face.

"Oh, Leo. Half the time ya fall asleep watchin' Johnny Carson and ya can't tell me ya really say your prayers as you're driftin' off to never-never land," Kerry chided her.

"Well, maybe not every night — just some nights. But I always say a word for Edgar before I fall asleep. It makes my dreams more pleasant," Leota said, tapping Kerry on the knee with her small, thin hand.

Her matching set of wedding bands always clinked together when she did that and it was such a familiar sound to Kerry's ears, a sound she could recall before memory began for her. It brought forth the great warmth of distant, familial understanding, like the crackling of a floor furnace at dawn on a winter morning and the smell of bacon and coffee permeating the air while soft, muffled voices drifted through her grandmother's house. She could vaguely recall the low timber of her grandfather's voice and the features of his face, with his thick, wavy hair. He was only a blur of an image to her, yet he was a presence in her memory.

"Well, I'd best go back. Dab a little rouge on those cheeks for me before you come out," Leota said. She turned back to face Kerry before opening the door to the study. She looked so small to Kerry, with her white hair so perfectly in place and those huge, magnified green eyes all a-twinkle. "Ya know, I've often wondered where the hell your mother got those big boobs anyway. Musta been from Cora," she chuckled.

Kerry burst out in laughter and ran to hug her grandmother, finding her light as a feather in her arms. "You're really somethin', Leo. I love you," Kerry said.

"S'pose I love you, too," Leota answered, standing up on her tiptoes to buss Kerry on the cheek before leaving the room and closing the door behind her.

Kerry dried her hair quickly with her blow-dryer, applied a small amount of makeup to her face, and returned to the party where everyone had gathered around the piano.

Julie and Leota shared the piano bench together. Their slender fingers were poised above the ivory as Jeff stood beside them monitoring his wristwatch. Ethel had had to settle for a long cotton kaftan to wear and her hair had dried into a softer, more natural style than the one she'd originally come in with at the beginning of the party. Her face was sparkling clean and Kerry thought to herself that it was probably the first time in fifteen years or more that she'd seen her sister without globs of eye makeup on.

Kerry was quite taken with how lovely Ethel really was. She still had that glow of peaches and cream. She pushed her way in to stand beside Ethel behind the piano bench.

"I knew you'd come out smelling like a little rose," Ethel sneered softly to Kerry. "At least you had dry clothes and some makeup to put on. I could just die," she winced.

"Yep, you sure could've," Kerry replied as Jeff began the countdown for midnight. Kerry turned her eyes down to her mother's blond French twist and snickered to herself.

"Five, four, three, two, one!" Jeff shouted. When he hit the one Shelton began popping the corks of the champagne bottles with Puttnam and Raleigh's help, while Leota and Julie hit the chords on the piano and started everyone off on "Auld Lang Syne."

Fletcher brought a glass of champagne to Kerry and lightly placed his arm around her shoulders as the second verse of the song came up. No one ever remembers the second or third verses to that song, but on this night the words seemed to come back to them — especially to Leota, who was reading the lyrics from the sheet music.

> *And there's a hand, my trusty friend,*
> *And give us a hand o' thine . . .*
> *We'll take a cup o' kindness yet*
> *For auld lang syne.*
> *We'll take a cup o' kindness yet*
> *For auld lang syne.*

The room exploded with laughter and applause after the second chorus. Kerry turned to find herself in Fletcher's embrace and he bent his face down close to hers, pausing for a moment before kissing her firmly on the lips.

"Dammit, Fletcher," Kerry said, struggling a bit in his arms.

"It's New Year's — you're supposed to kiss the one you love on New Year's," Fletcher said softly, and he bent down to kiss her again.

She did not struggle the second time, nor was she surprised that she remembered the feel of his lips against hers.

"You're supposed to kiss the person closest to you at New Year's, dummy, not the one you love," Kerry teased after the spell was broken.

"Well, I thought I'd do a little of both. Besides, I don't think either one of us had that custom quite right," Fletcher said with a grin. He laughed softly and the sound of his laughter brought a tear to Kerry's eye, which she quickly wiped away.

"You played that beautifully, Mother. Happy New Year," Julie said, giving Leota a light squeeze around her shoulders.

"Well, ya didn't do so bad yerself," Leota said, pushing the piano bench back and standing up to greet the kiss on the cheek from Jeff.

Julie swung her legs around the edge of the piano bench so she could face the party and Jeff sat down next to her, handing her a full glass of champagne.

"Here's to ya," Jeff said, lifting his glass to Julie's.

"Here's to you and all the lovely parties you've missed," Julie said in return.

Jeff winked at her, took a sip of his champagne, and said, "Well, like I said, I went to Mexico for Christmas this year."

"Well, you haven't been in Mexico for the last fifteen years!" Julie said sarcastically.

"So I haven't," Jeff bantered, lightly kissing Julie on the cheek as Ruben approached them. He bent down to buss the hostess on the cheek and shake Jeff's hand.

"Happy New Year, Julie. Such a pleasant party. Millie and I have had a wonderful time," Ruben said as Millie came to stand next to him. She bent down to kiss Jeff on the cheek.

"Jeff, it's so nice to see you. Why, it's just been years," Millie said, patting his shoulder.

"Millie, get your wrap, please. Time to go," Ruben said jubilantly.

"But, Ruben, it's only just turned midnight. One more dance, dear," Millie coaxed, looping her arm in his.

"All right, dear. One more dance," Ruben blushed.

"And one more glass of champagne," Millie said, holding her empty glass out to him. He tenderly took it from her hand and stroked the petals of the orchid as he did so.

"Such a lovely flower," Ruben commented as he turned to head for the bar. Julie caught his arm before he could take a step.

"What would you like to hear for that dance, Ruben?" she asked.

"How about that record you played earlier of Count Basie and his orchestra?" Ruben said with a wink.

"That's a long record, Ruben," Millie teased.

"I know," Ruben said, bending down to kiss his wife before strolling to the bar.

NOT LONG AFTER MIDNIGHT, Raleigh bundled Leota and Cora up in their coats and, sporting Candice on his arm, he left the party to drive the two elderly women home. The Fergusons followed quietly behind him.

Rodney woke the children and Ethel, carefully pulling their coats onto their sleepy bodies, and they filed out the door just before one in the morning. Justin had his blanket tucked close to his mouth and he turned around to Julie sitting on the piano bench to mumble "Happy New Year, Granmutha" as Rodney grasped his free hand and gently pulled him along.

Margaret and Puttnam were staying over in Julie's guest room, leaving the twins to sleep on their pallets in Julie's front room, which was somewhat of a den. Puttnam and Margaret went in together to check on the two redheads and found them sound asleep with toys strewn around them on the floor. They both bent down to straighten the blankets around the children; Margaret wrenched a Barbie doll from Virginia's hand.

"What the hell is this?" she whispered, placing the doll in the toy box.

"Ssshh. It's a Barbie doll," Puttnam said. Puttnam never could whisper.

"I didn't know they still made those horrid things," Margaret winced. She smiled then, reached out for Puttnam's hand, and they retired to Julie's guest room, bidding good night to the lingering guests as they passed through the living room.

They made love for the first time in weeks that night — all night. Margaret fell asleep resting her head on Puttnam's shoulder as he wept softy to himself. "I haven't lost you . . . I knew I hadn't lost you . . . you are my life," he tried to whisper as Margaret stirred, squeezed him gently, and nestled her head closer to his ear. He dropped off to sleep listening to her soft breathing and they remained tangled together until Puttnam's snoring called for Margaret to roll over to her side of the bed sometime around dawn.

Jeff offered a ride to Fletcher, who had been left behind by his parents. Fletcher had a hard time tearing himself from conversation with Kerry by the fireplace. She'd given him her phone number and promised to join him at Puttnam and Margaret's for dinner. Jeff stood at the door in his tux, tapping his foot impatiently, waiting for the two young people to say their good nights.

Jeff did not return to his hotel room that night after dropping Fletcher off at the Seibels'. Kerry heard him open the front door softly and the sound of her mother's voice greeting him as he closed the door behind him.

Kerry smiled to herself as she slipped into her nightgown. She walked over to the desk and turned on the fluorescent lamp, then returned to the switch by the door to turn off the overhead light. She had a ritual of checking what she'd written in the day just before going to bed. She sipped at the last of her champagne, picked up her glasses from on top of the typewriter, and sat down in the chair to read her work.

She gently pulled the sheet of paper from the typewriter and glanced over the lines at the top of the page. She found several typos immediately and was thoroughly disgusted with herself for the work she'd put down that evening. Just as she was about to crumble the paper and toss it in the trash can by the desk, she noticed the bold capital letters at the bottom of the page. "PHIL JESSEPS. TELL HER I'LL CALL LATER. NEW YEAR'S. TELL HER, HAPPY NEW YEAR," Kerry read in disbelief.

"Oh, damn you, Ethel," Kerry complained under her breath. She tossed the paper in the trash can, pushed her chair away from the desk, and glanced over at the clock on the wall. It was three A.M. in Austin, four in the morning in New York — too late to call.

She stood at the window for several minutes, with the blinds opened slightly, watching the winter sky. She felt so lonely and could not understand the loneliness.

She lay awake for a couple of hours in the darkness pondering her heart, realizing that all that was decided before tonight was now an indecision and that morning would not ease that difference.

NEW YEAR'S DAY was a dreary haze of drizzle as the gray skies returned before noon. Jeff took the entire family, including Margaret, Puttnam, and the twins, out to eat Mexican food at the family's favorite restaurant in downtown Austin.

It had been many years since they had all sat together in this restaurant, exchanging healthy familial banter and passing baskets of chips and platters of corn tortillas around the table. When Edgar had been alive this restaurant had been the family's weekly haunt on Sunday afternoons. They had each visited the restaurant separately through the years, trying to rekindle that same glow, but had instead merely gathered individual memories of the place and its atmosphere.

Ethel was quite hungover, and considering that she hadn't been allowed that much to drink in a few months, her condition was understandable. April sat next to her, smacking on a beef taco, which Ethel found nauseating. She dipped her white cotton napkin into her ice water, turned her chair so as not to have to face her daughter, and applied the cool cloth to her forehead to relieve her splitting headache. Raleigh teased her relentlessly about her hangover, until Julie nonchalantly kicked him in the shin beneath the table. She never even paused in her conversation with Cora, who sat to her right, as she administered the blow to her son on her left.

Cora and Leota had made a small pot of black-eyed peas. After lunch everyone gathered at Leota's to watch football and she demanded that they each consume a small portion of the black-eyed peas to ensure them a healthy and prosperous year. Everyone was stuffed with Mexican food and they all groaned in protest as Leota forced the small bowls of mushy black-eyed peas on them. Ethel flatly refused to eat hers.

The New Year would come and go, as new years hurriedly pass into the old.

Resolutions

THE SPRING PASSED MILDLY in 1976. Margaret English actually enjoyed the spring semester, with her classrooms full of freshly tanned faces and open minds. When the month of May rolled around, yawning with sleepy eyes beneath the Houston heat, she could hardly believe the semester was finished and it was time to pack her bags for her summer in New York.

Puttnam did not pout or show any visible signs of disapproval over her decision to go. He made the leaving easy for her in hopes that in doing so she would feel comfortable when she returned. He was almost certain she would return.

Kerry plugged along through the spring with a worried heart. She spent a great deal of her time with Fletcher. They found few barriers in reestablishing their relationship, except that Kerry now maintained a certain amount of caution with him. He was aware of her friendship with Phil Jesseps. Kerry was not capable of hiding such things from one so close to her.

She continued to write to Phil, yet she did not visit him, and he in turn did not come to see her. He was a place in her heart which she could not grasp in understanding. He always remained somewhat of an unknown — something she never truly held on to, so, therefore, she could not let go. Though Fletcher held the majority of her thoughts, Phil was an image that came to her in her dreams and brought tranquility and quiet. The dreams made her feel as though she weren't tethered to the ground by gravity, and when she awoke she could swear she felt herself drop softly back into her bed.

MARGARET BECAME CONCERNED over Kerry's emotional state. Kerry refused to speak at length about what was troubling her and insisted on concentrating on discussions about Margaret's pending trip to New York.

One night in late April, Kerry and Margaret sat out on the screened-in porch at Margaret and Puttnam's place. It was late and the twins had gone to bed. Puttnam was still down at Burley Hall and would be for hours, as he was trying to get his books up-to-date. The night air was still and humid as Margaret swung in her hammock and Kerry sat in a lawn chair with her feet propped up in the wood-frame windowsill. They were sipping red jug wine and smoking cigarettes. The neighbors could hear their light laughter filtering through the night like the sweet morning songs of whippoorwills. Margaret was casually clad in an old pair of cutoff blue jeans and one of Puttnam's old Burley Hall T-shirts with the sleeves rolled up to her shoulders. She wore no makeup and her auburn hair cascaded across the right side of her face. Kerry thought she looked like a skinny adolescent all stretched out in the hammock with her arms folded beneath her head.

"So, you're headin' back into the lights in two weeks?" Kerry sighed, grabbing the edge of the hammock and swinging Margaret back and forth.

"Damn right. I'm so anxious to hit the streets and roll again. Ty's going to be in Europe for the first few weeks that I'm there, so I'll have his place all to myself for a while. I mean, can you imagine that? No small children, hopefully no barking dogs, and the best part: I don't have to drive for two whole months. I am so weary of Houston traffic jams on the Gulf Freeway. I have so many plans, Kerry, so many ideas about what I want to write," Margaret said, before taking a long drag off of her cigarette.

"Have you made plans to visit with Clare?" Kerry asked, still swinging the hammock.

"She's coming into the city for two days in July. I was so surprised when she wrote me that. I thought I'd have to go up to Saratoga and pry her out of her office and believe me, I was not looking forward to seeing dear Ernest on my summer vacation," Margaret chuckled.

"Well, I wrote to Phil that you were definitely coming. He's going to be in the city for most of the summer. Said you should call him," Kerry said. She took a long sip of her wine, let go of the edge of the hammock, and walked to the screen door, pushed it open, and gazed out at the stars.

"He wrote me — I forgot to tell you. His letter came on one of those days when Virginia was plowing through the house giving her best Shirley Temple performance and I forgot to mention it to you the next time we spoke," Margaret said, swinging her legs around over the edge of the hammock so she could sit up. "We're planning on going out to some baseball games and bars and stuff until Ty gets back," she added.

"That's funny. He didn't mention to me that he'd written to you," Kerry said, closing the screen door. She'd been swimming in the early evening and had not bothered to rebraid her hair, so hundreds of wavy strands had worked their way loose from the braid to frame her face while her bangs were shuffled over to the side of her forehead, giving her a slightly disheveled appearance. Her braid swung down over her shoulder and she toyed with the ends of it before shaking a cigarette from the pack on the table and placing it to her lips.

"He says you don't write very often anymore. In fact, he mentioned New Year's, since you've been seeing Fletcher. Have you let go of Phil?" Margaret asked, risking a prying question.

"They are two different things entirely . . . they are different feelings in separate places within me," Kerry said, placing her hands up on the screen with her fingers stretched wide on one hand and her cigarette balanced in the other. Margaret was surprised by her open reply and chose to pursue the issue.

"How are they different, Kerry?" Margaret asked. "How are they so separate within you?"

"One is old love, sacred, balanced; not in love but a fragment of one's self within someone else; within yourself. And the other is loving someone, being in love, with need for that love: holding it within your heart and protecting its valuable qualities, which are essential to your very survival. It would be so easy if one or the other of these things was simply infatuation or a passing fancy but it isn't so and I am so damn tired of the frustration of it all. It's hurting me so inside. Most people live out their lives and only come across one of the two. How the hell do you deal with both at once?" Kerry cried, leaning her forehead against the screen window.

"Oh, why the heck am I telling you all this? Ya can't solve it, ya can't talk it away. I have to make the choices and shuffle the emotions around in myself. There's not a person on this earth who can do that for me," Kerry said, turning to face Margaret with the hint of a smile on her face.

"No one ever said you had to make that choice. They are two different things. I understand what you were saying about their differences and there is no reason to make a choice here. No reason at all. Loving people, respecting people, and giving warmth to another human being with all you have to share and all that you hold dear is too rare in each of our lives for us to throw it away; to cast guilt upon its value is the sin of our parents. It's bad enough that they inflicted such things upon themselves. We should not allow those unjust value judgments and ridiculous moral codes to pass on for another generation," Margaret said, with her hair dipping across her eye.

"Oh, for God's sake, Margaret, this ain't philosophy we're discussin' here. These are real folks and regardless of how many sins our parents passed into our fat, greedy, little hands, they sure enough did pass them along, and life is meant to be comfortable. Life should be a center of learning from one's own mistakes and accomplishments. This is just a damn mess; it's not a mistake or an accomplishment. And why the hell can't I think like you do, anyway? Why can't I rest easy with these feelings of mine?" Kerry said, reaching for her glass of wine, which Margaret handed to her from the table.

"If they are strong enough to give it time, if you are patient and honest with yourself, each emotion shall fall into its proper place and each will remain a part of your life. No one will lose then, and life will be comfortable again. It will depend on their own ability to understand, on their own pasts and dilemmas and whether they learned from them, for surely you are not alone in this, in having a past, and will not be alone in building a past within your future," Margaret said. "It'll work out, you'll see. Answers will come flying home. Your heart will rest in your own windowsill someday."

"And if by some fluke Richard Nixon gets elected by a write-in vote next election, we'll all gather down at Burley Hall to throw a victory party for him, won't we?" Kerry said, plopping herself down in the lawn chair and lifting her wineglass to Margaret.

"Right!" Margaret chuckled, tipping her glass to Kerry in return. She stretched back out in the hammock, resting her wineglass on her chest as she stared up at the ceiling.

"Do you think you and Puttnam will ever actually marry, Margaret?" Kerry asked, toying with her braid.

"No, I don't think we ever will," Margaret said softly.

"Why not? You've always seemed to be suited for one another; so much a part of each other's lives as individuals. I mean, it seems like you're married," Kerry said with a sigh.

"Oh, I can't really think of a solid reason. I guess it's because 'there's light out there,'" Margaret giggled, imitating Kerry's accent as she spoke. They both laughed then and tipped their glasses to the ceiling.

Puttnam found them still chatting and carrying on when he arrived home at three in the morning. He kissed Margaret good night, checked on the twins who were safe in slumber, and went to bed, leaving the two women to share their souls out on the front porch where they stayed until dawn.

JUNE BROUGHT a period of solitude to Puttnam Burley. Suitcases were packed and the twins were shuffled out the door to go to Austin with Raleigh, where they would spend two weeks being treated as royalty at Leota's house.

Puttnam was reluctant to let them go, but Leota had asked him personally on the telephone and the twins had this memory for such things involving Leota. They waved goodbye to their father from the back seat of Raleigh's Toyota; their little red heads could barely reach above the windows. Candice had come down with Raleigh, and Puttnam's last thought before going inside was of how natural Raleigh looked sitting in a car with an intelligent, lovely woman in the passenger seat and two laughing children in the back.

He walked back inside, brushing his hair back from his forehead, and headed for the bedroom, where he turned on the air conditioner, closed the window, pulled Margaret's last book of published poetry down from the shelf, and relaxed on the bed to read. He wondered what would be within the pages of her next book. He still did not understand this one and he'd read it cover to cover at least a hundred times.

There was only one picture of Margaret in the house. It hung above Puttnam's bedside table. The rest of the house was full of photographs of the children, friends, and performers who had come to stay at their home, yet Margaret was shy of cameras and still images of individuals so there was only this one photograph that she would tolerate being up in the house. Puttnam leaned against the pillows he'd placed behind him as he read and occasionally he'd bend forward and turn his head back to gaze at Margaret's photograph. In spite of missing her and the sounds of the children, he was enjoying his time alone. He and Wiley had scheduled a poker game for next weekend backstage at the hall. Raleigh was coming down for it and Jeff had mentioned that he was interested, as well as all the bartenders from the club. What a time they would have, Puttnam thought to himself, leaning back on his pillows with Margaret's book in his hand and his feet crossed at the foot of the bed. He reminded himself out loud that he should call Fletcher in the morning and tell him about the game. Kerry had to review some soul across town that night anyway — maybe ole Fletcher would enjoy the company.

————

"I NEED TO STOP now, Uncle Raleigh," Virginia chimed from the back seat.

"Virginia, we just left the city limits. Ya haven't even been in the car for twenty minutes! Why didn't 'cha go before we left the house?" Raleigh protested, rolling his eyes in amusement at Candice.

"I did. I really did, Uncle Raleigh," the three-year-old Virginia said in defense. She was so tiny, with such shining auburn hair and ivory skin that Raleigh shook his head and smiled in sympathy with her as he watched her in his rearview mirror. She had an amazing capacity for language for a three-year-old, though she was very near to being four. She was just so small, much smaller than her brother, Tennessee, who rarely spoke at all.

"OK, Virginia. Just a few more miles, darlin'," Raleigh said, winking over at Candice, whose shoulder-length blond hair was flying in the breeze coming in through the open car window. She had her elbow resting on the car door and she tilted her head toward Raleigh in response to his wink.

"Think she can wait?" Candice asked with a snicker.

"She can wait. She's just showin' off," Raleigh laughed, glancing back at Virginia in the mirror.

"I am not, Uncle Raleigh," Virginia cried, folding her arms across her chest indignantly. She was a tad jealous of Raleigh's new companion, Candice, and was green with envy over the fact that Candice got to sit in the front passenger seat instead of her.

Tennessee was coloring in a coloring book with a set of felt-tip pens his mother had given him. He looked over at his sister with skepticism as she pouted in the back seat beside him.

Raleigh's Toyota rolled into Leota's driveway, spitting gravel into Leota's lawn just in time for lunch. Thomas Evans stepped out on the porch to greet them, with Cora peeking through the screen door behind him. Virginia squirmed impatiently while Raleigh unfastened her seat belt. Tennessee quietly examined the pictures he'd colored in his book, patiently waiting his turn for freedom.

Virginia took off like a lightning bolt for the house when she was freed. Thomas Evans caught her in mid-leap as she skipped up the front porch steps. Raleigh had difficulty unbuckling Tennessee's seat belt, yet the child still sat quietly, closing the cover of his coloring book carefully when he heard the seat belt snap open.

"I bet you'll be awfully glad to get out of this ole hot car, won't 'cha, Tenn?" Raleigh asked.

"Uh-huh," Tennessee answered, climbing out of the car. He walked around to the trunk and stood waiting for Raleigh to open it so he could get his little suitcase out. He looked up at Raleigh with his sky-blue eyes and smiled innocently, as if he knew some secret about life that Raleigh hadn't yet found.

"Ya must be in a hurry to get your things unpacked here, Tenn," Raleigh said with a chuckle.

"Uh-huh," Tennessee said as Raleigh opened the trunk, reached inside, and grabbed Tennessee's small canvas suitcase. He handed it to Tennessee and began pulling the rest of the gear out of the trunk. When he looked around, Tennessee was still standing next to him, holding his suitcase firmly in his right hand.

"Was there something else I could do for you, Tenn?" Raleigh asked, a bit puzzled by the expression of disappointment on the boy's face.

"Um, I think my daddy put my fishing pole in there so I could go fishing with Mr. Evans. I'll carry that too," Tennessee replied, changing the expression on his face back to his usual warm smile.

"Is this it?" Raleigh asked, pulling out the small cylinder-shaped case which housed Tennessee's miniature fishing pole.

"Uh-huh," Tennessee answered, his eyes lighting up at the sight of his most treasured possession. Jeff Foster had ordered that rod and reel from a mail order catalogue especially for Tennessee. He'd ordered one just like it for his grandson Justin, too.

"Well, ya happy now?" Raleigh asked as he jiggled the coins in the pockets of his shorts and smiled down at Tennessee's carrottop head. Tennessee was busy inspecting the case of his fishing pole.

"Uh-huh. Thank you, Uncle Raleigh," Tennessee replied, before sauntering off toward the porch, holding the cylinder case up in the air for Thomas Evans to see.

"Well, he sure doesn't waste words, does he?" Raleigh said to Candice, handing her the toy box Puttnam had packed.

"No. But then, neither do you," Candice answered, grinning at Raleigh.

AFTER LUNCH, Leota put the twins down for a nap, and although she could hear the pitter-patter of Virginia's little feet scampering around the guest room after she'd closed the door, she ignored the mischievous sounds, fixed up a fresh glass of iced tea, and went out on the porch to join Thomas and Cora.

"Are the children settled in?" Thomas asked with a toothy grin as Leota slipped down into her lawn chair, breathing a sigh of relaxation.

"Well, I think that young Tenn is already sound asleep but that little Virginia isn't about to catch a wink of shut-eye this afternoon," Leota replied, shaking her head.

"Maybe I should go have a talk with Virginia. They really should stick to their normal schedules, and Puttnam did say in his note that it was very important that they both take at least an hour nap each day," Cora said, standing to go inside. She smoothed down the hem of her housedress and patted her hair down around her neckline.

"Oh, it'll be all right. She just got here and we don't want to frighten her. Besides, I leave the discipline of the children to their parents these days. What good's it do to get old if you can't ruin somebody else's children for 'em?" Leota responded.

Thomas stood up from the back steps and walked around the flower beds, occasionally pulling up a weed or sprig of grass. Leota watched him in amusement, thinking to herself that it was just like Thomas to not be able to sit still for very long. He always had to be working at something or another.

"Well, now, I'd like to take young Tenn and Justin out to the fishin' pond day after tomorrow, if that's OK with you, Leota," Thomas said as he walked along the edge of the flower bed.

"Oh, that'll be fine, Thomas. Cora and I will fix up a basket lunch for y'all but you have to be careful with young Tenn in the sun. He has such fair skin and Puttnam's note said that he sunburns easily," Leota said.

"Well, I suppose I'll have to get some instructions from you on that, Leota. I've never had the fair skin problem, ya know," Thomas said with a laugh, bending down to pull up a long sprig of carpet grass out of the mint.

"Now that I think on it, Thomas, I guess ya haven't," Leota laughed.

Cora joined in on the humor with her own anecdotes and the three of them spent the afternoon bantering back and forth, with Thomas pacing up and down along the flower beds. They were enjoying their retiring years of leisure and all three were so excited about having the young twins in the house that it was difficult for them to let the two little people take their naps in peace. They were anxious for the little ones to wake up and romp around the backyard, breathing new life into their households. They longed to experience the next generation carrying on the old.

Raleigh had driven Candice back to her place on Riverside Drive. They argued the entire distance about whether or not they should live together, which Raleigh was against. He wasn't ready to live with anyone. He needed his solitude and privacy.

He dropped Candice off at her place and went home to work in his garden. The sun felt good on his shirtless back as he hoed the weeds between his tomato plants. The blossoms were just beginning to bloom on them and he tenderly checked each tiny yellow petal. His hands had always been so large, yet they were deft as those of an artist as he handled the foliage of his plants.

There was a huge sycamore tree in the south corner of his yard. Late that afternoon, Raleigh carted his canvas camp cot out to that corner and stretched out for a nap in the shade. He thought a great deal about his argument with Candice as he drifted off to sleep. He wondered whether he'd done the right thing in telling her they shouldn't see each other for a while. He was afraid she would never be able to understand his nightmares about the war. He fell sound asleep pondering Candice and the war.

He dreamed of being lost in the streets of Saigon. He dreamed of finding Candice in the street beside the delivery truck instead of Buster; he dreamed of loneliness so intense that he awoke at twilight with his arms wrapped tightly to his chest.

Raleigh ignored the dreams. He always put them aside when he stepped into the waking world. They had a tendency to linger in his memory as no other dreams could. In fact, he could rarely recall his pleasant dreams with any clarity. Only the nightmares remained vivid.

He folded his canvas cot up and carried it to the garage, finding a tear resting on his cheek when he stopped to open the garage doors. He brushed it off casually with his massive hands, shrugged his shoulders, and went inside to shower.

He had overcome the anxiety of the nightmares during his nap by the time he'd showered and shaved. He locked his front door behind him whistling, and hit the streets on foot to head for his favorite campus bars.

"What the hell do I need to live with somebody for? I do just fine by myself. Christ, who needs that kind of responsibility? Already did that once," Raleigh mumbled to himself as he turned the corner onto Guadalupe Street. He stopped just outside the door of one of the bars and glanced back at the University of Texas across the street, with its massive tower and blocks of buildings, thinking that someday, by God, he'd go back to school. He hit the door to the bar with the palm of his hand and it flew open with a familiar gasp. The television was blasting, conversations were loud and jovial, and the bartender slapped his bar rag against his own shoulder the way he always did when he greeted a regular customer. Raleigh settled in at the bar with a gin and tonic and turned his attention to the baseball game on television. The bartender stopped in front of Raleigh and lit a cigarette. He drummed his fingers on the bar as he blew his first puff of smoke into the air.

"Hey Rals. Ya haven't been in in a while. Good to see ya, pal," the bartender said. "Hey, I got this new joke ya gotta hear," he began, as Raleigh placed his elbows up on the bar and leaned in to hear the dirty joke.

Raleigh was still sitting at the bar when closing time came. The bartender busied himself sweeping up some broken glass beneath a table in the far corner of the room. Some couple having a domestic squabble had sat there earlier and the woman had knocked beer mugs and a pitcher onto the floor in anger. One of the old winos was passed out at the end of the bar with his head buried in his arms, and the rest of the bar had thinned out, with the exception of Raleigh and a few other regulars.

"Hey Rals, do me a favor, will ya? Wake that old fart up and tell him last call," the bartender barked out as he stood leaning on his broom.

Raleigh tried to stir the old wino and the grizzly little character just belched and dropped his head back down on his arms. The regulars began to file out the door, checking their wristwatches and smoothing down their hair as Raleigh tried to roust the old guy.

"What's a-matter? Can't get him to budge?" the bartender said, tapping Raleigh on the shoulder. "Well, here. Why 'on't 'cha get that side of 'im and I'll take this side. We'll just give 'im a ride out. Marvin, get the door, will ya?" the bartender hollered as he threw his bar towel over his shoulder and grabbed one arm of the wino while Raleigh grabbed the other. They escorted him outside with his toes gently dragging on the ground and sat him down against the building, where he slid down into a sitting position.

"Think he'll be all right out here?" Raleigh asked.

"Oh, yeah. The cops'll come along in a while and haul him in. He'll get a good night's sleep," the bartender winked.

"Well, I'd best be gettin' on myself. Take care, now," Raleigh said, slapping the bartender casually on the shoulder.

"Yeah, you too, Rals. Hey, thanks for the help, man. See ya soon, huh?" the bartender said, waving good night.

Raleigh stood there on the sidewalk for a moment, watching the streetlights and traffic, which was slower than usual since it was summer session at the university. He heard the bartender shout "HEY, WHO THE HELL CALLED THIS GODDAMN CAB OUT HERE? SUMBITCH IS AWAITIN'!" He glanced back down at the wino, who was slumped just below the windows of where the neon beer signs glowed twenty-four hours a day. They were somewhat like a candle there in the window, as the bar was a home for the lonely and those all alone.

Raleigh lay awake for a while after he got home. He got up and grabbed a beer from the refrigerator and laid back down in the dark with his arms folded behind his head. It was the first night he'd spent in a couple of months without Candice. He missed her now. He missed the sound of her soft laughter — she always laughed at his jokes — and he missed the scent of her soft, straight, blond hair. He felt alone without her, yet he'd already made his decision not to see her for a while.

After an hour or so when he still could not fall asleep, he sat up in bed and drained the warm beer he'd sat down on the bed table. He swung his legs over the side of the bed and tried to force himself to yawn, which he could not do since there was no one to catch a yawn from in the house. He got up and put on his khaki shorts and a cotton T-shirt.

He wandered around this empty little home, pulled another beer out of the icebox, and settled into his easy chair with Margaret English's last book of poetry. "Now that's someone I could live with," he thought as he glanced at her photograph on the back cover — someone else who clung to their own privacy and solitude.

MARGARET ENGLISH was having the time of her life in New York City. She spent her days wandering around the Village, sometimes stopping in Washington Square to observe all the hustle and bustle of summertime activity. She kept notes on everything she felt, tasted, and heard, as well as reflecting on all she'd encountered during the past two years while her pen was stilled.

During the early evenings she would sit planted behind Ty's typewriter and pound out her lines of poetry, held so long within her. She wrote as if her very life depended on the structure of those lines — which, in a sense, it did.

She went to baseball games with Phil and in the late hours of those nights they would slip into dark corner booths in the bars to listen to jazz. They became close friends who could laugh with each other over silent amusements and gestures. Margaret became so fond of him that she dreaded the end of the summer when she would have to return to Texas. Yet, she went back to Ty's alone each night, as this was not a prurient relationship at all; it was just a marvelous companionship that left her smiling and free from any sort of guilt or obligation. They found they could talk openly with each other about their personal problems. Problems seemed to fade into humor once they were spoken and heard in sincerity.

They phoned Kerry in the wee hours of the morning from a pay phone in a bar and the two of them cupped their faces into the phone, chuckling over how hard it was to get Kerry to focus on conversation when she'd been wakened from a deep sleep. Kerry could only grasp one or two words from each sentence they slurred into the phone, and while Margaret and Phil had bent over in laughter as they strolled along the sidewalks beneath the streetlamps, Kerry had woken at dawn feeling as though the welcomed sound of their voices had only been a part of her dreams.

Margaret phoned home every weekend to talk with Puttnam and the children. Tennessee was always so glad to hear her voice. He would stutter on the other end of the line and his mother would giggle over his endless chain of 'uh-huhs' at all of her questions. She missed them. Her heart began to long for the touch of their small, fragile hands, as well as the knowing affections of Puttnam. They were happier than they'd ever been, so strong in their love for one another that nothing ventured between them but miles. Puttnam was elated that the block was finally over; being apart seemed a small price to pay for the new strength he could hear in her voice. He made her promise she would go alone more often, where the lines could come forth in solitude and the bond between them could grow on its own free will.

Clare came to visit in July. They combed the city together, delighted to be reunited after such a long separation. The tiny, sparkle-eyed woman, whose short-cropped curly hair was now frosted with gray, had tugged Margaret's arm around the city with laughter and lighthearted gaiety. Margaret noted that Clare seemed much happier since she no longer owned *The Avalanche*. She could joke about its flaws now and openly voice her low opinion of Ernest's personality.

They spent two days sightseeing, both recalling memories of their younger years in the city. They went out to the Statue of Liberty on a sunny Saturday afternoon, blending in with the tourists and recapturing parts of themselves they had thought long gone. Margaret recounted the story to Clare of how Kerry had remembered the Emma Lazarus sonnet while standing at the railing in Battery Park and Clare had thrown her head back with delight over Kerry's sentimentality.

Phil played one night and the two women went down to hear him. Clare drank quite a bit of wine and was fairly tipsy by the time the evening came to a close. Margaret swung her arm around Clare's narrow shoulders on one side while Phil took her arm on the other and they chaperoned her to an all-night diner for coffee. They laughed and sang all the way, with the melodies seeming to dance in the step of Clare's path. They did not return to Ty's apartment until four in the morning. Clare collapsed in exhaustion on Ty's sofa. Margaret tenderly removed Clare's sandals and covered her with a light blanket before she retired in Ty's bed.

Clare woke with a whopping hangover, which she flaunted at Margaret by wearing her dark glasses around the apartment until noon. At three that afternoon Margaret escorted her by cab to the train station. They cried when they parted, promising each other that they would meet again in the city sometime in the future. They stood waiting for the train, concocting ways of dragging Kerry to the city with them. Clare waved goodbye as she boarded the train.

"Promise me you'll write more often — and Puttnam, too," Clare called out, a tear rolling down her check.

"I can promise for me. Puttnam doesn't write — he takes pictures," Margaret laughed, raising her hand in the air in farewell before turning to leave. This world, she thought, is so much a grasping for understanding promises.

Margaret did not remain totally guilt-free for the whole summer. Ty returned to the city in mid-July, bubbling with energy from his trip to Europe. Elizabeth had joined him late in the trip and had stayed behind to visit friends in Paris.

So, it came to pass that Margaret and Ty eventually found themselves in the same bed together. It was a welcome breath of fresh air for Margaret, one more distraction which she had not anticipated that made her trip all the more special. She remembered so well the rituals of Ty's lovemaking and accepted it with a casual heart reaching out in comfort. Puttnam was a bit shocked when she first brought the subject up over the phone. He'd cleared his throat repeatedly and finally put Virginia on the phone to babble on about swimming lessons. By the next day he had reconciled the situation in his own mind. He knew she was in love with him and that was all that really mattered. "Hell," he thought, "I didn't want her to be Betty Crocker. She's a poet, for Chrissakes — wouldn't want her any other way." He called her back that day to reassure her that he was handling the news just fine and as long as she didn't announce that Ty was coming back to Houston to live with them, he'd be OK. Margaret had chuckled at his remarks; thanked him for his understanding, which was so important to her stability; and told him at least ten times how much she loved him before hanging up the phone.

Ty was not so casual in his response to the situation, though he kept his elated heart to himself. Margaret had always filled a certain vacuum in his heart. The loneliest time in his life had been when

Margaret stopped dating him years ago. He had battled that loneliness for two years afterward and he had never found a replacement for that certain feeling he felt for her. He felt so at ease and confident lying next to her at night, with her auburn hair spilling across her pillow. She made his heart pound and his mind race with fantasies of a shared future.

It was so unlike Ty to fall prey to any sort of fantasy world. He was normally so bound to reality. He was, in fact, the skeptical one as a rule, with a detached bachelor's point of view when it came to love affairs. Since Margaret, there hadn't really been any love affairs — there had only been affairs. He convinced himself that he would persuade her to stay when the summer ended, and each day that went by made that fantasy stronger.

Margaret had no idea that Ty felt as he did. She was so absorbed in her writing and the phenomenon of being prolific once again that she totally bypassed what was happening. Her energy and creativity gave her a certain glow of aloofness, which made her even more appealing to Ty. She was the captivating enigma in Ty's life — one that he longed to have another chance at unraveling.

ONE NIGHT, when Ty was off reviewing an off-Broadway play, Phil and Margaret went out to the ballpark for a baseball game. It was the second week of August and the air was warm and sticky as they sat in the stands under the lights, crunching popcorn and shouting obscenities at the umpire. They'd both worn old blue jeans and sneakers to the game. Phil had on a white short-sleeved shirt and his New York Yankees baseball cap with the brim just a tad off-center and the sides pulled down close to his ears so that tufts of his soft, dark hair sprouted out around the edges. Margaret wore Puttnam's old Burley Hall T-shirt with the sleeves rolled up to her shoulders. When she stood up the hem of the T-shirt came almost to her denim-clad knees. She felt like a teenager that night, wrestling with Phil over the box of popcorn and splurging her diet on hot dogs and Cokes.

"God, Puttnam will never believe how many games I've been to. He'll be so envious. I can't wait to get home to hear his laugh when I tell him about all of this," Margaret chuckled to Phil as she dug into the popcorn box he was holding.

"Wait a second. I think I've misunderstood something here," Phil said, setting the popcorn box down between them. The look on his face was one of alarmed concern and Margaret's dimples quickly faded from her cheeks.

"There's something about the tone of your voice that tells me I've said something wrong here. Maybe I'm the one who doesn't understand," she said.

"You said you can't wait to get home. It's Ty who doesn't understand. He doesn't think you are going home. I mean, he thinks his home is now your home. Oh, that sounds redundant, doesn't it? I should mind my own business," Phil said somberly, reaching up to tip the brim of his baseball cap.

"It isn't even my business. Um, he hasn't said any of this to me. I thought he knew I would go. I never told him I would stay! I never even hinted that that was a possibility. It's been so wonderful to visit with him; he's on such a high from his trip to Europe and he's mentioned his lady friend, Elizabeth, so many times. Oh, no, this can't be what's going on in his mind. He got over us years ago. This is just good, clean fun for him, for the summer. I'm just a touchable friend," Margaret said, sighing in disbelief.

"I recall going through that time with him when the two of you parted the last go-round. He'll make it through this time as well. You have to be aware of how he feels, though. Sorry I brought it up, but he's fairly obsessed with this. He and I even had an appointment to go look at a larger apartment for the two of you day after tomorrow. Oh, what the hell. It isn't your fantasy, it's his. Perhaps this time around will give him a better understanding of what he's really lacking in his life — but then, who am I to speak? I need that something in my own life and can't seem to hold onto it," Phil responded, reaching in his pocket to retrieve a cigarette.

He passed one to Margaret, lit a match, and cupped his hands around the flame as they both leaned their heads into his cupped hands to light their cigarettes.

"What is it that he's missing in his life that you're missing as well? I mean, he's successful, you're successful; he's handsome and a delightful person to have as a companion. He's always had his pick of the ladies. What could either of you possibly be missing that you can't reach out with very little effort and find?" Margaret asked in puzzlement.

"Substance. The sharing of substance," Phil answered, exhaling a cloud of smoke. "With me, it's that same substance that I miss in Kerry."

"Yes, but Kerry will be back. She returns your feelings. She's spoken to me about what's troubling her, briefly, but she has discussed it. It isn't the same as what's happening here with Ty," Margaret said softly, leaning sideways to rest her elbow on Phil's shoulder.

"Kerry and I haven't seen each other in nine months. I think perhaps that she treads a bit lighter than you, Margaret. She doesn't leave a path to follow back when she goes," he said.

"Kerry has always relied on those she loves to pave that path for her. Her own life has no path. It is a straight line, and only by the efforts of those who love her does she ever let herself be carried away from that straight and narrow line. She has an eye for her work, which holds her heart and mind almost entirely, and the diversions of love do not come easy for her. They are a luxury and Kerry has always been most frugal in her spending," she said, pulling down on the brim of Phil's cap. "She'll be back, though," Margaret winked, her dimples returning to her cheeks.

She thought of home then — home now surrounded by a new understanding and appreciation. Home with Kerry a few blocks away, pounding on her Smith-Corona portable, and Puttnam snoring close beside her late at night. She thought of Virginia and Tennessee, nestled in next to her on the sofa, and Jeff Foster, whom she'd practically adopted as her own father. They were all her family now: Leota and Cora, Thomas Evans and Raleigh, Julie with her removed and formal aura, the Prestons with their continuing soap opera of Ethel's drinking binges, and Wiley, dear Wiley, the lifetime student of philosophy slamming the lids on the beer boxes each night down at Burley Hall. She wished that everyone could hold so many dear things in their heart and feel in common with those who had nothing in common. She wished she could leave that feeling with Ty, to be able to leave him something of that warmth. That was what she longed for at this moment.

"So, what should I do with Ty, about Ty — oh, for God's sake — for Ty? How can I make this easier for him?" Margaret asked in frustration as the crowd jumped to their feet around them.

"You can make it the best summer he's spent in many a year. It isn't your obligation to furnish happiness after you leave. You have given him that since you've been here. Elizabeth will be back in October. That isn't substance but it beats the hell out of hurting alone. Just come back sometime — HEY, THAT WAS RIGHT OVER THE PLATE! HEY!" Phil shouted down at the field.

"What?" Margaret said, trying to outshout the crowd and regain Phil's attention, which had obviously been lost to the game. She'd missed the last part of what he'd said.

"Watch the game, Margaret, watch the game! We'll talk later," Phil replied, patting her arm resting on his shoulder. Margaret gave him a deep chuckle and a buss on the cheek. Her dimples flashed as she reached up to yank the baseball cap from his head, ruffling his hair into a thousand directions.

She stood up with the crowd, waving Phil's cap, and hollered "WAHOO!" for Kerry, and though it didn't sound quite the same as it would coming from Kerry, it was the thought that counted.

They never got the chance to talk later, although Margaret was quite sure that Phil must've talked to Ty because Ty never brought the subject up at all.

She flew home on the twenty-third of August. Puttnam stood at the gate to meet her, with Justin wrapped around one leg and

Tennessee around the other. Virginia was perched in front of them, holding up a sign so large that it covered all but her eyes and her tousled auburn hair. Margaret saw those eyes and felt as though she was looking into a mirror of her youth.

The sign said "WELCOME HOME, MA!" Margaret dropped her bags and ran to fold her family in her arms. Justin stepped aside shyly and she reached out to pull him into the circle of hugs, too.

Of course, the homecoming didn't go quite as smoothly as planned, since Virginia wandered off while they waited in the baggage area for Margaret's luggage. She was searching for a water fountain and ended up getting herself lost in the crowd.

Margaret was beside herself with worry, thinking that the child had been kidnapped. Actually, it wasn't too bad a deal for Virginia, because when they finally found her a half hour later, she was perched up on the counter at one of the airline booths with her pixie legs crossed over the side. She was surrounded by airline employees catering to her every need, and instead of that drink of water she had originally gone in search of, she had a frosty can of root beer in her tiny hands.

Three Birthdays, August 1983

"SHHH! VIRGINIA, SIT YOURSELF DOWN over there by Justin. You have to be quiet or Leo will hear you when she comes to the door," Kerry scolded.

"But, it's my birthday, too! I've been sittin' in the car for three hours listening to Tenn play that stupid penny whistle," Virginia whined back at Kerry. Puttnam snapped his fingers at her and pointed to the empty space beside Justin on the sofa in Leota's living room.

Julie stood at the window, peeking through the venetian blinds. "Here they come! I just saw Thomas' car round the corner. Everybody to their hiding places!" Julie said, turning quickly from the window and running head-on into Ethel, who had been perched behind her.

Everyone scattered to their appointed places. Fletcher and Kerry hid with Tennessee and Margaret behind the swinging door to the kitchen; Puttnam, Virginia, Julie, and Ethel hid in Leota's front guest room; while Jessica, Raleigh, and Justin ducked into the bathroom. Rodney and April were the only members of the Preston household not present. April was away at summer camp and Rodney was in Dallas on "business."

They listened as Thomas' car doors slammed next door. Julie risked peeking out between the blinds to see Leota and Cora walking across the lawn, their arms stuffed with packages. Thomas followed just behind them, carrying three sacks of groceries. The windows were open as usual at Leota's house, and everyone in the house had to stifle their chuckles over Leota's comments as she approached the house.

"Now, Thomas, it certainly was nice of you to take Cora and me out shoppin' on my birthday. I guess all my young'uns forgot about me this year. Julie hasn't even called today," Leota barked, shuffling her packages into Cora's arms and reaching into the pocket of her skirt for her house keys. Thomas stood behind her on the doorstep, sweat pouring from his brow.

"It's early yet, Leota. Julie'll call later, and besides, the whole Houston gang is pullin' in here tomorrow," Thomas protested, winking at Cora as Leota fumbled with the door lock.

"This dadgum thing drives me crazy. Maybe I'll just get you to give it a little shot of some WD-40 later on, Thomas . . . I thought those twins woulda called me this mornin'. They always call first thing on our birthday," Leota complained, giving the door a swift kick in frustration.

"Well, now, just don't get excited there, Leota. Try it again, there. Those twins'll call. Just wait and see," Thomas said, trying to balance the three bags of groceries.

"Well, damn it all. It's just a cryin' shame when your loved ones forget your birthday," Leota said as the lock on the door finally clicked open. She pushed the door open and stepped back to hold the screen for Thomas and Cora.

"HAPPY BIRTHDAY, LEO/GRANDMOTHER!" the household hollered out. Virginia popped up first to hug Leota, who dropped her house keys in surprise.

"Lord have mercy, Virginia, ya little dickens! Ya like to scare me to death," Leota said, hugging Virginia, who was now taller than she was. "Now, just tell me whose idea was this?" Leota laughed, reaching for Justin and Tennessee.

The family surrounded her while hugs and kisses were exchanged. Leota brushed a few tears from below her glasses and went to the kitchen to help Thomas with the groceries.

"This is such a surprise! You kids really got the best of ole Leo this time. Why, I wasn't expectin' to have to put up with you little nuisances till tomorrow," Leota giggled as Justin, Tennessee, and

Virginia hovered around her. Justin and Virginia were about the same size, while Tennessee was a head taller than the two of them.

"We brought ice cream, and Kerry made a cake for us all. Dad even brought a case of champagne. Can we have some champagne, Leo?" Virginia asked. Her auburn hair was parted on the side and cut in the same style Margaret had always worn. It dipped pleasantly across her right eye and Leota reached out to push it back from her face.

"Oh, I suppose — that is, if it's OK with those nagging parents of yourn," Leota said, winking at Virginia as she pulled groceries from the bag.

"Happy birthday to you, Mr. Tenn," Leota said. "I can't believe y'all are eleven years old today."

Julie and Ethel came into the kitchen and pulled the cake out of the refrigerator. It was a strawberry cake with lovely white frosting and fresh strawberries placed around the edges. The lettering on the top read "Happy three birthdays, darlin's. 1983." Leota chuckled when she read the lettering, which was quite sloppily written in red. Puttnam leaned over Leota's shoulder to read the cake's inscription and he roared with his boisterous laughter.

"I didn't read that earlier. Kerry, when did you ever find time to learn how to bake cakes?" Puttnam hollered into the living room at Kerry, who sat next to Fletcher on the sofa. She'd cut several inches off of her hair over the years and had let her bangs grow out. Puttnam's gray-streaked hair was now longer than hers.

"Oh, I can cook sometimes. I do know how to turn the oven on, Puttnam," Kerry barked at him.

"Well, ya coulda fooled me. Thought the only thing you knew how to do was play guitar and work a typewriter," Puttnam hollered back.

"Hey, she knows how to swim, too," Ethel remarked with sarcasm. "Maybe we could get a good price for her if we put her up on the market."

Ethel was sober on this day. She'd lost a few pounds and was tan from lounging by the pool at the country club. She was dressed fashionably, in designer shorts and a polo shirt. She'd eyed the case of champagne anxiously when Puttnam had pulled the bottles out to put them in the refrigerator.

"Ethel, if ya coulda gotten a good price for me, ya woulda sold me years ago. I don't think the market's changed that much since the last time ya checked, darlin'," Kerry shot back at her sister.

Ethel laughed and walked to the door of the kitchen. "Well, you can't blame me for tryin', Kerry," she said, pushing through the swinging door.

Fletcher smirked on the sofa next to Kerry. His dolphin eyes followed Ethel out of the room. "I sure am glad she doesn't live at our house. Make sure we never give her our real address, will ya, Kerry?" he joked, taking Kerry's slender hand in his.

"Oh, didn't I tell you, Fletcher? Ethel's coming to spend a month with us as soon as we get back from Saratoga with Puttnam and Margaret," Kerry said with a straight face.

"You're kidding," Fletcher said, dropping Kerry's hand into her lap.

"I'm kidding, I'm kidding," Kerry consoled him with a light giggle as she reached out to retrieve his hand.

"Get the camera, Puttnam. Julie's lighting the candles," Margaret called out from the kitchen. Everyone gathered around the kitchen table where the birthday cake had been placed next to a tub of homemade ice cream, while Puttnam scampered into the front guest room to find his camera.

Julie placed the match to each of the three candles in the cake and they all began to sing "Happy Birthday" just a little out of sync with each other since Leota had so many different titles. Thomas Evans popped the cork on the first bottle of champagne and the bubbling liquid burst out of the bottle, spilling out onto Leota's shining linoleum floor. Puttnam snapped a shot of Thomas holding the bottle out from his body with a look of total surprise on his face.

They all adjourned to the living room with their cake and ice cream. Virginia was so proud of her plastic champagne glass full of champagne. Puttnam didn't tell her that hers was merely mock champagne. He'd tried to pass off the fake stuff to Ethel as well, but she shook her head in disgust. Ethel knew the difference between mock champagne and the real thing from a mile away. You couldn't fool Ethel when it came to alcohol.

Leota and Tennessee sat side by side on the sofa. "So, you're gonna get to stay here with ole Leo while your folks go up north on vacation with Kerry and Fletcher?" Leota said, patting his knee softly.

"Uh-huh," Tennessee replied between spoonfuls of ice cream and cake.

"Did you bring your rod and reel, Tenn?" Thomas asked from the easy chair across the room.

"Uh-huh," Tennessee grinned.

"Well, we're just gonna have us a time right here at our own vacation," Leota chimed with her green eyes flashing through the lenses of her spectacles.

"Always do," Tenn agreed, making his first real statement of the day.

Whey they had finished their cake and ice cream, Cora suggested that they all go outside to sit in the shade on the patio. Margaret helped her collect the paper plates and plastic champagne glasses as everyone else filed out the back door. Thomas carried the box of birthday presents out to the patio, though Leota hadn't had a chance to wrap the gifts she'd bought for the twins that morning. Thomas grinned as he looked down in the box to see Leota's shopping bag, as it had taken her two hours in that crowded mall to make a decision on what to buy for the kids.

Justin distributed the gifts to the three of them. Leota tore into her presents with the same childlike curiosity as the twins. She and Virginia whooped and hollered with delight with each gift they unwrapped, while Tennessee simply nodded his head and grinned shyly each time he pulled a present from its wrappings.

The bows and wrapping paper lay wasted on the cement patio as Leota kicked her shoes off and slipped her feet into the new pair of house slippers Kerry and Fletcher had given her. She could always look forward to that new pair of summer slippers from Kerry each year; it had become a tradition between them.

The twins were delighted over the gifts Leota had gotten for them. She'd bought a hardbound copy of *Moby Dick* for Tennessee and a cotton sundress for Virginia. Virginia rushed inside to try it on while Justin and Tennessee huddled together to examine the pages of *Moby Dick* and the other presents he'd been given.

Thomas took the men out to the garden to show them what remained of the summer crop. Kerry watched them from the back porch steps with a smile on her face. Margaret sat beside her on the porch and they turned to exchange glances.

"I can't believe Puttnam has talked Fletcher into going on that hiking trip while we're up north. Fletcher hates to camp! His idea of roughing it is having to stop off at a Motel Six instead of a Holiday Inn these days," Kerry chuckled.

"Well, Puttnam needs help with his camera gear for this one and Fletcher said he really wanted to go. Puttnam's not the best camper in the world these days himself. We'll see how many nights they actually spend in that bulky old army tent Puttnam borrowed from Wiley. Gets awfully cool at night in the Adirondacks," Margaret smirked.

"Kerry, what's the plan here now since y'all are here a day early?" Leota asked.

"We thought we'd drive as far as Texarkana tonight. Fletcher made motel reservations there at the Holiday Inn," Kerry giggled, poking Margaret gently in the ribs.

"Now, just what's so damn funny about that?" Leota said in confusion, as two jets boomed above them, shattering the tranquility.

"Oh, it's nothin', Leo. Just a joke," Kerry replied, though Leota couldn't hear a word she was saying above the roar of the airplanes.

"I'm going to get the keys from Puttnam so I can walk down the block and bring the van back to the house," Margaret said, standing up to stretch her graceful arms.

"All right," Kerry mumbled, watching her walk through the lawn out to the garden. She sat observing them from her place on the back porch. Raleigh was off by himself inspecting the tomato plants. Puttnam was engaged in conversation with Fletcher and Thomas. He paused and leaned down to listen to what Margaret was saying to him as she stood by his side. Kerry watched him fish in the pocket of his jeans for the keys to the van and bend down to kiss Margaret on the cheek as he handed them to her.

Fletcher looked the same as he had for ten years, Kerry thought to herself. Through the years he had been the one thing in her life that grew but never changed. She watched him smile at Puttnam as Puttnam flipped his ponytail back over his shoulder and pushed the hair back from his face. Fletcher had always been so observant of other people's idiosyncrasies and since he had very few of his own, they were a great endearment to him. Kerry rested her head in her hand, with her elbows firmly grounded on her bare knees. She thought of the years past and the changes the love between her and Fletcher had withstood. It was forever a solid love, though it would change again and again throughout their lives.

Fletcher came back from the garden to sit down beside her.

"I love you," he whispered in her ear.

"I love you, too," Kerry said, kissing him lightly on the cheek. She met his eyes and was lost for a moment in contentment and wonder.

"So, Fletcher, you're a-fixin' to drive a couple of thousand miles," Leota said cheerfully.

"Yes, ma'am. This is the big one," Fletcher laughed, tugging at his beard gently.

"Well, y'all be careful. Ya never know what can happen on the highway these days," Leota said, shaking her head.

Fletcher smiled at her as Margaret pulled into the driveway with the van. Its bright blue paint sparkled in the sunlight.

Justin came to stand beside Leota. His shiny, dark hair was cut short for the summer and his olive complexion had deeply tanned to a golden brown, with the exception of his sunburnt, upturned nose.

"Grandmother, may I take Tenn and Virginia down to the park for a while?" Justin asked, shuffling his feet on the cement with his hands buried in the pockets of his shorts.

"Well, I suppose if you're tired of this party, it's OK with me," Leota answered, brushing a smudge of dirt from his cheek.

Virginia overheard Leota's answer and ran inside to put her shorts and sneakers back on. Tennessee gathered up his presents and took them into the house. He came back outside smiling and joined Justin at the end of the patio to wait for Virginia.

After they had gone, Julie left to take Ethel and Jessica home, as Jessica had a date that night and was anxious to get back to the house so she could shampoo her hair. Leota marveled at how much Jessica resembled Ethel in her teenage years, with her peaches-and-cream complexion and her soft, sculpted figure.

Raleigh stayed behind so that he could take Justin out to a movie later in the afternoon — that is, if he could manage to talk Leota into letting the twins go, too, since he knew it would be a battle to try and split up the three children today. *Raiders of the Lost Ark* was showing down at the mall theatre and Raleigh hadn't seen it yet.

Leota went inside and made a thermos of iced tea for Margaret to put in the van. She poured a glass for Thomas as well and placed a healthy sprig of mint on the edge of the glass. Thomas thanked her when she walked out onto the porch to hand it to him.

As they were loading the van to leave, Cora noticed that Margaret was the only one who didn't have any sunglasses. Though Margaret protested, Cora ran back inside and returned with a funny pair of shades with wing tips laced in rhinestones.

"Now, don't you lose those. I've had those ugly things for thirty years or more," Cora said, handing the shades to Margaret, who sat with Kerry in the middle passenger seat.

"Oh, I'll take good care of these," Margaret said, putting them on and flashing a dimpled smile at everyone. They all laughed so hard that the van shook and Puttnam was so tickled he could hardly get the key in the ignition.

"Oh, they're really you, Margaret," Kerry teased, snapping the road map in her lap. Fletcher sat in the front passenger seat. He folded his arms across his chest, glanced back at Margaret a few times, and chuckled in amusement, shaking his head from side to side.

Raleigh, Thomas, Leota, and Cora all followed the van down the driveway to the front of the house, waving goodbye. The haze floated across the asphalt as Puttnam pulled out into the street, put the van in gear, and drove off toward the park so they could say goodbye to the children.

"Well, all I've got to say is, it's a damn good thing they're not headed west," Leota said, locking arms with Cora as they walked back to the house. Thomas and Raleigh fell in step behind them and exchanged bewildered glances at each other over Leota's comment.

"LOOK, THERE'S VIRGINIA," Fletcher said, pointing off to the side of the road.

"What's she coming back so soon for? Uh-oh. Looks like a temper stomp if I ever saw one," Puttnam said, wiping the sweat from his forehead.

"Oh, let's not even stop, Puttnam. Let's let Leota handle it," Margaret pleaded.

"Shame on you, Margaret. That's your daughter out there," Puttnam grinned into the rearview mirror. He pulled the van over onto the shoulder of the road beside Virginia as she brushed tears from her cheeks and then doggedly placed her hands on her hips. Kerry slid the van's side door open, directly in front of Virginia.

"Virginia, what's the matter, darlin'?" Kerry asked as Margaret slumped down into the seat.

"It's Justin and Tenn. They won't let me play tetherball with them!" Virginia cried.

"Well, take it from an old tetherball pro: it's much safer to observe," Fletcher mused out his window.

"Oh, how would you know, anyway?" Virginia said, breaking down into sobs, which shook her thin frame as her thick, wavy hair slipped across her right eye. "It's not fair," she cried, brushing the tear away with the back of her hand.

"Virginia, you go on back to Leo's and wash your face. Get her to fix you a nice glass of that mint tea and pretty soon you'll forget all about the 'titherball' game," Puttnam snapped impatiently.

"It's *tether*ball, Dad . . . and besides, I'm only eleven years old. I'm not supposed to drink iced tea because it has caffeine in it," Virginia barked back.

"Well, I think you oughta turn yourself around and go right back down to that park, darlin'. You tell those two numbskulls that it's a public park and that tetherball pole belongs to everybody," Kerry said, closing the side door to the van.

"Thanks, Kerry," Virginia grinned, turning on her heels to stomp off in the direction of the park. They drove on past her and she waved a cheerful goodbye high in the air.

They pulled up in front of the park, where Puttnam leaned on his horn to get the boys' attention. The boys looked up impatiently, waved goodbye, and went back to their tetherball game.

The highway was steaming in the hot August heat and the sky was filled with large, puffy white clouds against the neon-blue backdrop as they rolled along, heading north for Texarkana.

Puttnam and Fletcher were absorbed in discussing their hiking trip, while Margaret and Kerry sat in the back trying to decide on a special celebration they could arrange for Clare, since she was retiring from *The Avalanche* in September. They traded suggestions and joked back and forth about how to get rid of Ernest for such an occasion. Kerry finally clicked her fingers after a long silence and grasp Margaret's shoulder with enthusiasm over an idea they had both overlooked.

"Hey, let's go to New York City, Margaret!" Kerry cried out as her face lit up and she unknowingly kicked a small tear into the roof of Wiley's army tent, which was stored beneath the seat. Margaret grinned in agreement, flashing her dimples at Kerry. They shook hands there in the back seat of that bright-blue van, with the wind kicking up the waves of Margaret's auburn hair and the asphalt stretching out before them like a ribbon laced with golden threads.

———

NOTE TO THE READER

Nanci Griffith was born in Seguin, Texas, in 1953, and raised in Austin. She was a child and young woman of the '60s and '70s. As a girl she was drawn to the singing of Carolyn Hester, a fellow Texan who was enjoying national success as a folk singer. She was also drawn to the fiction of Thomas Wolfe and Carson McCullers.

Nanci soon started writing her own songs, which resulted in her first album, *There's a Light Beyond These Woods*, in 1978. At the same time she began working on a novel, *Two of a Kind Heart*, loosely based on her experiences growing up and growing into the counterculture of the '70s and early '80s. Her musical career and songwriting soon took over her life, and the novel, while finished, was never edited or published.

Nanci and I started working together in 1984. We recorded two albums, *Once in a Very Blue Moon* and *The Last of the True Believers*, which led to her being signed by a major record label. We remained very close friends and eventually we reunited to record her Grammy-winning album *Other Voices, Other Rooms*, followed by *Other Voices, Too*. Nanci's music touched the hearts of countless thousands of people. After her untimely death in 2021, *Two of a Kind Heart* was bequeathed to me, which indicated to me that Nanci would have wanted it to be published at last.

— JIM ROONEY, 2023

In addition to working as a record producer with Nanci Griffith, Jim Rooney is known for his producing work with John Prine, Iris DeMent, Hal Ketchum, Peter Rowan, Tom Paxton, Tom Rush, and many others. He has written three books about music: Bossmen: Bill Monroe & Muddy Waters *(JRP Books),* Baby, Let Me Follow You Down: The Illustrated Story of the Cambridge Folk Years *(with Eric Von Schmidt; University of Massachusetts Press), and* In It for the Long Run: A Musical Odyssey *(University of Illinois Press).*

THERE'S A LIGHT BEYOND THESE WOODS

There's a light beyond these woods, Mary Margaret.
Do you think that we will go there,
And see what makes it shine, Mary Margaret?
It's almost morning, and we've talked all night,
You know we've made big plans for ten-year-olds,
You and I.

Have you met my new boyfriend, Margaret?
His name is John, and he rides my bus to school,
And he holds my hand.
He's fourteen, he's my older man.
But we'll still be the best of friends,
The three of us, Margaret, John, and I.

Let's go to New York City, Margaret!
We'll hide out in the subways
And drink the poets' wine, oh,
But I had John, so you went and I stayed behind.
But you were home in time for the senior prom,
When we lost John.

The fantasies we planned, I'm living them now.
All the dreams we sang when we knew how,
Well, they haven't changed.
There's never been two friends like you and me,
Mary Margaret.

It's nice to see your family growing, Margaret.
Your daughter and your husband there,
They really treat you right ...
But we've talked all night
And what about the light that glowed beyond
Our woods when we were ten?

You were the rambler then.
The fantasies we planned, well, Maggie,
I'm living them now.
All the dreams we sang, oh, we damn sure knew
How, but I haven't changed.
There'll never be two friends like you and me,
Maggie, can't you see?

There's a light beyond your woods, Mary Margaret.

— NANCI GRIFFITH, 1978

TWO OF A KIND HEART

Copyright © 2023 by James Rooney

JRP Books
139 Star Mountain Road | Sharon, Vermont 05065

SOFTCOVER: ISBN 978-0-9854399-1-0
EBOOK: ISBN 978-0-9854399-3-4
Library of Congress Control Number: 2023939119

Copyedited by Karen Francomano
Design, photograph, and illustration by Susan Marsh
Typeset in Arno Pro by Matt Mayerchak

"There's a Light Beyond These Woods" written by Nanci Griffith
and published by Nanci Griffith / Griffmill (ASCAP)

FIRST EDITION

Printed in the United States of America

Made in the USA
Columbia, SC
26 September 2023

23410855R00196